Also By Dorothy Clarke Wilson

Hilary: The Brave World of Hilary Pole

Jezebel, Wicked Woman of the Bible (formerly: Jezebel)

Lady Washington

Lone Woman Doctor (formerly: Lone Woman: The Story of Elizabeth Blackwell, The First Woman Doctor)

Palace of Healing (formerly: Palace of Healing: The Story of Dr. Clara Swain, The First Woman Missionary Doctor)

Queen Dolley (formerly: Queen Dolley: The Life and Times of Dolley Madison)

The Awakening of Jesus (formerly: The Gifts)

The Brothers: James and Jesus (formerly: The Brother)

Wheel Chair Doctor (formerly: Take My Hands: The Remarkable Story of Dr. Mary Verghese)

Woman of Mercy (formerly: Stranger and Traveler: The Story of Dorothea Dix, American Reformer)

MOSES
THE PRINCE OF EGYPT

DOROTHY
CLARKE
WILSON

This book is a publication of StoryWorkz, L.P
http://www.StoryWorkz.com
Email: publisher@StoryWorkz.com

Dorothy Clarke Wilson's Website
http://www.DorothyClarkeWilson.com

UNITED STATES OF AMERICA

First StoryWorkz, L.P. Edition 2012
Copyright 1957, 1985 by Dorothy Clarke Wilson
as *Prince of Egypt*

Library of Congress Cataloging-in-Publication
Data is available

ISBN: 978-1-938659-03-4

PART I

1

That magnificent mechanism, the Egyptian army, was in confusion. Bowmen who had faced, unblinking, the poisoned arrows of desert savages turned blanched faces to one another. Charioteers who had fearlessly stormed the fortresses of the terrible Kheta trembled. Officers of noble birth wearing on their helmets the golden bee or lion, insignia of special courage, fumbled their jeweled lances. Even the foreign slaves and mercenaries yielded to the contagious panic. The news spread through the camp like fire through dry marsh grass. *The royal sacred falcon was missing.*

The Good God himself, whose correct name was Pharaoh, Seti I, His Majesty Horus, the Strong Bull, Lord of the Diadem of the Vulture and of the Snake, King of Upper Egypt and King of Lower Egypt, Son of Re, Beloved of Ptah, Offspring of Amon, and Emperor of the World from the Fourth Cataract to the Euphrates, appeared as little perturbed as any. He listened with aloof indifference to the desperate protestations of the priest responsible for the bird's safekeeping.

"Stop the man's blabbings," he directed Rahotep, his fan bearer, equably. "What difference does he think it makes that he has attended six generations of sacred falcons without a single one escaping? If a man takes six steps in safety, does that keep the seventh from plunging him into an abyss?"

Rahotep's face, framed by the corkscrew ringlets of his elaborate wig, was ashen. "His Majesty Horus, the Strong Bull, speaks wisely as always," he asserted hastily without conviction. "But the Good God can hardly have comprehended the enormity of this happening. If he would permit the divine wisdom to wing itself down from that lofty pedestal where it surveys the comings and goings of gods and men—"

"The divine wisdom can function very well without wings," interrupted Seti dryly. "The only pedestal it occupies is this ebony monstrosity which some misguided cabinetmaker had the effrontery to call a chair. What possessed me to bring it along on this campaign is beyond me. No matter how well the thing is padded, the cobra heads always manage to get their fangs into my back."

"If the Strong Bull needs more cushions—" The fan bearer struggled between his normal anxiety for the Good God's comfort and his present dire preoccupation. The latter won.

"The sacred falcon is missing!" he blurted with unconcealed terror. "Horus has deserted us! Here in the desert among our enemies he has flown away and left us unprotected. Our chariots will founder, our spears fly wide of the mark, our arrows fall without barbs. Victory has departed from us."

"Silence, fool!"

The aspect of the pharaoh suddenly changed. The thin lips, habitually curved in a somewhat melancholy smile, became almost as straight as the spare, erect body. Sparks kindled in the gentle, almond-shaped eyes an unexpected keenness, linking them in close kinship with the beaklike nose. But the voice of Seti continued calm and cool, like a thing detached from his body.

"Am I Horus?" it interrogated briefly.

The relief of the group before the royal chair, flinching in expectation of divine vengeance, was ludicrous. Before the startled fan bearer could gather his wits to assure the pharaoh that of course he was Horus, that in a hundred temples in Egypt he was being worshiped that very moment as Horus, someone in the tent laughed. It was a natural, spontaneous sound, as foreign to the atmosphere of regal sanctity as a buffoon at a funeral. Instantly the hands of the guards tightened on their lances. The mouth of the fan bearer fell open. Even the terrified priest ceased his contortions. But from his manner Seti might not have heard the sound.

"Am I or am I not Horus?" he repeated. Then, taking the answer for granted, "How then can you say that Horus has deserted you when he is sitting here on a chair in this tent—uncomfortable though the chair may be!"

Without losing its immobility the spare figure seemed to relax and the lips reassumed their melancholy smile.

"If the sacred falcon is missing," added Seti with casual equanimity, "then find it. A bird in a cage is worth more to Egypt than a careless man's head in a basket."

After the poor priest, his terror fully restored, had stumbled to his knees and backed out of the tent, Seti sat for some moments in silence. Then he turned his eyes deliberately toward the spot to the right of his chair where the royal princes sat.

"Who laughed?" he demanded abruptly.

Of the three young princes sitting side by side on cushioned stools, two, the oldest and youngest, possessed certain features in common: small, slightly elongated head, low but strongly arched forehead, narrow slate-colored eyes set close to aquiline nose and

8

accented by prominent cheekbones. But the differences between them were greater than the similarities. The older, Prince Amon-nebet, sat with shoulders slightly stooped and head thrust forward on his thin neck, motionless except for the two first fingers of his long, slim right hand, which toyed with the crisp pleats of his linen skirt. While the narrowness of his eyes seemed to spring from a mood of gentle contemplation, that of the younger prince's found its source in a sharp wariness which attempted to see everything without while hiding everything within. The difference in age—perhaps a half dozen years—created the least disparity of all, for even now, at twelve, the eyes of the younger reflected at times a cynicism which more than compensated for his lack of years. The boy opened his lips to speak, then pursed them expectantly as the third prince rose from his stool and approached the royal chair.

"May the Son of Re shine kindly upon me," he murmured, kneeling and bending his awkward body until his forehead brushed the floor, "his servant is the one who laughed."

His voice, low and hesitant, was further muffled by the thick crimson carpet. Seti leaned forward, his small eyes sharpening.

"What's that?" he demanded. "Speak up, man, and don't swallow your words."

Rahotep regarded the recumbent figure uneasily, and the guards exchanged glances of consternation. The youngest prince noted their concern, and, his lips tightened in displeasure, he sprang to his feet.

"If it please my father, the Golden Horus, the Strong Bull who uplifts the world upon his mighty horns," he announced glibly, "Prince Moses wishes to inform the Offspring of Amon that it was he who committed the grave indiscretion—"

"Be quiet, Ramses." Seti's calm tone abruptly dammed the flow of words. "Let Prince Moses speak for himself. And let his brother, the Son of Amon, be the judge of whether he has committed an indiscretion. Now then!" The hands of the pharaoh moved forward, their long fingers closing over the carved sphinxes' heads that formed the arms of his chair. "So it was you who laughed. Pluck that stumbling tongue of yours from the carpet before it gets tangled like a boat among the reeds, and tell me why."

The youth lifted his face, the blood which had rushed to his bowed head staining his bold, straight features almost as deep a crimson as the rug. The single side lock of braided hair, the mark of his rank as a prince of the royal house, bobbed awkwardly forward against one high, bony temple, and he pushed it back under his linen headdress. His wide-spaced black eyes moved slowly upward, past the royal footstool, past the bright fixed stares of the uraeuses wreathing themselves in embroidered coils about the royal skirt, over the linen-shrouded breast crowned with its golden circlet, and came to rest on the chiseled features of the man who bore the title of lord of all the earth.

Seti's gaze engulfed him, and, as always, he felt himself sinking into some ultimate finality. Like a bird beating its wings to free itself from a net, he struggled to tear away his gaze, even as his reluctant tongue struggled to put his confused thoughts into utterance.

"Now," the placid pools drew him still farther into their depths, "why did you laugh at me?"

"Not at you," the youth began bravely enough, then stumbled, conscious of his error. "I mean—not at the Strong Bull, the Golden Horus."

"At whom, then?"

"The others. All of us." With one desperate beating of his will he managed to wrench his gaze from the almond-shaped snares. At the same time his tongue also seemed to find release. "Because they looked so afraid. When Seti frowned upon them, they paled and trembled, as if expecting him to wield a thunderbolt. Then, when the thunderbolt turned out to be but a simple question, they looked ludicrous with their mouths so foolishly gaping."

"And you," probed the calm voice of the pharaoh, "when Seti frowned, were you not afraid?"

Again the youth felt his gaze being drawn toward the unfathomed pools, and his eyes clung desperately to the two emeralds shining just above the king's forehead in the head of the golden cobra, symbol of the royal power over life and death.

"No," he said clearly. "I was not afraid."

Rahotep gasped, and the fingers that carried the plumed symbol of his exalted rank as fan bearer on the king's right hand trembled. With one accord the double row of guards on each side of the chair moved closer, ready to anticipate the king's slightest gesture when he should decide what punishment to inflict for the sacrilege just uttered. But their movements were reluctant, for the young prince was their favorite. Only Ramses showed no dismay. A smile flickered about his sensitive, full-lipped mouth and kindled a flame of excitement in his eyes.

But the gesture did not come. His fingers still curved about the sphinxes' heads, Seti slowly leaned back against the cushions, wincing

10

as he sensed rather than felt the fangs of the cobra's head. But his eyes, almost as expressionless as the sphinxes', remained fixed on the face of the youth at his feet.

Moses deliberately lowered his gaze from the emeralds to the almond-shaped pools. To his amazement he no longer felt drawn into their depths. He probed into them fearlessly and discovered that what had seemed to be finality was only emptiness. Beneath the mask of his tranquility Seti was no strong bull, no golden Horus rising at dawn to cross the heavens in his flaming chariot. He was a tired, middle-aged man, disillusioned and very lonely. And he was finding it a new and pleasant experience to meet the gaze of young eyes that could look into his own without fear.

The slender fingers traced and retraced the vacuous features of the sphinxes' heads, then formed a curt gesture of dismissal.

"See that the falcon is found," Seti ordered Rahotep abruptly.

2

The life of a royal prince, Moses contemplated moodily, had its disadvantages. Lying on his cushioned couch in the sumptuous tent reserved for himself and the younger son of Seti, head elevated above a smooth wooden arc, his garment of transparent linen gently ruffled by the movement of the huge fan in the hand of White Elephant, his Nubian slave, he tried to assume the accustomed dignity of the Egyptian nobleman at his midday rest. But there was no cushioned prison or stiff wooden pillow to set barriers for his racing mind.

The voice of Khamus, Ramses' aged nurse and tutor, rose and fell monotonously as he conscientiously utilized the afternoon rest period for the mental enrichment of his young charge. He was reading today from the ancient maxims of Ptahhotep, so familiar to Moses that, given the first three words of almost any one of the wise sayings, he could have finished it without thinking.

"Let not your heart grow proud because of your riches," the cultured voice admonished the young prince in words as old as Egypt's pyramids, "for it is god who was the author of them."

Was Ramses listening, Moses wondered. Or, like himself, was he wishing he were out with the slaves and common soldiers searching the hills for the lost talisman of Egypt's glory? His proud features were enigmatic, but the heavily lidded eyes glowed with excitement. Lying like that, the bold lines of his jaw somewhat softened by the subdued light, the young prince looked startlingly like his older sister Nefretiri. Her eyes too were like jewels in an exquisite setting. But they were not slate-colored. They were a sparkling black with a hint of green when the sunlight struck them, particles of warm jet shot through and through with jade and gold.

The watchful White Elephant noticed the sudden wave of color flooding his master's face, and his hand made a wider, more agitated arc. It was no easy task keeping the feathered fan suspended high in the air and moving at an even tempo for hours at a time, and the Nubian slave derived little benefit from the currents he generated. His squat black body, mute testimony to either the humor or the wishful thinking of the parent who had named him White Elephant, glistened with sweat. The cramp in his arm brought an involuntary grimace to his wrinkled features. Moses noticed the expression instantly.

"I've had enough of being fanned," he complained impatiently. "And the sight of that bobbing feather on your head wearies me. Stretch that ugly black body on the matting, so I won't have to look at it."

Wondering why he had yielded to such a foolish impulse as to feel pity for a slave, Moses surrendered himself to unaccustomed discomfort. Heat drew him into a stifling embrace. The cushions beneath his back and shoulders felt like steaming compresses. His light linen garment clung to his perspiring chest and limbs. He sank into a dull torpor through which the droning of Khamus' voice sounded a steady rhythm with the beating of his pulses.

"Good words shine more than the emerald, which the hand of the slave finds on the pebbles."

When did a slave ever find an emerald? mused Moses as he slipped into oblivion. When...

He awoke with the sudden realization that the voice was silent, that a fresh breeze was blowing from the sea, and that his name was being whispered sharply.

"Moses!"

Prince Ramses was standing beside his couch, the excitement which had been smoldering in his eyes ready to burst into flame. "Come! We're going out to hunt for the falcon, you and I. We must hurry!"

Moses struggled to lift himself from the sodden pillows. There was something about the manner of the young prince that compelled obedience. Then his reason returned. "But—"

"I have it all arranged," the boy pursued swiftly. "Khamus and White Elephant are both asleep. My brother Amon-nebet is with our father, the king. I've bribed my slave Obal and threatened to have his tongue cut out if he speaks so much as one word. And see!" From under his arm he triumphantly produced some soiled scraps of cloth. "Obal got them for us. They're part of the loot the soldiers took from the Shasu. If we put them on, nobody can tell us from the slaves who tend the asses. And I know where there's an opening in the shields. Hurry!"

When Moses made no motion to comply, the young prince stamped his foot impatiently. "What's the matter?" His thick lip curled. "Afraid of the Shasu? Scared to go outside the encampment?"

Moses flushed. "I'm not afraid of the Shasu," he asserted hotly. "But any man would be a fool to make himself responsible for taking a child into danger, especially if that child happens to be the favorite son of Tuya."

The braided side lock of the young prince fairly bristled. "The son of Tuya is not a child," he whispered harshly. "Anyway, I shall go whether you do or not. And if anything happens to me, I shall tell the whole court that I begged you to go with me and you refused. Besides," the corners of the full lips suddenly quirked upward, and the imperious manner was displaced by a mischievous, boyish charm, "you know you want to help find that falcon!"

They disrobed in hurried silence, stealing cautious glances at the two sleeping figures. Moses grimaced distastefully before pulling on the short dirty garment, but Ramses showed not the slightest hesitation.

"How do I look?" he demanded, striking a pose and grinning wickedly. "Like one of the Shasu?"

"No," returned Moses, "and neither do I. We're much too clean."

Dropping to his knees, he turned back a corner of the heavy matting and, scraping together a handful of earth, rubbed it into his arms and legs, then, more reluctantly, into his chest and neck and face, where it stung unpleasantly. Ramses hastened to follow his example.

"There! Look at me! Even my father Horus would not know me!"

It was so. The long regal lines of the princely head looked dwarfed beneath the coarse, flat headdress, the bold features nondescript. Ramses, son of His Majesty Horus the Strong Bull, and favorite offspring of the queen consort Tuya, was indistinguishable from one of the slaves who fed and loaded the asses. Moses stared at him in amazement. Had he also undergone this same transformation? What was the difference, then, between a prince and a slave? He felt suddenly confused and dismayed.

"Come!" ordered Ramses with a wave of his hand, thereby giving a partial answer to the unspoken question. For he had laid aside, along with his princely cleanliness and garments, neither his manner of peremptory command nor its accompanying regal gestures. "Follow me and do just as I say."

As the young princes emerged from the semidarkness of their tent, the splendor of the vast military pageant struck their eyes with a brilliance that was almost blinding. Banners of crimson and gold floated on tall staves above canopies that vied with the sky in their deep cerulean hues. The golden symbols of Amon, Re, and Ptah flashed in the sun; while in the space before the royal tent the king's two-wheeled chariot, its wooden frame coated, even to graceful fluted spokes, with a smooth gold-silver veneer, outshone the sun itself.

"The guards," murmured Ramses, his haughty manner quite departed. "Keep your head down."

But the royal bodyguard, engrossed by the recent excitement, contented themselves with a brief, "Get along there, asses' dung!" or, "Out of the way, you entrails of a wild sheep's carcass!" and an occasional prodding with their spear points in the vicinity of the dirty, naked feet. One such thrust caught Ramses in the heel, bringing a faint trickle of blood, and he would have turned furiously on his assailant if Moses had not grasped his arm.

"I'll have him slain for that," Ramses muttered, "I'll order his tongue torn out and the soles of his feet branded with hot irons!"

"But he did not know you were the king's son," protested Moses reasonably. "And it is you he is doing his best to protect."

Ramses looked unconvinced, but he resolutely averted his eyes from the trickle of blood. Though tightened lips indicated that the incident was unforgotten, his eyes were soon gleaming again with excitement. From the crimson-dyed pavilion that housed the sacred falcon issued the shrill, moaning voice of the unfortunate priest raised in prayers and chantings, and before the entrance had gathered a motley crowd of officers, common soldiers, and mercenaries.

"Lift me up so I can see," ordered Ramses to a burly mercenary.

Moses caught his breath in alarm, but fortunately the mercenary was good-natured. He hoisted the dirty, ragged figure to his broad shoulder, held him there for a satisfactory interval, then set him down.

"His falcon is really gone" announced Ramses excitedly, when they had left the pavilion behind them. "His gold cage is empty. And the chain that fastens his left leg to the ivory horizontal bar is broken. That means he's still wearing part of it. It should be easy to spot a pure-white falcon with a chain of gold hanging to his leg and a jeweled collar about his neck."

"Yes!" said, Moses, feeling a pang of pity for the luckless creature. He remembered seeing him one day on his ivory perch, beating his splendid wings up and down, up and down.

The suspected displeasure of Horus, divine hawk-headed slayer of Egypt's enemies, had infected the discipline of the whole encampment. The young princes, to whom the vast spaces beyond tie rings of officers' tents were alien territory, looked with fascinated amazement at the seeming litter of confusion.

But as they observed more closely a certain order emerged. Freshly scrubbed war chariots were ranged in neat ranks, the horses that were to draw them pawing the ground contentedly close by. Row after row of two-wheeled baggage carts were being loaded, checked, and hauled away. Naked boys were loosing the fastening pegs of small pack asses and fitting them with double panniers, taking time out to settle their quarrels by jabbing at each other with the pins, while the stubborn little animals added to the excitement by prancing about and rolling in the dirt. An endless procession of slaves, most of them children, moved between the cistern and the water carts, backs bent double beneath bulging skins.

"Here, you! You there with the gaping mouth! Shut your filthy face and get busy!"

Moses' arms closed automatically about the empty waterskin that was suddenly thrust into them. He felt the sharp contact of a heavy sandal with his buttocks and a rough grasp on his shoulder swinging him into line among the water carriers. Stumbling along, keeping his eyes on a bony sweating torso which had a curious crisscrossing of blue marks between the shoulder blades, he wondered if Ramses was also in the line. Were the young prince gifted with a sense of humor, they could have great sport recounting the adventure in the royal harem. The Princess Nefretiri would laugh her soft, merry laugh, and the green particles in her eyes would sparkle as brightly as the facets of an emerald.

"Imagine a prince carrying water!" she would ripple gaily. "What did it feel like, Moses? I've always wished I could know how it felt to be a slave."

He was spun suddenly out of his reverie by the stinging bite of a lash.

"Step lively, you doddering ass! What you waiting for? Somebody to push your stupid head into the cistern?"

Moses hastily filled his waterskin and, hoisting it to his shoulders, staggered after the procession. He knew now what made the crisscrossing of blue marks on the bony torso in front of him. At least the clammy weight on his shoulders would save him from further assaults of the lash. But he was wrong. Again and again the stinging coil swept about his hips, his calves, his ankles, until finally the petty officer who wielded it passed on to other lagging victims. Once Moses caught a glimpse of a familiar face peering at him between the spokes of an oxcart wheel, and he knew that it was Ramses and that the young prince was laughing at him.

The clammy burden was removed from his back and another empty skin thrust into his arms. Again the procession made its staggering round. And yet again. Sweat poured from his body and filled his eyes so that only the coolness of the moist sand on his feet told him that he was keeping to the right path. Yet each time he passed the row of oxcarts he was conscious of the eyes peering mockingly between the wheel spokes. He stopped counting the number of times he went around, filled his skin, shouldered its clammy weight, deposited it, received another, filled it, staggered...Finally the spokes with their mocking face rose out of the ground and came toward him, became giant-size, began whirling in the air faster and faster until they turned into thousands of shooting sparks and suddenly vanished. He was lying in the bottom of a deep sand pit, and somebody—it sounded like Ramses—was calling down to him from miles above, at the top.

"Quick! Crawl behind this cart and don't move until they've all gone by. There! Now follow me. Keep close behind that drove of oxen, then make a dash across that open space. Now! There, I guess we're out of sight."

"What happened?" asked Moses dazedly.

"You fell. And one of those filthy creatures kicked you out of the way before the big brutes with the whip saw you." Ramses laughed loudly. "Did you look funny carting that bouncing carcass on your shoulders! What a story to tell back in the palace! I wonder what my sister Nefretiri will say!"

Moses was silent. His back and limbs were beginning to smart again from the strokes of the lash, and his tongue felt thick and heavy.

"That officer with the whip knows his business," continued the young prince more seriously. "He is a good servant of my father. I shall see to it that he is rewarded."

Hot anger flamed through Moses' weakened body. "Rewarded!" he choked.

"Why not? As you yourself said of the guard, he had no way of knowing that the lagging feet he was tickling belonged to a prince."

"But," Moses protested weakly, "you don't know who he is. You couldn't even remember what he looks like."

"Oh, yes, I could," replied Ramses confidently, a sudden gleam in his eyes. "No matter what happens, I never forget a face."

Guards pacing about the heavily laden carts containing the fruits of Seti's latest Asiatic campaign skirted the area hastily, casting curious glances at the vast array of plunder and tribute. Strange sounds—stampings, neighings, whinnies, chatterings, snarls, occasionally an earth-shaking roar—issued from that section where rare animals, gifts of petty Asiatic monarchs to the lord of all the earth from the Fourth Cataract to the Euphrates, were kept closely confined.

"When I am pharaoh," announced Ramses calmly, "I shall not carry about a foolish falcon as the symbol of my victories. I shall have—" He lifted his face speculatively, just as an especially bloodcurdling roar rent the air. "I know. I shall have a tame lion, and his name shall be 'Tearer-to-Pieces-of-His-Enemies' and he shall follow me about everywhere."

"When you are—" Moses stared at the young prince uncomprehendingly. "But—" He stopped abruptly.

The words had already formed on his lips: "But you know very well you're not going to be pharaoh. Even if your sister Nefretiri were not heiress to the throne, your half brother Amon-nebet is your father's favorite." But he did not say them. For they had entered the area where the prisoners of war were kept.

They were herded together like cattle, each one chained by his hands and feet to two others, in a space barely large enough for each to stand upright: fierce fighters of the wandering desert Shasu in their short jerkins and caps, their fierceness quite departed along with their battle-axes; bold chieftains of the Upper and Lower Retenu, stooped now and weak from hunger and long marching; even a few of the terrible Kheta, no longer awesome, proud red and blue fringed uniforms stripped down to shirt and loincloth, habitually shaved yellowish faces haggard beneath a thick growth of stubble.

One prisoner, a boy wearing, like themselves, the Shasu cap and jerkin, was at the moment being chained to the wheel of a chariot and flogged. The soldier who wielded the lash punctuated each stroke with a loud incrimination intended for the ears of the other prisoners.

"Fool! Devil! Filthy swine! Try to run away, would you? Amon curse you! Ptah rend your limbs one from the other! Re burn your flesh alive!"

Moses stopped short. Fascinated, he watched the serpent like coil as it rose and fell. Strange waves of emotion passed through his body.

"Come," said Ramses, pulling at his arm. "The guards will see us. The Shasu think we belong to them."

He was right. Some of the prisoners in jerkins and caps were pointing at them and calling excitedly in their harshly guttural dialect. Moses turned reluctantly and followed his companion between a double row of chariots, beyond which rose the outer bounds of the encampment, a high wall made of great shields of piebald skins planted firmly in the ground. Triumphantly Ramses pointed to a small opening near the bottom, and in another moment he had fallen flat on his stomach and wriggled through it

Moses followed. As he rose to his feet, shaking the clinging particles of earth from his ragged jerkin, he had a strange feeling that by some mysterious transformation he had also shaken off his identity. He was no longer Moses, royal prince of Egypt, adopted son of the noble princess Sitra, foster brother of Seti, the Strong Bull, lord of all the earth. He was a son of the Shasu, a vagrant child of the desert. This wild, desolate country was his homeland, his heritage, and somewhere, beyond the burnished copper rim of the horizon, a black goat's-hair tent was waiting for him beside a distant watch fire.

3

"Someone is following us," observed Ramses with more of annoyance than alarm.

The young prince was tiring of the adventure. His tender feet were bruised and swollen, his legs scratched by thornbushes, the dirty jerkin drenched with sweat. His eyes smarted painfully from the ovenlike glare of sunlight on bare rocks. He had long since ceased to scan the burning sky for a white bird flying low because of the weight of a gold chain on one of its legs.

Moses wheeled abruptly, his body becoming as motionless as the furrowed cheek of the wadi in front of them. It was an alert stillness, born not of fear but of a perfect integration of the senses. As Ramses had lost zest for the adventure, the older youth had gained it. Though his feet were equally tender, his step was firm and his brown legs seemed to pass through thorn bushes unscathed. The jerkin fitted easily, almost jauntily, on his shoulders, and the keen eyes, lifted unblinkingly to the suns hot glare, seemed to have absorbed something of its clarity and brilliance. While he stood motionless, the sound came again, a clatter of small pebbles behind them.

"Down behind these rocks," he ordered Ramses. "Flat on your stomach. Quick!"

It was strange how well he knew just what to do. Even while he peered warily over the edge of the narrow shelf on which their flattened bodies were huddled, his hands were reaching for rocks, swiftly sorting them as to size and shape and cutting edge. Instinctively he knew that a flat stone with a sharp point made a better missile, if used properly, than a larger round one, and when he found one that fitted his palm, he held it in his right hand, fingers relaxed, every muscle coordinated with his steady gaze and ready to spring taut at an instant's notice.

Though they were not far from the encampment, the wadi they had penetrated was as wild and lonely as a spot in the middle of the desert. They had entered it to escape detection by a contingent of Egyptian soldiers emerging with a great fanfare from the single entrance of the camp and marching with a mighty flourish of trumpets toward the desert. The chariot of Amon-nebet, Seti's oldest son, had led the procession, the young prince's undersized body looking absurdly insignificant beside the burly driver. Ramses, watching from the shelter of a wadi crevice, had flushed darkly.

"Reed-necked skin and bones!" he had muttered. "Thinks he's Horus himself riding the chariot of the sun across the sky! I'll grant he looks like a hawk with that hook nose and skinny neck, but if he thinks he's going to be lord of all the earth—!"

Moses had been too busy considering their quandary to concern himself with the jealousies of the sons of Seti. He had suddenly realized that their chief danger lay not in marauding natives but in plundering Egyptians. To all appearances they were Shasu, should they be captured, it would be little satisfaction to know that their tormentors would be executed with the cruelest torture as soon as the identity of their victims was discovered. They might be dead or worse before that happened.

"We must go up this wadi," he had told Ramses as soon as the soldiers had passed, "and stay in it until it's dark enough to find our way back to camp undetected. I guess we aren't quite as clever as we thought we were."

But Moses had not regretted the adventure. Even now, hand closed over the most primitive of weapons, eyes fixed intently on the ragged silhouette of sloping ground around which the approaching danger, Shasu or Egyptian, would at any moment make its appearance, he felt an emotion akin to exultation. He had never before lain so close to the bare earth. The dead gorge was no longer a lifeless place. Its withered furrows flowed with bright cascades of a thousand changing colors. Its silence was broken by an orchestra of sound: the swelling crescendos of expanding rocks, the faint drumbeat of insects' wings, the soft twanging of heat waves on the wiry stems of dry scrub. It was these barely perceptible sounds, hardly more than rhythms, which possessed reality, not the more audible warnings of a human presence.

"They're coming closer," whispered Ramses.

Moses scarcely heard the distinct clatter of falling pebbles. Following a sudden impulse, his gaze left the sloping ground and traveled up the wrinkled face of the wadi, up and up.

"Look!" With his free hand he grasped Ramses' arm.

High in the sky above the desert a white bird was flying. It hung poised in the intense blue like a perfectly carved inlay of ivory on a globe of sapphire. So clear was the atmosphere that each feather seemed sharply defined, the line of each graceful talon etched in firm outline. The slanting rays of the sun flung a collar of gold about its neck, forged bright golden coils which trailed in long streamers from its outthrust talons.

"The falcon!" breathed Ramses with avid excitement. "I can see the jeweled collar and the gold chain hanging to its leg!"

But Moses knew he was wrong. This creature bore no encumbrances of gold. It had never known imprisonment. In its exquisitely poised body, its splendid outflung wings, it was completely free. An exultation such as he had never known possessed him. The stone dropped forgotten from his hand. Up and up the bird mounted into the path of the setting sun, and his spirit mounted with it, riding triumphantly on a wave crest of unfathomable blueness. Then suddenly both white wings and sunlight vanished behind the dead, wrinkled features of the wadi. He was back again on the shelf of rock, and Ramses was clutching his arm.

A small landslide of pebbles slid down the face of the wadi so close that a few puffs of dust appeared along the ragged silhouette. Their pursuer was climbing up the side of the wadi as they had done. At any moment he would appear within their line of vision. Deliberately Moses reached again for the rock and fitted it carefully into his palm. Ramses began to whimper childishly.

"Quiet!" Moses mouthed the word silently.

A hand appeared in one of the jagged fissures, then a long lean arm, both surprisingly black. Moses lifted his own right arm, and, swinging it in a slow arc, held it poised above his head. Their one chance lay, he knew, in taking the pursuer by surprise. After the first strategic missile, his small pile of stones would give little competition to either the Shasu's short metal battle-ax or the Egyptian's bronze, sickle-shaped sword.

The black hand and lean arm were succeeded by what looked like a large wad of knotted wool surmounted by a bobbing ostrich plume and this in turn by a squat body, fully nine tenths naked. A sudden exclamation escaped Moses' lips, and at the same moment the stone slipped from his hand.

"White Elephant!" he cried in a loud voice.

The plume bobbed violently, and the wrinkled face split wide open, displaying a wide gap in the yellowed teeth. The little Nubian scrambled up the side of the wadi on all fours, filling his hands with rocks as he came. These he laid in a little pile before Moses, then, still beaming, obligingly prostrated himself to receive what he considered to be his proper punishment.

"Great lord printh big angry bad thlave," he lisped cheerfully in his stumbling Egyptian. "Bad thlave wake up crawl like worm find lord printh. Great lord printh hit bad thlave hard rock. Break back if want."

"He ought to be flogged to a pulp," said Ramses angrily, "giving us a scare like that. Doesn't he know a slave gets his tongue cut out for running away from camp?"

White Elephant did know, and a pink protrusion through the gap in his front teeth indicated his willingness to comply with this requirement also. He even picked up the stone that had dropped from Moses' hand and shrugged his shoulders apologetically because he had no weapon with a keener edge to proffer.

Ramses lifted one of the stones. "He's your slave," he said curtly. "But if you're not going to punish him, I will!"

Moses' hand shot out and closed firmly about the young prince's arm. "Put that down," he ordered briefly.

Ramses dropped the stone, but his lip curled and his eyes were sullen.

It was White Elephant who led them back to the camp after nightfall and who found the opening in the wall where the shields did not quite overlap. Without him they would have been lost in a maze of rutted desert paths.

The Tower of the Lion, the round, high, impregnable fortress that Seti had built to guard the Lion's Pool, one of the series of oases that marked the ten days' march between Tharu on the border of Egypt and the southernmost walled city of Canaan, was an even more imposing spectacle by night than by day. Surrounded by tier upon tier of marching guards, its surface of whitewashed bricks gleaming in the light of their torches, its massive battlements were visible far across the desert. Above the wall of shields the gaily colored fabrics of the royal tents and shrines were outlined against the night sky by their encompassing watch fires.

A spirit of holiday festivity pervaded the encampment. The long campaign was nearing its end. Tomorrow at dawn the last lap of the march would be undertaken. There was no further need for conservation of supplies. While the officers banqueted in their tents, common soldiers supped less sumptuously on Syrian bread, lentils, and garlic. Wine flowed freely. Discipline was relaxed. Some of the less desirable of the female captives, previously reserved for the use of officers alone, were now relinquished to the common soldiers, and since most of the prisoners were males, competition over the matter of precedence and length of privilege was keen. The camp resounded with the echoes of quarreling and more or less good-natured drunken brawls.

Fortunately for the two princes and their Nubian guide, the guards also were indulging in a bit of joviality, and their entrance through the gap in the wall was as inconspicuous as their departure had been. Were the vanquished desert tribes to come in any number tonight, thought Moses as he crawled between the wheels of deserted chariots, they might well be able to challenge the dominion of the lord of all the earth.

There was no revelry in the area where the prisoners of war were herded. Most of the guards still on duty were either clustered about burning torches playing checkers or lying on the ground in a drunken stupor. But the captives showed no inclination to take advantage of the relaxed surveillance. Their bodies lay huddled together in the darkness. Since no man had enough room to stretch himself full length on the ground and was forced to seek rest by leaning in sitting posture against his neighbor, there was a continuous uneasy motion like the fluctuation of waves. It filled the night air with a murmurous undertone as pervasive as the stench of unwashed bodies and the filth in which they lay.

The intrusion of a different sound attracted Moses' attention, and as he turned toward it curiously he stumbled over a bulky object on the ground. He knew instinctively that it was a human being and that the moaning sound he had heard issued from its lips. He remembered the Shasu boy who had been lashed to the chariot wheel and the serpent like coil whipping again and again through the air. Stooping, he passed his hands over the still figure, encountering first warm, moist flesh, then cold metal, and he knew that the chain fastening the boy's body to the wheel had not been unloosed.

Feeling the exploring fingers, the figure stirred and began to talk wildly in a voice deliriously high and penetrating. Instantly White Elephant was by his master's side, his fingers clamped over the young Shasu's lips.

"Lord printh run behind chariot" he muttered. "Quick. Guard come, printh look like thlave boy. Bad."

Moses hastened to obey his slave. Following Ramses by a circuitous route toward the center of the encampment, he heard the oaths of the guards behind him and knew that he had escaped just in time. Presently White Elephant appeared like a watchful black shadow beside him.

There was another reason why the camp was indulging its thirst for celebration. The royal sacred falcon had been found. The hawk-headed one had withdrawn his disapproval. Outside the shrine devoted to his sacred person a throng of worshipers were gathered, and inside, confined in his golden cage and chained securely, the bejeweled bird was being stuffed with delectable balls of paste by a grateful priest. While two royal princes and the flower of the imperial army had been scouring the desert and searching the lofty heavens, the lost glory of Egypt had been hiding behind a pile of rubbish in a corner of his tent, tail drooping and head tucked beneath his feathers.

4

Moses lay on his bed in the royal tent and watched the flickering light from the open lamp play on the folds of the canopy above his head. There was no reason why he should not be able to sleep. Yet he was as wide awake as when, a few hours previously, he had lain on a narrow shelf of earth in a desert wadi and watched a white bird winging its way upward into the path of the sun.

He had seen birds fly before—hundreds, thousands of them: snow-white herons mirrored in the placid waters of the Nile, cranes and hoopoe birds and wagtails, white-billed ducks rising gracefully from their swaying nests in the tops of slender papyrus reeds. What was there in the flight of one white bird to make it seem that in all his fifteen years up to that moment he had never once sensed the glory of freedom, the pure beauty of motion? And what did the flight of a bird have to do with the fact that a boy was at that moment lying chained to a chariot wheel, flesh swollen and lacerated, babbling incoherently about some place called "home?"

Moses knew only a few words of the Shasu dialect, but he had recognized this one in the boy captive's delirious outburst. *Home.* That was why he had run away, of course. To the Shasu this barren desert country with its stunted scrub, its leprose soil, its desolate wadies, was home. And Moses understood how he felt. Yesterday he would have been unable to do so. But this was today. And today he had done many things which he had never dreamed of doing. He had laughed in the presence of the pharaoh. He had worn the ragged jerkin of a slave and carried a bulging waterskin and felt the biting teeth of a lash on his back. He had walked barefoot through a blistered waste of thorns and dry broom and peeling rocks. And he had seen a white bird flying.

Ramses, he was sure, had already forgotten the adventure. With the washing of his body and the donning of his perfumed white garments, the young prince had completely resumed his proper role. He lay now on his couch, breathing deeply and evenly, aloof and untroubled. It would always be so with Ramses, provided he could get his own way. He would probably lie just so in his final voluminous wrappings in the Valley of the Dead at Thebes, his proud, handsome features as unravaged by a lifetime's experience as they were now untouched by the emotions of a single day.

Tomorrow, doubtless, like Ramses, Moses would forget that the day's events had ever happened. He would put on his clean garments and his elegant sandals. He would ride in his chariot behind the king's older son and review with indifference the loaded wagons of booty and the endless procession of prisoners chained one to the other. And if he saw a white bird mounting upward into the path of the sun...

Suddenly Moses rose from his bed. Noiselessly he slipped the linen robe from his body and, fumbling under his couch, found the wadded bundle of soiled rags. This time he donned them with no emotion other than haste and caution. Satisfying himself that White Elephant, sprawled on the mat near the tent entrance, was really soundly sleeping, he crept carefully outside. Several of the attendants on duty were snoring. Moses waited until the pacing sentry had his back turned, then slipped across the brightly lighted area into the shadow of the shrine of Amon. Here he lay flat on the ground, until the sentry passed again.

Once he was outside the royal area, progress was easy. One ragged slave more or less among the many who were kept laboring through the night attracted little notice. The working area of the camp, it seemed, did not sleep on comfortable folding beds between linen sheets. In fact, it did not sleep. The naked donkey boys were still quarreling and prodding each other with their fastening pins as they filled the panniers with staggering loads of provisions. Soldiers were still shouting, oxcarts still creaking, horses still whinnying and pawing, chariots still being polished. And in the area where the captives were herded there were still the indescribable stench, the solid mass of human bodies, the seething restlessness.

Moses moved more carefully now. He crawled between the wheels of chariots on his stomach, crossed the spaces between the rows on his hands and knees. When he reached the place where, as he remembered, he had heard the low moaning, he dropped flat on the ground and remained motionless. The guards were still playing checkers under a flaring torch, and for some moments he studied their movements, noting that their voices, though cautiously subdued, were unnaturally high, their hands unsteady. They had reached that stage of drunkenness where their perceptions were slightly dulled but their emotions, once aroused, would flare hot and unrestrained. His every movement must be careful, but the success of his purpose depended not on him but on the still figure that he could barely discern in the shadow of the chariot wheel a dozen feet away. Inch by inch he crawled across the intervening space. At arm's length from the boy he paused but did not reach out his hand to touch him.

"Home," he whispered softly in Shasu, then slowly repeated all the other words he knew in the desert dialect. "Sky. Tent. Water. Earth. Bread. Home."

Again he repeated the list softly, but no sound came from the still form. When he spoke the word "home" for the third time, however, he thought he detected a slight motion in the shadows. Again he crawled forward, this time on his knees, until he was bending over the recumbent body, but still he made no effort to touch it.

"Home," he whispered again, his lips close to the boy's ear. "Tent. Bread. Home. Home. Home"

"Home." The answer came back clearly but in the same soft whisper. And Moses' pulses leaped, for he knew that the boy was conscious and that his delirium had passed. He was suddenly aware of a pair of bright eyes gazing at him through the semi-darkness.

He worked quickly now but silently. It took him an eternity, it seemed, to find the fastening of the chain and another to unloose it. The clinking of the bronze coils sounded as loud in his ears as the beating of war drums, but it was apparently drowned in other sounds, for the guards remained indifferent. The boy's wrists and ankles were bound tightly with rope, and he struggled with the knots until his fingers felt numb and his nails were broken. Finally he succeeded in loosing the rope about the ankles, but the knot fastening the wrists proved too stubborn. The boy would have to move as well as he could with his hands tied behind him. That is, if he could move at all. Moses lifted the feet and limbs, but they felt like lifeless sticks in his hands. He chafed them gently, then more vigorously, until he could feel strength flowing beneath his fingers. The boy, fully conscious now, tried to help him, moving his legs up and down and twisting his body, but the effort was painful, and his breath began to escape in little gasping sounds.

"Sh!" warned Moses, watching the guards apprehensively.

Suddenly he dropped flat on the ground and crawled between the chariot wheels, trying to burrow into the sand and make himself as inconspicuous as possible. The guards had hastily left their game, hiding their checkers in the sand, and, staggering to their feet, had seized their lighted torches and begun dutifully to make their rounds. An officer's voice rang out sharply some distance away.

"Here, you drunken sluggards! What do you think you are? Wet nurses to a cradle full of babies? Let one of these prisoners get away and you'll be a juicy picnic for the vultures!"

The darkness bloomed into activity, as guards with torches busily and noisily policed their areas. From beneath the chariot Moses watched the approach of four stocky, unsteady legs, outlined in a little pool of flickering light. They came so close that he could see the fine white ridges where the plaited thongs of sandals pressed into the flesh. When they paused close to the chariot, he lay in an agony of apprehension, certain that the beating of his pulses, echoing in his ears like hammers, would reveal his presence. He twisted his head so he could see the boy's prostrate figure and was relieved to note that he had put his ankles tightly together and was lying completely motionless. If the guards did not come any closer, they might not notice that the chain was unfastened.

"Look! What's that thing by the chariot? A shadow?"

"You're lucky if shadows is all you see! After the wine you guzzled, it should be horned snakes and—By Horus, there is something!"

"I know. It's the Shasu who ran away. The boys left him there after they flogged him."

"Maybe we ought to put him back in line. Save trouble in the morning."

"Save more trouble, maybe, if we wait. Leave him for the birds."

"He's not dead. Hear him breathing?"

"Maybe he will be if we wait."

"Hold the light up while I check on his chains."

"Oh, why bother! He's trussed up like a cooked goose. The inspector's gone. Let's get back."

"All right, but look out with that torch! I don't want my eyes burned out."

"Hold it yourself then. You're as drunk as I am. Let's get out of this hole. It stinks like dead swine."

Moses waited until they had returned to their shelter and he could hear them swearing truculently because they could not find the checkers they had hidden. In their present condition, he decided, the task would consume a good hour. The young captive was waiting for him, his eyes wide open.

"Home?" The whispered question was followed by a torrent of words in Shasu.

"Home," replied Moses simply.

Placing his hands beneath the boy's armpits, he tried to drag him over the ground, but he dared not stand upright, and with his heavy burden it was impossible to make much headway. To his relief the young captive soon began to help himself, crawling on his knees and hitching his body along by a series of short, jerking motions, but his weakened condition and bound hands made progress slow. Moses could now crawl ahead, leading the way between the rows of chariots. The journey seemed interminable, and more than once he feared they were traveling in circles. He wondered if he had remembered the way, counted the rows of chariots correctly, or if, having remembered, he had kept a straight path between the wheels. It would be so easy to miss the small opening in that endless array of tightly fitting shields, far easier than to find it.

Finally the end came, and they emerged into a narrow open space, the stout rampart of interlacing shields in front of them. Feverishly Moses searched for the small hole near the bottom of the wall, feeling the rough surface with his hands because it was too dark to see clearly. When he finally found it, the relief was so great that he sank back weak and shaken, the sweat pouring from his body.

"Home," he whispered, pointing to the shadowed space. "Desert. Sand. Tent. Water. Home."

After the boy had gone, Moses lay quietly on the ground. Later, in the dimness of his tent, clothed again in clean linen and lying between cool sheets, he would try to think lucidly about this strange thing he had done. But now he could not think. He could only feel. He lay very still and let the shapes and sounds and aromas of the night play upon his senses.

He was poignantly conscious of raw sand pressing into his flesh, of cool air fanning the moisture from his face. His nostrils quivered beneath the commingled smells of horses, human sweat, and leather. The distant howling of a jackal sent a tingle up and down his spine. He felt a sudden stab of regret that for him the strange adventure would have no finish. He would never know whether the little captive had found his home or not.

But in this he was wrong. For when the Egyptian army broke camp at dawn on the following morning, the lord of all the earth, his princes, and the mighty host of his followers, rode past the figure of a young Shasu who had tried to make his escape during the night and had been caught by the guards a short distance from the camp. He had been impaled on an upright stick beside the road as an example to all the world of what must happen to any individual who dared defy the will of the pharaoh. Already the vultures were circling about his mutilated body.

5

Seti, the Strong Bull, the Mighty Horus, the Golden Hawk, Creator of the Two Lands, the lord of all the earth, was returning in triumph from his latest foreign tour of inspection. Not since the first years of his reign, when the disgrace of a half century of military decadence had been gloriously wiped out by the resubordination of her Asiatic empire, had Egypt given her conquering pharaoh such a welcome.

A new song by the court poet was on every tongue.

> "Behold, Seti comes with the glory of the sun!
> He rejoices to enter the fight.
> He loves to encounter the foe.
> Blood is the joy of his heart.
> Rebellious of heart are his foes;
> Their heads he lays low at his feet.
> An hour of battle to him is more than a day full of joy!"

Fast runners reported the progress of the mighty cavalcade along the final lap of its journey, and by the time the first clouds of dust appeared on the eastern rim of the desert the road west of the border was lined with hundreds of pilgrims. From the massive battlements of the fortress of Tharu bright banners floated, and its long marching walls and bastioned towers bristled with the glittering lances of mercenaries in full uniform. When finally the vanguard of the vast procession arrived, dusty and weary from its last long trek, there rose a cry of rejoicing which could be heard far out on the desert.

First to cross the bridge in the train of the advance guard were the Syrian captives, marching single file, each chained to the one before and behind, their arms either pinioned behind them at the elbows or crossed and tied together above their heads. Their long black hair and matted beards and striped woolen garments elicited shrieks of derision from the clean-shaven, white-robed Egyptians. The crowds cast shrill taunts at the proud rebel princes of the Retenu, their jeweled headbands awry, their rich, bedraggled garments trailing about their ankles. They rained coarse jests on the unsightly bodies of women, clothed only in their long hair and the caked dust of the desert. But the most pointed gibes were saved for the small group that marched stolidly at the end of the procession, powerful shoulders squared, short, squat bodies unbent and apparently unwearied, their fewness in number and proud demeanor mute testimony that beyond the tents of the Shasu and the walled cities of the Retenu and the rich seaports of the Phoenicians lay the dominions of the terrible Kheta, their heads unbowed, their knees but slightly bent before the lord of all the earth.

Clods of earth struck the stocky figures and sent them reeling. The gibes and epithets were but louder and lustier for being self-deceptive.

"Behold how the mighty Kheta lick the dust!"

"Amon and his son Seti have crumbled them to powder!"

"Flatter than their own flat foreheads have the Kheta fallen!"

But there was no self-deception in the acclaim that greeted the next major division of the procession. The crowds stared with avid eyes at the array of plunder and tribute stored in chests and sacks or piled high beneath sheltering animal skins. There would be casks of olive oil and corn and honey from the city states of Canaan; from the towns of the Amorites gold vessels inlaid with jewels, fine-woven embroidered stuffs, and chariots adorned with silver and gold; from Phoenicia silver and precious stones, furniture of carved ivory, copper, lead, and cedar.

The loaded wagons passed over the bridge, and the throng held its breath, then burst into a storm of cheers that seemed to make the solid masonry of Tharu tremble.

"Hail, Seti! Son of Re, Offspring of Mighty Amon! Golden Horus, rising on the wings of the morning and sailing your shining bark high in the heavens! The sun himself is your father! Hail, Seti, Conqueror of Darkness, Rider of the Golden Falcon!"

The spare features with their hint of gentle aloofness did not appear to belong to a man to whom blood was the joy of his heart or an hour of battle more than a day full of joy. And indeed Seti at that very moment was congratulating himself that his fighting days were over. He had had more than enough of battle long ago during the first years of his reign. The only reason for his undertaking this last campaign was the youth who rode in the chariot just behind him. He had wanted to assure himself that his oldest son would inherit security along with the double red and white crown which he intended at all costs to place on his head. He did not propose that the young prince should have to begin his reign, as he had done, by resubjugating Egypt's vassal provinces. For him it had been a tiresome and unpleasant task. For Amon-nebet, the scholar and dreamer, it would be a self-destructive one.

So deeply was Seti immersed in his thoughts that he did not notice the sudden waning of applause at the appearance of his oldest son's chariot or the storm of approval that greeted Prince Moses, who followed. The garlands rained down on the youthful figure whose eyes lighted eagerly at sight of familiar landmarks, who returned their homage with genuine, if reticent, smiles of appreciation, and who drove his own horses instead of committing their reins to his driver.

"Welcome home, Prince Moses!" shouted the people. "May Amon bless you with long life and riches!"

But Ramses, riding in his chariot behind the two older princes, noticed, and his eyes first brightened with satisfaction, then narrowed in wary disapproval. It suited his plans very well that his half brother, Amon-nebet, should not find favor with the people. But the popularity of Prince Moses was both disquieting and difficult to understand. He was certainly not unusually attractive in appearance. His body was too long and loose-jointed and angular. His features were too dark and heavy, boldly sculptured like those of the Asiatic princes who passed through Tharu each year to bring their homage and tribute to the court of the pharaoh.

Asiatic. That was the word that described him. Swiftly Ramses reviewed in his mind the rumors concerning Moses' parentage. While there was but one actually known fact, that he was the adopted son of Princess Sitra, Seti's royal mother, for years the court had buzzed with conjectures. Some said that he was the son of the great pharaoh Harmhab by a favorite concubine; others that, like Sitra herself, he was blood descendant of the fabulous Ikhnaton. But the most popular rumor asserted that he was actually the son of Sitra by a Mitannian prince who had journeyed to the court during the late years of Harmhab's reign and whose philanderings were even now the source of excited whisperings in the privacy of the harem.

The slate-colored eyes suddenly gleamed. It was this very mystery about Prince Moses' origin, decided Ramses with an astuteness far beyond his years, which accounted for his popularity. If it could once be ascertained and published throughout Egypt just what his parentage was, especially if such a discovery should reveal a lack of royal blood...

"Look! There's the little one!"

"Imagine a baby like that fighting battles!"

"See how straight he stands. Pretending he's driving like Prince Moses!"

"Hail, Ramses! Welcome home, little one!"

Ramses sensed the spirit of good-natured raillery, even though most of the comments were indistinguishable, and his face flushed darkly. He stretched himself high on his toes, clinging tightly to the reins to keep his balance, and set his features straight ahead as his father did, looking neither to right nor left. He wished he dared command his driver to give the reins completely into his hands, but he knew the power of the horses.

Slowly the blood receded from his temples. Very well then. He was a child. His time had not yet come. But it would come. Perhaps now he was small in stature, but he would grow. He would grow until his figure filled the whole of Egypt and stretched its shadow to the north and south and east and west, farther than that of Seti or of Harmhab or even of the mighty Thutmose. And no one, certainly neither a puny bookworm nor a princeling of doubtful origin, no, not even the great god Amon himself, was going to stop him.

After the desolation of the desert the fertile Valley of Goshen seemed a veritable garden of the gods. Moses gazed about him in delight. The heaviness that had settled on his spirit since they had broken camp at the Tower of the Lion suddenly lifted. It was as if the adventure he had shared with Ramses in the desert had never been. It was one of the mirages that had tortured their aching eyes over and over again during the ten days' march between the outpost of Canaan and Tharu. There had been no creeping forth from his tent at night with the coarseness of dirty rags chafing his clean flesh; no rising in the morning to see black shadows circling about a naked body. And the only white birds that possessed reality were the lazy herons perched along the banks of the canal.

He was glad to be home again. His lungs drank deeply of the sun-drenched air and of the fragrance of fresh garlands piled on the floor of the chariot about his feet. The fevered restlessness of the long days in the desert ebbed slowly, and a pleasant feeling of lethargy stole over him. Unconsciously he slackened the pace of his horses and let his chariot fall farther and farther behind that of Amon-nebet. Here in this land of sunshine and flowers there was no urgency, no haste. As it was now, so it had always been. So it would always be. These might have been the same white herons that had stood lazily sunning themselves on the bank of the canal when the mighty Snefru reared the first fortresses at Tharu. And these stooped bodies toiling in the brickfields beside the road, naked or clad only in breechclouts, might be the selfsame laborers who had mined the mighty blocks for Khufu's pyramid.

No, not just the same. He looked at them more closely, then turned questioningly to Nefu, the young captain who stood beside him in the chariot.

"Some new breed of slaves?" he inquired curiously.

The captain shrugged. "They all look alike to me. Same dirt, same empty faces, same—" He looked more closely. "By the holy mother Isis, these are different! They still have their beards!"

It was more than beards, however, Moses decided, that differentiated these laborers from the thousands of other serfs whom he had seen in the mines and quarries and brickfields of Egypt. Handing the reins to Nefu, he directed his full attention toward the toiling figures, determined to discover just what the difference was. For one thing, he noted, they were not habitually stooped. The moment one of them set down a loaded basket or lifted his body after the placing of a mold, his shoulders automatically straightened.

Then, too, their movements were awkward. They were not used to making bricks. Their rows of freshly molded rectangles were neither straight nor well spaced, their calculations as to how large a mass would fill a mold by no means accurate. Even the motions of their feet as they trampled the mud in the kneading pit were lumbering and awkward.

"Squatters," observed Nefu contemptuously. "Filthy tenders of sheep and goats. I'd heard the pharaoh was using them to build his new city up here in the Delta. It's a wonder they don't get those dirty beards caught in the mud. Filthy foreigners! You'd think after being in a civilized land this long, they'd learn to live like men!"

Distaste was suddenly mingled with Moses' curiosity. He had noticed these squatters before when passing through the valley, watched them sitting in the openings of their ugly black tents or mud hovels, seen them herding their awkward goats and cumbersome, broad-tailed sheep into shelters made by draping papyrus mats over their long, ungainly crooks. The Delta, and especially this long fertile triangle extending from Tharu to its apex, was full of these seminomads who had drifted in from Asia and settled close to the border. Some of them—families, clans, occasionally even whole tribes—were continually knocking at the gates of Tharu, begging asylum from famine, pestilence, or other hostile nomads, and the policy of Egypt had been lenient toward such peaceful invaders. They had been permitted to pitch their tents, or, as they became more civilized, build their rude huts and tend their flocks, unmolested as long as they remained by themselves and yielded a good portion of their produce to the tax collectors. They also made an excellent buffer between the Egyptian state and other marauding desert tribes.

Being nomads, most of them soon drifted back into Asia again, but some clans had lived in the fertile valley for generations, even tracing their lineage back to the era of the hated Hyksos, the Asiatic conquerors who had swept into Egypt, seized the sacred diadem of the vulture and the snake, and worn it for a century or more upon their unholy, bearded heads. Occasionally, reminded of this experience by a slight excess of striped turbans and stubborn black beards, Egypt had risen in a brief surge of panic, rigidly regimenting these alien minorities or hustling them from her borders, but for the most part she had treated them with contempt and indifference. Now, it seemed, Seti had conceived the idea of utilizing their man power.

Revulsion swept through Moses, followed by a sense of pride and well-being. The gods had truly blessed him. It was good to be a prince and to belong to the chosen race which Ptah, the divine artificer, had conceived and created. Other peoples of the earth had been given names according to their place and kind: Libyans, Nubians, Phoenicians, Amorites. Even these contemptible squatters had names by which they called themselves: Bedouins, Arabians, Hebrews. But those in whose veins the blood of pharaohs flowed, who were nourished by the life-giving energy of Re and reborn after death in the likeness of the risen Osiris, had no need of a name. They alone were *men*.

"Look at the stubborn fools!" muttered Nefu angrily. "What's the matter with their construction bosses? Can't they even keep the swine off the road when a royal procession passes?"

Quickly lowering his eyes, Moses saw that the road ahead was lined on either side with a slowly uncoiling chain of figures, heads and shoulders hidden beneath huge baskets of black mud. Seti and his glittering equipage had completely disappeared.

"Get out of the way, you offal from a swine's dirty belly! And when a prince of the royal house passes by, put your face in the mud as well as your feet!"

Seizing his whip, the young captain swung it in a swift arc. It whined through the air and curled smartly about a pair of naked calves, buckling them sharply to the ground. The basket tipped forward, its contents spilling in a black soggy mass over the head of the fallen figure. Moses was aware of a pair of eyes blazing up at him through sodden streaks of earth.

"I didn't expect him to take my advice so literally," chortled the captain in high good humor. "Guess he'll have a bit of trouble combing that dose of mud out of his crazy beard."

Moses was silent. Now he knew what that intangible something was that made these laborers different from all the others he had noticed. He had seen it in the eyes of the kneeling figure. It was rebellion.

"Pull to the side!" warned Moses suddenly.

Seizing the rein nearer to him, he gave it such a sharp, swift tug that the right horse reared. The light chariot lunged to the side and barely escaped overturning. There was a howl of pain as one of the brown stooped figures crumpled beneath the descending hoofs. But the impulsive gesture had been none too soon. Missing their left wheel by but a few inches, the chariot of Ramses swept past them.

Ramses himself held the reins. He stood with feet wide apart, head flung proudly back, on his handsome features an expression of triumphant confidence that contrasted ludicrously with that of his terrified driver, who crouched on the floor clutching the light rail. Swerving to the left, the excited black stallions plunged forward, their hoofs mowing a swath in the long line of plodding laborers. Further excited by the shrill screams of their victims, the rearing beasts lunged first to one side of the road, then to the other, the stooped figures crumpling beneath them like slender reeds.

But Ramses remained unperturbed. His hands, though lighter and less skillful than those of his driver, were sure and steady on the reins. Slowly the plunging animals responded to the unaccustomed but dynamic touch. Wild eyes subdued, necks proudly arched, shining flanks quivering, they swung obediently into rhythm. The light chariot stopped careening and flashed triumphantly down the road, each wheel a swift-spinning disk of gold. Ramses' full lips curled into a slow, exultant smile.

"By the sacred crocodile!" exploded Nefu weakly after he had succeeded in getting his own horses under control and back to the center of the road. "What happened?"

"The prince decided to drive his own horses," returned Moses briefly.

The confusion about them increased rather than lessened. Moans and screams from the wounded laborers were punctuated by staccato commands from a construction boss attempting unsuccessfully to keep discipline intact. The road ahead and on either side of their chariot was suddenly dark with a horde of naked figures working swiftly and silently, closing the eyes of the dead, digging with bare fingers into the mounds of bruised flesh and massed clay and reed, hoisting the crushed bodies to their shoulders. The sight filled Moses with an overpowering nausea, and he closed his eyes.

"Let's get out of here!" he said thickly to Nefu.

He was conscious of the shouts of soldiers and knew that a path was being cleared ahead of his chariot. Another moment and they would have left the revolting scene behind them. Tensing himself for the jolt of their first movement, he waited for the whine of Nefu's whip. It did not come.

"I tell you, drive on!" he commanded sharply.

"Look!" said Nefu.

Moses opened his eyes. A woman was standing in the road directly in their path. The spears of a half dozen guards were within striking distance, but none made an effort to touch her. Indeed, their almost diffident restraint gave the mistaken impression that it was she, not the royal chariot, whom they were there to protect. Moses noted in his first startled glance that she was both young and beautiful. Naked from shoulders to waist and from knees to ankles, her straight slender figure was rich with the bloom of early womanhood. The black clay that covered arms and limbs and furrowed the rest of the half-naked body with caked streaks of grime hid none of the voluptuous curves nor dulled the warm tints of smooth golden flesh.

"Sweet Hathor!" exclaimed Nefu. "Will you look at those breasts and thighs! She's the goddess herself with no cow's head to spoil her! Would I trade my commission for a job as construction boss of this outfit!"

Moses scarcely heard. He saw only a pair of wide blazing eyes that looked straight into his, so compelling in their intensity that he could not tear his own away. A snake's eyes had once held his gaze like that He had stood before a golden cage in a temple of Buto, the serpent-goddess, and tried desperately to tear his eyes from two glittering beads of flame. The sweat had stood on his forehead, as it did now, and a burning dryness had settled in his throat. The nausea in the pit of his stomach spread in an enveloping coldness over his whole body.

Without releasing his gaze, the woman moved forward until her knees brushed the crossbar to which the harnesses were fastened. The great stallions pawed the ground nervously. But she showed as fearless a disregard for them as for the guardsmen's spears. Her right hand remained closed over a lump of moist clay, but with her left she reached up carelessly and grasped the nearer stallion's bridle.

"They'll kill the crazy bitch!" muttered Nefu, pulling the reins so taut that his knuckles showed white. "Mother of Horus, what a woman!"

Moses grasped the rail hard with both hands. He had to hold fast to something to keep from sinking into the cold flood that seemed to envelop him.

"Coward!" The woman spat out the epithet and it hung like a palpable substance in the air between them. The words that followed were spoken in broken Egyptian, but so interspersed with some obscure desert dialect that they came to Moses' ears in disjointed snatches, whipping his dulled consciousness like the sharp strokes of a lash.

"*You*...gold-bedecked puppet...pampered princess' darling...pet baboon on the end of a string...don't know what it is to do a day's work...get those pretty fingers dirty...make bricks out of human flesh instead of clay...you and your kind...no wonder you're sick to your stomach...turn tail and run like a coward...day will come when you'll really be sick...wish you'd never been born...day will come when you'll no longer dare...you who ride now in the chariot will be crushed beneath its wheels...will wipe the dirt out of your eyes...like *this!*"

The final words darted from the woman's lips like a snake's hiss, and at the same moment she lifted her arm and flung the handful of wet clay straight into the young prince's face. Stunned and blinded, still clinging to the rail, Moses heard the shouts of guards, felt the chariot lunge forward beneath him. By the time he had caught his breath and wiped the sticky particles from his stinging eyes, they had left the noise and confusion behind. Nefu cast him a hasty side glance in which discreet amusement was properly concealed beneath indignant outrage.

"Daughter of the she-cat Bast!" he exclaimed with undeniable relish. "Her tongue should be pulled out by the roots, her eyes burned with live coals. Her limbs should be fastened to a pair of tigers and torn one from the other. What a pity, though—such beautiful limbs!" He pulled regretfully on the reins. "Shall I turn about and see that all these things are done?"

"Yes," said Moses, his anger fanned by the suspicion that Nefu was secretly enjoying his predicament. "If one of those heathen squatters thinks she can defy a prince of Egypt—!" He choked suddenly. Some of the gritty particles had got into his mouth, and an especially large one seemed to have lodged in his throat. He had just remembered that if they returned he would have to look again on those mounds of bruised flesh and massed clay and broken reed.

"No!" he directed sharply. "The guards will handle her. They know how to deal with rebels."

"If they catch her," chuckled Nefu. "One minute she was under the horses' heads, the next she'd completely disappeared. I'd swear the earth came up and swallowed her. Who was she, do you think? Bast or Hathor? Or a little bit of both?"

Moses did not reply.

PART II

1

Moses was submitting to the ministrations of one of the temple barbers when the message came that he was to report in the chamber of the high priest at sundown. Although it was still before dawn, he instantly began to conjecture as to the purpose of the summons. Did the Great Seer have some special mission for him? Was he to be promoted at last to an official position among the priesthood? or reprimanded because he had not properly fulfilled his duties as Chief of Scribes? Before his questionings could be satisfied, the great god Re whom he served would have passed through his daily threefold pilgrimage: been born out of the night as Harmachis, risen at noonday to the full glory of his strength as Khepri, and descended to his death in the west as Atum. It was a long time to wait.

The agile little barber, who dutifully appeared every third day in Moses' apartment with folding stool and sharp razor of firestone, suddenly waved his murderous instrument in triumph.

"Atum be praised!" he exclaimed. "The lord prince, the Chief of Scribes, is a man full grown at last. Today for the first time I must put the razor to his cheeks!"

White Elephant hastened to produce a bronze mirror and stared admiringly while his master strove with attempted nonchalance to locate the barely visible light-brown tufts. In spite of his apparent indifference it was with an undeniable thrill that Moses felt the unfamiliar tingle of firestone on the flesh above his cheekbones.

His routine ministration finished, the barber lifted his little oil cruse, and, pouring a rich stream, massaged it with gentle motions into Moses' short, curly hair. "Soon," he said flatteringly, his voice almost as smooth as the contents of his cruse, "I shall be shaving not only the body and face of my lord prince but his head also. Is it not so?"

"Perhaps," replied Moses, the color mounting in his tingling cheeks. The barber was right. Three days from now, when the process of shaving his body was again consummated, the curly locks might be replaced by a completely bald pate, one of the distinguishing marks of a full-fledged priest. Regarding his image critically in the mirror and secretly admiring the luster of his curls, he wondered how he would look were he completely bald, and his enthusiasm for the priesthood momentarily waned.

For two years, since his return from the campaign with Seti in Asia, Moses had been fulfilling his apprenticeship as scribe in the College of Priests at On. Though his education was formally finished, he continued his studies under his old teacher, Maruma, and acted as his assistant. Since it was the will of the Princess Sitra that he should enter the priesthood, he had no other choice, nor, indeed, any other desire. He fretted only at the delay. Now, he hoped, the long-expected day had come.

The barber fussed nervously with his equipment, cutting his wrist on the sharp edge of his razor as he restored it to its leather case. His work was finished, but still he lingered, shifting his weight uneasily from one foot to the other.

"If the young prince w-would be so k-kind," he stuttered, "when he c-comes into the c-court to admit the army of unfortunates to the m-mighty *kherhab*—"

"What's that?" Moses emerged from his reverie with a start.

Small beads of moisture appeared on the barber's forehead. Still stuttering, he managed to frame his request. He was the father of a child, he explained, a little girl named Cool Breeze. Each night before putting her to bed her mother had striven to protect her from the evil ones, calling through the open door: "Run out, you who come in darkness, who enter by stealth, your nose behind you, your face turned backward! Come you to harm this child? I will not let you!" These and other spells had the fond mother repeated each night, but all to no avail. The evil ones had entered into the body of Cool Breeze and filled it with a raging heat which not even her namesake, the refreshing north wind, could quench. Each afternoon her mother had brought her to the temple court at the hour when Maruma treated the ills of the unfortunates, but she had not gained admittance. He knew that he was only a miserable barber and he could have his ears cut off for his presumption, but if the young prince who was the right hand of the *kherhab* and who admitted the unfortunates into his presence—

Moses' impatience changed to instinctive sympathy as he viewed the little barber's distress. "Tell your wife to bring the child to the temple court this afternoon," he said kindly. "If she gets there early, she should have no difficulty gaining an audience."

"B-but—the lord prince does not understand. Always she gets there early, yesterday even before dawn. It is that she has not the price—"

Impulsively Moses drew from his wrist a bracelet of twisted gold threads strung with beads of carnelian and lazuli, and placed it in the menial's hand.

"Tell her to bring this with her when she comes this afternoon. But be sure she gives it to no one but me. A jewel like this might tempt even a holy priest, to say nothing of a doorkeeper."

He realized his mistake the instant the words were out of his mouth, before the barber, his eyes incredulous, had prostrated himself, and then, stammering his gratitude, had seized his stool and basket and hastily backed from the apartment. The temple of Re would never see him again. Before the sun had risen he would have pawned the trinket, bundled his family together, and left the gates of On behind him forever.

Moses opened his lips to bid White Elephant follow the fleeing man and apprehend him. Then he closed them again. White Elephant was busy. He was down on his knees scrubbing the carpet where the blood dripping from the barber's wounded wrist had left a crimson stain.

The red granite obelisk with its crowning pyramid of pure gold shot a resplendent welcome to its patron lord as his shining bark bore him triumphantly through the celestial ocean above the red cliffs of the eastern desert. At the same instant the City of the Sun sprang into life. As if kindled from the fiery tip, one by one the lesser symbols of the great god—lions, eagles, sphinxes, falcons, winged disks of pure gold—leaped into brilliance on every roof and wall and parapet. Even the mud hovels of the poor outside the temple area blazoned their allegiance in the small gilded scarabs or bulls or lions affixed to their flat thatched roofs.

In the colonnaded court where the worshipers were gathered Moses stood beside Maruma, the reciter-priest, and lifted his voice in the hymn of greeting to the sun. It was the hour of the day which he liked the best. The triumphant beating of sistrums, the smell of sweet incense, the blazing glory of the newborn sun—all filled him with a sense of high fulfillment. Sometime, perhaps, when he was old like Maruma, his eyes also would become weak and watery from constant gazing on such shining splendor. But not yet. Boldly he lifted them, wide open and steady, from the great circular altar of alabaster, up the massive gold-sheathed columns, on to the kindled peak of the lofty, flame-hued obelisk. At such a moment, it seemed, he could lift them even farther and gaze unblinking on the blinding glory of the sun-god's bark itself.

Together with his soaring vision rose the words of the noble awakening hymn:

> "Hail to thee, beautiful god of every day,
> Rising in the morning without ceasing,
> Not wearied in labor.
> Thou art a craftsman shaping thine own limbs;
> Fashioner without being fashioned.
> When thou sailest across the sky, all men behold thee!"

On this particular morning the court was thronged with people, since, though it was not a feast day, the bark of the god was to be brought forth from its inner shrine and borne in regal procession through the temple area. For the Grand Vizier of the north, whose seat of government was in On, was about to make a journey through his cities, and he wished to discover if the favor of the god would accompany him.

When the short, stocky high priest appeared between the columns, leading the procession, Moses felt Maruma stiffen. "Pompous little interloper!" he heard him mutter.

There was not a priest in the court that morning whose hands did not clench at sight of Amonemheb, the second priest of Amon, clad in the short, narrow, linen skirt with its border of embroidered flowers and seed vessels, the panther skin studded with gleaming stars slung about his shoulders. But their resentment was a private indulgence, like Mamma's mutterings. It was Amon now who commanded and Re who obeyed. Though On might still be the seat of Egypt's wisdom, it was toward Thebes that the wealth of Egypt poured. And wealth, it seemed, not wisdom, was in this modern day the source of power.

What did Re himself think about it, Moses wondered. Riding in his magnificent bark behind tall banners, hidden beneath the crimson-velvet canopy, his wooden servants kneeling about him under huge lotus blossoms, was he content to follow his rival's lesser priest, like a sun making obeisance to a candle?

Two lines of priests supported the fragile poles of the divine bark on their shoulders, sensitive to its slightest pressure. If the god weighed heavily upon them as they passed the spot where the tip of the obelisk cast its shadow on the court, his favor would rest upon the Grand Vizier and his expedition. If lightly, the journey would be presaged by misfortune. The maidens of the god's harem danced joyfully about his bark, cast lotus blossoms in its path, and twanged their sistrums. But the faces of the priests were as immobile as the gleaming hawk's head on the sacred prow. They kept their eyes fixed on the loaded wagons that bore the Grand Vizier's tokens of appreciation to the sun-god: vessels of gold and silver, statues of ivory and ebony, bronze daggers, a cartful of rare animal skins, another of dressed geese and choice cuts of beef, a dozen casks of mixed red and white wines.

As the bark approached the fateful spot the excitement of the worshipers grew intense. The drivers of the wagons paused, open-mouthed; the maidens forgot to jangle their sistrums. Only the Grand Vizier, standing beside his coachman in his low, gilded carriage, a row of fan bearers on either side of him, his jeweled collar a gleaming ruff about his thick neck, watched the ceremony with aloof disinterest. It was almost as if he knew, thought Moses, exactly what was going to happen.

The prow of the god's bark dipped suddenly downward and the foremost bearers stumbled to their knees. Simultaneously the priests behind them grasped the supporting poles more firmly, bracing their legs and squaring their shoulders. As the apex of the triangular shadow rested its significant finger on the crimson canopy, the weight of divine favor became intolerable. The priests staggered forward, then one by one sank to their knees.

A great cry rose from the assembled worshipers. Re had again proclaimed his divine will. He had made himself heavy on the shoulders of his servants. The success of the Grand Vizier was assured.

"Blessed be Re!" intoned the aged Maruma piously. "Happy is the man on whom the sun of divine favor has fallen!"

Moses' lips moved with the rest but without their usual fervor. A startling suspicion assailed him. Had there been a good reason, perhaps, for the Grand Vizier's indifference? Was it the will of the god or the wagonloads of rich delicacies that had pressed heavily upon the shoulders of the priests of Re?

While his office of Chief of Scribes was largely honorary and involved few specific duties, each morning Moses made a tour of inspection of the halls where the state archives were preserved and the temple scribes, seated cross-legged in orderly rows on the floor, plied their routine tasks. It was one of his pleasantest activities.

Ranofer, the master scribe, his wrinkled old face wreathed in welcoming smiles, came to meet him. He spoke in a soft, wheezing treble, like wind blowing gently through hollow reeds.

"The young prince, beloved of Re, is most gracious. His servants have looked forward to his coming as a thirsty traveler anticipates a cooling stream. But in his absence," he continued more practically, "their hands have not been idle."

Moses smiled indulgently. "I'll wager they haven't. And you know very well my coming makes no more difference than a drop of water in an overflowing cup. How do you do it, Ranofer?"

"Do what?" wheezed the old man gently.

"Make your students believe that copying old dead marks on a shard or a piece of papyrus is the most fascinating task in all the world?"

"Old? Dead?" The pale glimmer in the watery eyes brightened. "The writings of the ancients? Next thing, my son, you'll be telling me that the sunrise is old—"

"I know, I know." Moses soothingly patted the thin, clawlike hand, its fingers curved, even in repose, to fit the contours of a brush. "You don't have to convince me, Ranofer. I was one of your pupils."

"So you were. One of the best I ever had." The old man chuckled. "Even if you asked some questions you shouldn't have."

Moses curiously regarded the bent heads, the rapt faces, the swiftly moving brushes. Looking over the shoulder of one of Ranofer's ablest scholars, now a professional scribe, he marveled at the skill of his facile fingers. The wells in his palette contained at least a dozen different colors of ink, and he shifted his brushes with amazing rapidity.

"O Devourer of Shades," read Moses over the scribe's shoulder, "I have not stolen. O Eyes of Flames, I have not played the hypocrite. O Cracker of Bones, I have not told falsehoods. O Swallower, I have not blasphemed. O Eater of Hearts, I have not made conspiracies..."

Moses could glibly have finished the recital of the Repudiation of Sins, all forty-two of them, with his eyes shut. The famous chapter containing them, from the sacred Book of the Coming Forth of the Day, had been the first textbook of every Egyptian highborn youth for well-nigh a thousand years. But the blended colors of the beautiful, flowing script, together with the tiny painted figures depicting the judgment scene, fascinated him.

"You are an artist as well as a scribe," he commended earnestly.

The scribe raised his head. "The prince is kind," he murmured. "I do only what I am paid to do."

Deftly he added the finishing strokes of color to the robes of the twelve gods who served as judges in the scene of acquittal.

"How do you know he's going to be acquitted," demanded Moses suddenly, "this man for whose coffin you are making this roll? What makes you so sure he has committed none of the forty-two sins?"

The scribe was young, but the eyes he lifted to Moses' were as old as Egypt herself, There was no future in them, only the long past.

"The man is rich," he said simply, "like the young prince himself. He is paying a high price for the roll."

Moses went back to Ranofer. "What becomes of the poor man," he demanded abruptly, "who can't afford to buy a beautifully written chapter from the Book to put in his coffin?"

"Why—why—" he blinked warily. "The fact that a man cannot buy his salvation is proof that he does not deserve it. The poor lack the favor of the gods in this life. How can they expect to gain it in the hereafter?"

"Which is more important," persisted Moses, drawing his brows together until they formed one continuous line, "not to commit the forty-two sins or to buy yourself a beautiful papyrus roll saying you haven't committed them? What I mean is—"

He stopped suddenly at sight of the old man's face, its eyes burning so brightly that it seemed as if the thin, yellowed papyrus of its flesh would kindle from them and be consumed.

"Don't!" wheezed the voice. "Take the path as it comes to you, my son, and look not in envy toward him who walks above you nor in tenderness toward him who walks below. Happiness lies not in understanding but in accepting. I used to ask questions too, when I was young, and *I know.*"

2

When Moses finally entered the chamber of his teacher Maruma, the strong, sweet pungency of myrrh from the noonday sacrifice still lingered in the air. It was their custom to study together for an hour during the early afternoon, before the unfortunates should be admitted for healing and while most of the occupants of the temple area were enjoying their midday rest. Maruma seldom slept. His thirst of his spirit and the energy of his body were boundless.

But today Moses found him sleeping. So unusual an experience was this that Moses stood staring for long, wondering moments at the tall, straight figure lying on the couch, trying to discover in the massive head, the thin features tapering into sharpness at the chin, the long sensitive fingers, the secret of his teacher's wisdom and power over men. For Maruma was the wisest man in On, and On was the center of the wisdom of Egypt, perhaps of the world.

But lying here so, his eyelids closed like curtains drawn over his spirit, he did not look wise. He looked weak and defenseless. The roll he had been reading had dropped from his hands. Even the long ebony rod, which many people thought to be the secret of his power, looked strangely dormant lying at his side, its finely carved snake's head as lifelike as the outspread fingers which had so recently grasped it.

Once Moses' attention had fixed itself on the rod, he could not tear it away. He had never seen it so closely before. When Maruma held it in his hands, it possessed strange powers. If he wished, he could cast it on the ground and it became a living snake, writhing and hissing so that people ran from it in terror; then, when he picked it up, it became again but a carved piece of ebony. Many people said that it was by the power of this rod that Maruma performed the acts of healing for which he was renowned throughout the city, but Moses, who helped him in the preparation of his medicines, knew that this was not entirely so. If the rod were such a source of power, why did he not stretch it out and heal the unfortunates with but a touch instead of spending long hours in study and experimentation? Why had he not used it to gain for himself the one prize on which he had set his heart, the high priesthood of Re?

"By the power and in the name of Re!" chanted Maruma when he cast down his rod and caused it to become a snake. "He it is who is king over all the gods!"

Fascinated, Moses stared at the long, slender column of ebony. In response to some ungovernable impulse his hand moved toward it. Slowly his fingers closed about the finely wrought snake's head. It felt smooth and cool, and at the contact something like a quiver passed through his palm, up his arm, and into his body. The rod seemed strangely light for ebony and possessed a certain resilience that was at variance with the inert deadness of wood.

His every nerve tingled with excitement He was conscious of some strange leashed power, but whether it flowed from the rod into him or from him into the rod he could not tell. Suppose he were to cast it on the floor as Maruma did? Would it slither away among the painted reeds and grasses on the smooth tiles, perhaps turning upon him venomously? Or would it lie stiff and inert?

"By the power and in the name of Re!" he whispered. "He it is who is king over all the gods!"

The hot tingling in his body changed to coldness. Almost without his volition his fingers unclasped, and the rod dropped from his hand. There was no resounding clatter as it struck the floor, only a soft thud. It lay for a moment straight and motionless, a slim piece of ebony. Then a slight tremor seemed to pass through it, moving in a barely perceptible wave from sculptured head to rounded tip. Slowly it coiled into a mounded spiral, up-reared its head, and darted a small forked tongue three times into the air; then uncoiled and slid away across the tiles. At its approach the painted reeds and grasses seemed to bend and sway, making a path through which the undulating form might pass.

Moses stared at it as if hypnotized. If the snake had turned upon him and coiled itself ready to strike, he could not have moved.

"Pick it up," ordered the voice of Maruma quietly. "It's non-poisonous. Seize it firmly by the tail."

It was a voice that Moses was accustomed to obey without question. Crossing the room quickly, he grasped the elusive shape and held it with a firm hand. His power, if power it had been, was gone. The thing he held was still a writhing snake, not a rod of ebony.

"Now bring it to me!" Maruma commanded abruptly.

Automatically Moses obeyed. He watched Maruma's fingers close in a caressing gesture about the glistening body, heard him utter little crooning sounds as he stroked it with his other hand. Slowly it straightened, then stiffened, like black liquid hardening in a mold, became a rod again.

"So," said the priest tonelessly, "it is not enough that I should teach you the secrets of the ancients. I must confide to you the secrets of Maruma also."

"No!" said Moses. "I did wrong to touch the rod. May Re smite me for my presumption! I have pried into the secrets of the gods themselves."

"Come with me," said Maruma.

He led the way into his inner chamber. Moses followed, trembling. He knew of no other pupil of the great teacher who had penetrated beyond the richly embroidered curtain. It was a small room, hardly more than a cubicle, very hot and dim. The only light entered from an outer courtyard through a few thin slits high up in the wall. There was a mingled odor of incense, ink, old papyri, medicines, and some strange sharp animal scent which he could not define.

A cage of woven rushes stood in one corner. Maruma lifted the lid. Unaccustomed to the darkness, Moses discerned at first only a vague duskiness; but gradually he became conscious of movement, then of shape, finally of a pattern of black twining coils. He drew back in horrified amazement. Without a word Maruma slipped the rod inside the cage and closed the lid.

They had returned to the outer apartment before Moses realized the full significance of the episode. "Then—it was never a rod at all!" he marveled. "It—it was a snake all the time."

"An unusual breed of cobra," explained Maruma, "which a tribe of natives above the cataracts has tamed and trained for centuries. There are only a few of them in Egypt, and all of them except these are in the custody of the prophets of Buto, the serpent-goddess. Not a one of the prophets of Amon knows the secret. And none other of the priests of Re—except you."

"I am not a priest," murmured Moses. It was not what he should have said. He should be expressing his gratitude to his beloved teacher for sharing with him this most precious of all his secrets, but there was no gratitude in him, only a curious emptiness.

"You will be," said Maruma confidently. "You will be first a *uab*, and then a *kherhab*, like me. But you will not stop there. There is something within you, my son, that not even the power and wealth of Amon will be able to crush. You don't realize it yet, but it is there." His voice sank to a whisper. "You can be the high priest, the Great Seer himself."

Moses was silent. This morning at dawn the prophecy would have awakened in him a tumult of longing and expectation. But now it aroused no warmth of emotion. So he was to be the high priest of Re. He would wear the panther skin studded with gold stars proclaiming him to be "chief of the secrets of heaven," and he would march at the head of innumerable processions in the name of a god who made himself heavy with favor in proportion to the gifts men brought him. His eyes would become so weak from looking at the sun's reflection that he could not bear the vision of the sun itself. He would be as wise as Maruma and be sought by unfortunates from all over Egypt who were able to pay the price. And he would keep pet snakes in order that he might impress men with his wisdom and authority. Suddenly he laughed aloud.

"And I thought it was the power of Re!" he said mirthlessly.

As the sun-god in his golden bark sailed steadily through the ocean of the heavens toward the completion of his daily journey as Atum the Decrepit, the pile of offerings outside the audience chamber of the *kherhab* Maruma grew as steadily higher. The line of unfortunates was longer than usual, for it was the beginning of the season of inundation, when many hostile spirits were driven by the rising of the river to seek new abodes in the bodies of men and women.

Today Moses must be more than a mere assistant to the *kherhab,* meeting the supplicants at the courtyard gate, accepting or rejecting them according to the value of their offerings, and conducting the favored ones into the master's presence.

"Another case of Nile scab," time after time Maruma would diagnose the case wearily. "My assistant also knows the secrets of Re. He will drive the evil spirit from your body." And Moses would place upon the spotted, inflamed flesh a poultice made from the healing lotion which Isis herself had once made for the suffering Re, a compound of wax, honey, date wine, rancid fat, and boiled horn.

Maruma was right. Moses did know the secrets of Re, and in this emergency his hands were almost as skillful as his master's. With competent fingers he splinted a broken arm. He washed a badly burned chest in the milk of a woman who had borne a son, reciting over it the magic words of healing once spoken by Isis: "My son Horus, it burns on the mountain, no water is there, I am not there, fetch water from the bank of the river to put out the fire." He painted sore, running eyes with a goose's feather dipped in a solution which he himself had made and strained through a cloth the night before.

The heat of the overcrowded apartment, the sight and smell of festering bodies, the odors of medicines with their components of stale fat and bone dust and animal excretions, all made his senses swim. He was glad when from time to time he could return to the outer courtyard, sun-blistered though it was, and draw a few breaths of purer air.

It was late afternoon when he remembered the little barber. Hastily he scanned the dwindling line outside the gate. His suspicions had been correct. There was no woman waiting with a child. He should have set White Elephant on the barber's trail at once. It might be that Ranofer was right, after all. Perhaps the gods did allot wealth and poverty to men according to their virtues. It would simplify life exceedingly to think so. If the barber was at heart a miserable thief, it was right that he should not be able to purchase freedom from the demons of fever.

The twelve gold and silver vessels which contained Maruma's blended medicines—one for each of the twelve vessels which led in pairs from the heart to all the members of the human body—became depleted. Hastily Moses aided him in preparing other mixtures: ointment of stibium for the stiffened neck; seeds of the plant shepen mixed with fly dirt for quieting the crying of children; poultices of lizards' blood, rotting meat, and antelopes' excreta; plant seeds pounded to powder and heated to produce a steam which the sufferer from stomach complaint might inhale; old manuscripts soaked in oil to be used as compresses. Over each medicine Maruma piously recited the magic formula without which no medicine could be made effective. So fatigued was he that the words were scarcely more than a mumble.

"That Isis might make free, make free," he chanted weakly. "That Isis might make Horus free from all evil that his brother Set has done to him when he slew his father Osiris...1"

Finally Moses ordered the gates to be closed. He led the weary Maruma back into his apartment and settled him on his couch. The priest's face was drawn and haggard.

"You should not have labored so long," chided Moses. "I'll order the slaves to bring oil and wine and some soft pillows."

"No—pillows!" protested Maruma. "Always thought cushions—for weaklings. If a man needs pillows to support—backbone in this life, how does he think—can keep his *ded* upright in life to come?"

"There's no danger of yours ever bending," said Moses affectionately. He adjusted the wooden curve more comfortably beneath the massive head and loosened the clinging folds of the linen scarf. "There are other magicians in the temple. You should not have tried to do so much."

"For the glory of—Re," murmured Maruma. The long, straight body relaxed. Though he seemed to be slipping slowly into unconsciousness, words still issued from his lips.

> "Thy dawning is beautiful in the horizon of heaven,
> O living Aton, Beginning of life!
> When thou risest in the eastern horizon,
> Thou fillest every land with thy beauty.
> Thou art beautiful, great, glittering, high over all the earth,
> Thy rays, they encompass the lands, even all that thou hast made.

How manifold are all thy works!
They are hidden from before us,
O thou sole god, beside whom there is no other..."

The murmur drifted into silence. His pulses pounding, Moses stared at the closed eyes, the motionless lips. "Did you say Aton?" he burst out sharply.

Maruma's eyes flew open, their clouding film quite dissolved in the sudden brightness of his gaze.

"You did!" Moses answered his own question in a harsh whisper. "You spoke the forbidden name! You said—"

"Hush!" warned Maruma. He glanced swiftly about the apartment. "Your ears deceived you. It was Amon of whom I spoke."

"It was not Amon," said Moses boldly. "Say it again, master. It is more beautiful than the hymns of Re."

"Thy dawning is beautiful in the horizon of heaven,
O living Aton—"

"Stop!" commanded the priest hoarsely. "You just imagined that I said those words. If you heard them, forget them."

But Moses would not be silenced. For years he had wanted to learn the truth about the heretic Ikhnaton and his sun-god Aton, whom he had made supreme above all the gods of Egypt. Now the questions tumbled from his lips. Had Ikhnaton really believed that there was only one god, whose being was the heat of the sun and whose symbol was its disk? Had he actually succeeded in erasing the name of Amon from every inscription in Egypt, including those containing the name of his own father, Amenhotep? Was Merire, the high priest of Aton, still alive and practicing the strange faith in defiance of the priests of Amon? And how could Moses find out everything there was to know about Ikhnaton and his fascinating heresy?

Moses could not, it seemed, if the information was to be derived from Maruma. The priest closed his lips tightly and stiffened his body into a rigid solidity of negation. Knowing that the weary *kherhab* would no longer dare trust himself to unconsciousness in his presence, Moses regretfully slipped away.

One of the temple attendants was waiting for him outside the apartment. He had turned away the rest of the unfortunates, as bidden, but there was one woman who would not go. She insisted on seeing the right hand of the master.

Moses frowned, but he accompanied the attendant to the gate. The woman was crouching on the ground, her figure as patient and immobile as the small, carved sphinx's head on the gatepost against which her forehead rested. Moses felt that he had seen her again and again that afternoon in the same position without being actually cognizant of her presence.

The attendant gave her a contemptuous kick. "Well, daughter of a river rat, here he is. Don't keep the lord prince waiting."

The woman raised her head and dropped from a squatting to a kneeling position, holding her hands clasped tightly between her naked breasts. Moses stared for a long moment at the outline of the sphinx's head graven into her forehead before recognizing it as the imprint of the carving against which her head had rested. She held out her hands, and the slanting rays of Atum the Decrepit seized the thing within them and made of it a dazzling splendor of gold and blue and crimson.

Moses took the bracelet. "B-but—" he stammered, "the child— the—the little one called Cool Breeze. I—I thought—"

The face which the woman lifted was like that of the carved sphinx's head, calm and inscrutable and heavy with a vast patience.

"Cool Breeze is dead," she said simply.

The bronze lamps were being lighted when Moses came from the chamber of the high priest. Bravely the devout occupants of the City of the Sun sought to compensate for the absence of their god, but their pitiful little flares were a meager substitute. The city lay crouched in the dusk like a child afraid of the dark, deserted by its protector. Later the stars would come, but until then the City of the Sun would hang uncertainly in the balance between life and death. They called it the "hour of the stifling," this brief pause of emptiness after the bark of Atum the Decrepit descended to its long voyage through the darkness.

So he was not to become a priest. It was the wish of the Princess Sitra that he should pack all his possessions immediately and return to Memphis. Why? The Great Seer had not known, or at least had not cared to say. A pity that the princess had not seen fit to consult the god before making her decision. Amon-Re would most certainly have made himself heavy in her behalf. But since she had not seen fit, perhaps the lord prince would like to leave some little token to insure the god's continued favor, some changes of raiment, perhaps, or even that bracelet trinket he held in his hand!

Moses felt no particular emotion. He was like the City of the Sun in its "hour of the stifling," empty both of regret and expectation. He went to his apartment and ordered White Elephant to pack his personal belongings. But the bracelet of gold threads strung with beads of carnelian and lazuli he himself wrapped in a small package and gave careful directions for its disposal.

It was to be delivered, not to Amon-Re, as the high priest had suggested, but to a humble temple barber.

3

The Princess Sitra was preparing to go forth to battle. Her weapons were ranged in orderly rows on a table of inlaid cedar, innumerable little jars and boxes and bottles fashioned in strange shapes and filled with a variety of fluids, pastes, and granules. In her hand Sitra held the most potent weapon of all, the broadsword of her collection: a round mirror of polished bronze. Her slender fingers curving about the full-breasted Hathor which formed its handle, she studied her image dispassionately.

She was not one to blind herself to facts. The features that she saw reflected were still evenly formed, noble in contour, but no longer beautiful. Even her husband, Ramses, were he still alive, would not think so; and certainly not the jovial, transient prince from the Mitanni. At least she did not need any of that sickly green paint which most women daubed on their lids to make their eyes look larger and more brilliant! Even now, after more than a quarter century, they were as thick-lashed and sparkling as when they had captivated the court in the early days of Harmhab. How was it the Mitannian prince had described them? "Pools of liquid jet with a fire blazing at the bottom." He had composed lines about her hair too, but she did not care to remember them, for they were no longer true,

Sitra frowned "Tomorrow," she said to Beket, who had been her personal slave for forty years, "we will go back to the old remedy. I believe I have more gray hair than ever since you started using these new treatments from black bulls' horns. The court physicians all say there's nothing better than the blood of a black calf boiled in oil."

"Except the fat of a black snake," agreed Beket calmly, unable to resist a complacent patting of her own ragged but unsilvered locks.

"If you're implying that's what kept those tatters of yours from turning gray, then you're a fraud," replied Sitra bluntly. "You're so afraid of snakes you shiver every time you touch this perfume bottle twined with the gold uraeus."

"Her-royal-highness-Princess-Sitra could of course speak no untruth," retorted Beket with a brusque irony which transformed the apparently obsequious remark into a good-natured, "You're a liar."

Though outwardly their relationship was that of princess and menial, there existed between them a fellowship not only of intimacy but of conspiracy. Beneath the conventions there flowed a stream of understanding, augmented now by the swift currents of the secret they shared.

The slave's fingers hovered over the array of bottles. "Would the daughter of heaven desire any special perfume?"

Sitra shrugged a pair of shoulders that were still as smooth as golden-brown satin. "Something—anything—it doesn't matter. What's in that green bottle with the petals on top?"

Wordlessly Beket reached for the fragile container and removed its cover. Instantly a subtle fragrance filled the chamber. The little interplay of words had been superfluous. Both mistress and slave had known that for the coming interview with Queen Tuya, Sitra could wear but one perfume, the special blend of spices and incense and cypress blossoms of which she alone knew the formula and which the young queen had tried for years to imitate.

"He will be here tonight," said Sitra. "If all goes well, we should be leaving for Thebes shortly."

"And if the queen refuses?" prompted Beket gently, applying a drop of the precious liquid to a golden ear lobe.

"I shall see to it that she does not refuse," returned Sitra confidently. "You see, Beket, I have one advantage. I know what Tuya's plan is, to get rid of Amon-nebet and put her insufferable little Ramses on the throne. But—she does not know mine."

"The mother of the Good God speaks wisely, as always," murmured the slave. The brown mask of servility melted from her face. "I wonder if he's grown any taller!" she mused. "It's been nearly two years since we've seen him. He grew over two inches while he was off in those heathen deserts fighting. I'm glad you're going to make him a soldier instead of a priest. He'll look so handsome in a uniform. And it would have been such a pity to shave off those curls. At least you know they're there, even if he does have to wear a wig. Remember how soft they were when he was a baby—like the finest linen threads?"

Again donning the mask, the slave regarded the mistress critically. She adjusted the heavy gold collar above the transparent folds of linen which covered the straight shoulders and full, firm breasts. With skillful fingers she rearranged the long scarflike headdress of gold inlaid with little circles of bright glass and carnelian so that the two black wings of hair showed fewer streaks of gray. Dipping her ivory stylus into the blue faience jar, she deftly added another touch of black antimony to the arching brows and thick lashes. Lastly she took a small ball of crushed incense sweetened with honey and slipped it between the carefully rouged lips.

Sitra rose slowly from the cushioned chair. "Go tell the servants of Queen Tuya that the mother of Seti comes to inquire after her health."

Beket bowed low. "The daughter of heaven is most considerate of the welfare of others," she replied humbly.

The two women smiled at each other. Then together they moved across the floor, the slave's bare feet and the mistress' richly sandaled ones treading soundlessly upon a paradise of painted pools and green waving grasses and lotus blossoms. An auspicious setting surely for the first steps in a long and carefully wrought plan, the goal of which was the placing of the Princess Sitra's adopted son, Moses, on the throne of Egypt!

"You are suggesting that I send Nefretiri to Thebes for the Feast of Opet in my place?"

"Yes," replied Sitra gently. "Though we can all see and rejoice that your health is so much better, it would be folly, my child, to attempt a long journey so soon. And who could take your place better as the divine consort of Amon than your own daughter?"

Sitra lowered her eyes discreetly in order that the young queen might not see the triumph in them. It was going to be easy, far easier than she had thought. Tuya, the strong-willed, the arrogant, lay weak and defenseless on a sickbed. A high, unnatural color flowed beneath the rouge on her thin cheeks. So wasted was the long, graceful body that the bent backs of the Asiatic captives supporting her couch, had they been human flesh instead of carved ebony, could scarcely have been conscious of her weight. For the first time since Seti had mounted the throne with his beautiful bride, Sitra knew that she was stronger than her willful daughter-in-law. Before she left the chamber she would not only have obtained her objective, she would also have discovered what Tuya was hiding under the coverlet.

But the battle was still before her. The young queen's eyes were dark with suspicion. "You have never been my friend," she said with blunt directness. "Why are you so anxious for Nefretiri to go to Thebes in my place? There must be some reason."

Sitra returned her gaze steadily. "My dear child," she said gently, "how can you say that? Believe me, I was thinking only of you and— yes, I will admit it—of the pride and honor of the harem. It hardly seems fitting for one of the lesser wives, perhaps a concubine, to take the queen's place as consort of the god."

The bright spots flared in Tuyas cheeks. "I—I hadn't thought— What concubine would dare—"

"Probably," Sitra replied with composure, "the mother of Amon-nebet. Since her son is the oldest-born and the king's favorite—"

"No!" screamed Tuya. "She shan't! I—I won't let her. How dare that ugly little grasshopper think she can take my place! It's she who has given me this sickness, I know it is! Her slave told my slave that she had a wax image of me and that she sat for hours paring it away with a knife until—until there was nothing left of it!"

"Hush!" murmured Sitra with genuine sympathy, her fingers almost unconsciously seeking the contours of the hard object beneath the coverlet.

"But she shan't kill me, she shan't! I won't die just because she wants me to, do you hear? I tell you, I won't, I won't, I won't!"

Her voice rose to a shrill scream, bringing a bevy of slaves running to the side of her couch. Exhausted by the outburst, Tuya sank back trembling among the cushions. Sitra calmly motioned the slaves away, then gently arranged the pillows more comfortably, chafed the thin arms, and, removing the heavy vulture headdress, smoothed back the damp hair. She was not pretending now. She felt a motherly solicitude for this unhappy woman who was the wife of her son and the mother of his children. Nevertheless, she intended to utilize the moment for her own purpose.

"You shall work a spell on her," she said soothingly, "something far worse than having her flesh pared away. I know. We shall burn her, you and I, with red-hot irons. We shall have a little wax image made of her—"

"Not of her," breathed Tuya softly.

"No," responded Sitra swiftly. "Not of her. Of Amon-nebet. Because if he were gone, Ramses might well be his father's favorite.

Then he could marry his sister Nefretiri and become the true heir to the throne."

Tuya gasped. Her eyes were both frightened and wary. "How—"

"How do I know that is the one thing you want most? Because..." Sitra had the good grace to lower her eyes again. "Well, isn't it possible that I might wish that very thing myself?"

"But—I can't understand—"

"That I might prefer to have a prince of true royal blood follow my son on the throne than one who derived his claim from marrying your daughter?"

Suddenly Tuya made a decision. She reached beneath the coverlet. "See!" she whispered triumphantly.

The object which she revealed resembled a big wax doll, head, grotesquely large for its body and neck ridiculously long and thin. In spite of its exaggerations, its likeness to Prince Amon-nebet was unmistakable. Its painted features had been badly mutilated as with a sharp instrument, and there was a deep depression near the crown of its head. No words were necessary. Any woman in the harem, in Egypt, would have understood that Tuya was attempting to destroy the young prince with a magic spell.

"Ramses shall be king," said Tuya with a blaze of defiant conviction. "I shall get my way if I have to die and journey to the land beyond the Lily Lake with its horrible monsters and deserts and fires and its great serpent Apap. I shall go to Re myself and ask him to make Ramses king."

The fires of her passion burned out, Tuya languidly bade the slaves bring them refreshment. Then, while they drank date wine and tasted delicately of assorted cakes and glazed fruits and sweetmeats, the mother and wife of Seti concealed their animosity beneath a thick sugar-coating of polite affection. They fed each other tender morsels of food; they murmured gentle phrases; they twined garlands of fresh flowers about each other's arms and neck.

When Sitra returned to her apartment, she found Beket in dutiful attendance, her masklike face properly servile, the eyes which peered through it demanding and curious.

"Did the queen of heaven enjoy a pleasant pilgrimage?" the lips of the mask inquired obsequiously.

"Tell me quick what happened!" the eyes commanded boldly.

"The Princess Nefretiri will go to Thebes for the Feast of Opet," replied Sitra. "I myself have promised to accompany her. And—" the black eyes gleamed their triumph, "I shall make all the necessary arrangements for securing a military guard for her protection."

"And the captain of that guard—"

"Hush!" said Sitra.

She knew that she should feel completely satisfied. Every detail of her carefully wrought plan was falling into its prescribed pattern. The cup of triumph was brimming at her lips. But strangely enough she did not feel like drinking of it, for she knew that it held a trace of bitterness at the bottom. In spite of her strength and Tuya's weakness she was afraid. For the mother of Ramses had one advantage. To insure the success of her plan she was willing to journey to the land beyond the Lily Lake with its horrible monsters and deserts and raging fires and its devouring serpent Apap.

4

It was good to be at home again in the palace at Memphis. Each morning Moses awakened in the familiar room which adjoined Sitra's apartment, falling easily into the simple habits he had formed long ago as a child.

Now, as then, he lay quietly in order not to awaken White Elephant, who slept on his pallet close to the arched doorway leading to Sitra's private garden. He watched until the gray fingers of light plucked the darkness from the narrow slits high up in the wall, then followed with his eyes as they groped about the room picking out an object here and there: first the graceful round wooden columns with their flutings of pink and blue and gold; then, unerringly seeking the most brilliant objects, the gilded chair whose back and arms were the outspread wings of a bird, and the low table with the top made all of bright bits of glaze and polished blue and red and yellow stones.

As the light became stronger, he began eagerly to pick out the painted figures on the walls. Sitra had possessed an uncanny knowledge of the interests of boyhood. Under her direction the court artists had captured the wonders of far horizons: hunters riding hard across the desert, a water sportsman spearing a lumbering hippopotamus, lions and leopards roaming the jungles, and monkeys swinging by their tails. When, a little later, he would slip from beneath the sheets to undergo his morning toilet at the hands of White Elephant, his bare feet would tread the surface of blue-green pools beneath which long grasses rippled and bright fish swam.

But the Princess Sitra was equally clever in devising amusements for a youth in the first full flood tide of manhood.

"Forget the future for a little!" she had admonished him lightly soon after his return to Memphis. "It's enough now that I have decided you are no longer to train for the priesthood. I don't know why I ever wanted you to be a musty old priest anyway. Stop asking questions now and enjoy yourself."

It was a relief to stop asking questions. He had been doing nothing else, it seemed, since that last day in the temple at On. Quiescently, without emotion, he let Sitra's amusements flow over him as the waters of the Nile flowed over the parched, cracked soil of Egypt.

He sat in the place of honor at a banquet attended by all the young nobles of Memphis and ate delicate morsels of roast goose and wild duck and pigeons which tasted like sawdust in his mouth. The fragrance of the lotus crown about his head, perfumed constantly by a melting cake of sweet-smelling unguent, brought no responsive quiver to his nostrils. Even the sinuous naked bodies of the dancers, the excited pulsing of sistrums and tambourins, the amorous invitation of soft harps and guitars swelling into perfect rhythm with the movements of warm golden flesh, failed to stir his senses. The ribald jests of his childhood playmates flowed about the table as freely as the wine, but they seemed to enter no farther than the outer portals of his ears.

"Give me the one with the long hair and the girdle of flowers! I like mine more mysterious."

"Why do they put all that oil on their bodies? Makes them slippery!"

"Come closer, you with the crimson-tipped breasts! Give me a smell of your lotus, and I'll give you a sip from my wine cup."

"With those bodies of Hathor they should have cows' heads, but, by Amon, I'm glad they haven't!"

"How about it, Moses? Homesick for the priestesses of On?"

Moses smiled and uttered some inane reply, but it was as if he stood apart and watched the scene objectively from a distance.

He rode in a festive barge along the swelling Nile and up the canal to the Land of the Lake, where Sitra had planned an enormous house party on the lake shore. Amon-nebet was one of the group, and, to Moses' surprise and gratification, a swift intimacy developed between himself and the oldest son of Seti. It was both satisfying and stimulating to find another person who not only laughed at the same things he did but who could also remain gratifyingly silent.

They sailed and fished together and bathed in the clear blue waters, then wandered for hours without speaking through the bewildering courts and chambers of Amenemhat's labyrinthine temple, or chattered unimpressed as they gazed up at the two gigantic quartzite statues of that ancient pharaoh standing just outside his huge retaining wall in the midst of the waters.

"That's just the sort of thing Ramses will do if he ever gets to be pharaoh," observed Amon-nebet wisely. "Make two of him everywhere and make them just as big as possible."

They crossed the lake one day in a light sailing craft and visited the ancient temple of Sob, the crocodile god. An aging priest conducted them solemnly to the sacred pool where an immense beast, the earthly embodiment of Sob, snatched greedily at the offerings of his few faithful devotees. Great spiked jaws lazily agape, ears hung with gold and crystal rings and paws adorned with sparkling jeweled bracelets, the divine amphibian moved sluggishly about his rich domain of granite and alabaster.

"He's getting old," the ancient priest confided. "Nearly two hundred years, they say." His voice sank to a whisper. "The coffin is already prepared. Twenty feet long and covered entirely with gold. He will be buried close to the tomb of the great Amenemhat himself."

The two princes listened with solemn gravity. Only when they were well outside the temple did Moses trust himself to look at his companion. To his intense satisfaction he discovered an answering gleam of hilarity in Amon-nebet's eyes. They waited until they were well out on the lake and the slaves were busy with the sailing rigging, then burst into uproarious laughter. But the older youth quickly sobered.

"Do you—ever feel ashamed," asked Amon-nebet in a low voice, "of—being an Egyptian?"

Their glances met in swift understanding. "I know what you mean," replied Moses. "That horrible scaly creature crawling about on his belly! A god!"

"Yet he's lived longer than any man alive," mused the other softly. "He was splashing about that tank with those jewels on his crusty hide before Ahmose drove out the foreigners, before Thutmose lived and conquered Syria and died."

"That isn't living!" burst out Moses. "If you were to die tomorrow, you'd have lived longer than that brute could live in a thousand years. And that isn't Egypt, either." In his nervous excitement his speech became jerky and halting. "Egypt is—more than sacred snakes and—bulls and—crocodiles. It—it's the wisdom of Ptahhotep, and—and the patience of the slaves that built the pyramids, and the courage of men like Menes and Thutmose and—and Ikhnaton—"

He stopped suddenly, for Amon-nebet had turned toward him with an expression of abject terror. His eyes bulged in their long, almond-shaped sockets. His nostrils were dilated. Why—why did you say that about—my dying tomorrow?" he demanded in a hoarse whisper. "And then—you mentioned—*him*—"

"Mentioned whom?"

"Him. That—that heretic."

Moses was distressed and puzzled. "But—surely you know I didn't mean anything. I'd have said the same thing about myself. What's the matter, Neb? What makes you look so?"

The older prince was breathing heavily. "Haven't you noticed," he whispered, "that I—look like—like—"

Moses stared at him, suddenly comprehending, taking cognizance of the elongated eyes, the narrow face with its high cheekbones, the prominent chin protruding almost ludicrously from the thin, slanting neck. "You do! How strange I never noticed it before! You look almost exactly like Ikhnaton!"

"Hush! Don't let anybody hear!" Amon-nebet's glance darted warily toward the slaves, but the terror had left his face. He spoke in excited whispers. "Nobody has noticed yet. But sometime they will, and then who knows what will happen? There are people who hate me now. They want to kill me, I'm sure of it. And I don't want to die. I'm afraid. I'd never get across the Lily Lake. I'd wander around forever in the dark on its banks. If I were only big and strong and brave like you, I'd be willing to die."

"You're not going to die." Moses placed a steadying hand on the trembling wrist. "You're going to be pharaoh of Egypt and a good one too. And I'm going to tell you a secret. If it were I, I'd be proud, not ashamed, if I thought I looked like Ikhnaton. No matter what he believed, he was the bravest man Egypt has ever known."

The color flowed slowly back into Amon-nebet's thin cheeks. Before they reached the palace across the lake, he was laughing with Moses again.

Only once was Moses afraid that his friend's instinctive sharing of his own moods would fail to stand the test.

With the other young noblemen of Memphis they had gone on a long hunting excursion into the marshes along the borders of the Delta. Very early one morning he and Amon-nebet propelled their light bark through the thick white mists, finally coming to rest among the tall, slim reeds of papyrus. Patiently they waited, throw sticks in hand, ears alert for the sound of the flutter of wings.

Slowly the mists turned golden, became faintly rifted, then suddenly swept aside as the sun broke through. Scarcely a boat's length away a covey of wild birds, a thousand it seemed, lay at rest on a bright shaft of blue in a nest of gold rushes. Moses' hand tightened on his throw stick. His arm described a swift arc, then remained motionless. He stood quietly, every sense attuned to the miracle of beauty, yet apprehensive, waiting for the whine of Amon-nebet's throw stick to break the spell.

"If he throws," thought Moses. "If he throws—"

But Amon-nebet did not throw. Silently the two princes stood watching, until with a swift upsurging of wings and a noise like the rushing of many waters the birds rose in a body and mounted upward on a crest of sunlight.

"How many did you get?" shouted a voice from beyond a thick forest of reeds.

The two young princes looked at each other and grinned.

"All we shot at," Moses shouted back promptly.

But in spite of his rich new friendship with Amon-nebet, he remained impassive, the deep inner core of his being dry and parched and untouched. Though he knew now that he was to enter military service, beginning with a commission in the royal guard, he contemplated the prospect without reluctance or enthusiasm. Both past and future were equally colorless and void.

Until one day he passed inadvertently through a narrow gateway and saw a woman bathing in a garden...

The gateway should have been guarded, of course, but since Queen Tuya's illness her attendants had become lax. Even her famous hedges, symmetrically clipped in the shape of animals, looked a bit run to seed. But that was no excuse for entering the forbidden precincts. Had he been thinking intelligently, or, in fact, thinking at all, Moses would have realized that the small opening in the thick green wall surmounted on either side by a crouching lion sculptured of tender green leaves led to Tuya's private garden. But he was not thinking. He was letting his steps stray and his senses be stirred as they would by the colors and sounds and smells of a garden at the height of its early-morning perfection.

So when he stepped through a flowering hedge and saw the gaily painted kiosk and sunlit pool with the most beautiful statue he had ever seen sculptured in glistening bronze exactly in the center of it, he stood unabashed, staring with frank delight at the naked female figure, his eyes absorbing each perfect detail with the candor they might have accorded the petals of an exquisite flower: the rich curves of shoulders and breasts and thighs, the golden slimness of lithe limbs half hidden by the water, the grace of a slender arm outstretched to pick a lotus blossom.

Was it Hathor, Moses wondered, without her disfiguring cow's head? Or her still more voluptuous sister Anath of the north countries? And who could have performed the miracle? It was whispered that there had been artists in the days of Ikhnaton who could make figures so real that men swore they were living flesh. Was it possible that—

Suddenly there was a scream, and the pool was surrounded by excited, chattering females. Spray rose like a fountain as they plunged into the water. The bronze figure melted into startled motion, and Moses was burningly conscious of the gaze of a pair of half-strange, half-familiar black eyes before he turned, cheeks flaming, and fled back along the path.

At the narrow opening a guard was standing, his face gray with terror. He began to mutter incoherently. "Queen's private garden— strict orders—privacy not to be violated—young prince must remember from boyhood—"

Of course Moses remembered. His cheeks burning, he stammered his explanation. It seemed incredible, he knew, that he could have walked between the crouching lions without knowing it, but apparently he had done so. If only the guard would believe him—

The guard, who had known Moses since childhood, was quite willing to believe him, but unfortunately it did not solve the problem. If that was really a scream he had heard, it augured ill for both of them. In fact, if he wasn't mistaken, he could hear the patter of the feet of the seven Hathors even now approaching.

The instruments of destiny, however, proved to be singular rather than plural, a breathless female attendant dispatched to inform Moses that her mistress, the Princess Nefretiri, requested his presence in the garden.

The guards face brightened. "Perhaps she's not angry, after all"

"Perhaps not," returned the young attendant coyly. "But if it were I who had been caught bathing by a rude interloper who just stood and stared—"

"Heart and bowels of Ptah, it's worse than I thought!" The guard groaned but emerged from his misery long enough to reward the girl's coyness with a bold glance. "If it were you who had been caught— Oh, well, let's not go into that now. Unfortunately I'm the one who's going to be stripped—of my uniform." He sat down beneath one of the crouching lions. "I'll wait here. If the young prince returns soon, I shall know that this head is lucky indeed if it rests on these shoulders. If he's gone a long time, then it may still have the luck to rest sometime on a prettier pair."

Shrugging the attractive members thus singled out for attention, the young attendant led Moses into the queen's private garden, keeping a safe distance in advance as befitted the conduct of a virtuous young woman in company with a dangerous philanderer. Moses was not anxious to overtake her. His steps dragged on the red gravel path. His tongue felt dry and heavy, and he wished desperately for the guard's bright facility of speech.

It had been three years since he had seen the young princess. On his return from the Syrian campaign two years ago she had been vacationing with her mother at the Land of the Lake, and this summer he had looked for her in vain at all the court functions. Had she changed much, he wondered excitedly, since those informal years of study and play in the peculiar intimacy of the harem? Did she still like to play jokes on people, bending a prim, innocent face over her embroidery while the nurses vainly attempted to find the culprit, then dissolving into soft, merry laughter that was like the sound of silver bells? Were her eyes as sparklingly black as ever, with just a hint of green, as if they had been sprinkled with powdered jade? And had the slim, boyish body assumed the warmly rounded contours—

Remembering the sculptured perfection he had just gazed upon, he felt a renewed suffusion of warmth compounded of horror, shame, and—it must be confessed—exultation. His cheeks were still flaming with it when with startling abruptness he entered the gaily painted kiosk and came face to face with the Princess Nefretiri, heiress of the throne of Egypt.

"There's something oddly familiar about this interloper, don't you think, Memnet? Perhaps the way his brows grow so thick, like clumps of marsh grass? Or maybe the queer shape of his chin?"

The square, humorless face of Memnet, the princess' nurse since babyhood, remained grave. "If my lady will permit me to express an opinion," she replied bluntly, "he bears a remarkable resemblance to the princess' cousin Moses. In fact, if they're not one and the same, I'll swallow my own right arm."

"Mercy, Memnet!" The slender figure on the ebony and ivory couch gave a delicate shudder. "What an unpalatable diet! And you're going to have to do it too, because how could this wretched creature possibly be my honored cousin? Prince Moses was at least reared to be a gentleman. He wouldn't go sneaking around private gardens spying on ladies in their bath. Or—would he?" Elevating her daintily plucked brows, the princess appeared to reconsider. "After all, it's been years since I've seen my cousin Moses. And, come to think of it, he did act a bit oddly at times in the harem."

"He certainly did," returned Memnet tartly. "What mischief my lady couldn't think of, he always did."

Nefretiri lifted a languidly reproving hand, its slender fingers tipped with bright carnelian. "Please, Memnet, don't remind me. And have the goodness to remember that I am no longer a child. If I were to tell my lord Amon that you had spoken thus familiarly to his royal consort, Mut, he would probably strike you dead for your insolence."

Had he not been so engrossed in his own troubles, Moses would have derived keen satisfaction from the dark flush that stained the face of the old nurse. Having herself inherited a few drops of royal blood, Memnet had keenly resented her menial position and had compensated for her frustration by bullying the children of the harem.

But Moses was not thinking of Memnet. His eyes were fixed miserably on the exquisite profile which was already the delight and despair of half the artists of Egypt. Was she still the Nefretiri he had known? If she would turn her head ever so slightly so he could see her eyes, or curve the proud line of her lips into a smile— Yet he hoped desperately she would not. For a few seconds longer, at least, he could remember her as she had been, the sparkling eyes, the soft lips ready to bubble into laughter.

"Go to the palace, Memnet," commanded Nefretiri with languid indifference, "and bring some wine and little cakes and anything else good you can find. My bath has made me hungry. And if you tell my mother what has happened, I'll make you scrub the tiles of the palace courtyard when all the slaves are watching."

"But—" The nurse's flat features sagged, then settled into their rigid mold. Only the eyes betrayed outrage and frustration, and the broad back disappearing along the path spoke the defiance her lips would once have uttered. In spite of his misery Moses looked after her with satisfaction. But when the princess dismissed the rest of her attendants and they swarmed, chattering indignantly, out of the kiosk, he became suddenly indifferent to all except the proud, expressionless profile. The moment had come. Surely now she would turn her head.

But she did not. "Suppose the interloper explains," she said coldly, "what he was doing in the queen's private garden. And the explanation had better be good, or the guard will lose his head."

"I—I—The princess won't believe me—" Moses' throat contracted. He felt as if he were trying to talk with a large stone in his mouth. "B-but I didn't look where I was going. I was—busy thinking—"

"How very unusual!" marveled Nefretiri. "An accomplishment quite foreign to most of the men I know. You must be a stranger at court."

"But I—I—" The stone completely filled Moses' mouth, so that no sound came.

"I could swear you weren't thinking when I saw you," continued the cool voice imperturbably.

"B-but I was." A faint sound proceeded from the cavity beneath the stone. "I thought you were a—beautiful statue—the most beautiful one I had ever seen, and I wondered what—what artist could have carved you. And—I'm not a stranger, Nefretiri. If—if you'd just look at me—"

He awoke suddenly to the consciousness that she was looking at him, had been for some time, and that her eyes were dancing. The sound of merry laughter bubbled around him.

"Oh, Moses, you funny, serious old monkey! You didn't really think I didn't know you, did you? And you haven't changed a bit! You still catch your breath and swallow all your words when you're nervous. Don't tell me you're afraid of me, Moses! After all the mischief we used to plot together! Remember the time Memnet fell asleep in her chair and we found a henna pot and painted her arms and shoulders all over with stripes like a zebra?"

Moses' relief was so great that the floodgates of speech were released too abruptly, and the words poured forth in a torrent. "Please believe me Nefretiri it was just as I said I wasn't watching where I was going and then when I saw it—I mean you—that is—"

"Yes?" The black eyes probed mischievously into his sudden confusion. "When you saw me?"

"I—I didn't really think you were alive at all!"

"Really? Did I look so dead then?"

"No, I—you know I didn't mean—that is, I—"

She came to his rescue with another peal of laughter. "My dear cousin, don't take things so seriously! Can't you see I think it's a good joke? If I have to turn myself into a brazen statue to get you to pay me some attention, I guess it's worth it." The curving lips pouted slightly. "You might have considered it a duty, if not a pleasure, to pay the royal princess at least one formal visit after two years' absence. I could name other princes who show a much more—brotherly concern."

"I've been very stupid," replied Moses. "I just kept looking for you at every palace function and wondered why you never came."

The pouting lips relaxed. "Well, now you've come at last, don't stand there like a big, cold obelisk. Sit down here beside me and tell me everything you've been doing in the last three years." The black eyes, suddenly serious, looked full into his. "Have you stopped to think, Moses, that we're no longer children? We're—man and woman."

Moses left the garden as he had entered it, through the narrow opening between the crouching lions. The guard was no longer there, but a faint whispering and occasional giggle behind a nearby clump of flowering bushes indicated, possibly, that the fellow was so assured of the safety of his head that he was already engaged in placing it on a fairer pair of shoulders. And no wonder his mind had been set at rest, for, Moses discovered to his amazement, it was well past midday.

The passivity in which he had been existing was gone. He felt warmly, virilely alive. He was acutely aware of every small detail in the garden about him; the crunch of his sandals on the red gravel walk, the fragrance of roses and bittersweet, the bright sky painted with green inlays of palm fronds, the pattern of a lotus leaf on a reed-bordered pool. But he did not ask himself the reason why. It was enough for the moment to be alive again.

5

But the mood of well-being was not to last. He exchanged it a few days later for a tumultuous unrest which beset his emotions like a fever, plunging them into alternate extremes of warmth and frigidity.

He and Amon-nebet had gone with a group of young Memphis nobles on a hunting trip into the Valley of the Gazelles, a favorite resort of sportsmen far out in the desert west of the pyramids. In spite of its name the fleet-footed gazelle was only one of its tempting prizes. Prowling about the scant vegetation of its water holes were antelopes, hyenas, jackals, foxes, hares, and hedgehogs, and, just rare enough to make their pursuit the very essence of excitement, leopards and lions.

Queen Tuya had planned the party. Rousing herself to feverish activity on her couch, she had supervised each detail. While her thin body had seemed to shrink beneath the exertion, her mind had seemed to absorb all its waning energy. The party was the most brilliantly executed social event of the season.

On the third night, after a successful chase, Moses lay beside Amon-nebet on a cushioned mat outside their tent. Healthily tired and surfeited with the richest of food, they were enjoying all the comforts of the palace at home. Slaves were constantly at their elbows with fans and frosted goblets of wine. The fires were near enough to give them a sense of security but far enough away to leave their vision of the stars undimmed. If they turned their heads, they could see the naked dancers, whom Tuya had thoughtfully dispatched that day from Memphis, weaving golden patterns from fire to fire and group to group; or they could lie on their backs, gazing dreamily at Sirius and Orion, the souls of Isis and Horus.

When one of the dancers drifted toward them and bent to whisper seductively in his ear, Amon-nebet dismissed her with impatience. "Women belong in scented chambers," he said companionably to Moses, "not in the cool sanctity of the desert. Besides, when I think of Nefretiri, all the others look cheap and tawdry."

"Nefretiri," echoed Moses faintly. His pulses began suddenly to pound, beating so loudly in his ears that he was sure Amon-nebet must feel the ground throbbing beneath them. But if he did, the older prince gave no sign. They were completely alone now, having had enough of wine and preferring the faint stirring of the night air to the monotonous fanning of slaves.

"I'm going to tell you something," confided Amon-nebet with sudden intimacy. "Since my father told me his plans for me and Nefretiri, I haven't wanted to possess another woman. Is that strange?"

"No," Moses heard his own voice replying steadily. "It's not strange at all. I—I think I would feel the same way."

"I want to tell you something else," went on the older youth earnestly. "If I do marry Nefretiri and become pharaoh, I'll have you to thank. I'm no longer afraid the way I used to be. You're so strong that just being with you has given me strength."

Moses slept little that night. Lying motionless on his mat in the tent, he battled with emotions he had never before experienced: physical desire, jealousy, hatred. Each inflicted its peculiar torture. He would vision Nefretiri, golden and lovely as he had seen her that day in the garden pool, and his pulses would race until he seemed consumed with fire. Then he would picture her in the arms of Amon-nebet, and the heat in his veins would be replaced by a devastating coldness. Once he rose from his mat and crept to the other side of the tent where the young prince lay, and thought how easy it would be to snap the frail cords of the thin neck. He crouched there for long moments, muscles flexed and powerful fingers curved; then, weak and exhausted, crept back again to his mat.

He was able to think more clearly then. It was not Amon-nebet's fault that he, Moses, was in love with the heiress of the throne of Egypt, had loved her without knowing it since the days they had pitted their childish wits against the waspish Memnet. Of course Seti would wed Nefretiri to his beloved oldest son whom he wished to place on the throne. Why shouldn't he? What business was it of Moses'? He should be thankful it was to Amon-nebet she would be wed and not to the insufferable Ramses.

So finally he conquered the third of the strange new emotions, hatred, but the other two continued to torment him, as they were to do for days to come: flame followed by coldness, joy pursued inevitably by despair.

The camp came to life with a great fanfare. There was much excitement, for this morning two lions had been sighted by the scouts near a water hole on the other side of the valley. Bows were tested, arrows sharpened. Sensing the tension, the great greyhounds strained at their leashes.

Moses, usually in the forefront of the chase, today fell behind with Amon-nebet, who was never a bold hunter. On the level stretches the two raced along the desert floor side by side, their horses neck to neck, the spinning disks of their small two-wheeled carts making barely a mark on the hard-packed red earth.

"Let's keep on toward the dunes," shouted Amon-nebet when they came to the place where the rest of the party had turned on to the rougher path leading to the water hole. "This is better than hunting lions."

"Good!" agreed Moses. "Let's go *achech*-hunting instead!"

And, riding so, feet braced hard to keep his balance, hair leveled to the wind like his horse's mane, he did not consider it at all impossible that they should flush or even overtake an *achech* that fabulous but most swift of all animals, whose body was half bird, half lion. He might even be an *achech* himself, his mortal bulk become light because he had suddenly discovered the power to fly. Or was he really moving? Perhaps it was the desert that was racing past.

As the path narrowed among the dunes, it became rougher and less clearly defined. "Better slow down!" shouted Moses.

But Amon-nebet was reluctant to heed the advice. In the triumph of speed he had found a compensating sense of fulfillment. And for once he looked neither awkward nor ungainly. His thin body with its outthrust head lent itself to the poetry of motion as perfectly as did the horse's high-arched neck and rippling flanks. Watching his companion's horse draw ahead and pass his own, Moses felt a vicarious thrill of exultation.

Then as they passed a thicket of stunted tamarisks, he pulled hard on the reins and drew sharply to the left, for Amon-nebet had suddenly crumpled and fallen forward and was hanging precariously on the thin railing of his light wagon. Feeling his rein slacken, the horse reared and floundered, then, as something spun through the air from the direction of the thicket, charged wildly off among the dunes, the light wagon bobbing after him like a craft of frail papyrus tossed by angry waves.

He'll be killed surely! thought Moses, automatically whipping his own horse into swift pursuit.

Each moment he expected to see the crumpled figure detach itself from the wagon's rail and be thrown beneath its wheels, but by some miracle it clung to its frail support. The seconds dragged, seemed to lengthen into hours, but at last Moses knew he was gaining. Inch by inch he crept up on the careening wagon, moved warily in beside it, passed it. Then came the difficult moments of decision. If he waited too long, he might not be able to save Amon-nebet. If he stopped too soon, he might not have time to prepare himself properly. Now...Pulling sharply on the reins, he drew his horse to a trot and jumped backward from the wagon, falling headlong from the sudden impact. Fortunately he had made due allowance for the time it took to pick himself up, measure his distance, and place himself in the path of the approaching horse. Swiftness and sureness were all that counted now. He crouched and waited.

The beast came thundering toward him, saw the obstruction in his path, and swerved sharply. With all the speed he could muster Moses sprang to intercept him. He leaped for the bridle. There was only one chance in a hundred that he could grasp and hold it, but on that chance Amon-nebet's life depended. Moses' eye was good and his co-ordination perfect. He felt his fingers closing, his arm nearly torn from its socket. By the time the horse came to a quivering stop a few rods away, his whole body was shaken and bruised. He was sure his arm was broken. But there was no time now to investigate.

Carefully he lifted the limp body from the wagon rail, discovering why the young prince had not fallen beneath the wheels. One of his feet had become wedged in the railing between the spokes. The deep, three-cornered wound on the back of his head might have been caused by a horse's hoof, but Moses did not think so. Remembering the whining sound he had heard, he took time to examine the horse's side and found on the right flank a small wad of matted hair, the flesh beneath it still raw and bleeding. His lips set grimly.

He cleaned the wound on Amon-nebet's head as well as he could, lacking water, and bound it with a strip torn from his pleated overskirt. The ankle, he feared, was either broken or badly sprained. While he was bandaging it, the young prince stirred.

"O-oh, my head!" he groaned. Presently he opened his eyes. "What happened?"

Moses hesitated. "You—had an accident," he replied slowly. "Perhaps you grew faint. Anyway, you fell forward over the rail of your wagon, and your horse bolted and dragged you a long way. It looks as if he may have kicked the back of your head."

"No." Amon-nebet put his hand to the wound and winced.

"The horse didn't kick me. And I didn't faint. Something hit me on the head before I fell. You saved my life," he added simply.

"Your horse was struck too," said Moses, "by a rock, I believe, flung from that thicket back there. It was all carefully planned to look like an accident. Struck in the back of the head like that, you'd naturally fall over the rail, then when the horse went wild you'd be flung under the wagon wheels. The wound on the back of your head would apparently be made by the horse's hoof. Remember—you and I rode this way yesterday too, and the day before. It was all very cleverly planned."

"Yes," replied Amon-nebet. "I told you they wanted to kill me."

"Who?" demanded Moses. "Do you know?"

The older youth nodded, then clamped his lips together and closed his eyes. It was obvious that he had no more to say. Moses took him back to camp in his own wagon. Leaving a message for the other young nobles and taking with them suitable guards and attendants, they left at once for Memphis.

Only when he was back in his own room in the palace, having seen to it that his friend's wounds had been ably treated by the court physicians and that officers had been detailed to guard him day and night, did Moses remember that the man whose life he had risked his own to save was the one person in the world whom he had the most reason to hate.

6

Except for one small detail Sitra's scheme was working to perfection. Nefretiri was journeying with her on a royal barge to Thebes, and Moses was captain of the military guard that accompanied them.

It had not been too difficult to manage. The general in charge of royal troops at Memphis was building a new tomb for himself at Abydos and would gladly have upset the whole military machine for the privilege, graciously extended by the queen mother, of having his life-sized statue carved by the king's own sculptor. Tuya's insistence on witnessing the departure of the royal party from the palace balcony had necessitated a change of plans which involved dispatching Moses on a last-minute mission to Seti's new temple of Ptah, but even that emergency had been smoothly passed. The wasted face with its burning eyes and two bright spots of color had dominated the procession from the moment the first slave emerged from the palace door until the last guard passed through the gate.

But beyond the pylons was the domain of Hapi, the river-god, whom none dominated, not even the queen. Even in his months of weakness, when he crept through the land like a sluggish serpent, he was master, not slave. And now, swelled to a benign but eagerly rapacious monster, his belly gorged with the black richness which was to restore life to the shrunken earth, he was the destiny of mankind itself. Watching the naked slaves straining at the oars, Sitra had moments of misgiving. She too was battling against powerful currents. But her scheme was working—except for that one small detail. Could it be that her plan might be balked by the one liability which she had accounted her greatest asset, the stubborn will of Prince Moses himself?

"To Princess Sitra, mother of the God and Beloved of Amon-Re, fairest of all women in the Two Lands, greetings and regrets that his duties as captain of the guard prevent her servant Moses from accepting her invitation to dinner on the royal barge—"

Sitra bit her lip and crushed the small roll of papyrus in her hand. She lifted her arm to throw it from her, wondering idly if she could make it clear the oarsmen below and fall into the swirling water, but the effort seemed too great, and her arm relaxed, the wadded papyrus still clasped in her fingers. From the deck beneath came the sound of music and the patter of dancing feet, the throbbing of lutes and the tinkle of castanets interspersed with the bright cadences of the Princess Nefretiri's laughter. Reclining on her ebony couch close to the rail, Sitra could look down and see a small, crimson-clad foot gaily tapping time to the music on a little footrest of gold and ebony and ivory. She sighed. At Nefretiri's age she too had been tireless even on a summer afternoon before a refreshing breeze had risen. Nothing would have daunted her, certainly not the stubbornness of a square-chinned, rawboned youth.

Sitra's own eyes suddenly smoldered. She smoothed out the wad of papyrus, lifted her hand to the rail, and slowly, carelessly, loosed her fingers. It fluttered down and landed, as she had expected, a few inches from the little footrest. She saw a crimson-tipped hand pick it up.

A gentle breeze lifted the ruffle of the bright blue canopy above her head. The limp sail fluttered languidly. Presently it was riding, vigorous and full-breasted, on a brisk north wind. Sitra relaxed on her couch, smiling.

Moses flushed as his subordinate officer handed him the dainty roll of papyrus tied with a ribbon of intricately woven gold threads. Without lifting his gaze he knew that the young soldier's eyes held a faintly mocking glint.

"Perfume!" he would report later to an appreciative audience below deck. "Stank with the stuff. And pretty soon he'll send another message back saying his duties as captain are so strenuous he hasn't enough strength left to lift a wine cup!"

Moses knew what they were saying. It was not his princely rank which they resented nor his inexperience. They did not expect him to be captain other than in name and would gladly have conceded to him all the privileges of his office without any of its responsibilities. It was his vacillation which they resented, this unnatural mood of indecision which caused him one moment to summon every soldier for meticulous inspection and the next to walk the deck in aimless indifference to duty, which caused him to stand now, hesitating, an unopened roll of papyrus in his hand.

From where he stood, in the cabin entrance of the foremost guard boat, he had a clear view of the royal vessel sailing a short distance behind. Its curving prow, shaped like a gigantic lotus flower, lifted itself as gracefully as a maiden's slender throat. Colorful pictures adorned its sides. The great sail rode proudly on the wind, its richly woven hues of crimson and blue and gold flaunting their brightness on a scene already profligate of color. The hot shining clearness was riddled with sounds: the swashing of oars and the grunting of oarsmen, the gibes of soldiers and sailors, the staccato commands of a half dozen pilots, muffled mooings and stampings from a passing cattle barge. But Moses heard only one, a light peal of laughter as delicate as spun silver.

He had not seen Nefretiri since that day in the garden, but since sailing from Memphis he had been acutely conscious of her nearness. The knowledge that he was separated from her by but a brief width of water which he must not traverse was becoming more and more intolerable. Yet he was more determined than ever to adhere to his purpose. Nefretiri was the heiress of the throne of Egypt. She was soon to be the pledged wife of his friend Amon-nebet. He had no place in her future. For the sake of all concerned, himself included, he was determined never to seek her presence again.

But she came to him constantly without his seeking, induced by the slightest of pretexts—the glow of bronze in sunlight, the sound of light laughter across the waters, an elusive hint of fragrance. Suddenly remembering that Sitra abhorred perfumed letters, he looked more closely at the small roll in his hand. The ribbon was sealed with a bit of clay, but the impression upon it was not that of Sitra's seal. It was a representation of the goddess Isis holding the infant Horus in her arms.

With trembling fingers Moses tore open the seal. The words on the papyrus were briefly bold and black, belying the soft curves of the lips which had dictated them.

"So you turned out to be a coward!"

Moses stared at the script, his cheeks flaming. Then abruptly he left the cabin and strode down the deck.

"Have one of the small skiffs made ready," he ordered his subordinate officer, "and load it with gifts—flowers, wines, choice foods, the best the ship affords. I'm paying a visit to the royal vessel."

"B-but—" The officer's jaw dropped. "Where—how—"

"I don't care where or how," snapped Moses. "Send ashore for them if you must. But get them. And quickly."

"Yes, sir." There was no mockery in the officer's eyes now. He departed hastily to do the captain's bidding.

From that moment Moses forgot the future and lived only in the present. He spent long, lazy hours under the blue canopy on the cabin roof of the royal vessel, sipping date wine and occasionally munching a bit of fruit or a honey cake from one of the loaded trays which Sitra kept constantly at the elbows of her guests. He sat in cushioned ease at the banquet table in the sumptuous cabin, his emotions as pliantly yielded to the mellow warmth of their surroundings as the ball of fragrant ointment which a slave kept continually renewed upon his head.

Now that the one flaw had been remedied, Sitra's plan proceeded, perfect in every detail. Actors came in at the proper times and played their minor parts: harpists and singers and dancers; a juggler who plied his art with flowers; a minstrel who sang nothing but love songs.

But, so far as Moses was concerned, all of Sitra's elaborate planning had been superfluous. The presence of Nefretiri satisfied his every sense and emotion to its full capacity. It was the sight of her glowing, piquant features that lent sweetness to the hours spent at the banquet table, not the honey cakes which melted in his mouth.

Only the minstrel, plucking his little five-stringed lyre and striving gallantly to put the elusive drama into words, came near to disrupting it when he sang passionately the old love plaint of the peasant girl who went snaring wild ducks in the marshes:

"Caught by the worm, the wild duck cries,
But in the love light of thine eyes
I, trembling, loose the trap. So flies
    The bird into the air.
What will my angry mother say?
With basket full I come each day,
But now thy love hath led me stray,
    And I have set no snare."

"The wild duck scatter far, and now
Again they light upon the bough
    And cry unto their kind;
Anon they gather on the mere—

But yet unharmed I leave them there,
    For love hath filled my mind."

Listening, Moses felt a sharp stab of reality. Nefretiri was no peasant girl, worse luck! And he— What was he doing here lost in a romantic trance? The peasant maid had had to pay the price of her plaintive romancings when she had returned home with an empty basket. "What will my angry mother say?" She also had had a strong-willed Tuya or Seti hovering in the background, and doubtless an Amon-nebet too, whom the family favored. It was the peasant lover, not the bird, that had fallen into the trap.

"What fools those peasants were!" said Moses abruptly.

"Why?" demanded Nefretiri. The red-sandaled foot with which she had been tapping time to the music was suddenly still.

"Because," he replied carefully, "when the end of the day comes, it is all over and they have nothing left. The girl goes home to her angry mother with her basket empty, and then the trouble starts. You can imagine what happens."

"What?" asked Nefretiri.

The minstrel plucked agitatedly at the strings of his lyre. "If the noble prince does not like that song," he quavered, "the tongue of his slave is dripping with a thousand others."

But to the two who sat gazing at each other his voice might have been the chirping of an insect. Sitra too leaned forward and started to speak, then, her black eyes moving watchfully from one to the other, settled back again.

"What happens?" repeated Nefretiri.

Moses' dark brows drew together in a straight line. "The mother obviously has other plans for her daughter, which do not include this lover, whoever he is. Let's say she wants her to marry—a hatchet-faced farmer to whom they are in debt. And the father too has plans—"

"Let me," interposed the girl quickly. "The father wants her to marry a—an ugly hunchback with green eyes and a long neck like a crane's. And he will lock her in—in the granary until she comes to her senses."

"And the next day they won't allow her to go back to the marshes to snare birds," continued Moses gravely. "So she may never see her peasant lover again."

The green particles in Nefretiri's eyes glinted. "But at least they had that one day," she countered.

Sitra lifted a languid hand and picked a honey-coated date from the tray of sweetmeats. "There's one thing you haven't taken into consideration," she remarked casually, "and that's the maiden herself. Isn't it just possible that she may have a stronger will than either her father or her mother?"

She gestured to the minstrel, and his babbling voice gushed into the silence like a suddenly unstopped stream. "I will sing you a song of the maiden who wove for her lover a wreath of flowers," he chirruped with relieved abandon.

Listening to the tuneless cadences, Moses drifted back into the mood of voluptuous quiescence. The sun was still high in the heavens of their perfect day together. The peasant lover had not looked beyond the twilight, and neither would he. It was enough to be in his beloved's presence, to hear her bubbling laughter, to caress her lovely body with one swift motion of his eyes.

He was but vaguely aware of the constant shifting of scenery against which their absorbing little drama was played. Bright cities floated past. Frail villages of mud huts hung precariously to slender brown networks of dikes. Behind long, shaded avenues crouched ancient temples, somnolent and secretive, their gates guarded by pairs of carved giants sitting in rigid dignity. The river itself was as warm with life and color as a garden pool with fish. The shrill halloos of sailors, the trumpetings of pilots and warning shouts of polemen, the harsh gutturals of the slave drivers on the towpaths along the shore, created a melee of confusion. But to Moses they might have been sights and sounds in a dream.

Then abruptly, without warning, he became completely aware of his surroundings.

Late one afternoon, just as he was preparing to embark in the small boat for the royal vessel, they approached a sudden opening in the red cliffs which for miles had towered close to the river's edge. On their left lay a broad, pleasant valley scooped, crescent-shaped, from the desert, its fertile black and green richness strewn with the ruins of what had once been a beautiful and stately city. Its magnificent buildings were now bleak and desolate, brick walls gaping and roofless, gaunt towers and obelisks stripped of gold caps and jeweled inlays, gates sagging on their hinges—a vast corpse, its bones picked clean by the vultures and left to whiten beneath the pitiless sun.

With the sighting of the city the manner of both soldiers and sailors changed abruptly. All joking and ribaldry ceased. Even the pilot's shrill mouthings became muted. And when the brisk wind subsided without warning, leaving the vessel becalmed, terror suddenly stalked the decks. Hastily the great blue sail was lowered and wound about the mast. Without a single stroke of the lash the oarsmen sprang to their places, ready for the struggle with the midstream current. Occasionally above the subdued bedlam of sound the fear of a sailor or soldier became articulate.

"The criminal has cast a spell! It was he who made the wind go down!"

"They say if you see the sun set while you're passing it, you're a dead man!"

"I knew a sailor once who but set foot on shore in these parts and was swallowed to his neck. When his mates threw him a towing rope, he was stuck there firm as a rock. You can still hear him shouting when the river is low."

"By the whiskers of Bast, keep your eyes straight ahead! What you don't see isn't likely to kill you."

The glow of dreamy preoccupation faded from Moses' eyes. Abruptly he summoned his subordinate.

"What's the matter with the pilot?" he demanded sharply. "Those oarsmen needn't be rowing in midstream. Why doesn't he order them to pull over toward the bank?"

The officer's glance was wary. "Perhaps the captain has not made this journey before," he suggested hesitantly. "Perhaps he does not know—"

"That we are passing the ruined city of Akhetaton?" finished Moses bluntly. "Of course I know. What of it?"

"Please!" The officer's face was gray. He hastened to finger the little hawk-shaped amulet about his neck. "That name—Even the captain's lips must not repeat it."

"What would happen," asked Moses more gently, "if I were to order the pilot to seek quieter waters and anchor until the wind is again favorable?"

"He would throw himself overboard," replied the officer promptly, "rather than disobey the noble prince, our captain. But even if he were to give the order, the crew would mutiny."

"I see," said Moses. Dismissing his subordinate, he ordered the small boat to be made ready. The sailor who propelled him to the royal vessel was so nervous that more than once he almost dropped his short, broad-bladed oar into the water.

Moses went straight to the cabin roof top. Without glancing at Nefretiri he swiftly approached the great armchair in which Sitra was sitting, relaxed and motionless in the intense heat. Noticing the intentness in his dark face, her eyes flew open.

"Why—Moses—what—"

"I want you to tell me," he said deliberately, "all that you know about Ikhnaton."

Sitra's features remained serene, but the heavy fringes over her black eyes drew together. With a casual motion of her hand she gestured for the two Nubians, with their huge ostrich fans, to depart. "Sit down, son," she said calmly. "No, not the stool. The chair where you can sit back against the cushions. After you've cooled your blood with a goblet of white wine, we'll have a surprise for you, a new dance which they say all Thebes is raving about. It's called 'the wind,' and it's done by three maidens, two of them swaying like reeds—" She stopped suddenly, knowing that the idle prattle was a waste of time.

"Sit down, son," she repeated gently.

Moses sat down, but he did not lean back against the cushions. "You heard me," he continued stubbornly, "I've been trying for a long while to find out about him, but it's like finding the way into a sealed tomb. People won't even let you mention his name. He's always just that 'criminal of Akhetaton.'" With a brief, curt gesture Moses indicated the grim ghost city visible beneath the blue awning. "Well, there it is. I have to know the truth about it. The secret is hidden there somewhere. I'm going to find it if—if I have to swim ashore and go pawing among the ruins."

Sitra measured him thoughtfully between the drawn curtains of her lashes. She was dealing with the unknown now and must move cautiously. For it was not the voice of Egypt speaking. Egyptians sought truth only that they might live and die more profitably, not for the sake of truth itself. The Mitannian too had had the strange blood of Asia in his veins, and she had lost him.

"What makes you think I could tell you about—him?" she parried.

"He was your grandfather."

The promptness of his reply was disconcerting. Perhaps this was not the time for caution, after all. She had been cautious with the Mitannian prince. "So he was," she said simply. "Although it seems strange to call him that. He seemed so young."

"You remember him then?"

"Not much, for I was only five when he died. He used to come into the nursery or the garden and play with us. He loved children more than any man I ever knew. I can see him now, sitting in the summerhouse by the lake with us children all about him. We used to hang so many garlands about his neck that his slight body was almost buried. He wasn't a robust man," she went on reminiscently, "and not attractive to look at, though he wore a serene, kindly expression and there was a beautiful dreamy gentleness in his eyes. His head seemed too heavy for his body, and it jutted forward from his thin neck like—like—"

"Tell me about the god he worshiped," interposed Moses.

"Aton?" Sitra barely whispered the word, her glance guardedly circling the roof top.

"Is it true that Ikhnaton believed there was only one god?"

Sitra shook her head. "I don't know. I never could understand just what he believed, nor why the priests of Amon were so angry. After he died, they even broke into the tomb where he was buried with his mother Tiy and erased his name on his coffin, thus robbing him of eternal life. When the husband of my mother, Meritaton, became king, they made his brief reign a miserable farce, and they forced his successor, Tutenkhaton, to change his name to Tutenkhamon."

"But Aton, the one god," persisted Moses. "Doesn't his name recall anything to your mind? Aton, the glorious, the supreme—"

"Stop!" cried Sitra. The surface of her serenity suddenly crumpled. "Don't mention that name again! It brought Egypt nothing but trouble. Even the poor oarsmen are stricken with terror. They know that some ill fortune is likely to befall us as long as we are here in its shadow. For the love of Amon, don't try to penetrate its secrets!"

Moses returned to his guard boat intensely disappointed in his interview with Sitra. He had not known until now how consuming was his desire to discover the truth about Ikhnaton and his heresy. Maruma and Sitra were the only ones he knew who had known the "criminal of Akhetaton" intimately. Both had failed him.

As long as daylight lasted he stood in a secluded spot on deck, his gaze fixed intently on the distant shore line. Even in its stark emptiness it was a long and imposing panorama. When sunset finally gilded its grim outlines and darkness fell with the abruptness of a quickly drawn curtain, the oarsmen were still straining and panting on their benches below. In the darkness their terror seemed to assume bodily form, stalking the deck with every creaking board, pulling with strong, grappling hands in the opposing current.

Though he could see nothing of the shore line, Moses continued to stand motionless, his eyes straining toward it. When finally he saw a light moving high in the air, it took him some moments to realize its significance. Then his hands gripped the rail. Fascinated, he watched the point of flame, following its tortuous progress as it descended through a sea of blackness, occasionally disappearing, then continuing to flare steadily again, finally vanishing entirely.

When the moon rose a little later, full and lustrous, it revealed no ghostly outline of a ruined city. The mood of panic lifted abruptly. Groans and muttered prayers were replaced by lusty shouts and ribald jests. The prow of the leading vessel swung toward shore.

A gleam in his eyes, Moses summoned his subordinate.

"What now?" he demanded. "Surely those oarsmen can take a rest until morning."

The officer grinned. His respect had receded along with his panic. "Try and stop them! If we get them out of their wine cups by noon, we'll do well. We're heading now for the first towing station, where we'll drop anchor. The men will be going ashore. We couldn't stop them if we wanted to, and they deserve some relaxation. There'll be women at the station. And the wine casks are already unstopped."

"So we won't be moving on until noon or later," said Moses slowly. "How far is the towing station above Ak—the city we have just passed?"

"Only a few hundred strokes from the stele which marks the outer boundary. Perhaps a mile or two."

The gleam brightened in Moses' eyes. "Very well. Delay seems inevitable, as you say. However, we may as well take advantage of it.

Have one of the reed boats kept in readiness. I—may wish to return to the royal vessel."

"*Yes, sir!*" The officer winked deliberately. "The captain also has endured great strain."

The revelry continued for some hours after midnight. Moses waited until he judged by the sound that most of the crew had either gone ashore or drunk themselves into oblivion. The sailor designated to propel his skiff lay, as he had expected, in a drunken stupor. Carefully Moses lowered himself into the reed boat.

The royal vessel lay directly in his path, and he floated noiselessly into its shadow, keeping on the shoreward side to avoid the bright moonlight. Though he did not see the slender shape detach itself from the shadows of the deck just above his head, the sound of a low, familiar whistle caused his fingers to freeze suddenly on the oar shaft. It was part of a secret code he and a group of his playmates had devised in the harem nursery, and this particular signal meant: "Come here quickly. I have an idea!"

It came again, three low whistles with a slight trill at the end. Carefully Moses backed his skiff in its direction, conscious now of the slender shape in the shadows above him.

"Moses!"

"Nefretiri!" he whispered back. "What are you doing here?"

"Don't ask questions. Just keep the boat pulled close. I'm sliding down this rope. Here I come."

Automatically he lifted his arms, and the slender figure slid into them. He was vaguely aware of an intoxicating fragrance and of soft warmth against his body before she was out of his arms again and pushing him gently toward the boat's high stern. "Quick! Let's get away! Can't you take faster strokes?"

"Nefretiri, are you crazy?" Even while whispering his protests, Moses obediently quickened his movements. The light skiff slipped noiselessly through the shadows beside the vessel, then out into the moonlit space beyond. "What in heaven's name are you doing here!"

She settled herself comfortably on the thick mat which covered the tightly bound papyrus reeds. "I'm going with you, of course. I knew you'd come. I've been waiting there on the deck for hours."

"But—" Moses' senses were still whirling, "it may be dangerous, and when they miss you on the vessel—"

"They won't miss me. I left word that I wasn't to be disturbed in the morning, and, anyway, I gave Memnet a big sleeping potion. She may not wake up for days and days."

"Sitra—"

"Sitra won't know I'm gone." Nefretiri leaned backward, arching her neck until her hair brushed his knees and she could look up into his face. The moonlight made a golden blur of her features. "Don't you want me to go with you, Moses?"

His fingers closed hard about the oar shaft. His pulses sounded like drumbeats in his ears. Lifting his arms, he touched the shimmering water with a light, swift stroke, and the boat bounded forward.

From the shadows on the deck of the royal vessel Sitra watched them go. She felt baffled and helpless, like a man who has carefully constructed dikes to control the rising of the waters and sees them suddenly swept away by the very flood he has designed to exploit.

"Shall I call one of the sailors?" whispered Beket. "It still isn't too late to bring them back." As the black eyes of her mistress remained shadowed, she thrust her brown, wrinkled face into their direct line of vision. "Will they go to the evil city, do you think? Will it cast a spell upon them? Will it happen while they're gone, I wonder, the thing you've been waiting for? Will they find out they're in love with each other?"

Sitra made an impatient gesture. "Really, Beket! You are insufferable. If the Princess Nefretiri chooses to take a moonlight ride on the river, what possible concern is it of yours?"

"The queen of heaven is always the wisest of women," murmured the slave humbly. Then deliberately she winked one eye.

7

The sky above the ghost city of Akhetaton turned from pearl-gray to silver. In their shadowed, crescent-shaped tomb the bones of the dead city lay grim and exposed. Moses waited in an agony of anticipation. Presently the flaming disk whose radiant energy was the essence of the strange god Aton would blaze its way above the cliffs. Would it instill life into these scattered bones, as Isis had once breathed it into the assembled limbs of her beloved Osiris by blowing on them with her wings?

Nefretiri was also watching intently, but it was on the features of the man guiding the small reed boat that her sharp eyes were fixed. She was not at all disturbed that he appeared unaware of her presence.

Leaning back, she stretched herself full length on the mat, cupping the back of her head in the palms of her hands. She knew that she was utterly desirable and that not one man in a hundred could watch the coming of the dawn in her presence and remain oblivious of her charms. That Moses could do so was interesting, a bit challenging, but by no means disturbing. She did not want a hundred men. She wanted one. This one. She had wanted him since a certain day in the nursery when she had tried to persuade him to play a game of checkers and he had sat with his face buried in an old papyrus picture roll, completely indifferent to her demands. She had found a way to win him then, not immediately but in due time, simply by producing a more lavishly colored picture roll and sharing it with him. She had discovered then that the game of checkers had not really mattered.

Patiently she watched the coming of the dawn on the bold, intent features: high brows, strongly sculptured nose, firm chin emerging like mountaintops out of the shadows; the short curls to which the blackness of the night still clung; the sudden flash of light which would have blinded most men's eyes but which he gazed at without flinching.

Nefretiri could afford to wait. This time she held a more potent weapon than a lavishly colored picture roll. For the city which held Moses' attention was dead, but she, every beautiful vibrant inch of her, was very much alive.

"Hurry!" Moses urged impatiently. "We must be back to the vessels by noon, and we've only barely begun to search. See how high the sun is already!"

As she followed him through the neglected garden and into the little kiosk beside the dry lake bed, Nefretiri stifled the sharp words that rose to her lips. Her tender feet, used to the smoothness of a palace floor, felt as if they were on fire. She was sure her beautiful red-leather sandals were worn through on the bottom and that the flesh of her soles was raw. For the first time in her life she felt hot and uncomfortable without being able to summon a dozen slaves to alleviate her discomfort. But the face she turned toward Moses was still untroubled and eager.

"Haven't we seen enough?" she inquired hopefully. "All these palaces may have been beautiful once, but they're certainly not now.

Roofs fallen in, floors covered with rubble, even the paintings on the walls defaced!"

"They're not defaced here." Moses' eyes swept the walls of the little kiosk.

Nefretiri sank down on a beautifully carved double chair, grateful for the cushions heaped upon it but too weary to question how they had come there. She pulled off the red sandals and rubbed her burning feet. Then, noting that the eager, untroubled look was quite lost on her companion, she relaxed her features. It was apparent that Moses was not concerned with how she looked or felt. She was merely a convenient sounding board for his enthusiasm.

"Look! This is one place the vandals haven't touched. See the paintings on the walls? The faces aren't even scratched. It's just as it was when *he* was alive and used to sit here with his children. Look at those cushions on the chair where you're sitting! They still show the imprints of a human body."

Nefretiri started up hastily, her first impulse one of terror. She glanced about, half expecting to see ghostly figures lurking in the shadows, then noting that there were no shadows. It was the brightest and pleasantest room she had ever seen. Light poured in from innumerable apertures high up in the wall, not bright and glaring but softly muted as if it had been sifted through meshes of sunlight. Delicate fluted columns supported the gaily painted ceiling, their carved grooves inlaid with bits of bright blue and rose glaze, their edges picked out with gold. The floor was made entirely of smooth, cool tiles, as blue-green as the reed-bordered stream they were skillfully fashioned to represent. She felt its delicious coolness under her burning feet.

But it was at the painted walls that she stared with amazement. The man with the gentle, pensive features, his head slightly thrust forward on his slender neck, a laughing child on either knee, and the lovely woman leaning her head against his shoulder—surely they were not painted things! Unbelievingly Nefretiri tiptoed across the tiles and placed an exploring finger on the stuccoed wall.

"It's—really painted!"

"Yes," said Moses. "Ikhnaton believed that art consists in depicting things as they actually are. He was the first pharaoh in Egypt who wasn't always painted to look like a stone monolith, with his hands plastered to his knees and his eyes staring into space."

Standing on tiptoe, Nefretiri touched one of the golden disks that topped each grouping and traced one of its bright, threadlike rays to its end. "Look, Moses! Every one of the sun's rays ends in a funny little hand! Why are they there?"

"I don't know," replied Moses slowly. "That's one of the things I came here to find out."

The girl returned with relief to the softness of the double chair. It no longer seemed frightening that it bore the imprint of other human bodies. She even gave the dented cushions a playful pat.

"If the ghosts of Ikhnaton and his family are still here, they must have plenty of slave ghosts with them," she remarked lightly. "There isn't even any dust on the pillows."

Moses was instantly alert. "Of course! Nefretiri, do you know what that means? Someone has been taking care of this place. I didn't imagine that light I saw. Come, let's hurry on! It may not be much farther."

She shook her head. "I'm staying here. You go on and find out the secrets, if there are any. Then you can come back and tell me."

"But—I couldn't leave you here alone. Someone might come—"

There was no mistaking the eagerness in his voice. He wanted to be gone, either with or without her, preferably the latter, she suspected grimly. The women who loved Moses would spend a good bit of their lives in solitude cooling their blistered feet. Resignedly she drew her own to the smooth coolness of the ebony chair and, crossing her legs comfortably, leaned back against the cushions.

"Run along," she said sweetly. "If anyone comes to bother me, I'll scream so you can hear me all over this tumble-down place and come running. Just don't forget I'm here and go back to the boats without me. And don't stay too long. You might not always find me waiting."

Moses hastened back through the neglected garden; but now it did not look so neglected. He noticed small details that he had missed before: the marks of a reed broom on a gravel path, a pile of weeds carefully heaped beneath a bush. Amid the vast ruin they looked like the pitiful attempts of a child building toy dikes to stop the inundation. He took time to pull a dead branch from a pomegranate tree and toss it into the wild growth out of sight.

He went on into the palace. Here there were no marks of human presence. Time and the loyal avengers of Amon had been hard at work. Every detachable object of value had been stripped away. The floors were strewn with rubbish. His footsteps resounded emptily through the deserted corridors, startling the long silence and awaking mocking echoes of voices from the past.

"Akhetaton, great in loveliness," her poets had once written, "mistress of pleasant ceremonies, rich in possessions. At the sight of her beauty there is rejoicing. When one sees her it is like a glimpse of heaven."

Impatiently Moses searched the rooms, hundreds of them, it seemed. A sense of panic-stricken urgency possessed him. Presently he found his way to the temple area, where a scene of utter desolation met his eyes. Here Harmhab and the priests of Amon had done their work well. The brick walls lay in ruins. All that remained of the once magnificent mansion of Aton was a vast death's-head strewn with wreckage, its empty sockets bared to sun and wind.

Moses stopped short, disappointment chilling his whole body. This was the end of his search. If no spark had been kept burning in this most sacred place, then the moving light in the night had meant nothing. Some half-crazed vagrant, perhaps, or slinking tomb robber.

Through court after court he passed, among dim forests of colonnades which led only into other empty courts. Then, tired and disappointed, he retraced his steps and was about to return to Nefretiri when he noticed that his steps were following a clearly defined path no wider than a forearm's length but carefully cleared of all obstructions. He quickened his steps until he was almost running. Yes, it was most certainly a path, so well trodden that it formed a slight groove in the polished stone floor. It led with apparent lack of purpose around the temple proper to the rear of the great outer court, turning and twisting to avoid heaps of fallen debris, and ending in a small gateway in the rear wall.

His pulses pounding with excitement, he entered the outer court of a much smaller temple. Here there were amazingly few signs of devastation. The walls of white polished limestone were intact, the floor of the courtyard smooth and well swept, the columned gateway that formed the temple's entrance still imposing and complete with its five slender gold flagstaves. Swiftly he crossed the courtyard and passed through the pyloned gate. Before him lay a narrow corridor, at the end of which an open court was visible.

He moved more slowly now, his steps soundless on the polished tiles. Even before he had reached the entrance of the court and seen the figure of a man standing before the high stone altar, he heard the voice. So light and thin did it sound that it seemed a disembodied thing, yet every syllable was clearly distinguishable. With a thrill of excitement he recognized the words that he had heard whispered by the lips of Maruma.

"Thy dawning is beautiful in the horizon of heaven,
   O living Aton, Beginning of life!
   When thou risest in the eastern horizon,
   Thou fillest every land with thy beauty.
   Thou art beautiful, great, glittering, high over all the earth."

Moses listened, almost without breathing, while the hymn continued to its end. Then he realized that the figure by the altar was beckoning to him, and in a tumult of emotion he passed into the great open court. Questions burned on his lips. Yet he stood hesitating, reluctant to interrupt whatever ceremony the strange, solitary figure was performing.

But he need not have worried. The lonely worshiper continued his ritual as if he were quite alone, or, rather, as if the court behind him were filled with an army of devout worshipers and assisting priests and singers. Understanding, Moses felt a stab of pity, mingled with disappointment. The man was obviously mad. Was this venture also to end in failure?

But as the strange service proceeded, pity became displaced by other emotions. Moses found himself participating in the familiar ritual, and he discovered to his amazement that he had never before truly worshiped. Here there were no glittering falcons or obelisks or crescents to dazzle his vision, only the bare stone altar, the enfolding radiance of the sun, the bright clear blue of the sky above his head. And a voice clear as a bell but so light and thin that it seemed but an echoing pulsation of the enveloping warmth in which his whole being had become submerged.

"How manifold are all thy works!
   They are hidden from before us,
   O thou sole god, beside whom there is no other.
   Thou didst create the earth according to thy desire.
   While thou wast alone:
   Men, all cattle large and small,
   All that are upon the earth,
   That go about upon their feet;
   All that are on high,
   That fly with their wings.
   The countries of Syria and Nubia,
   The land of Egypt;
   Thou settest every man in his place,

Thou suppliest all their necessities...
How excellent are thy designs, O lord of eternity!"

The voice was silent. The man turned and descended the nine long steps of the altar. He came straight toward Moses.

"So you have come," he said simply. "It has been a long time. I have been waiting."

Moses stood speechless, absorbed in his first close inspection of the strange figure. Never in his life had he seen a human being so old yet so completely ageless. The bones of the nobly shaped skull were so sharply delineated that the flesh above them seemed transparent. Parchment-thin and silken-textured, it hung on the high cheekbones and tapering temples like fine, soft webbing. So deeply were the eyes embedded in the sockets that they seemed to possess neither form nor color, only a luminous intensity, as if they were being constantly fed by renewing fires from within. And they were not the eyes of a madman.

His clothes, while spotlessly clean, looked as old and fragile as his body. His pleated linen skirt was as yellowed as ripened wheat, and over one shoulder he wore a tattered panther skin adorned with little gold stars, like that of the Great Seer of On.

Moses caught his breath. "You—you're Merire!" he stammered.

The old man bowed with great dignity. "And you?"

"Moses, a prince of the royal court, the adopted son of the Princess Sitra."

A twinkle appeared in the cavernous depths. "I remember Sitra. She was dark and sprightly, like her mother, Meritaton. The king, the spirit of Aton, used to call her his 'golden lotus flower.'"

Moses continued to stare at him. No wonder he looked older than any man alive! For Merire, the high priest of Aton, had been old when Ikhnaton had lived, a half century ago.

"W-why did you say you had been w-waiting for me?" he stumbled. "You d-didn't even know my name. You'd never heard of me before."

"But I knew you would come."

"H-how could you? I didn't know myself."

"I knew you would come," repeated the old man steadily, "because in half a hundred years some man is sure to be born who asks questions."

Moses' eyes blazed. "Tell me about Ikhnaton" he burst out eagerly, "and the god he worshiped. I've asked Maruma and Sitra, and neither of them would tell me."

"They are afraid," replied Merire.

"But you—you're not afraid. You will tell me."

The old man shook his head. "No. I shall not tell you."

"B-but—" Confused and disappointed, Moses stared at him helplessly.

"I shall *show* you."

Beckoning him to follow, the aged priest led the way to the rear of the open court, where a columned gateway gave entrance to another narrow corridor leading to a small roofed hall sown as thickly as a forest with tall colonnades. At the end of the hall was a small closed door. As they approached it, Moses' excitement mounted to a new intensity. Beyond that door was the most sacred room, the holy of holies, which only the priests were permitted to enter. Here the statue of the god was kept, his daily toilet performed, his garments changed, his sacred bark held in readiness for his journeys. The room would be small and dark, as befitted the abode of a god, dimly redolent of mystery and incense.

"I shall show you," the old man had said.

Moses' eyes burned, and there was a suffocating lump in his throat as he drew nearer and nearer the closed door. Was he about to look on the earthly image, not of Re but of the even more elusive and mysterious Aton, concerning whom his followers had made that preposterous claim: "Thou are the sole god, beside whom there is no other!"

Merire placed his hand on the gilded panel. "Come," he said.

Gasping with astonishment, Moses lifted his arm to cover his suddenly blinded eyes. For it was no small dark room they entered but another open court, its white walls and polished floor bared to the bright light of the morning sun. "B-but I thought—" he stammered.

Untouched by the invading brightness, the old priest's eyes gazed at him steadily. "You thought what, my son?"

"That—that this was the most holy place."

"And so it is."

"B-but the small dark room—where the image of the god is kept—"

"There is no small dark room in the temple of Aton," replied the priest. "He who shines in the heavens is not worshiped in secret but openly, where every eye can see. And he has no image to be washed and dressed and painted and carried abroad on the shoulders of men, that he may view his domains and visit those of other gods. For there are no gods except Aton, the creator of life and of beauty, the giver of all good."

Moses lifted his face. His eyes were no longer dazzled by the brightness. He opened them wide, letting the golden radiance fill them, until they felt like brimming pools of light, until his whole being seemed immersed in a flood of warmth, through which the gentle voice sounded clearly but as from a great distance.

"The symbol of Aton is the gold disk, whose rays are the life-giving arms and hands which support and sustain his creation. But it is the god we worship, not his symbol. Lift up your arms, my son."

As Moses obeyed, the burning radiance became more than he could bear. He closed his eyes. But the light was still there, a blazing golden disk that whirled and throbbed and vibrated, then splintered into a thousand dazzling separate rays, each ending in a tiny, outstretched hand.

Nefretiri was tired of being wise and patient. In fact, she was tired of the whole adventure. She wished she were back on the comfortable deck of the royal vessel, a cool glass of wine at her elbow, the gentle motion of fans constantly stirring a fresh breeze about her supine body. In all her life she had never experienced such discomfort. The bright sun shining on the water hurt her eyes. Her thin garments clung to her flesh. Her nostrils rebelled at the strange odors thrust upon them: the faint mustiness of water-soaked papyrus, the hot strong smell of the rising river sated to the brim with rich silt and vegetation.

And her feet still hurt. The crimson sandals were nearly worn through on the bottom. If it were Amon-nebet there in the stern, he would not be staring at the diminishing sky line with such indifference to her presence. At the thought of Amon-nebet a spark of triumph kindled in her eyes. She wondered if she should tell Moses her newly discovered secret. Sometime, perhaps. But not yet.

"Tell me more, Moses," she begged, leaning forward on the mat and opening her eyes wide with what she hoped was a semblance of eagerness. "What happened after you left the temple?"

She might have spared herself the effort, for he still did not look in her direction.

"After we left the temple," he said, "Merire took me up into the cliffs behind the city and showed me his tomb."

"He took you inside?" There was no need of pretense now. The girl's voice revealed her curiosity.

"Yes. We went inside. The entrance is so well hidden that the despoilers of the other tombs never found it."

"What does it look like? Weren't you afraid to go into it?"

"No," replied Moses. "There is nothing frightening about Merire's tomb. There are no ugly statues about, for Ikhnaton and his followers didn't believe in making images. And the walls are covered with beautiful pictures like the ones we saw in the kiosk, natural, lifelike scenes of the way men lived in Akhetaton. And when Merire is finally laid to rest in his coffin, there will be no magic spells buried with him."

Mischief sparkled in the girl's eyes. "If Ikhnaton's picture is on the walls of Merire's tomb, then they aren't all beautiful." She giggled. "If I'd looked like him, I wouldn't have wanted to be painted the way I really was."

Still he did not turn to her. "Ikhnaton believed," he said soberly, "that there is beauty in all reality."

"Moses!" She spoke with sudden urgency, determined to make him give her his full attention. "Want me to tell you a secret? I made a discovery when I was sitting there so long in the kiosk."

"What was it?" he asked, his eyes still on the far horizon.

"Amon-nebet looks exactly like Ikhnaton. He's the living image of him."

She had hoped to gain his attention for the moment, but she was unprepared for the swiftness with which he turned toward her, the dark concentration with which he bent his gaze to hers.

"No! Don't say that!"

"But it's true. Why shouldn't I say it?" There was triumph in her voice now as well as urgency. Even antagonism was preferable to indifference. She returned his gaze with provocative challenge.

Moses' hands ceased their rhythmic motion. He dropped to his knees on the mat so his eyes were on a level with hers. "Because," he said earnestly, "Ikhnaton's name is hated in every corner of Egypt. Can't you see what might happen if people discovered Amon-nebet looked like him?"

"No. What?"

"They might hate Amon-nebet too. They might even make it impossible for him to become pharaoh."

Nefretiri leaned forward. "And suppose they did," she prompted softly. "Would that be so very terrible? Would we mind so much, Moses, you and I?"

She could hear his sharply indrawn breath. "Amon-nebet is to be pharaoh of Egypt," he replied steadily. "It is the wish of Seti his father. And you are to be his queen."

Triumph swept through the girl's body. The moment had come at last. Thank the gods, there was no longer need for patience! But for wisdom, yes. So much could happen in a moment. The history of a nation could be changed, the hope of a lifetime gained—or lost.

"No," she said slowly. "I shall never be Amon-nebet's queen. No one can make me. I'd rather die."

She felt his hands gripping her shoulders. "You really mean that? Look at me! Look straight into my eyes."

She did so, opening her own wide, glad that there was no longer need for patience or concealment, even for wisdom. The hands on her shoulders pressed so hard into her flesh that she felt a faint throbbing of pain, but she welcomed it, exulted in it. Never again would she feel a distaste for aching feet or the discomfort of hot clinging garments or the smell of the swollen river.

"Why?" he demanded in a hoarse whisper.

"Because," she said steadily, "it's you I love, Moses. It always has been. You must know that."

Bereft of its oarsman, the little boat had become caught in an eddy and was turning slowly round and round. But Moses did not notice. The only currents of which he was conscious were the waves passing through his fingers from the smooth flesh of the shoulders beneath his hands, and the only eddies worth considering were in the black, green-flecked pools into which his own unbelieving eyes were probing.

It became suddenly unimportant that she was intended to be the future wife of Amon-nebet or that she was the heiress of the throne of Egypt. He took her in his arms.

PART III

1

Seti was tired. He was always tired after he had spent a long time in Thebes. He felt like one of those strange treasures which the Peoples of the Sea sometimes brought to the Two Lands, a shellfish which kept creating for itself newer and more splendid abodes while still burdened with all its outworn dwellings of the past.

By the time he had risen and eaten his frugal breakfast, listened to the reading of the most important dispatches and dictated his replies, his head was already aching. Outwardly as composed as usual, he submitted to the ministrations of the numberless lords and lordlets of the royal toilet, but his mind was a whirling confusion of the duties he must perform throughout the day.

Riding in his glittering palanquin along the broad avenue of rams and sphinxes, he fretted at the impeding crowds and at the slowness of the distinguished courtiers who bore him on their shoulders. It consumed hours of precious time making the daily morning pilgrimage across the river to the temple of Amon at Karnak, but he dared not omit the ceremony. The priests of Amon were jealous of his every movement. They resented his building operations in the Delta, believing, and rightly so, that it was another attempt to transfer the center of power from Thebes to a new city in the north. To pacify them, Seti had not only increased their gifts from the crown to staggering amounts but continued with his father's plans for one of the most pretentious building projects that had ever been known in Thebes—a gigantic pillared hall to be reared in front of Amenhotep's mighty pylon—such a stupendous triumph of masonry, if it was ever finished, that even Amon with his insatiable belly must be satisfied.

If he doesn't choke on it first, thought Seti.

If it was size and quantity the priests of Amon wanted, they were certainly getting it. The colonnades would be the largest ever reared by human hands and as thickly sown as trees in a forest. On their swelling capitals a hundred men could stand, and the architraves which roofed it would each weigh a hundred tons. But to Seti it would be the height of ugliness. He derived an ironic satisfaction from the fact that while the greedy priests were gulping down these huge, unmasticated mouthfuls, a creation of genuine beauty, his own funeral temple, was rising, stone upon graceful stone, at Abydos farther down the Nile.

"Thus speaketh the great god Amon-Re unto the Good God Seti: 'My beloved son of my body, Lord of the Two Countries, my heart rejoices when I see thy beauty. I give thee years of eternity and the joyful government over the Two Countries...'"

His gentle, melancholy features as immobile as a mask, Seti listened in an agony of impatience to the long prayers. Through the smoke rising from the sacrifice on the great stone altar, his somber eyes met those of Amenernhat, the high priest of Amon, and they measured each other in silent challenge.

"A very pretty ceremony," commented the bits of hard metal with ironic triumph, "and one that delights the people. They like to believe that their king is all-powerful and derives his power from the gods. But you know and I know the priests of Amon really rule Egypt."

As the service dragged on, Seti's flesh beneath the circular gold collar became drenched with sweat. His temples throbbed under the high, gold-encrusted cap, and the heavy jeweled apron which was the latest version of the first pharaoh's loincloth hung in a paralyzing weight about his hips and knees. Perhaps, once the approaching Jubilee was past and Amon-nebet appointed his successor, he would cease to be driven by this terrible urgency. But until that time neither his mind nor his body would know rest. His enemies might be in the temple, among his government officials or the palace staff, even in his own household. He must not relax his vigilance for a single moment.

The space in front of Amenhotep's massive pylon was black with human figures. Seti barely glanced at them through the curtained windows of his palanquin. The daily inspection was a perfunctory routine. The priests of Amon had their own building superintendents and foremen. All he had to do was furnish the funds for the gigantic enterprise.

But when the royal procession reached the outside of the huge north wall, which was nearly finished, it was another matter. Seti parted the curtains and leaned far out. For here was portrayed in immense sculptured reliefs the story of his own conquests, their colors as arrestingly vivid as Egypt herself, set like a blazing jewel in the red-gold of the desert.

He looked toward the scaffold where a group of sculptors and painters were still working, and his excitement became a glowing satisfaction. They were doing their job well. No one would ever suspect that the figure of Amon-nebet standing beside his father in the scene of his battle with the Libyans had been inserted at a later date. The sculptured lines were a superb imitation of the original. The colors blended perfectly.

As he leaned back against the cushions, Seti let his tired muscles relax. It was a good omen. After all, why should he be disturbed? Was he not Seti, the Good God, the Strong Bull, the Beloved of his Father Amon-Re? He would accomplish what he had set out to do. He would build his city in the Delta. He would prove himself stronger than the priests of Amon. And he would place Amon-nebet, his son, upon the throne of Egypt.

The mood of defiant self-sufficiency persisted even during his distasteful interview with Baka, his foreman of building operations in the Delta. The news that Baka had brought with him to Thebes was not good. In fact, the work was almost at a standstill. And all because of those stubborn squatters whom Ptah had seen fit to endow with asses' skulls instead of heads and with cloven hoofs instead of hands. If the Strong Bull, the Golden Horus, the Son of Heaven, would recall, Baka had not approved of drafting them as laborers in the first place.

Seti did recall. He seemed to remember also that Baka had made some sworn commitment to the effect that he would have the squatters making bricks even if it meant chopping off their beards to aid the process.

"Yes," replied the foreman. "I tried chopping off their beards, with the result that longer ones have grown in their places. And by the swollen breasts of Hathor, I believe if I'd tried chopping off certain other of their unholy appendages, they'd have found some better way of spawning!"

The thin lips of the Good God drew tightly together. There were other appendages, he reminded Baka grimly, which a man might spare with even less of equanimity. He doubted if even the brashest of Egyptian foremen could devise an effective substitute for living without his head.

Oh, but the Strong Bull, the Golden Horus, the Creator of the Two Lands, had misunderstood his miserable servant. Baka was by no means admitting failure in his commission. All he needed was a little more authority, and he would soon have the despicable apes begging to make bricks, yes, even the most stubborn brood of them who called themselves the Children of Joseph!

Seti ended the interview abruptly. Baka should have his way. Let him handle the squatters as he pleased, with the aid, if he wished, of a detachment of troops from Tharu. What Seti wanted was bricks, and he wanted them quickly, for the swift completion of Per-Ramses was of vital necessity to the success of his plans. Amon-nebet must not be forced to drag this vast shell of the burdensome past behind him. He would wield his scepter in a new city as far from Thebes as possible.

The feeling of urgency was again upon him. Yet for a long time after the departure of Baka he still sat idly on the Great Seat of Horus, his fingers gently stroking the carved sphinxes' heads on its arms, his feet resting on the inscriptions proclaiming the names of all the enemies he had conquered.

And then the letter was delivered. He sat holding the neat, sealed roll in his thin fingers, resenting the intrusion. Then, recognizing the seal, he tore it open.

"Shall I summon a scribe?" asked Rahotep anxiously.

Seti, fumbling at the heavy linen wrappings, did not hear him.

"To the Son of Amon, Beloved of Re, the Golden One of Horus..." Impatiently the king's eyes leaped over the lengthy salutation, eagerly combing the neat strokes of the script for some more personal message than a report of Amon-nebet's official duties at Memphis. Near the end of the letter he found it.

"I believe that my father, the Strong Bull, should know that an attack has been made upon my life. A few weeks ago while I was hunting in the desert a stone was flung at me from an ambush and another stone cast at my horse, so that he would run away, thus making my death appear an accident. Had it not been for the courageous action and quick thinking of my cousin Moses, who loves me like a friend and brother, I would now be battling with the monsters that wait for men beyond the Lily Lake. At great danger to himself he stopped my horse, and he cared for my wounds and brought me back safely to Memphis. I do not know who would desire to bring about my death..."

In spite of the heat Seti shivered as if a cold gust had struck his flesh. He had known for a long time that this moment might come. A clever woman who was ambitious for her son would stop at nothing. Swiftly, the cold urgency still gripping his body, he planned his course of action. Amon-nebet must be brought at once to Thebes and kept under close guard. His marriage with Nefretiri must be arranged, the Jubilee hastened. The priests of Amon must be diplomatically constrained, if necessary by further gifts and promises, to approve his plans. More endless details, which he dared not trust to his officials. For who could tell which one of them might be in league with Tuya? If only there were someone in all his vast entourage whom he could completely trust!

"Had it not been for the courageous action and quick thinking of my cousin Moses..."

Seti's eyes narrowed thoughtfully. Moses, his mother's favorite protégé. He had not seen Moses for years, not since the Asiatic campaign. A tall, awkward, rawboned youth, as he remembered him, with none of the compact grace of an Egyptian, but a lad with a mind of his own, one who had dared to laugh out loud in the presence of the pharaoh. A good education too. A pupil trained in the university at On would never let himself become a satellite of the priests of Amon. After all, why not? If the story about the Mitannian prince was correct, and, knowing Sitra, Seti did not doubt it, it was possible that he and Prince Moses had the same blood in their veins, and if a man were to find loyalty anywhere, he might expect it in his own brother. Again he scanned the letter.

"Moses, who loves me like a friend and brother..."

The hands that gripped the carved sphinxes' heads slowly relaxed. The jeweled sandals ceased their nervous tapping. Seti drew a long breath. For the first time in weeks he believed he would get a good night's sleep

2

Moses still could not believe his good fortune. He had answered the imperative summons from Seti with intense misgivings, fearing that the king had heard of his understanding with Nefretiri, and prepared to resign not only his commission but his privileged position as a prince in the royal household.

Even his informal reception, in the king's own private apartment rather than in the audience chamber, and the dismissal of all attendants, including the ubiquitous Rahotep, did not dissipate his fears. Naturally Seti would not wish to discuss a matter of intimate concern before even his most trusted officials. When Moses bowed before him and began to murmur the usual perfunctory hymn of praise that prefaced all conversation with the Good God, Seti cut him short with an impatient gesture.

"That's enough. I know everything you're going to say. If I were dying and needed a draught of medicine to save my life, I'd have to listen to a long psalm before getting it. By Amon, sometimes I envy the peasant who grubs in the earth all day! At least he can eat his bread in peace and lie down to a good sleep at night."

Moses forgot his fear. He was conscious only of Seti's trembling hands and of the twitching muscle in his forehead. "You're tired," he said gently. "Don't try to talk for a little. Whatever business you have with me can wait. If you will permit me, I believe I can make you more comfortable."

He adjusted the cushions behind Seti's back, careful that the carved figures on the ebony and ivory chair were buried beneath many soft thicknesses. Gently he loosened the high, stiff headdress and with a fold of his own clean linen overskirt wiped back the clinging strands of short hair. Then he unlaced the jeweled sandals and massaged the chafed flesh. And, as when he had performed the same services for the weary Maruma, he felt the tensed muscles relax. It was not until he lifted his face and noticed the somber eyes fixed on him that he realized what he had done. Color flooded his cheeks. He dropped the king's foot as if it had been a hot coal. "I—the M-mighty One of Horus must forgive me," he stammered. "I—I forgot for the moment that the K-king of Heaven is not as other men. I was thinking only of his comfort. It—it was unpardonable."

"Why should it be unpardonable to want me to be comfortable?" asked Seti. As he sank back among the cushions, a sound, suspiciously like a chuckle, issued from his throat. "I believe you actually did forget who I am."

Moses flushed again, but his voice was steadier. "I saw only that the S-strong Bull was tired."

"Get off your knees," ordered Seti abruptly, "and sit on that stool where I can look at you."

Moses obeyed. In spite of his uneasiness he moved with dignity and submitted unflinchingly to the prolonged, probing gaze.

"What do you know of your origin and background?" asked Seti with sudden bluntness. "How much has the Princess Sitra told you?"

Moses' heart pounded. Was he to discover the secret about himself at last? His throat contracted so that he could hardly speak. "N-not much. In fact, almost n-nothing," he replied faintly.

Seti stroked his chin. "There's a rumor that you're actually Sitra's son by a certain prince of Asia who—er—failed to confine his Egyptian visits to wholly diplomatic ventures. Do you know anything about the truth of this rumor?"

"No," replied Moses steadily. "Nothing." So Seti knew no more about the secret than he himself did. He could not have told whether the discovery left him more relieved or disappointed.

"We were living in the Delta at the time my mother adopted you," continued the Good God reminiscently. "She was occupying the royal palace at Bubastis while my father commanded the garrisons at Tharu, so naturally they did not see much of each other. Harmhab had been having trouble with the squatters in the rich lands along the eastern branch, and my father was kept exceedingly busy." Seti's features momentarily darkened. "By Amon, I can sympathize with him! We've been impressing them for labor in the new building projects in the Delta, and it's like trying to yoke a hippopotamus to a plow. At the rate they're going, the city will be a hundred years in the building."

Moses noticed with concern the beads of moisture that dotted the high, thin forehead.

"Surely the Good God can leave all these matters to the wisdom of his faithful officials," he said soothingly. "Among the many hundreds who count it their privilege to do his bidding there must be someone he can trust."

Seti relaxed again, drawing a long breath of relief. "That's right," he murmured. "Someone I can trust. How stupid of me to have forgotten!" He continued to stare at Moses fixedly for some moments. "And you are that very person," he said at last, with simple finality.

Moses gasped. "I—"

"You saved the life of my son," continued Seti, "at the risk of your own. You love him like a friend and brother. Is it not so?"

Moses' head was whirling, but he returned the gaze of the dark eyes steadily. "Yes. It is true. I do love Amon-nebet."

Without sacrificing its proud erectness Seti's spare body yielded itself completely to the softness of the cushions. "Yes. I can see you do. You and I together. I his father and you his friend and brother. You shall help me protect him, care for him, make his path easy. And because all I do is for his sake, you shall stand beside me and help me in all that I do. Because you are his friend, you shall be my friend, my *nearest* friend, than whom none in the Two Lands is more highly honored. Let it be recorded this very hour what the tongue of the pharaoh has spoken."

Moses had entered the king's chamber fearing that he was about to face severe censure and the loss of his privileged position. He left it heralded by an imposing array of runners and fan bearers calling his name and chanting his praises, with a new gold collar about his neck and one of the pharaoh's own signet rings on his finger.

Surely he would awaken and find it all a dream. But not yet. In the half light of dawn he lay in his great four-post bed under its canopy of blue tapestry and watched his new apartment in the palace which Seti had given him take concrete shape about him.

Even the gauze net that draped his bed could not hide the fact that the room possessed solid substance. The massive furniture looming into his vision might well have been designed for a human hippopotamus. A vast couch of ebony set with enormous inlays of ivory and gold stretched forth arms the size of tree trunks. A richly carved folding stool as large as a small banquet table swam into shape through the shadows, its huge gold hinge pins shining like the watchful yellow eyes of a crouching beast. Even the magnificent papyrus columns with their intricate stripings of gold and bright faience managed to look ponderous rather than cheerful.

Could one awaken and still keep on dreaming? If so, then he had been doing it repeatedly dawn after dawn for many days: the first moments of startled consciousness, of wondering where he was; the slow awareness as the furnishings took form in the dusk about him; the sudden realization that all this wealth, this splendor, belonged to him, Moses, who was no longer a mere prince but the friend of the pharaoh, his fan bearer upon his right hand. And not friend merely, but—that most coveted of all titles—*nearest friend.* And tomorrow the greatest honor was to be paid him that could be conferred on any Egyptian. No, not tomorrow. *Today.*

Sunlight poured suddenly through the narrow open slits at the top of the chamber. Lifting himself abruptly, he reached for a gold tassel and gave it a determined pull. A rivulet of sound cascaded through the apartment.

Instantly the palace sprang into life. A bevy of servants darted toward his chamber, bearing freshly washed and pleated garments, sandals, wig, anointing oils and perfumes, gold collar, bracelets, and anklets. A dozen slaves darted into action in the great dining hall close by, and in the kitchen at the rear the tempo of activity quickened. The small boys standing over the immense limestone hearth poked their long forks into the huge kettle of meat with accelerated vigor. Even the geese turning slowly over the fire seemed to heed the summons of the bell and stretch their plump bodies to bursting. Sharp commands whipped through the palace, the stables, the gardens, like the strokes of lashes and more often than not accompanied by them.

"Imbecile! Excrement from an ass's carcass! The collar of gold and precious stones! Not that thing of paint and paste!"

"A dozen more ewers of fresh water for the master's bath! And see that they're well perfumed with the essence of roses!"

"Flowers! Flowers and more flowers! Wreaths for the jars in the dining hall, fresh buds wet with dew for the master's tray, garlands to braid in the horses' manes! Pick faster, offsprings of a swine's filthy belly!"

"Quick, you maidens with the sistrums! Be ready with your music when he steps from his bedroom! This is the day of the master's gilding!"

But in the apartment adjoining the great dining hall there was neither noise nor confusion. White Elephant hovered about morosely, his wizened face like a thundercloud, while a half dozen competent experts, usurping his monopoly of long years' standing, washed, dressed, oiled, combed, perfumed, and bewigged his master. Now and then he uttered indignant animal-like sounds which gave expression to his jealous sentiments.

Moses submitted to the ministrations with less impatience than usual. He even watched critically in the mirror while the king's own wigmaker set on his head an elaborate creation of long curls and spirals, each one plaited with a strand of pure gold. It was not so unbecoming, he discovered, as he had feared. Its long, flowing lines softened the angular boldness of his features, and the single tight row of ringlets shortened his overhigh forehead.

"There!" announced the keeper of the wardrobe at last with satisfaction. "The friend of the pharaoh will blind the eyes of all the princes who dare to gaze upon him. The birds of the air will fly low and say one to the other, 'Who is this new Horus coming forth to greet the dawn from his chamber?'"

All of this merely indicated to Moses' practiced ear that his toilet was completed and that he presented a decently creditable appearance. As he rose to his feet, excitement surged through his veins. But he could not have told which roused the keener emotion, the fact that he was about to receive "the gold" from the king's hand or the possibility that he might again see Nefretiri.

The journey up the river, short though it was, was slow. Half the noblemen of Thebes, it seemed, had assembled in their pleasure boats to catch a glimpse of the king's new protégé. Comments floated about as profusely as bubbles on the swollen stream.

"Must be a favorite, all right. Even Rahotep, the king's mouth, didn't ride in the royal vessel when he got his gilding."

"Seems to me I've heard of Prince Moses. Isn't he the one—"

"How long ago? A prince of the Mitanni, you say?"

"Look at him sitting there so high and mighty under his canopy! Thinks he owns the whole of Thebes, no doubt."

"He will own plenty of it before the day is over."

"If you ask me, some folks have all the luck!"

Even here, riding on the cabin roof of the king's own vessel, Moses still had a feeling of unreality. He fingered the thick, gold-embroidered tapestry that lined the blue-silk canopy, but it was so soft that it seemed almost to possess no substance. Even the ship's massive figurehead rearing itself high above his head on the great carved prow, the statue of a fierce wild bull trampling men under his feet, seemed but an ephemeral projection of the sun's bright rays. He looked slowly over the teeming surface of the river and along the far eastern bank, where high above the quays and the slow-moving sails of the shipping vessels the sky line of the city lay carved in brilliantly painted relief on a solid sheet of sapphire. Here surely there was reality, for Thebes was old, perhaps the oldest city in the world. It had been old when Ptahhotep had written his words of wisdom and when Khufu had built his pyramid. But across the shifting currents of the river with its kaleidoscopic pageantry, it looked neither old nor eternal. It might have been a bright-hued painting or even a mirage.

Suddenly Moses realized that nothing had seemed real since the time he had turned from that other shore line farther down the river and taken Nefretiri in his arms. In that moment he had been near to discovery. Then abruptly he had been plunged into a swift tide in which turbulent emotion had submerged clear thinking. Before the amazing certainty that she returned his love all other discoveries had paled into insignificance. His attempt to revive the memory of his quest in the ruined city only reminded him that while he had been searching she had been waiting for him, lovely and desirable, in the kiosk, and that all those precious moments of intimacy had been wantonly wasted. Later, snatching at the few crumbs of privacy which the decks of the royal vessel had accorded them, he had chided himself bitterly for the sweet loaf he had thrown away!

But the crumbs too had been sweet: the warm caress of a glance, the touching of hands on the stem of a wine goblet, the exchange of a kiss through the medium of a lightly tossed flower, the passing, under the guise of politeness, of a sweet morsel of fruit from her lips to his. And then, on the last evening of the journey there had been those brief stolen moments of ecstasy when Sitra, professing a satiety of dancing and music and feasting, had dismissed both servants and entertainers and then obligingly fallen fast asleep. Yes, and snored too, Hathor bless her!"

"If the nearest friend of Horus, the Strong Bull, will forgive the impertinence of his humble slave, I might remind him that the Lord of the Two Lands is waiting."

Moses roused himself with a start, to find his scribe Tutu regarding him with his usual cold, nearsighted scrutiny, in which sardonic amusement was veneered by a studied servility. He flushed guiltily, wondering how long the vessel had been sitting motionless at the dock while those slightly rheumy eyes had been probing into his most intimate thoughts. Tutu, it seemed, had an uncanny ability for knowing what a person was thinking. His neat, flowing script often appeared to anticipate the spoken words of dictation, for after Moses, who found letter writing difficult, had painfully formulated a sentence, his scribe was more likely than not to remark a bit contemptuously: "Let the friend of the pharaoh proceed. His wise words are already written."

"Let us go," said Moses, attempting to make his voice sound casual. "As you say, our delay may keep the Great One waiting."

"And his family," added Tutu humbly. "What a pity that Queen Tuya will not sit in the balcony beside the Strong Bull to stir the king's nearest friend with a glimpse of her beauty! But doubtless some other lovely female—one of the king's minor wives, perhaps, or—even his daughter—"

Moses felt himself flushing again and despised himself for his weakness. Tutu could not possibly know of the romantic interest existing between himself and Nefretiri. Or—could he?

"Hail, Moses! Beloved of Amon! Nearest friend of the pharaoh!"

"Strew flowers in his pathway, and hang garlands about his neck!"

"May his mouth quaff the sweetness of red wine each day and of red lips each night!"

"May his slaves be crushed like stones in a mortar by the heaviness of the pharaoh's gifts!"

Riding high in his glittering palanquin on the shoulders of a dozen burly Asiatics, Moses accepted these acclamations of the crowd for what they were worth—scarcely more than the already wilting flowers that fell through the curtained apertures. Few of these Theban noblemen were here because they wished him well. Their curious, avid glances spoke far more eloquently than their words.

"So you're going to be gilded, are you! What have you done, we'd like to know, to deserve it?"

"Who are you, anyway? Son of a Mitannian prince, they say. And what does that make you? Nothing but a queen's pet bastard!"

"You may be the king's favorite today, but that isn't saying what you'll be tomorrow."

"Don't let this fool you. We'd as soon be flinging mud at you as flowers."

Bright banners streaming, sistrums twanging, fans swaying like the spread plumage of tropical birds, the festive procession swung up the tree-lined avenue and through the great double gate. Here there was a mighty cheer as the ancient palace of Amenhotep sprang into view. At the palace door the slaves lowered their huge bodies to the ground, and Moses stepped from the palanquin. Accompanied only by the most important nobles and preceded by the military guard and royal fan bearers, he passed into the outer vestibule, through the vast reception room and banquet hall, and into the great inner court, at the end of which, ensconced in the high, gorgeous balcony of malachite and ivory, the King of the Two Lands sat waiting with a beautiful woman by his side.

Moses' muscles froze. The floor with its alternating tiles of silver and azure swam like a billowing sea before his eyes. Just when he had decided that he could not possibly make the long journey across that heaving sea, a gently ironic little sound came to his ears.

Tutu, thought Moses grimly, *clearing his throat. He's probably hoping I'll make a fool of myself.*

His vision cleared. The tiles ceased to heave. He walked steadily toward the gaily painted pillars which upheld the little balcony. Not until his feet rested on the shining gold disk where the recipient of "the gold" stood to receive the abundant gifts which the king showered on his favorite did he lift his eyes to the two figures kneeling on its bright cushions.

With a sudden feeling of emptiness he saw that the woman by Seti's side was not Nefretiri.

"Ten chains of gold beads, three arm bands of gold and jet and ivory, twelve finger rings...check! Two small lions, pectoral of woven gold set with lotus blossoms of lapis, carnelian, and agate, three

110

ointment vases of lapis lazuli...check! Two silver arm clasps, collarette of tubular gold beads with red carnelian and blue glaze rosettes, one necklace of large gold flies, one Syrian dagger, handle of ivory, blade inlaid with figure of lion chasing bull, six vases of gold, silver, and electrum...check!"

The voice of Tutu the scribe possessed a soft smoothness, a richly lubricated quality, as if he dipped each word in oil before uttering it. Only one syllable rose above the monotonous intonation, like the name of deity recurring again and again in the mumbled prayer of a priest. *Gold.* Moses felt as if he were swimming in it.

"Put gold on his neck and on his back and gold on his feet, because he has found favor in the sight of the Lord of the Two Lands."

Seti's command had certainly been obeyed. He himself had showered golden ornaments on his new favorite—jewels, weapons, trinkets, every imaginable sort of treasure—until the floor of the court inside the golden disk had been covered with them. Necklaces and bracelets and anklets and girdles had been hung upon him until Moses had felt like a vast, trussed mummy equipped with enough implements to last him through eternity. And even now, with the day long since over, he could not escape the imprisoning flood. He must sit here in his apartment in the hot glare of lamplight, entombed in the midst of his new treasures, and listen to the unctuous voice of Tutu. If he heard the word "gold" just once more, he would pick up the nearest object on the table at his side—a beautiful little carved monkey with a lotus blossom in its mouth—and throw it as far and as hard as his strength would permit.

"One wine goblet with bowl of pure *gold*, base of onyx set with leaves of *gold* and topaz, handles of twisted *gold* twined with wreaths of *gold* lotus flowers, stem of jade inlaid with *gold*...check!"

Moses' fingers closed about the monkey, but he did not throw it. Instead, he sat staring at its counterpart, a giant edition of the ebony miniature suddenly materializing on the floor almost within arm's length of his chair. He frowned with annoyance. The intrusion of White Elephant's grotesque body into this ceremony was a sufficiently grave error in itself, to say nothing of the disgraceful antics he was performing. Crouched on all fours, the little Nubian was indulging in a series of violent but silent contortions, each obviously designed to attract Moses' attention and land him a bit nearer his master's chair.

Like his ebony counterpart, White Elephant had something in his hand, but it was not a lotus blossom. Still frowning, Moses studied the object more closely. Then, turning his eyes deliberately toward Tutu's monotonous voice, he slowly reached his arm over the side of his chair and let it fall full length. Presently he felt warm breath on his hand, and his fingers closed about a round object. When he glanced down again casually, the dark shadow had disappeared.

"One broadsword with blade of bronze, handle of carnelian inlaid with *gold*...check!"

Moses unfolded the tiny roll of papyrus, and as he read the brief message his eyes lighted with an excitement which all the rich gifts of the pharaoh had not been able to arouse.

"Meet me in the garden of the temple of Mut tomorrow at dawn. White Elephant will show the way. Do exactly as he tells you."

3

In the hour before dawn the river was a strange underworld. No cheerful vessels with bright-hued sails dotted its surface. Dancing and song and laughter seemed as remote from its sunless expanse as in the depths of a tomb.

But there was no dearth of activity. The quays lining the east water front swarmed with shadowy figures bent on mysterious missions that could not wait the coming of dawn. Even the river itself, swollen now almost too ripened fullness, reflected the hour's stern desperation of purpose. For a small reed boat piloted by a little Nubian and ridden by a nondescript figure who bore no burdens, it had only the contempt of the strong for the weak. Seizing the boat in mid-current, it spun it dizzily around, licked it tentatively with hungry lips, then, apparently in the act of swallowing, spat it disdainfully into calmer waters.

"Move closer to the shore," commanded Moses. "I want to know what those men are doing."

It was a world which he had not known existed. The shadowy outlines were familiar enough—high Phoenician galleys loaded with timbers and chariots, Cretan ships with their colorful, widespread sails, triremes from the Islands of the Sea, crude cattle boats, lumbering barges. But here in the half darkness they had suddenly become human flesh. He could hear labored breathing, almost feel the sweat pouring from naked bodies, sense the groaning strain upon already tortured muscles as the great kegs and chests, the trunks of cedar, the mammoth limestone blocks were pried and hoisted, shoved and dragged from barge to temple warehouse.

"Remember," warned White Elephant in his gentle, monotonous treble, "printh no more printh. Printh common worker, dig in dirt."

Moses remembered, and his attention shifted abruptly. He looked down with instinctive distaste at his brief skirt of coarse linen. Even in the semidarkness he could see the grimy streaks of the unpleasant substance which White Elephant had insisted on rubbing into his feet, legs, arms, and upper body.

"Too clean. Thoft thkin not burned black with thun. Not look like digger in dirt."

Well, he looked like one now, all right. Only once before could he remember being actually dirty—when he had stolen out of the camp with Ramses on their foolish search for the white falcon. But he had been a mere boy then, keen for adventure, not the nearest friend of the pharaoh, one of the most important persons in all Thebes. And he had not been going to meet Nefretiri.

"I hope you know what you're doing," he said sharply. "If this is a trick, I'll have you flogged until your back looks like a zebra's."

The Nubian grinned, his teeth gleaming in the surrounding dusk. "Printh wait," he lisped soothingly. "Dark now but dawn come thoon. Girl like flower come too. White Elephant know."

"Girl like flower." It described Nefretiri perfectly. In spite of the mud slowly caking into his pores, Moses' flesh tingled. He was going to see Nefretiri again!

Impatiently he watched the dark bulk of thickly clustered buildings on the high bank give way to the sweeping brush marks of shaded boulevards and palm and olive groves. Pair after pair of colossal statues loomed out of the dusk, stared at them with a glassy fixity, and vanished. The temple of Mut, the consort of Amon, was at the south of Karnak. White Elephant guided the small craft expertly into a narrow arm of the swollen river and beached it neatly in a secluded spot close to the high brick wall. Moses followed him along a path beside the wall until they came to a small gate, which swung easily in its socket, and they passed inside.

"Wait here!" whispered the slave and disappeared.

His heart pounding, Moses waited. He was evidently standing in the temple garden, for before him stretched orderly rows of luxuriant trees, separated from each other by neat paths of red gravel. In the distance, beyond a double row of palms rose a cluster of staves and domes and obelisks, already gold-tipped from the morning sun. A lake glimmered among the trees, and bright flower beds showed bright splotches of color.

"Here!" breathed White Elephant, reappearing with startling suddenness and thrusting something into his hands. "Take path ahead. Turn right. Find people working in flower bed. Take hoe. Work hard. Come back here. White Elephant wait."

Bewildered but keenly expectant, Moses moved forward along the ribbon of red gravel, stepping gingerly on his sensitive bare feet. At the end of a row of trees, he hesitated, then, remembering the injunction to turn right, he followed another path which brought him abruptly to the vineyard in the center of the garden. Here he found himself plunged into a scene of intense activity.

It was the season of the harvest, and already, with the sun barely risen, the day's work was well under way. Women, naked to the waist, were filling their reed baskets under the trellises, assisted by small children who climbed nimbly up the wooden posts and picked the rich purple clusters from the topmost vines. In a cleared spot men were standing in a wine press, their naked, olive-skinned bodies sweating deep-crimson rivulets. Close by four husky workers were forcing the last drops from a sack of already pressed grapes. Each holding fast to one end of long sticks tied to the bag's two ends, they twisted the pulpy mass round and round like women wringing a wet garment.

Moses regarded the scene with both curiosity and consternation. It was the first time he had witnessed the processes that preceded the storing of the rich wine in the great wreathed jars adorning the dining halls of the nobility, and he was fascinated. But he had come here to meet a princess, not to stare at peasants. This place was as public as a bazaar.

"Here! You there with the hoe! By the sacred bull, who do you think you are! Prince high-and-mighty? Amon blast your lazy hide!"

Moses felt a stinging pain which started at his ankles and traveled upward to his calves. The red-faced foreman punctuated his oath with a final searing stroke of his lash.

"Gaping lout! Get along there to your digging where you belong!"

Moses stumbled and fell to his knees. Staggering to his feet, he turned in blind anger toward his assailant. Hit the nearest friend of the pharaoh, would he, address him like a common laborer! Power flowed through him, concentrated itself in his finger tips. The red face swam before his eyes. He was crouching like an animal ready to spring when he remembered where he was and why he had come. Abruptly he

114

turned and walked along the path. Now that the anger was gone, he felt weak, as he always did after one of his fits of temper.

Suddenly he found himself walking on the edge of a tiled pool swarming with bright fish and dotted with lotus blossoms. But he looked in vain for a kiosk or some flowering shelter in which Nefretiri might be hidden. In the flower beds at his right some half-naked slaves were on their knees grubbing in the dirt, but there were no other signs of life. Totally confused, he was standing uncertainly by the pool wondering what to do next when a low, familiar whistle came to his ears. He looked about him dazedly. The sound repeated itself a second time before he realized that it came from the direction of the kneeling figures.

When he saw her, he cursed himself for his stupidity, for the coarse linen skirt and the thin coating of grime failed completely to conceal her golden loveliness. Disregarding all the other slaves, he went straight to her side.

"Nefretiri—"

"Quick!" she admonished him in a sharp whisper. "See what I'm doing? Loosening the earth about these little plants. Take your hoe and get busy."

Obediently Moses dropped to his knees. Tentatively he thrust the hoe into the dirt among the green shoots, but his hands were awkward and succeeded only in dislodging a shower of black earth.

"No, no, not like that! Watch me!"

Moses needed no second invitation. His eyes hungrily absorbed every detail of the grimy figure. Flowers and jewels, he discovered, had concealed her beauty, not enhanced it. She needed them no more than a sunlit day needed candles. Jewels, flowers! Why, she had been born wearing them! Her lips were bright bits of carnelian, her hair pure jet, her small ear lobes delicate carvings of ivory, her breasts two golden lotus flowers just ready to burst into bloom...

"Quick! The head gardener's coming. For Hathor's sake, don't let him notice you!"

The blissful rhapsody ended abruptly. By the time the warning shadow of the gardener drew near, he was earnestly, if still awkwardly, loosening the black earth with his hoe, handling the tender plants with careful though inexpert fingers.

"There!" whispered Nefretiri when the shadow had passed. "We have only a few moments. I must be back in the temple to lead the procession and play the sistrum. Tell me quickly what's happened. Why have you been made the nearest friend of the pharaoh?"

She listened attentively while he told her, the two bright bows of carnelian tightening into an arrow-straight crimson line. "So," she said slowly when he had finished, "my father has made you his favorite because you saved the life of Amon-nebet. That's—" she laughed softly—"that's really very funny."

"I don't see why," replied Moses. "Amon-nebet is my friend. Your father thinks I may be able to help him when he becomes the pharaoh. What's funny about that?"

Nefretiri deftly patted the earth about the green shoots. "Nothing," she murmured. "It's really not at all funny. It's merely—amazing."

"Amazing good fortune for us, perhaps," returned Moses eagerly. "As the nearest friend of the pharaoh I should be entitled to a wife of high birth, perhaps even a king's daughter. Since making me his favorite, Seti has often told me to ask for anything I want. Perhaps if he knew that it was against your will to become the wife of Amon-nebet—"

"No! He must never know! Do you understand? Seti must never discover the truth about our love for each other. It would mean ruin for all our plans."

"But—" Moses fumbled with the hoe, "how can he help knowing? When you refuse to become Amon-nebet's queen—"

"Look!" whispered Nefretiri suddenly. "The gardener's back is turned. Let's run for that clump of trees—"

In the shelter of a cluster of feathery acacias Moses took her again in his arms, not gently this time, with the deference due to royalty, but urgently, almost roughly. They were no longer prince and princess; their love had become something simple and honest and elemental, like the fragrance of fresh earth still clinging to their fingers. Her breasts, unencumbered by linen or jewels, were soft and warm against his flesh. The red lips crushed beneath his own were unsweetened by any more subtle perfumes than youth and health and sunshine.

"Sweetest of all lotus blossoms, loveliest of the jewels which Ptah fashioned to wear about his neck, little flower which brings fragrance to the nostrils of Amon—" He stopped abruptly. The tender diminutives and pretty phrases which had seemed in keeping with a starlit river and muted lyres did not belong to this moment of reality.

"I must go back," whispered Nefretiri breathlessly, "and be the goddess Mut again and dance and play with the other women. I don't like being Mut. I'd rather belong to you than to Amon."

Jealousy flamed through Moses. He gripped her shoulders. "Come with me now," he said with impulsive urgency. "The boat is waiting outside. We can go somewhere and live like peasants just as we are now. White Elephant will help us. Other people in Egypt do it, thousands of them. I—I'd even be willing to be a slave if we could be together."

She laughed and slipped out of his grasp. Then she came close to him and spoke earnestly. "We'll be together," she said softly, "and we won't have to be slaves, either. Just promise to tell no one about you and me. And trust me, whatever happens. Even if it should look for a time as if I were going to be Amon-nebet's wife, remember what I told you, that I never shall be. I'd die first. But I don't mean to die. I mean to live—with you, Moses. Promise?"

"I promise," he replied steadily.

He tried to draw her again into his arms, but she pushed him resolutely away. "Go quickly now. The gardener will be coming back. Take that path there among the trees. It doesn't pass the vineyards. White Elephant will be waiting."

She watched him go, the green and gold flecks in her eyes dancing. Would he have promised, she wondered, if she had told him the details of her plan? How strange, but how very fortunate, that he could have grown up in the midst of court intrigue and still remained so innocent! At least his innocence was not a sign of weakness. He was the strongest person she had ever known. And fortunately she had wisdom enough for both.

4

As the days passed and the swollen belly of Hapi the river god waxed slowly toward its complete fullness, the eyes of Tutu the scribe lost some of their cold boldness. He no longer anticipated the words which his young master might wish to have inscribed on the rolls of papyrus stretched across his knees. He waited respectfully, his brush poised, until the words were uttered. And he became more and more reluctant to render an appraisal.

"But," Amenemhat the high priest, his true master, adjured him impatiently, "you've sat at the fellow's feet for days. You've been with him in every waking hour—"

"Almost," corrected Tutu with his meticulous scruple for detail. "There were a few hours one day between dawn and the middle of forenoon when he escaped me. I'm still wondering—"

"What's happened?" demanded the high priest abruptly. "You surely should be able to tell by now whether he's loyal to the interests of Amon. You were sure enough about him when you first became his scribe. Couldn't find words to express your contempt for his empty brain and stumbling tongue!"

Moses sensed the change in his scribe, but he made no effort to penetrate the barrier of restraint between them. Friendly or hostile, Tutu's eyes were far too penetrating. Reluctant to probe too deeply into his own thoughts and emotions these days, he was even more reluctant to permit another to do so.

But he had less and less time for introspection. His days were so full that at first he seemed to be borne along like a leaf in a powerful current. He accompanied Seti on his daily trip to the temple and on his tours of inspection, sitting silently in the background while the king consulted with his officials, dictated innumerable letters, and held interminable interviews.

Then all at once he was no longer silent. His voice, hesitant and stumbling at first but with undeniable authority, was dictating messages to the two viziers and their local governors, to the princes of the Retenu and the Libyans and the Mitanni. Alone in the king's audience chamber he was receiving envoys from Kush and Asia and the rich land of Punt. His palanquin, not Seti's, was riding at the head of the daily procession of inspection. At his simple gesture words were inscribed in stone which would apprise the world for centuries, perhaps millenniums to come, that "this monument was restored by Seti I, in the tenth year of his reign."

Gradually he ceased to be like a leaf spun by a powerful current from one eddy to another. Rather he was like the river itself, rising into increasingly turbulent activity, responding to a power and a destiny within itself of which it is as yet but dimly conscious. And, as for long centuries men had watched on its banks and measured by each fraction of an inch the mysterious rising of Hapi to his fullness, so now certain ones watched the rising of this new swelling stream and made their comments.

"He's stronger than I thought," reflected Tutu, gently tapping the handle of his brush against his small white teeth. "And he does not yet know his power. But when he awakens—what then?"

"Insufferable bastard," murmured young Ramses into his wine cup, his narrow, slate-colored eyes fixed moodily on the guest of honor at the royal banquet table. "How long must I wait for the fires to spend themselves? If I were a fool, I would rise up this minute and pour water on them, proclaim him for what he is, an impostor without a name. But I am not a fool. Therefore I shall pour oil on the fires and make them serve my purpose." He lifted his goblet high, careful that his action was noted by the approving eye of Seti. "Hail, Moses! Place your lips on the rim of my cup, that we may drink together like brothers!"

"Look at him," breathed Sitra to her slave Beket. "He might be the pharaoh now, except for the crown. It wasn't the way we intended it. The gods have interfered. Suppose they also have their plans. Suppose—"

"If only he didn't have to wear that ugly wig!" mourned Beket.

Only Seti, sitting at last in uninterrupted leisure in his garden, was almost completely satisfied. "My son will sit like this," he reflected with tranquillity. "He will have time to listen to the rustling of the grasses and the mating songs of the birds and the plashing of wings in a quiet pool, knowing that another's ears are tuned to the wearying complaints of people. All is well now. My plans cannot fail, unless—*unless*—"

Hapi had attained at last to the full vigor of his glorious manhood. Joining with the parched earth in the lusty heat of desire, he had sown his rich male seed in her womb with lavish abandon.

Now, all desire fulfilled, his splendid virility began slowly to languish.

At their appointed stations along the mighty artery the scribes of the twenty ancient Nilometers, divining in their great marble wells an anxious nation's future of hunger or abundance, recorded their findings with mathematical precision.

"The belly of Hapi has waxed full," they reported with satisfaction. "With his swollen breasts he gives suck to an abundant offspring. An excellent inundation. Sixteen ells."

"The gods have heeded the command of their divine master Seti," approved the keepers of the royal granaries. "An excellent inundation indeed. We must raise the price of seed corn."

"The golden smile of Re is upon his children," commented the managers of the royal treasury piously. "A very excellent inundation. Throughout the length of the Two Lands we must raise the taxes."

But from the throats of the multitude there rose a wordless plaint which was older than the creaking lament of the shadufs, endlessly rising and falling with their dripping burdens. Up and down the long narrow country it swept, swelling from an inarticulate murmur to a mighty wail, the origin of its burden as ancient and shrouded in mystery as that of the treasure-laden river at whose swollen breasts all the children of the Two Lands suckled.

"Osiris!" it mourned with one voice. "Osiris our lord is dead!"

It was the hour of the fellahin, that vast multitude which for countless generations had been hands and feet and straining sinews for a corpulent and lazy body. Freed from their months of enforced labor in building project and mine and quarry, their tiny plots of land not quite dry enough for sowing, they became suddenly individual and articulate. Tools were laid aside. Brown bodies, normally bent to a curve, slowly straightened. The pounding of mallets, the whining of lashes, the grinding of stone against stone, even the interminable creaking of the shaduf, ceased. With one accord all who were able to do so flocked to the sacred city to keep the feast of their favorite god, Osiris.

"I am not going to Abydos this year," announced Seti calmly, his spare limbs pleasantly quiescent on a cushioned bench beside his garden pool. "I have no mind to see the unwashed hordes gaping at my beautiful new temple, and the Mysteries have always bored me. Moses shall go in my place. He will make a very excellent Horus."

And a very popular one, thought Sitra with satisfaction as she languidly removed a honey cake from the loaded tray. Aloud she said: "A wise decision, I should say. The Son of Heaven does well to spare his strength. And, besides, Amon-nebet may arrive from Memphis at any time now. It would be a pity for his father not to be here to receive him."

Sailing down the river on the *Star of the Two Lands,* Moses felt the contagion of mounting excitement. All of Egypt, it seemed, was journeying to Abydos. In spite of the captain's bellowing voice and the pilot's sonorous orders, progress was slow. The fellahin, their thick knotted muscles adjusted to the patient rhythm of the shaduf and the creeping pace of monoliths, were not swift at their oars. Their small, crowded skiffs bumped awkwardly against each other, and occasionally a high reed prow brushed the gleaming gold flank of the royal vessel. But when this happened the spears of the guards stationed on the lower deck were ready. The offending craft received thrust after vicious thrust, which more often than not upset it and plunged its terrified occupants into the water, where they became targets for further playful spear thrusts.

Seated in his high cabin beneath the awning, Moses watched them painfully right their mutilated craft, drag themselves dripping and often bleeding to its flat surface, and submit doggedly to further proddings until they had gained a safe distance or the guards had tired of their sport. To his amazement there was neither anger nor rebellion in their faces, only a stubborn patience.

Have they no feelings at all? he wondered. *No emotions?*

He had wondered the same thing before on his tours of inspection—in the mines and quarries to the south and east of Thebes, in the immense tomb that Seti was carving out of the mountains of the western desert. Only last week he had been standing in the great unfinished hall in the temple at Karnak watching these same fellahin drag their mammoth burdens of stone up steep mountains of sand, seen them clinging like flies high up in the vast forest of columns. One of the flies had been brushed from a towering stone trunk, had come hurtling down almost at Moses' very feet, and he had stared horrified at the pulpy mass with its gushing bowels. But the fellahin had displayed no emotion. Stolidly they had lifted the obstruction to their wooden shovels and deposited it in the great vat of mud and gravel which a yoke of patient oxen was slowly churning into mortar. The construction foreman had whipped their deliberate motions into swifter action and apologized profusely for the inconvenience caused the friend of the pharaoh.

Remembering, Moses felt his skin prick with sudden coldness. The foreman had been such a little man. Any pair of hands that had helped move those trunks of stone could have snapped him like a reed. And beside the handful of foremen and the small armed guard the toiling fellahin had been as the sands of the sea. Just as now, here on the river, their little skiffs outnumbered the gaily painted vessels as the seeds of a tree outnumber its fruit. Just as throughout the length of Egypt—

"Suppose," his thoughts took shape, "they should decide not to work for us any longer? Suppose they should become tired of being poor one of these days and should awaken—"

"They did once," said Tutu quietly.

Startled, Moses looked down at the scribe sitting cross-legged on a mat at his feet. Unconscious of having spoken the words aloud, he found the bold gaze suddenly disconcerting.

"Who—what—" he murmured faintly.

"The fellahin. They did awaken once. Surely one so well tutored in Egypt's history as the friend of the pharaoh should remember."

Moses did remember. It had been hundreds of years ago, at the end of the Old Kingdom. No historian had recorded exactly what had happened or why the fellahin had revolted. But they had dispossessed the rich men and the priests, and for two centuries or more they had governed the Two Lands.

"'The land is lost,'" quoted Tutu with somber relish, "'the sun has ceased to shine.'"

Moses' mind leaped to other ancient sentences which he had never before understood. "'The poor triumph,'" he repeated with awakening comprehension. "'They cry: Let us put down the mighty! He who had not where to lay his head has now a bed. He who found no shade sleeps under trees, and he who had shade flees through wind and weather. He who had no bit of bread to eat has now a granary. But the great hunger and weep...'"

Sudden understanding struck Moses. The "Dark Age," historians had called it. But they had recorded only one side of the story. For the fellahin had not known how to write. If they had, perhaps the mournful dirge might well have been a paean of victory.

He turned impulsively to Tutu. "Why—" he began and stopped. Even silken walls had ears.

"Why do not the fellahin awaken again?" the scribe supplied gently. "Why have they been sleeping for nigh a thousand years, as they will continue sleeping for a thousand more? I can tell you."

"Why?" demanded Moses.

"Because after the first revolt the rulers of Egypt were wiser than their predecessors. When they stripped the fellahin again, they left them the one thing necessary to make the poor man contented with his lot."

"What?"

"Religion," replied Tutu simply. "The promise of equality in the hereafter and the hope of immortality."

Osiris was dead. He had died long ago at the hand of his wicked brother Set, who had by a trick enticed him into a beautiful casket, nailed down the lid, and set his body afloat on the river, where it had drifted to the Great Sea. But now he had died again, as he did each year when the river which was the blood stream of his flesh began slowly to ebb. And as Isis, his sister-wife, had gathered together the dismembered fragments of his sacred body and breathed life into them

122

by blowing on them with her wings, so now the children of those ancient Mysteries sought by their re-enactment to secure a promise of resurrection.

Osiris was dead. But he had returned to life. Egypt too was dying, her blood stream draining slowly away until her flesh should become a shriveled corpse. But in the springtime the life-giving flood would again pour through her veins. All men must die and come at last to the narrow cleft behind Abydos leading to the western desert. But by the Mysteries of the holy mother Isis and her blessed son Horus there was promise of life beyond. The suffering Osiris had also passed through the terrifying cleft. He had become the first of those in the west, king of the glorified. Because he lived, they should live too.

Moses entered into the ceremonies of the great autumn festival with an abandon which Tutu found amusing.

"Anybody would think the friend of the pharaoh had never seen the Mysteries before," he commented tolerantly. "I can understand a man's getting excited over Abydos. Even a prosaic scribe like me is tempted to write poetry about Seti's new funeral temple. But how a cultured prince can keep from shuddering at the crudities the priests are forced to practice for these swarming fellahin—"

Moses did not attempt to explain. In fact his emotions were inexplicable to himself. He knew only that he felt a peculiar, satisfying sense of unity with the eager, hungry multitude who swarmed into Abydos with their more favored countrymen, thrusting their unwashed bodies past Seti's graceful pylons, smudging the fair white limestone, pointing stained brown fingers at his delicate, painted reliefs.

Unlike his fellows of the nobility, who ventured forth only in their chariots to watch proceedings from a distance, Moses mingled with the crowds. On the eve of the festival, like all good fellahin, he went out under the full moon and partook of the roasted pig, symbol of the evil Set, who had hunted Osiris by moonlight, discovered his body, and scattered it abroad.

Squatting on the ground in a circle of nondescript worshipers, Moses felt a premonitory thrill of excitement. Was it possible that these humble, ignorant fellahin had discovered the answers to questions he had long been asking? They had discarded Re, riding high in the heavens, as too remote. To Amon they gave only lip service and the sweat of their bodies. Aton, with his tiny, delicate gold hands, was but a name to be hated and feared. But the life-giver, the restorer, who endowed the familiar black earth with fertility—him they could understand.

"Osiris," they mourned, beating their breasts and bending their knees until their heads touched the ground. "Osiris our lord is dead."

"Either he is more clever than I thought or more confused," reflected Tutu, watching his young master. "A man who seeks to make himself popular with the fellahin might be very useful to the priests of Amon—or very dangerous. Let us wait—and see."

Already the days were shortening, the trees beginning to shed their leaves. The refreshing north winds had ceased to blow. And in the court of the temple at Abydos the priests of Osiris took a huge golden ox and covered it, even to its horns, with a coat of black linen in token of the darkness that had descended on the Two Lands.

Osiris was dead. On a huge makeshift stage within the temple, priests and priestesses and people portrayed the Mysteries of his life and passion. Amid the wailing of the multitude the god met his death at the hand of his enemy Set, and the members of his body were scattered. Tearing aside his mummy wrappings, his sister-wife Isis received from his dead loins the seed which conceived within her the divine Horus. So, frenziedly, did the multitude attempt to assure for themselves this promise of fertility. Giant phallic emblems were borne through the streets. In the temple gardens without waiting for the privacy of darkness men joined their bodies with those of women. With a fierce urgency impelled by the memory of parched, cracked earth and pangs of hunger, the male devotee of the dying god sowed his seed with a lavish abandon, and the female, reminded of earth's imminent sterility, opened herself wide to receive it.

Osiris was dead. Wide-eyed and apprehensive, they accompanied the holy mother Isis on her search for his dismembered body, swaying and chanting in triumph when its parts were finally assembled and enclosed in a life-sized effigy of wax and perfumes and bound in mummylike wrappings.

"You have taken back your head," they murmured raptly. "You have bound up your flesh. You have regained your members."

Wailing and beating their breasts, they followed the magnificent gold coffin out of the city to the holy sepulchre in the desert. Weeping, they cast their votive vases on the mound which had grown to a mountain through the centuries, gold and porphyry and alabaster mingled with crude shards. Officials in gold collars and noblemen in spotless linen rubbed shoulders with begrimed peasants in an effort to catch a glimpse of the great stone image lying on its bier.

Osiris was dead. And he must be made to live again. Not next spring when the waters again began to rise, but now. Back in the temple on the improvised stage, day after day, act after act, the drama swept forward to its climax.

"Come! Come to your dwelling!" implored the holy mother Isis, kneeling, hair unbound, her arms encircling the statue in its clinging shroud. "Look at me! It is I, your sister, whom you love. You whose heart no longer beats, oh, come to your dwelling!"

"Come!" echoed the swaying multitude. "Oh, come to your dwelling!"

Osiris was dead. The entreaties of Isis had failed to awaken him. The incantations of the priests were of no avail. The suspense of the multitude became unbearable. The miracle had always happened before. The Nile had always risen. But perhaps this time...It was not a play. Their eternal destiny was at stake. They could wait no longer. A hoarse cry burst from their mouths.

"Horus! Horus can awaken him! Find the blessed son Horus!"

And at last Horus came, a taller and stronger Horus than usual, who brought a tremendous cheer to their lips. They had seen him earlier in the play, without his hawk-headed mask, and they liked a Horus who did not hold his head high as if he owned the earth but who smiled a bit diffidently. They rather liked, too, the way he half stumbled over his words. It made him seem more human.

A red bullock was slain. Seizing the lifeless statue, Horus laid it in the skin of the dead beast, and the multitude cheered, understanding. Set too had had red skin and red hair. "You are the bull of the sacrifice!" they cried. Surely now Osiris would live. But no! Removed from the bullock's skin, its long shroud unwound, the figure of the god remained still and lifeless.

A tense silence fell on the multitude. They watched with bated breath while Horus moved his fingers slowly over the statue, pressing here and there, describing magic symbols, and finally, placing his arms about it, gathered it into his firm embrace. About the smooth, carved lips appeared a flicker of movement. The head slowly turned. An arm was lifted. A long shudder of ecstasy swept over the multitude. Then a great cry burst forth.

"Horus! Horus has saved us! Osiris was dead, and now he lives. Osiris our lord is alive!"

Wearily Moses removed the hawk-faced mask. It was intended for a smaller head than his, and the sides of its narrow dome had pressed sharply into his temples. Through the tiny slits of eyes he had barely been able to see sufficiently to press the statue in the right places and release the hidden springs. Tutu watched him shrewdly.

"The Strong Bull should be pleased with you today," he said. "Also, which is even more important, the priests of Amon."

Moses turned slowly, his face expressionless. "Why should the priests of Amon be pleased with me?"

"It is a good thing for the fellahin to have a hero among the nobility," returned Tutu, "especially at a time when taxes have to be increased." He chuckled. "You actually had me sitting on the edge of my cushion up there in the balcony, believing my eternal destiny depended on whether that statue waggled its forefinger."

Moses left his scribe's presence abruptly, his enthusiasm completely gone. Riding from the temple to the royal lodgings in his curtained palanquin, he wondered how he could have had the slightest desire to mingle with the wretched fellahin. Already their ecstasy, their unity of emotions, had vanished. Huddled in knots along the streets, they wolfed the last fragments of the free bread and salt fish and onions which Seti had generously provided for the festival. Like bent reeds released from the hand's straightening pressure, their bodies were slowly returning to their usual stooped postures. The sight of a passing temple dancer, voluptuous breasts bared and full hips swaying, elicited but a few avid glances. Excess was again a luxury which only the rich could afford. In a world of hungry mouths and thirsty soil the vigor of manhood must be hoarded as jealously as the precious water in the buckets of the ever-creaking shaduf.

The hour of the fellahin had passed. It was the priests' turn now. They moved among the lingering crowds, displaying their wares of amulets, scarabs, and sacred papyrus rolls.

"Woe to him who takes his staff and travels up the long western valley if he carries not in his hand the witness of his innocence! New copies of the sacred chapter, all grades and all prices!"

"When your soul is weighed in the balances, whose voice will speak to deliver you from the devourer? For the denial of all forty-two sins, three copper uten, ten only for one uten!"

"See, the name of the innocent soul is left blank. Any scribe of the temple can fill it in for you. A small payment—"

"What! Not even one uten? Then come back after harvest with a dozen full measures of barley. Half your crop, you say, after taxes are paid? Suppose it is. Would you rather have a full belly now or feed on the blessed Maat in the hereafter?"

Moses drew the curtains of his palanquin more tightly. The swaying movement of the slaves on whose shoulders he rested brought a feeling of emptiness to the pit of his stomach.

Osiris was dead.

5

The day had come. Eagerly, through the delicate gold meshing of his high casement windows, Seti watched it dawn. He had not been able to sleep. Over and over in his mind he had reviewed the details of his elaborate preparations: the obelisks, the inscriptions, the route of the procession, the list of invited guests at the banquet where the approaching marriage of Amon-nebet and Nefretiri would be announced, the words which he must speak when he presented his oldest son at the altar of his father Amon-Re for confirmation.

"Hear my words, all you holy ones assembled. Let Thoth, the god of wisdom, write them on his tablets. This is my son, yet not my son. From the loins of our father Amon was he conceived..."

The priests were powerful and at the moment restless. During the last few months his gifts to Amon had been decreasing. The revolt in southern Nubia had deprived the treasury of much rich tribute. To be sure, he was dispatching a regiment shortly to quell the rebellion, but it would be months, perhaps years, before its return. He had diverted large sums for his funeral temple and for this Jubilee. Suppose at the last minute the priests should oppose the choice of Amon-nebet. It would be easy—a slight juggling of the oracles. A faint aroma of clover, and the sacred ram would as soon turn left as right. At the thought cold sweat broke out on Seti's body.

The day had come. In the women's quarters Sitra forced Beket to change her wig three times, and even then she was not satisfied.

"No, no! Not those tight ringlets. They look like the broad side of a sheep. Try the blue one with the beaded braids of gold. Beket, you clumsy grandmother of a donkey! You pulled my hair!"

"May the daughter of heaven forgive this miserable worm," countered the slave cheerfully. "May a serpent swallow me for my stupidity."

Beket was in an amiable mood this morning. She was inordinately fond of parades, and today's exhibition promised her appetite a gorging satiety. Moreover, taking advantage of her mistress' preoccupation, she had rubbed into the royal scalp a liberal quantity of oil from a black snake killed at midnight, an achievement which filled her with an unholy triumph. The change of wigs, usually an irksome task, offered another welcome opportunity to inspect the graying locks.

"If we continue with this treatment," she remarked smugly, "my lady's hair will soon be as black and soft as a raven's wing."

"It should be," returned Sitra absently. "The stuff is ill-smelling enough."

The suspense was agonizing. Had she done right in leaving the execution of her plan to the ingenuity of a mere child? She had been so certain that Nefretiri would devise some scheme of getting her way. In fact, she was still certain. And if Nefretiri failed, there was still Tuya, who had not been content merely with making dents in a little wax image. But Tuya had failed once. And Nefretiri might not always get her own way. And the time was getting short. By nightfall Amon-nebet would be crown prince of Egypt, unless—

The day had come. From the shelter of his four-post bed Ramses regarded it indifferently. It was a pity that all days in Egypt were so much alike, glaring sunlight and cloudless skies. When he became pharaoh, he would have some mechanism devised by which rain could be made to fall gently on the roof of a kiosk, starting and stopping at his command. Some new kind of shaduf, perhaps, with a few dozen slaves to operate it. He liked the sound of rain.

So this was the day his half brother was to become betrothed to his sister Nefretiri and be made crown prince—perhaps. He still did not believe it would happen. But suppose it did. Let Amon-nebet be pledged to the royal princess and thus establish his right to the throne beyond question. He would never marry her. Let him have the double crown remodeled to fit his silly little sloping head. He would never wear it. Destiny would not permit.

"From the time that I was in the egg," murmured Ramses softly to himself, "the great ones sniffed the earth before me. From the time that I was in the egg—" He repeated the words again and again, liking the sound of them. He must remember them. They would do well for an inscription.

Yes, let Amon-nebet have his little day—if he could. Tomorrow would belong to Ramses.

"The great ones sniffed..."

The day had come.

"I shall see the stranger alone, Memnet," ordered Nefretiri sharply. "He is—he is a merchant, and he has some jewelry I wish to buy."

The nurse's square face set stubbornly, her small eyes more curious than suspicious. "I didn't see his merchant's pack."

"He is a merchant of—of very small gems," explained the princess with more than her usual patience. "And—and they are so valuable that he won't show them to anybody when there are people around." As the woman still lingered, her color rose sharply and she stamped her foot. "Did you hear me, Memnet? Leave the apartment, I say!"

Alone at last with the visitor, a short, thickset man with shifting eyes and a livid scar embedded like a white palm frond in the flesh of one cheek, she turned on him angrily.

"Fool! Imbecile! Why did you come here? Don't you know the procession is about to start and my palanquin is waiting? We settled everything that day in the garden at the temple of Mut. You know exactly what you are to do, and you've been paid to do it."

"Ah, but the princess is mistaken," murmured the visitor, bowing until his short, tightly curled wig brushed the carpet. "Everything is settled, yes. I know what I am to do, yes. But the pay—no."

Nefretiri gasped. "What do you mean? You know very well I gave you more than you deserved."

"The princess gave me nothing."

"Why, you—you—" She stopped abruptly, her dark eyes narrowing. Deliberately she removed her gem-encrusted pectoral and tossed it to him. "So it wasn't enough. Very well. But if you fail to do exactly as you promised or if you ever breathe a word about this business, I shall have that ugly body torn into so many pieces the birds won't be able to find them. Now—go!"

The pectoral disappeared in the folds of his voluminous garment. "The princess will not be disappointed. When the forefront of the procession reaches the outer court of the temple and approaches the great altar—"

"Hush!" warned Nefretiri sharply.

The day had come.

"Are you awake?" spoke Amon-nebet softly when the high apertures were still so deep-gray as to be almost black.

"Yes," replied Moses. He had barely closed his eyes all night. It had been Amon-nebet's wish, not his, that he should share the latter's apartment during the period of the Jubilee. If he had had his way, he would have shut himself within his own palace, encountering not a single human being until the festival was over.

"I suppose I should be excited," mused Amon-nebet half to himself. "But I'm not. The only thing that matters is that three moons from now, when the festival is over, Nefretiri will be my—my wife." He spoke the word as a man might call a bird to him, softly for fear of frightening it away. "I don't suppose you could possibly understand how I feel about Nefretiri."

Moses made a choking sound. He did not trust himself to speak.

"It—it's like watching a bright bird flying high up in the sky, so beautiful it makes your whole body ache with joy, and then finding it suddenly close to you, fluttering against your breast. You—you see what I mean?"

"Yes" replied Moses in a low, strained voice. He felt wretched. He wondered if he should tell the young prince the truth—that the wings would never flutter against his breast except in a wild beating of rebellion. She had said she would die before she became the wife of Amon-nebet. Had she meant it literally? There had been no hopeless resignation in her that morning in the temple garden. The memory of her flesh against his coursed through him, changing the coldness within him to flame.

"Sometimes I dream of—of holding her in my arms," went on Amon-nebet almost in a whisper. "And then I wake up with my heart pounding so I can hardly breathe. Tell me—I'm not dreaming now, am I, Moses?"

Moses wet his lips. His body felt cold again. "No, Neb. Of course you're not dreaming."

"Maybe she's awake too. Do you suppose she's excited, Moses, the way I am, because this is the day?"

"I—I don't know, Neb."

Nefretiri awake? If so, what was she thinking? Was she even now making plans to go to Seti and persuade him to release her from this impending bondage? Surely he would listen to her, especially if she offered to relinquish all rights to the throne for the sake of freedom. But—why had she not gone to him before? Or had she perhaps gone and he had refused her? Was she even now in desperation planning to fulfill her passionate pledge that she would rather die...

"Moses." The gentle, almost apologetic voice probed insistently through the enveloping coldness. "I must ask you something. It's important. I—I have to know."

"Yes?" breathed Moses with sudden premonition.

"I'd rather die," continued the young prince simply, "than to make her unhappy. Do—do you think she'll mind very much my—my being so ugly?"

Moses drew in his breath sharply. The gray fingers were groping their way into the room now, picking out objects here and there. With pitiless candor they stroked the young prince's profile on the blurred canvas, accentuating the sharply sloping line of forehead, the upthrust curve of chin. Moses regarded it for a moment in silence.

"You're not ugly to me, Neb," he said gently.

6

"Sed," they called the great Jubilee, Feast of the Tail, commemorating the day thirty years before when the reigning pharaoh had first donned the lion's tail. As a matter of fact, it had not been thirty years since Seti had assumed the royal appendage. He had had to juggle his figures considerably to present even an excuse for a jubilee at this time, settling finally on the date when his father Ramses *might* have been made general of Harmhab's army. The populace, however, was little concerned with either history or arithmetic, and for three months of parades and free bread would cheerfully have sworn that he was a blood son of Khufu. The priests of Amon, to whom the gratification of the pharaoh's wish meant a source of profit, were delighted to wink at the slight disparagement.

Exactly at the hour of noon Seti was borne from the palace, shining like the sun, and carried in his glittering palanquin down to the river, where the *Star of the Two Lands* waited to carry him across to the temple of Amon. Crowds thronged the banks on both sides of the river, swarmed into pleasure vessels, filled reed boats to sinking, or cast themselves fully clothed into the water. Their shouts hurt his ears as the glaring sun on the ripples hurt his eyes.

"Hail, pharaoh! Strong bull of a glorious mother!"

"The great day has come, the turn of the ages! No more hunger, no more sorrow!"

"Hail, Seti, live forever! Live a million years!"

Seti did not want to live a million years, much less forever. He had little concern beyond this festival, indeed, beyond this one day. Not that his responsibilities would end then; they would be even greater. But the driving urgency would be at rest. He could devote himself with a clearer mind to preparing for his son a more comfortable throne than he himself had occupied. This Nubian revolt, for instance. The spirit of rebellion must be quelled once for all. The tribute from Nubia was precious; more, with the increasing demands of the priests, it was a dire necessity. He must discuss again with Moses the leadership of the regiment which was soon to be dispatched. Before he had reached the eastern bank of the river where his chariot was waiting, Seti's brain was again whirling.

Triumphant and glittering, the procession swept up the sphinx-lined avenue toward the massive pylons of the Luxor temple, then swung north along the great thoroughfare to Karnak. Not since the days of the fabulous Amenhotep, whose image they bore between their forepaws, had the huge stone rams lining the road cast their vacant eyes on so splendid and brilliant a sight: the deep greens of palms and sycamores and acacias, the burning topaz of an unclouded sky, the rainbow hues of flowers, the rich sepias of polished woods and gleaming leather, the reds and yellows and purples of tufted harnesses and waving plumes and pennants and gorgeous outspread fans.

But even as the sun's full blaze consumes and absorbs into itself all the dawn's many hues, so Seti in his chariot burst on the vision of the crowds with a glory dispelling all color. Spotless and glittering, a sunburst of gold about his neck, his chariot of pure electrum gleaming with a blinding brilliance, he surmounted the horizon like a living Re, driving his splendid steed into the heavens. Shielding their eyes, the crowd burst into cries of rejoicing.

"Seti! Son of the Most High!"

"Strong Bull with horns of gold! Let thy sacred feet trample us!"

"Blessed are the breasts which suckled thee!"

A frown marred the placid smoothness of the divine forehead. Amon-nebet should be receiving the plaudits of the multitude today, not he. The crowds had a new Horus to acclaim. How would they greet him? Indeed, how had they been greeting him? Amon-nebet's carriage was directly behind him. If he had been listening sharply instead of riding along immersed in his own thoughts...Eagerly he pricked up his ears.

"Hail, Moses! Friend of the pharaoh, beloved of Amon-Re!"

"Fair as Horus when he steps from his chamber!"

"Give us a smile, Moses! The maidens would rather have smiles from you than jewels!"

Hot jealousy swept through Seti. What had he done? Exalted an obscure princeling of doubtful origin that his own son might be abased? How stupid of him! Very likely his courtiers were all laughing at him, these same courtiers who were now so vociferous in their praises of his nearest friend!

But not for long. They could not ignore the crown prince of Egypt. Let them wait a few hours, until the divine oracle had proclaimed that Amon-nebet was the eldest son of Horus; until the priests of Amon, standing on their golden pedestals, had released four wild geese in the four directions of the compass, to carry to all the gods the news that Seti, Son of Amon, had set upon his son's head the white as well as the red crown!

Up the great avenue of sphinxes surged the crowd toward the lofty pylon of the Karnak temple. Here Seti and his sons and courtiers dismounted from their chariots, proceeding on foot into the more sacred precincts. Beyond the pylon in the great inner court Amenemhat, the high priest, stood waiting. At the other end of the court Amon, hidden behind the curtains of his gorgeous bark, came slowly forth from the deep forest of pillars to meet his son.

Moses, close behind Seti and Amon-nebet, kept his eyes anxiously on the latter. In spite of his regal attire, the young prince looked oddly small and defenseless. Amon-nebet was frightened. But what did he fear? Was he remembering the stones flung at his fleeing horse in the desert? The crowds were pressing into the great court. Already the spaces between the lofty columns were alive with swarming people, waving plumes, arid fluttering pennants. It would be easy for a missile to spring through the air, hit its mark, and betray not the slightest sign of its origin.

Sharply Moses scanned the heaving sea of faces, but they swam before his vision, as featureless and indistinguishable as separate waves. He was vaguely conscious of a face here and there: a guard's, scowling and intent; a high official's, fat and soft and lazily appraising; and one completely devoid of expression, its flabby cheek crossed by a livid scar which looked like a palm leaf inlaid in ivory.

Moses felt a fierce desire to protect the slight figure walking hesitantly across the great court of the temple. At the moment he would willingly have stood in the young prince's place, taking upon himself any dangers that might be lurking in those restless, heaving waves, any sorrow or disappointment—yes, even the scorn and cold contempt of Nefretiri.

And then it came. Not a whining missile. Only an innocent pointing finger and a voice rising insistently above the restless confusion of the waves.

"Look! The heretic! That heretic of Akhetaton! Returned to us in the flesh! Look, I tell you! That heretic—"

Moses stood motionless, his feet frozen to the silver tiles of the great court. The waves too seemed to hang suddenly suspended, uncertain whether to break or to recede. The silence in the court was like a vacuum. Then, almost imperceptibly, the waves again began to murmur, tentatively at first; then they picked up the cry, tossed it avidly from crest to crest.

"That heretic! That heretic of Akhetaton!"

"By Amon, he does look like him!"

"Osiris defend us; he's returned!"

It was not the sight of Amon-nebet's stricken face which released Moses' muscles but the sound of Ramses laughing softly behind him. He sprang toward the pointing finger. But it was too late, of course. There was no one there except the bewildered guards and the man with the scarred, vacant face. Moses seized him by his coat.

"Did you see who he was—the man who pointed?" he demanded hoarsely. "What did he look like? Which way did he go?"

But the man only gaped at him foolishly, his small eyes shifting loosely in their sockets. Resisting an impulse to bury his clenched fist in the soft cheek with its embedded palm frond, Moses released his hold abruptly. He turned back toward Amon-nebet. One glance was enough. He covered the distance between them in three strides.

"Neb!" he exclaimed sharply, catching the slender prince in his arms. "He's sick," he told Seti briefly. "I'm taking him back to the vessel."

Amazingly it was Ramses' staccato commands to the guards that cleared the way. *I misjudged him,* thought Moses absently. *He is really concerned about his brother. But—I could have sworn it was he who laughed.*

They made their way back along the edge of the long procession, their shoulders brushing those of the eunuchs who bore the gilded palanquins in which the ladies of the royal family were riding. Moses did not notice the parting of silken curtains above their heads, the watchful gaze of a pair of black eyes shot through with triumphant glints of green. By the dead weight in his arms he knew that Amon-nebet was unconscious.

"Lift his head," he ordered one of the guards. "Place it against my shoulder."

The guard stuttered incoherently. Moses caught the words "struck dead" and "curse of Amon" before the man turned and fled. Grimly he shifted his burden so the limp head fell forward instead of back. He understood now why a path had opened so readily. Stark terror showed on every face. The people believed that the wrath of Amon had fallen on the young prince because of his suddenly discovered resemblance to the hated heretic. At once Moses realized his grave mistake. He should have used all his strength and persuasion to make Amon-nebet remain at the head of the procession and continue with the ceremonies as planned. The priests would not have had time to revise their procedure. But it was too late now. Grimly he made his way through the ominous gaping in the crowd.

Outside the great pylon he stumbled toward the row of waiting chariots, picking one at random. "The prince has been taken sick," he told the driver abruptly. "Take us to the royal vessel as quickly as possible"

The panic had reached here also. The driver took one look at the unconscious figure, and his face blanched. "That isn't sickness," he muttered. "It's the curse—"

Seizing the reins, Moses shouted a curt command to the horses, and the restless animals sprang forward, necks arched high and colored plumes waving. Holding Amon-nebet's limp body balanced against his knees, he managed to guide the swaying chariot down the broad avenue leading to the river front. The *Star of the Two Lands* was waiting, as he had expected, at the temple quay. There were many hands to relieve him now. A dozen slaves, among them White Elephant, clustered about, chattering excitedly, lifting the still unconscious figure, loosening its heavy gold collar, carrying it into the cabin where a soft couch was waiting.

"Neb!" Moses repeated the word patiently again and again, while his fingers slowly chafed warmth into the chilled limbs. It was like trying to penetrate a thick wall that had no opening. Amon-nebet did not want to be awakened. As warmth was restored to the slight body, its limpness changed to stubborn hardness. Its breathing became slow and labored.

"Neb! Can't you hear me? It's I, Moses. There's no one here but me. You can come back now. Neb!"

The wall finally crumbled. After one last convulsive tightening the tensed muscles slowly relaxed. The clamped lips parted in a long, shuddering sigh. Amon-nebet opened his eyes.

"It happened," he said simply. "I knew it would."

"Yes," replied Moses. "Now there is nothing left to fear."

"Nothing—to fear?"

"It's the thing you've always dreaded most, isn't it?" returned Moses steadily. "Now it's happened. Before nightfall every man in Thebes will know that you are the living image of Ikhnaton."

"Don't!" Wincing, the young prince lifted his hands to cover his face. "And don't look at me. I—I can't bear to be pitied."

"I don't pity you." Deliberately Moses took the fumbling fingers in his own strong ones, leaving the cowering features unsheltered from his steady, relentless gaze. "I envy you."

"Envy—"

"Yes. You have the good luck to look like the bravest man who ever lived, and you've been given the chance now to prove that you are like him. It wasn't the people who hated Ikhnaton. It was the priests, and they hated him, not because he worshiped another god, but because he took away their power. He was strong, not weak, and you can be like him."

Hope flared in Amon-nebet's eyes. "I can still be—pharaoh?"

"Why not? Your father's wish is still law in Egypt. It may be a long battle, but it will be worth the trying."

"And—have Nefretiri for my wife?" Unconscious of the sudden silence Amon-nebet gripped Moses' cold hand. "Moses, I've just remembered! *He* had a wife who was beautiful, whose name was almost like Nefretiri's! And she loved him in spite of his ugliness." Excitement had risen within him, momentarily.

"Yes," said Moses. He felt the fingers relax, saw the light of hope in the fevered eyes flicker and die.

"But I'm not strong," came the despairing whisper. "I'm weak. Even though there's nothing more to fear, I'm still afraid. Without you to help me—"

Moses pressed the faltering hand reassuringly. "I'll help you, Neb," he promised steadily.

With a great effort Seti turned his head so he could see the face of his younger son. "You mean you have evidence that Moses was responsible for the—the thing that happened in the temple?"

Deliberately Ramses averted his face, knowing instinctively that the sight of his handsome features, so unlike those of his brother, would at this moment arouse irritation in his father.

"The Strong Bull misunderstood his son," he said gently. "The most insignificant of the sons of Horus remarked merely that the action of his cousin Moses was suspicious."

"In what way?" asked Seti. Though it required but little energy to move his lips, the words consumed a vast amount of effort.

"Well, if the Strong Bull will turn his mind backward, he will recall that my cousin Moses seized my brother and bore him away before it could be ascertained whether he was really ill or not. I myself followed him to see what he was about, but he was too quick for me. He acted like a man intent on a set purpose, as if he had planned each step deliberately."

"My son was sick," murmured Seti, again with a great effort. "I saw his face. He would have fallen at my feet."

"But surely not sick enough to warrant the interruption of his appointment as the future pharaoh." The young prince paused discreetly. "But doubtless I do my cousin a grave injustice. He has certainly made himself popular with the people. If my father will recall, judging by the ovation he received, it might have been he, not my brother, who was to be named crown prince."

Seti did indeed recall, and again jealousy swept through him. Ramses was right. If it were not for Moses, Amon-nebet would now be confirmed as crown prince. The adulation of the crowds, the voice in the temple court, his summary departure—all pointed to his complicity. Perhaps even the rescue in the desert had been part of the plan.

"If there were some service he could perform," suggested Ramses in a voice so soft that it seemed merely an extension of Seti's thoughts, "some place far enough away so he could cause no more harm, something perhaps a little—dangerous."

"Nubia!" replied Seti, not realizing that he had spoken the word aloud. Of course. Moses was just the man to head the campaign to quell the rebellion. He would return with the rich tributes necessary to satisfy the new demands from the priests as the price of their continued support of Amon-nebet. And if he did not return—

Seeing that the Strong Bull's eyes were closed, Ramses crept noiselessly away, a smile on his handsome features. For even though his destiny was assured by all seven Hathors, it did no harm to help their good work along a little.

7

Moses' last night in the palace which Seti had given him seemed almost as unreal as his first. Given him? Lent would have been the better word. He could tell by the oblique glances and the frenzied activity of cleaning and polishing that already the vast staff was making preparations for another possible occupant. Occasionally he overheard a whispered comment.

"...wondered how soon the pharaoh would get tired..."

"...to Kush! The last one went only to Elephant Island. The farther they go the worse..."

"...wonder what awful thing he did..."

"...all those gifts! Pity to keep them locked up in chests...lucky if he finds them all here when he returns..."

"*If* he returns, you mean."

So they believed he was in disfavor with the pharaoh and that he was commanding the army being sent to Kush as a punishment. Perhaps it was so. But punishment for what? He did not know. His interview with Seti had not been too revealing.

"This Nubian campaign must succeed. One of our richest dependencies is refusing to send tribute. You know what that means. Especially now when the priests of Amon will be demanding more—and more—and more."

Moses had been too stunned to think clearly. "The S-strong Bull is always wise in his d-decisions," he had stammered. "B-but—Amon-nebet—he d-depends on me—"

"My son will be well cared for in your absence," Seti had assured him. "I might remind you that your presence has not always afforded him complete protection."

Moses wandered restlessly through the empty rooms of his palace. He was leaving Thebes at dawn tomorrow. As the hours slipped away, the unrest within him grew slowly into panic. He had had word neither from Amon-nebet nor Nefretiri, though earlier in the day he had dispatched messages to both through White Elephant. Again and again he had tried to gain access to Amon-nebet's apartment, but each time he had failed.

"The young prince is indisposed," the attendants had informed him with finality. "It is the command of the Good God that he shall not be disturbed."

From Nefretiri there had been complete silence. He could not believe that she would permit him to pass out of her life for months, perhaps forever, without at least a farewell message, but apparently it was so. Finally he stopped pacing and went to his own apartment, but not to sleep. Dismissing the small army of attendants, he watched them depart without regret. Nor did they display the slightest hint of emotion. To all of them he had been merely a body to wash and oil and perfume and dress.

Both unrest and panic had given place to an empty, despairing quiet. He sat waiting, but without expectancy, for White Elephant to return. Perhaps he would bring a message, perhaps not. It did not really matter.

A sudden sound caused him to lift his eyes. He sprang to his feet. "Nefretiri!"

"Hush! Not so loud! Unless you want all Thebes to know that you entertain princesses in your bedroom at midnight."

"Wh-where did you come from? How—"

"White Elephant brought me. He's waiting outside, watching to warn us if anyone comes. I hope you've sent away all the servants."

"Yes. I've—sent them away—but—"

"I waited until now on purpose, until White Elephant was sure it would be safe. He gave the gatekeeper something to make him sleep. He—he'll probably be sleeping most of the night."

As Moses started toward her, she slipped out of the dark cape that covered her from head to foot. Long before his arms could reach her, his burning gaze enveloped each separate inviting feature of her loveliness. He drew her to him ungently, as he had done in the temple garden, drinking deeply from the sweet open goblet which was her lips, pressing his fingers into the warm flesh until they discovered an answering pulsation to the throbbing hunger within his own body. After the despairing emptiness, the assuaging flood of emotion was almost too much to be borne. There was no room for thought or reason. He was holding in his arms neither the betrothed wife of Amon-nebet nor the heiress of the throne of Egypt, but the woman he loved. And she had come to him on this last night, deliberately.

"Moses." Her voice was soft but insistent. "I want to talk to you. There are some things we must say—before—"

His arms loosened reluctantly. "Well?"

"I'm sorry you have to go to Nubia. Will you be gone long?"

His voice was thick with emotion. "Only as long as it takes to go to the ends of the earth and back."

"It won't last forever. And—perhaps it will be better to have you away from Thebes just now, while—things are working out. They will work out, Moses, I'm sure of it. For us, I mean."

Again his arms reached out for her with hungry impatience. "When you're going to the ends of the earth," he said hoarsely, "it doesn't seem very important that things may work out sometime. It's—tonight that matters."

"I know, but—there are hours and hours to dawn. Listen to me, Moses." Her hands were still hard and resistant against his breast.

"I'm listening."

"You must go to Nubia and do all that my father expects of you—and more. Don't let anything stand in the way of your success, Bring back more treasure, more slaves, than have ever been seen in Egypt before. You can do it. You have a power over people. You can be as great and as strong as Amenhotep or Thutmose."

He drew her to him in spite of her resistance. "I don't want power and greatness," he said huskily. "I want you."

"You shall have me, and greatness and power also," she whispered, "if you'll just do what I say. By the time you return my father will have forgotten he suspected you of betraying Amon-nebet that day in the temple."

"What—did you say? You mean Seti suspects me of doing that—that cruel thing to Amon-nebet?"

"Why—yes. Didn't you know? Everyone else in the palace does. That's why he's sending you away."

"He b-believes I'd do a-a thing like that—" The words choked in his throat— "to a f-friend I love and p-promised to protect?"

"But it doesn't really matter, Moses, can't you see that?" Her small hands, still hard against his breast, drew now rather than repelled. "It's better this way. As long as he suspects you, he won't know who really—"

She stopped suddenly, her hands slowly loosing their hold on his linen tunic, knowing that she had made a mistake but instantly rallying all her instinctive resources to rectify it. Moses had always been unpredictable. Perhaps that was why she had first found him so

140

intriguing. But it was disconcerting that in a single moment his eyes could change from the heat of passion to such sudden coldness.

"You mean that you—know who did it?" he demanded.

"Did what?" she parried.

"Cried out in the temple court that Amon-nebet was the living image of Ikhnaton. Or hired someone to do it."

She wished he had given her more time to think. His sharp questions, the intensity of his gaze, put her strangely on the defense. And she did not feel at all defensive. She felt triumphant.

Suddenly Moses' hands were gripping her shoulders. "Of course you know," he said with a quietness that belied the iron grasp of his fingers. "Why shouldn't you? It was you yourself who did it! You've been meaning to do it ever since that day in Akhetaton."

"Yes!" She lifted her head proudly, her eyes shooting green sparks of triumph and defiance. "Of course I did it. How did you think I was going to be able to keep my promise?"

"Your—promise—"

"Didn't I tell you I would rather die than become the wife of Amon-nebet?"

He gripped her shoulders more tightly. "Was it you who tried to kill him in the desert?"

"No! Believe me, I swear to you by Thoth, I never tried to kill him! There are others who hate Amon-nebet."

"Who?"

Nefretiri looked frightened. "How should I know?"

"But you do know. Tell me."

"Well—my mother Tuya for one. She wants to put my brother Ramses on the throne, and if she did I'd have to be his wife."

Moses let his arms fall heavily at his sides. "Amon-nebet," he murmured. "Poor boy, no wonder he was afraid!"

"Why should you think of him?" demanded the girl. "You and I are all that matter. It's not our fault if he looks like the heretic, but we'd be stupid if we didn't take advantage of it. Look at me, Moses! Put your arms around me. What's the matter? Don't you want me?"

"Want you!" Something like a groan burst from his lips. "Does a thirsty man want water?"

"Then take me—take me, Moses—"

The touch of her soft flesh pressing against him was like fire in his veins. His senses swam in the heady fragrance of the fresh flowers she wore about her neck. He had only to bend his head to press his thirsty lips to the rim of the goblet. In fact, he need not even bend his head. She was lifting it toward him, bringing it nearer and nearer his lips.

Deliberately he took her by the shoulders and pushed her gently away. "No." His voice sounded strange, like an echo from a hollow space. "You and I are not all that matter. Amon-nebet is more important than we are. Because you have hurt him and I have promised to protect him."

She did not believe him at first. She laughed lightly, then stormed, and finally wept.

"Oh, Moses, you fool! You stubborn, stubborn fool! I come to you with all I have to give, and you scorn me like—like a common dancing girl! Oh, I should hate you, despise you! But I don't. I love you."

Patiently, not trusting himself to touch her, he tried to make her understand. There was still a chance of redressing the wrong she had committed. It might very well be in her power to restore the confidence she had taken away. She must become the wife of Amon-nebet.

Tutu was restless. He had no relish for the trip to Nubia and felt that he was getting much too old and stout for military campaigns. Ironical that the last night for months when he would be able to lie in his own comfortable bed he was unable to sleep! However, he derived a somber satisfaction from such ironies, especially one that proved as profitable as this one. So fortunate too that Moses spoke the name of the cloaked and hooded figure whom he conducted to the palace entrance some hours before dawn! Otherwise the slightly nearsighted scribe, hidden behind a fat column in the outer vestibule, would have thought her any common dancing girl.

And he had believed the friend of the pharaoh impervious to the charms of women! Tutu, the discerning genius! He scoffed at himself good-naturedly. Should he tell Amenemhat? No. That is, not just yet. A secret kept was likely to be worth more than one shared, if one watched and waited and used it to good purpose. Perhaps the trip to Nubia might not be so bereft of profit, after all. A man to whom the Princess Nefretiri chose to pay nocturnal visits might be worth following to the ends of the earth.

PART IV

1

There was mutiny among his soldiers. Moses did not blame them. He was glad that they had spirit enough left in them to rebel.

"If the friend of the pharaoh were an older man, he would have foreseen that such unprecedented action would result only in disaster," Ahmose, his captain, reminded him with more impertinence than a subordinate would ordinarily dare employ. "No doubt the ways of the great conquering pharaohs were old-fashioned, but at least they arrived at their objective. They didn't lead their armies into a serpents' nest!"

Moses barely stifled a sharp rejoinder. "Get back to your inspection," he ordered curtly, "and see that the men proceed faster with their weaving."

The captain's lips curled. "Child's play," he muttered. "If you think you can keep grown men playing at making baskets out of sedge grass—"

Moses turned on his heel and went back to his tent. Perhaps Ahmose was right. It did seem presumptuous for a mere youth to pit his judgment against that of the great Thutmose or Sesostris. But some stubborn instinct deep within him still told him that he had acted wisely.

The center of the rebellion was at Saba, close to the Fourth Cataract, the farthest point up the Nile to which Egyptian dominion had ever extended. One pharaoh after another—Thutmose, Amenhotep, Harmhab—had followed the river up its narrow green path between the deserts, waiting for the flood season to make certain stretches navigable, dragging their boats on land around the boiling rapids, painfully traversing each hazardous mile of the river's long, curving detour. Moses proposed to cut straight across the desert toward the Fourth Cataract. It had seemed the only sensible thing to do, and he had wondered why no commanding officer had ever thought of it before. The desert could be no more relentless a foe than the river, which had already taken heavy toll of both boats and men. They would avoid the long waiting for the spring floods, and they would strike the rebellion first at its roots, without dissipating their strength in lesser encounters along the way. White Elephant, who was as at home in this hostile country as a monkey in a palm tree, had given the plan his unqualified approval.

"Black man find way," he had nodded. "White Elephant lead. Find way with eyeth clothed. In dark."

The little Nubian had indeed revealed an uncanny aptitude for finding the way, even if it had been no triumphant charge of a victorious army. Foot by foot, sometimes inch by inch, they had followed an apparently blind trail: through glaring stretches of yellow sand; up wild, gloomy wadies engulfed in rivers of petrified rock; along naked skeletons of granite and basalt and syenite, their bones sharpened to a cutting edge by centuries of wind-driven sand. But he had led them unerringly from oasis to oasis, and, though they had often sucked the last drops of moisture from their empty skins, never had they been long without water.

Now White Elephant was gone, together with the other Nubian guides who had been impressed into service from the last settlement where the army had encamped. He had disappeared in the night soon after the advance patrol had reported that the stony plateau lying just ahead was infested with a fierce and dangerous breed of serpent and dragging the dead, bloated body of their leader to prove it. Moses knew where he had gone. In fact, he himself had sent him. But he dared trust no one with the knowledge, not even his scribe Tutu.

From the entrance to his tent Moses could see Tutu within. The scribe's plump figure had become gaunt, and the hand that held the brush trembled. But the characters he inscribed on the roll in his lap were as faultless as if they had been intended for a king's coffin.

"The gods have deserted us," he wrote in his fine flowing script. "They have abandoned us on an island of palms and acacias in the middle of this Land of Ghosts. Our death will be all the more horrible because it will be a lingering one, food being plentiful. We shall die not of hunger or thirst but of madness. Amon-Re returns each day to taunt us, sending his burning wrath down upon us. Anubis, the pathfinder, howls at us mockingly from the desert. Apap, the mighty monster, has sent his serpents to devour us.

"We have camped here for nearly three months," continued the scribe in a more practical vein. "Of the three thousand men who left Egypt, not more than two are left. The reinforcements that joined us in northern Nubia deserted us soon after we left the river for the desert. They were wiser than the men of Egypt. They knew the power of the gods who dwell in this Land of Ghosts.

"I believe that Moses is mad. He has ordered the men to cut the long grasses that grow along the edge of the oasis and weave baskets of them. Yet he does not look like a man gone mad. I'd swear his hand was steadier and his eye clearer than they ever were in Thebes. And he still manages to keep the army in perfect discipline. In spite of their panic the men listen to him. He walks through the camp and talks with them like any common soldier. When he sees two men disputing, instead of ordering them flogged he sits down with them and tries to help them settle their differences.

"We live from day to day like a man caught between a lion and a precipice. Moses tells us his wretched slave and his miserable guides will return, but few believe him. And if they do, what then? One thing is certain. We cannot go forward. Apap himself crouches ready to devour us. Could we find our way back to the river alive? The men are becoming more and more mutinous. If Moses does not act soon, someone will steal into his tent at night and kill him..."

Moses knew what Tutu was writing. He knew what the soldiers were thinking. Turning again from his tent, he looked out over the encampment. Color, sharp and intense, smote his eyes: the rainbow hues of tents and pennants, the vivid blues and greens of clear pools and grasses and feathery tamarisks; the bright sharp thrust of palm leaves against hard-glazed sapphire. He never tired of this miracle of abundant life in the midst of desolation. He liked it best at night when the stark black rocks surrounding the valley were muted by the moonlight into alabaster, and the palm fronds lay against the softly burnished sky like inlays of pale ivory.

But today he was oblivious to beauty. It was the moving figures in the valley that held his attention: the sentries, nervously pacing; the squatting basket weavers on the edges of the pool; the shrill, gesticulating officers. His men had nearly reached the breaking point. If he did not give the command to retreat and try to lead them back to the river, they would compel him to do so. His most trusted officers might be leaders in the mutiny, his own guards their tools. It was possible they might try to kill him this very night.

It was easy to understand how they felt. Hardened soldiers as they were, they had suffered experiences that might well have driven them mad long before this. Day after day they had grappled, hand to hand, with the fierce, hostile desert—its blinding glare, its thirst, its lurking marauders, animal and human, and, worst of all, its strange unseen gods, having irrevocably left their own on the riverbank behind. And all

147

to what purpose? That Seti might have a thicker crust of gold on the columns of his funeral temple and the priests of Amon more intricate inlays of ivory for their chairs.

For Moses there was a more compelling purpose. He must succeed in his mission for Amon-nebet's sake. Seti would need all the riches of Kush, and more, to persuade the priests a second time that his oldest son should be made his successor. They had hated Ikhnaton with a deadly hatred. And Amon-nebet was his living image. Seti believed that he, Moses, was responsible for the misfortune that had befallen his son, and perhaps he was right in part. It was Nefretiri's love that had driven her to such desperate measures.

The thought of Nefretiri was still like a knife thrust in an open wound. She had come to him during those last brief hours and he had sent her away. Now he would never possess her. Night after night he lay wide awake, remembering, listening to the howling of the jackals, and cursing himself bitterly. Why was he so different from other men? What was this strange compulsion within him that kept him from possessing a woman merely because he felt that she owed a debt of honor to another? Amon-nebet would never have known. Not a prince of Egypt but would have thought him stupid even to question his right. And not a god would have cared a whit one way or the other.

"*I ought to hate you,*" she had said, the green flecks in her eyes shooting sparks. "*If another man had scorned me like this— But it isn't another man. It's you. And I don't hate you. I'd lie down in the dirt and let you walk over me. All right. Have it your way—now. What do you want me to do?*"

Weeks had passed since then. Had she kept her promise, he wondered, so reluctantly given? Was she even now the wife of Seti's oldest son, thus securing his position as future pharaoh of Egypt? Even though the thought filled him with torment, he hoped so. But he must also fulfill his part of the bargain. With the treasures of Kush he also must purchase security for Amon-nebet.

There was a commotion at the other end of the valley oasis, where an opening in the overlapping piebald shields formed the entrance of the encampment. The shouting of the sentries was drowned in a sudden unintelligible hubbub. Water carriers dropped their skins. The weavers beside the pools tossed aside their grasses, reared themselves on their bare heels, and ran shouting at the tops of their voices. Discipline had vanished. If an enemy invading the camp was causing the tumult, he would find, not an orderly and well-armed array of soldiers, but a mob of excited schoolboys elbowing each other for a front-row view at a feast day parade.

Watchful, alert, Moses stood in the entrance of his tent and waited. Whatever the cause of the sudden tumult, its perils were insignificant beside the dangers lurking in the excited crowd which rushed to meet it. The moment of crisis had come. But with an instinctive astuteness he did not go to meet it. He waited for it to come to him.

It came. The shouting grew louder, the excitement more intense, and the crowd swept en masse toward his tent. Suddenly it parted, and an amazing procession bore down upon him. At first glance it looked like an army of grotesque hybrids, half bird, half man, but as it approached, gradually the details became more distinct. White Elephant was in the lead, a great bird astride his shoulders, its long legs dangling almost to his knees, the bobbing feather in his woolly knot of hair surmounted by its long, curving beak. Behind him marched at least fifty other Negroes, each bearing a similar burden and each grinning as broadly as White Elephant. The shouts of the soldiers became articulate.

"The ibis! The sacred ibis!"

"The gods are with us again!"

"By Amon, no harm can come to us now! We're saved!"

"Let them go! Untie their wings!"

"They'll lead us out of this Land of Ghosts, back where we came from!"

"Back! Let's go back—back to the land of the river!"

Moses lifted his hand. This was the moment for which he had been waiting. He had sent White Elephant back to the river for a few ibis, and the faithful little Nubian had brought back fifty. Moreover the men, recognizing them as sacred birds of Egypt, had welcomed their coming as a good omen. But they still must be persuaded to go forward, not back. Words surged through his mind, tumbled to the threshold of his lips. He knew suddenly that there was power within him, power to mold the wills of these men to his. He had only to pour forth his racing thoughts. His lips felt stiff and dry. He opened them, but no words came. Desperately he tried again.

"M-men of Egypt—"

His voice sounded like wind blowing through a puny reed. A hand clamped itself tightly about his throat. Then he saw that it was at White Elephant the crowd was staring, not at him. Reaching into the pocket of his leather apron, the little Nubian had drawn out what looked at first glance like a smooth bronze coil of rope. He dropped it on the ground, and instantly the men closest to him, remembering the black, bloated body of their snake-bitten comrade, recoiled in horror. Swiftly White Elephant removed the straddling creature from his shoulders and released the cord that bound its wings. There was a flash of bright hues as the great bird darted forward, struck unerringly at the glistening coil, and, clamping its bill about its writhing smoothness, shook it violently. There was a triumphant cheer as the serpent slowly disappeared down the long, curving throat.

"Blessed be the sacred ibis!"

"The gods of Egypt have swallowed the king god of Kush!"

"It's a sign!"

"Let's go on, not back! The gods are with us!"

Thanks to the genius of White Elephant, the wild scheme that Moses had conceived as a last expedient succeeded. Better yet, it became the men's own plan.

"If our general, the friend of the pharaoh, would permit us," proposed Ahmose with enthusiasm, "we could put the ibis in the baskets the men have made, take them with us as we march forward, and release them when we come to the land of the serpents."

"An excellent idea," said Moses approvingly. "Whoever thought of it should be commended."

The subordinate flushed with pleasure. "It's nothing," he returned deprecatingly. "It was our general who had the real inspiration. It was a stroke of genius marching straight across the desert. I wonder that no pharaoh ever thought of it before."

2

No wonder the defenders of Kush declared Saba, their capital city, impregnable! For two months the Egyptian army, swelled now to a great host by the Negro prisoners they had captured in surprise attacks along the way, had been encamped on the river-bank overlooking the city, waiting for the defending troops to meet them in combat. In spite of White Elephant's frantic objections and against the advice of Ahmose, Moses climbed again to the high rocky bluff where he could gain a clear view of the city's walls.

"Lord printh make too beautiful target," protested the little Nubian earnestly, clambering up the steep rock behind him. "Men thee him, throw thtoneth, thend arrowth. Lord printh fall flat-tho!"

"Let them," returned Moses briefly, giving the dramatically recumbent figure of his slave but a passing glance. "We've waited long enough for them to show some signs of fighting. If I thought it would rouse them to a little action, I'd try swimming across."

"No, no! River full of crocodileth! Lord printh thlapped hard with tail, like thith!"

Leaving the black extremities waving wildly in mid-air, Moses continued to the top of the bluff. It was just after sunset. The sky was aflame with a wild beauty. Even the river beneath, still agitated from its recent battle with its agelong enemies, the rocks, was touched with color. It swept between its gray banks in a yellow, foam-flecked flood, its myriad little waves glimmering in a constant play of lights and shadows.

As always in the presence of beauty, Moses felt a compelling urge for participation. Deep gratitude welled up within him. He longed for communion with the mysterious, creative source of such beauty, but, as always, the longing was followed by a vague emptiness. Communion with what? with whom? Ptah, the fashioner, wrapped in his swaddling clothes in Memphis? Amon-Re, who cared more for the gold buried in these desolate hills than for the transient glow his disappearing bark might leave trailing behind it? With the mysterious, radiant Aton? Or—

Deliberately Moses turned his attention to the city he had failed to conquer. Built on a small island in the middle of the river, its walls rose sheer and straight, washed glass-smooth by the turbulent waters. He knew how smooth and straight they were, because his men had tried to climb them. The defenders in the square stronghold above had merely laughed, not even bothering to fling stones down upon them.

As smooth and straight, thought Moses, studying them curiously, *as the polished stones of the pyramids. They're as clever at building as we are. Only wiser. They build to protect the living, not the dead.*

He had tried all the methods known to modern warfare; building reed boats and crossing under cover of thickly woven roof shelters held high over the men's heads with poles; scaling the walls with ladders; assailing the fortresses with heavy barrages of arrows! hurling battering stones for days on end at single strategic points of the wall in an endeavor to weaken it. But all to no purpose. It was a small city, hardly larger than an Asiatic castle. Water, of course, was unlimited, but its food supply must be getting low. The tiny garden plots that sustained it were all on the mainland. And, in addition to its usual inhabitants, it was supporting all the refugees who had fled up the river ahead of his conquering army. Yet it exhibited no sign either of distress or of resistance.

So close was he that he could see the features of the people moving about in the turreted strongholds. One of them, leaning far out through a narrow opening, wore a round gold collar like an Egyptian pectoral, and he could have sworn it was a woman. He watched until the bright colors had faded into pale gray-blues and violets, the island city become a faintly looming shadow. Then, with the faithful White Elephant still dogging his heels, he returned to the encampment.

A stranger was sitting in the center of a group of soldiers gathered about a campfire. Though his face was burned black by the sun, his features were not those of a Nubian. There was no mistaking the narrow, slightly slanting eyes, the thin lips, the long, hooked, aristocratic nose. This man was an Egyptian and one of no mean birth. What was he doing here in this desolate outpost? Curiously Moses paused in the shadows beyond the firelight, where he could observe without being seen. The stranger was talking, holding his listeners, a group of hardened mercenaries, enthralled. His voice was cultured and gently modulated, and he was speaking in pure Egyptian.

"So I journeyed until I came to the place of the joining of the male and the female, the father and mother of the great waters, where he who is strong with the full vigor of manhood plunges joyfully to plant his rich seed in the quiet, receptive body of his mate. And because I too was young and virile, I turned to the left and took the path which he had followed. On and on I journeyed, up and up, through the land of the rushing blue waters, until I came to the place of his exultant boyhood, his romping, merry childhood, his triumphant birth, and, finally, his wild, tumultuous conception, from the mating of the winds and the mountains."

"There are many strange things in the land of the great blue father of rivers," continued the gentle, vibrant voice. "Monsters with invisible bodies and forked tongues of flame that strike men dead where they stand. Mountains that vomit up fire and smoke. Cataracts whose roar is louder than a thousand lions. Trees so big the arms of a hundred men could not encompass them—"

Moses moved on to his tent. Ahmose was waiting for him there, his voice hoarse with excitement.

"A messenger has come from the city. He says the queen sent him. He has been waiting to see you."

"Send him in to me," said Moses quietly.

Seen more closely, by the light of the flaring lamps, the stranger was even more of an enigma. It was hard to tell whether he was unbelievably old or incredibly young. His face was almost as leathery and finely crisscrossed with wrinkles as an elephant's skin, yet the hands were smooth and graceful. And the eyes, set deep and wide apart, were as alert as those of a young child. His dress was a strange combination of Egyptian and Nubian. Over a short leather skirt he wore a coat of linen with full, flowing sleeves. His throat and breast were covered with a round gold collar, as elaborate in design as one a pharaoh might have worn, and his long, thin hair, gathered into a knot on top of his head, was fastened with bright ostrich feathers dyed a half dozen different hues. With a mocking twinkle in his eye which belied the humility of the act, he bowed low until the plumes swept the ground.

"Prince Moses, the mighty warrior, the friend of the Strong Bull, who scatters all his enemies like dust before his breath, welcome to the miserable land of Kush. May your feet never find rest except upon the necks of the conquered! May the tears you shed be turned to silver! May the water to which your lips are pressed become pure gold!"

Moses laughed. "In other words," he returned promptly, "may my feet never find rest, may I shed many tears, and may I never slake my thirst."

The two exchanged a glance of complete understanding mingled with both caution and respect.

"The friend of the pharaoh has astuteness of mind as well as strength of body," murmured the visitor. "A rare quality in a prince of Egypt."

"You should know," retorted Moses, "for you were one once yourself. Who are you?"

"Suppose—suppose you just call me—Sinuhe."

Sinuhe. Of course he should bear the name of the fabulous wandering hero of Egypt's most beloved adventure tale, even though it was obviously not his own. "Did you really find it?" demanded Moses eagerly. "Did you follow the great river to its end—I mean its beginning?"

"Ah!" The slanting eyes kindled. "I see we have more in common than the struggle to possess a few mud hovels. You also have asked questions. And, like me, you are uncertain as to which is the end and which the beginning. Suppose I say that I found the beginning of something and the end of nothing."

Again something flashed between them like a spark struck from the contact of rock and metal. "You mean—" began Moses. "How did you get here?" he demanded abruptly. "The men have orders not to let anyone land, and we've had guards patrolling every inch of the shore day and night."

"We have our ways," smiled Sinuhe. "And even if we had not, we are quite capable of subsisting inside our city walls for years on end if necessary. It's quite hopeless, you know. There's no possible way of conquering us—unless—"

"Yes?" returned Moses steadily.

"Unless," continued Sinuhe equably, "you permit the people of Kush to confer upon you a very great honor. The city of Saba and all its wealth will be yours for the taking the moment you are willing to accept its queen as your wife."

Moses stared uncomprehendingly. "The moment I— Are you mad?"

"Not at all. Why should a simple proposal of marriage suggest the idea of madness? The friend of the pharaoh no doubt has many wives. Surely one more—"

"I have no wife," replied Moses briefly.

"No? Then so much the better." The visitor shot his host a shrewd but amused glance. "If we could discuss the matter in a slightly less constrained atmosphere—say, over a bottle of good wine—"

The wine was brought. His eyes sparkling with anticipation, Sinuhe received from White Elephant the slender silver goblet, and, tasting it, smacked his lips. "There are two things I have missed since I turned my back on Elephant Island," he murmured reminiscently. "One is good wine. The other is *not*—as you are expecting me to say— beautiful women."

Moses flushed. "But I didn't—"

"And if you are worrying lest the queen of Saba lack the golden complexion and slender grace of the daughters of the Two Lands, don't let it disturb you. Tharbis is neither old nor ugly. Odd, isn't it," he pursued, sipping thoughtfully, "that the children of the Black Land should have golden skins and the children of Nubia, the Land of Gold, should be black? One of the creator's little jokes, whoever he was. Not Amon nor Re nor Ptah, I'm sure of that. They have no sense of humor."

Moses stopped his nervous pacing, but his mind was still whirling. "Y-you actually mean this seriously?" he demanded. "The queen of S-saba has sent you to me with a p-proposal of—of—"

"Of marriage," supplied Sinuhe helpfully.

"B-but why?"

"Why indeed?" The visitor sighed over his empty goblet, but his slanting eyes were twinkling. "Suppose the queen is looking from the windows of the stronghold when the gallant young general is walking along the riverbank. Suppose she is so impressed with his strength of body and nobility of countenance—I can hardly say beauty—that she falls madly in love with him. There, there! Spare the painful blushing! I didn't suppose young Egyptians knew how to blush these days. I can think of a better reason. Suppose—suppose she is tired of being queen of a little Nubian city, even one as rich as Saba. Suppose she has been taught from infancy by an Egyptian, who has imparted to her all the wisdom that he knows but, being only a simple adventurer, is unable to satisfy her thirst for knowledge. Suppose for years she has desired to gaze on the pyramids, to bathe in the Fayum, to dwell in the land of Thoth and Maat, not as a slave but as a princess..."

Moses slept little that night. While Sinuhe lay comfortably on a mat, gently snoring, he walked up and down, up and down, outside his tent The proposition which the amazing stranger had made to him was so monstrous, so unexpected, that he had no power to think clearly.

"Take your time, take your time," Sinuhe had told him blandly. "As long as the wine lasts and this black monkey remains at my elbow to pour it, I'm in no hurry. Though I'll admit your hesitation amazes me. I wonder if you heard me aright. I'm offering you victory, man. Suppose an unexpected marriage does go with it? What's a wife, more or less, to an Egyptian prince?"

Sinuhe was right. It was a choice between victory and defeat. The city of Saba was impregnable. Moses knew that now. He could camp here for months, years perhaps, and unless a miracle happened, the proud walls across the stormy flood would remain undented. But the miracle had happened. He had only to speak a few brief words, and the treasures of Kush would pour in a golden stream into his lap. Why then should his body become weak and cold with sweat, his throat choke, his will grow suddenly stiff with rebellion?

I take you, Tharbis—

Tharbis. Not an ugly name. He repeated it aloud, and its syllables mingled in his ears with the sound of the rushing river. There was within it a note of wildness, almost of harshness, like the screaming of the goatsucker or the hoopoe bird. Not soft and gently rounded, like "Nefretiri." *Tharbis.* The tropical night pressed upon him, heavy and black and clinging, fraught with strange cloying scents, the stars girding its dusky neck like a collar of jewels. He found it hard to breathe.

A blurred face appeared. "There's a rumor in camp a truce is to be arranged," said Ahmose. "The men are like wild animals—can't wait to get into the city—babbling about the women. If it isn't true, I believe they'll kill us. What shall I tell them?"

"T-tell them?" echoed Moses. The blurred shape swam before his eyes. He wanted to lift his clenched fists, to pound it to a pulp, "Amon curse the cowardly swine! Tell them—" His voice choked, "Tell them—n-nothing."

The face disappeared, and suddenly he wanted to laugh. Life was full of such ironies. There was not a soldier in camp but would gladly have accepted defeat as the price of a woman, while he rebelled at accepting a woman as the price of victory! He wondered what Ahmose, what Sinuhe, would say if they knew he had never yet possessed a woman. The priestesses of On had been his for the taking. The palaces of Memphis and Thebes had been as completely provisioned with female slaves as with wine and rich foods. Yet he had desired only one woman. And now she could never belong to him. Was she already, he wondered, the wife of Amon-nebet?

Amon-nebet. The mere thought of the name steadied him. He had come to Nubia with but one purpose. How, even for a moment, could he have forgotten it? For Amon-nebet's sake the gold and ivory of Kush must be fed into Amon's greedy, open mouth that his vision might become dulled to the features of the son of the pharaoh. He must help Nefretiri atone for the wrong they had both done. What happened to him did not really matter.

He went into his tent. The man who called himself Sinuhe lay on the mat in deep slumber, graceful hands outflung in a gesture of pure abandon. Moses wakened him abruptly.

"It means full surrender?" he demanded without preface.

"Full surrender," replied the visitor promptly.

"Immediate?"

"As soon as you comply with the conditions. You will march into the city on the first day of your marriage festival, which will be celebrated at once."

"The amount of the indemnity?"

Sinuhe shrugged. "Whatever you choose. The city will be yours. Load it on a barge and take it all to Thebes if you wish—and can. Provided Tharbis accompanies you as your honored wife—and Sinuhe as her trusted attendant."

Moses felt an unexpected stirring of pleasure. "Then you are coming too?"

"Why not? There comes a time when it's easier to journey down the river than up." He shrugged again. "And besides, the wine is good here, I find."

Moses' glance kindled. "You said there were two things you have missed since you left Egypt. What is the other?"

"Serenity."

"Serenity!" echoed Moses in amazement. "In Egypt?"

Sinuhe smiled. "You did not find it there? Then you are not at heart an Egyptian. A people that live only in the past know little of disquiet and unrest. They belong to those who live for the future."

3

It was the seventh and last day of his wedding festival, and Moses had not yet seen his bride. But the moment could not be postponed much longer. As bridegroom he had ridden through the gaily festooned streets of Saba in the final grand procession, accompanied by his male friends, including Tutu, Ahmose, Sinuhe, and a hilarious company of his soldiers—all, in fact, who had not succumbed along the way to drunkenness or more pleasant diversions—and had arrived at the modest palace which, on his triumphant entrance into Saba, had been assigned to him. At the very moment his bride, accompanied by a similar procession of riotous female attendants, was approaching by a different route. He sat now among his companions in the banquet hall, smiling woodenly at their ribald jokes, ears strained to catch the first shrill accents of excited female voices. It seemed the longest hour he had ever spent.

"Maybe her Kushite majesty has changed her mind," suggested Ahmose with a boldness compounded of wine and excitement. "Maybe she caught a glimpse of the groom through the slits in that barbaric reed basket these savages call a palanquin. Oh, well, let her come or not. Who cares? We have the city. Of course it would be too bad to disappoint the mighty conquering general!"

"She will come," said Sinuhe confidently, his hand still amazingly steady as he refilled his goblet from the flower-wreathed jug. "Not a bad celebration for the wilds of the Fourth Cataract, what? I'll wager the crown prince himself won't have a more elaborate wedding. Thank old Sinuhe for that! Tell me, did we lack anything that Thebes could have provided? Acrobats, mountebanks, wrestlers, dancers, food, good wine? I'll admit you had to supply the wine yourself, but what's the difference?"

Tutu drank little and said less, but his eyes rested on Moses with a cold boldness far more eloquent than words. "So," they said mockingly, "you think you're fooling people, do you? Others, perhaps, but not me. This isn't the sort of marriage you had planned. What would the daughter of the pharaoh think of it, I wonder? Ah, I see you are wondering too. A pretty bit of irony—exchanging the loveliest princess of Egypt for a black daughter of Kush! How the noble friend of the pharaoh has fallen!"

Moses touched his dry lips to his goblet, but he did not drink. The shouting of the soldiers outside became so loud it drowned out all other sounds. Deliberately he turned his eyes from Tutu's mocking gaze. By closing his senses to his surroundings he could almost negate their reality.

The past seven days, with their splendid barbaric pageantry, did not exist. He was not sitting in a mud house in Nubia. He was in his own palace in Thebes. It was the day of his wedding, yes, but not with a strange, dark-skinned savage of the daughters of Kush. It was for the golden Nefretiri that he waited. Her attendants were anointing her body with perfumes and unguents, braiding the long, shining strands of her hair and intertwining them with flowers, accompanying her in carefree procession through the streets of Thebes, stopping beneath the latticed windows of his palace. So vivid was the illusion that he could hear the shrill cries of her female attendants, followed by a breathless, waiting silence; then the bride's own clear voice lifted in her wedding song:

"I come to you as the flower turns to the sun;
   As the mountain stream hears from afar the song of the river
   And hastens to merge its flow with the Father of Waters;
   As the wild duck harks to the trumpet call of her mate

And mounts up to meet him on swift wings;
Like a bird homing to its nest, I come to you!"

He had not supposed Nefretiri could sing like that, in a voice rich and full as the sound of the river in floodtime, with the wild cadence of the cataracts added to its melody.

"My heart is a pathless waste, a fireless hearth,
The parched earth panting for the flood's embrace,
Until I see your face, beloved; then lo,
The rushing tide, the flame, the sweet oasis,
A garden of flowers which are yours for the plucking!
I come to you, my love! I come to you!"

Sinuhe touched his shoulder. "Is it not customary in Egypt for the bridegroom to go forth to meet the bride?"

The illusion was gone. He felt himself lifted and borne forward by a hilarious bevy of his attendants, like a reed on the crest of a wave. He was conscious of a shifting sea of black, smiling faces, of the blaring din of drums and pipes and sistrums, before the procession swept on into his own apartment. Moses felt weak with relief. The inevitable encounter had been postponed a little longer. In the confusion he had not even been able to distinguish the features of his bride among the laughing faces.

"Well?" Sinuhe's dark eyes were close to his. "What do you think of her? Didn't I tell you she was not so ugly?"

Before he could answer they were caught in the full tide of the final festivities. Sinuhe had provided all the accoutrements of a respectable Egyptian wedding, with native embellishments. Drunkenness rioted with obscenity, Hathor and Bast cohabiting shamelessly with the more savage god beasts of the jungle. The blessing of the gods of fertility, both Kushite and Egyptian, was invoked by suggestion and symbol. Corn was strewn on the floor and sprinkled liberally with water, gigantic phallic emblems hoisted on poles and lewdly manipulated with strings. Naked female slaves, baskets of sprouting corn swinging from their hips, slipped through the lolling groups with labyrinthine motions.

Moses grew sick with revulsion. This was not marriage as he had dreamed of it. It had nothing to do with the pure flame of emotion which he and Nefretiri had kindled, any more than had the strange, dark-skinned woman waiting in his apartment.

It was over at last. The wineskins were drained. The ribald jests subsided. The princes of Nubia and the officers of the Egyptian army either slipped into pleasant oblivion or stole away to await their turn with one of the obliging slaves. With one final outburst of hilarity Moses was dragged to the closed door of his apartment and thrust inside. He felt a moment of panic. He knew that if his life depended upon it, he could not speak. And even if he could, what would he say? What did a man say to the queen of a strange country whose face he had never before looked upon but who had just become his wife?

With a surge of relief he discovered that he would have a few more moments of reprieve. A young girl, presumably a slave attendant, was seated on a mat outside the entrance to his inner chamber. He hoped the sounds of revelry had been muted before coming to her ears. They had not been fit for a child to hear, especially one as frankly innocent as this one seemed. The single garment she wore, a simple tunic of linen cut more loosely than the transparent, tight-fitting dress of the Egyptian woman, was devoid of ornament. No flash of ring or necklace or anklet interrupted the golden-brown duskiness of her flawless skin.

She doesn't need jewelry, thought Moses absently, *any more than a sky needs painting.*

She was not beautiful like Nefretiri. Her eyes were set very wide apart, like those of an alert animal designed to look both ways at once, and her small nose, neither aquiline like the Egyptian's nor broad and flat like the typical Nubian's, began in one neat single stroke but pertly turned up at the end. Her lips, firm and straight instead of gently curving, were, like the smooth cheeks, untouched by artificial color. They parted now, with slow deliberation, as the girl lifted her eyes to the face of the newcomer and studied it silently for a few moments with unabashed curiosity.

"You're Moses. I've been waiting for you. It's seemed a long time. There are so many things I want to ask you."

His relief was mingled with bewilderment. What sort of country was this, where the slaves addressed the husbands of their mistresses as equals and were taught to speak perfect Egyptian?

"Sit down here on the mat beside me. You look just as I thought you would. I couldn't see you very plainly from the tower."

She made room for him on the mat beside her, and he sat down. It was good to let his tense muscles relax. "If—if you think she won't m-mind—"

"She?"

160

"My—my—" His voice stumbled. "I mean the queen, your mistress."

"Oh!" She was silent for a moment, her eyes searching his face curiously. They were brown eyes, he noticed, very clear, unbroken by any sparkling flecks of green or amber. "No. She won't mind."

Her voice was surprisingly rich and full for that of a child. Moses had a fleeting impression that he had heard it before, but he could not remember where. He did not try to remember. He was sure the memory was connected with something disturbing, and at the moment he felt completely at ease both in mind and body. This simple child was no woman to make him tongue-tied and self-conscious, no Nefretiri to stir his senses. Even her casual movements were unhurried and deliberate. In her presence he experienced an odd feeling of serenity and fulfillment.

"Tell me about Egypt," said the girl eagerly. "There are so many things I haven't been able to find out. Is there really a great god of stone who sits in the desert and watches what men do, his countenance like that of a king and his body like that of a lion? And are there mountains which men have made with their own hands, as high as those in which the Blue River is born? And is it there that the souls of men enter through the narrow gate into the west, where the thirty-two monsters lie in wait to devour them? And how do they know that there are monsters there? Has anyone ever seen them? Please, Moses, quickly! Tell me everything you know!"

He laughed indulgently. "That wouldn't take long."

She leaned toward him, her every motion still unhurried, but with a sudden urgency in her voice. "Don't laugh at me. I can't bear it if you laugh. Have you not felt, ever, that there were things you must know or something would burst within you? What lies beyond the mountain, perhaps, or—why men die digging yellow dust out of the ground?"

Moses sobered instantly. "Yes," he said. "I'm sorry. I shouldn't have laughed. I have felt just that way."

He answered her questions then as well as he could, amazed that a mere child, much less a barbarian slave, could be conversant with such names as Ipuwer and Hammurabi and Ptahhotep. Though his body remained at ease, his mind was as agreeably alert as in the stimulating society of his teacher Maruma,

"Where did you learn all these things?" he asked at last, curiously. "And who taught you how to speak such perfect Egyptian?"

The brown eyes locked briefly with his, then fell. Had Moses imagined there was a hint of mischief in them? "Suppose we say it was my—my mistress who taught me."

He sprang up. The warmth of ease had left him. "I—I must g-go," he stammered.

She stood beside him, taller than he would have thought, the top of her dusky head reaching almost to a level with his shoulders. "Where must you go? And why?"

"In th-there where m-my—" the words choked in his throat—"where the queen is waiting."

"Do you really like queens?" she asked, her small nose wrinkling. "I don't. They are such stupid creatures. Please don't go." Her voice became childishly eager. "There are so many things you have not yet told me. And there are things I must tell you too, and show you. Did you know that if you stand on the highest turret of Saba and stretch your arms high, like this, you can brush your fingers against the stars? And if you listen very hard, you can hear the singing and shouting of the waters as they leap the cataracts?"

Moses knew now where he had heard her voice. "You were the one who sang," he said wonderingly.

"Yes." She began to sing again, softly.

"B-but I don't understand." He looked at her in bewilderment. "Were you singing the song for—for her—for my—my—"

"Yes. For her. For your bride. Your *wife.*"

Placing her hands on his shoulders, she lifted herself suddenly on tiptoe and pressed her lips to his. He felt a swift pulsing of warmth and looked down at the girl in startled wonder. For the kiss she had given him had come not from a child but from a woman.

"Who are you?" he whispered. "What is your name?" This time there was no mistaking the mischief in her eyes.

"Tharbis," she replied.

4

Not since the days of the great Thutmose had so much wealth poured toward Egypt from the Land of Gold. Tharbis, queen of Saba, leaving the government of her city to an unloved brother, was glad to empty its treasures into the lap of her new husband. Lashed to the surfaces of tough woven sailing rafts and covered tightly with protective sheaths of leather, the riches of Kush rode safely down the narrow, winding green strip of river valley between the blazing gold of the deserts, sometimes on the turbulent breast of the river, sometimes on the swaying black shoulders of the slaves who were themselves its richest portion.

Tutu was in his element. His hands ceased to tremble, and his well-nourished body reassumed its plumpness, with some additions. As the piles of treasure mounted and new boats were loaded at each stopping place, fabulous figures flowed beneath his fingers.

"One thousand elephant tusks," his brush would glibly record the day's accretions. "Two bales ostrich feathers, three boatloads ebony logs, two thousand Negro slaves, sixty panther skins, sixteen apes of a kind no pharaoh has ever seen, a thousand long-horned oxen, gold..."

Gold. The natives grubbing in their tiny garden plots knew what the Egyptian wanted. The news of his coming swept down the river with the first "teardrop" which brought the promise of the coming flood. Panic-stricken, they fled into the eastern desert, where, feverishly, they delved into long-unused shafts, wrested from the rock the broken lumps containing the strange yellow veins of metal, and washed and washed them until there were left only the pale flakes which seemed to them of no earthly use but which the Egyptian seized with greedy eagerness. But if they had hoped by this palliative to satisfy his deeper hunger for their own black bodies, they were doomed to disappointment. When he had passed, the eternal creaking of the shaduf was mingled with the shrill wailing of those whose husbands and sons and brothers had been forged into the lengthening chain of captives.

"From this spot, to all eternity," one conquering pharaoh had inscribed on a granite column just below the Second Cataract, "no Negro shall sail down the Nile." As a free man, the conqueror had meant, of course. Not as a slave.

Slowly the triumphant caravan moved down the river, like insects crawling along the back of a coiled serpent, gorging themselves constantly on other lesser insects, lords of their breed but never masters of the monster along whose treacherous back they moved. One flick of his tail, a motion of his darting tongue, merely a slight shifting of his heaving body, and it was as if they had never been. But he was for the most part indifferent, letting them slip about on his glistening coils as their insect ancestors had done; past the turbulent Third Cataract, where Thutmose had stabbed the king of Nubia with his own hand; past the giant columns which proclaimed the glory of

Amenhotep and Sesostris to a handful of naked, gaping peasants; on through the narrow cleft between the deserts.

Moses had not wanted to visit the gold mines. Any, the viceroy of Kush, anxious to find favor in the eyes of the king's nearest friend, had insisted on the expedition. They had traveled east for days, coming at last to a small settlement of stone huts in an unsheltered valley deep in the burning desert. The water from the previous winter's scanty rainfall had been collected in two large cisterns, close to the sloping tables which served for gold washing.

Here in this desolate place a hundred or more slaves, men, women, and children, labored in the heat beneath the whips of a handful of Egyptian overseers. Following the veins of quartz deep into the heart of the mountain, they first burned the hard stone brittle by fire, then, toiling by the light of little lamps, hoed it out with iron picks, while children carried away the pieces. Outside in the burning sun women and old men crushed the pieces in stone mortars, then pounded them to dust in mills. The dust was then placed on the sloping tables and washed until only the fine glinting particles remained, to be collected finally and kept for five days in closed clay smelting pots.

"The foremen have to watch them like hawks," said Any, "or they will drink the water that runs from the washing tables. But they've found a clever way of curing them. See that man chained to the rock in the hot sun within a few feet of the cistern? He hasn't had a drop to drink for two days, yet he can both see water and hear it dripping. Clever—what?"

Moses looked at the crouching figure, then quickly averted his eyes. But the brief glance had recorded the details: bloodshot eyes, swollen tongue, cracked lips trying frantically to suck a few beads of sweat from the parched flesh. "Yes," he said. "Very clever."

"He'll think twice after this before he takes more than his half cup a day," chuckled Any. He wet his lips and hopefully watched his distinguished visitor for signs of approval. He was tired of being viceroy in Nubia and wanted a good report taken back to the pharaoh. "The output is twice what it was when I came here," he continued eagerly. "They were giving the men too much water and didn't have enough to wash the gold."

"Didn't the men object," asked Moses, "when their supply of water was reduced? After all, it isn't pleasant to be thirsty."

Any's moist eyes blinked. Then he laughed loudly. He would not have supposed the stern-faced young general had such a sense of humor. A slave objecting! He laughed even louder. It was really one of the funniest jokes he had ever heard. Someone should draw a picture of it—a slave sitting down on his job with a solicitous overseer standing beside him with a tray of fine foods and wines. He was going to get along well with the general. He might even dare to suggest that his name be mentioned as a possibility for vizier. He clapped Moses intimately on the shoulder.

"I see what you mean. A man does get thirsty in this furnace. As soon as we get back to the pack donkeys we'll open a couple of wineskins."

Moses was glad when the trip was over. Entering the encampment, he made straight for his tent, avoiding the heavily guarded strings of Any's pack animals which were adding to his treasure stores the precious harvest of the mine he had just visited. He wanted to forget the mines and everything connected with them as soon as possible.

Confusion suddenly loomed in his way. A crowd of hooting officers and soldiers were gathered about some central focus of interest. The air was redolent with oaths, shrill whistles of derision, and catcalls.

"That's the way! Flay the demons out of the stinking swine!"

"By Amon and his ram's head, we'll show these heathen!"

"Open him up and see if he has an ass's belly!"

Moses pushed his way determinedly toward Ahmose, who stood, arms folded and a broad grin on his face, in the center. "What's going on here?" he demanded.

The subordinate, still grinning, snapped to attention. "One of the new captives got away," he explained, "but the guards caught him. We're just teaching him a lesson."

Moses looked at the slim figure on the ground, writhing beneath the strokes of the lash. He noticed that the face of the man who wielded it was smiling. The broad red welts on the slender back swam before his eyes and he could not have spoken if he had tried. But there was no need for words. His left hand shot out and seized the uplifted arm, while his right tore the lash from its grasp. With a swift gesture he spun the surprised guard to his knees and whipped the thin coil again and again across his back.

"There!" Pulling him again to his feet, he gave him a push which sent him reeling. "You know how it feels. At least next time you won't feel like laughing." He turned abruptly to a gaping Ahmose. "Unloose the slave's chains. Get the blood washed off his back and his wounds rubbed with oil. And be quick about it!"

He stood watching while his dazed subordinate hastily executed his commands. The circle of onlookers had warily widened their orbit and now maintained a tense, curious silence. He was completely unaware of their presence. When the red welts had been washed with oil and the slave lifted to his feet, Moses turned again to Ahmose.

"Give him food and water," he ordered curtly, "enough to last him for several days. After that take him to the edge of the encampment and let him go."

Then he turned abruptly and strode away. This time the crowd parted as if by magic, dissolving into a confused blur of incredulous features. Out of the blur one face swung slowly into focus. Tutu's. Something in its sardonic scrutiny cooled the fever within him. As always after one of his hot bursts of temper, he felt suddenly drained of all vigor.

"The friend of the pharaoh has been too long in the heat of the sun," said the scribe slowly. "Let me accompany him to his tent and apply a quieting lotion to his head. It's no wonder he is not himself, after all those long hours in the desert."

"I am quite myself," replied Moses curtly. "And I need no lotion."

He brushed past the scribe and went on to his tent, his one desire to be alone. Behind the curtain, in the small inner compartment, he sank down weakly on a bench, dropping his head in his hands. When he lifted it, Tharbis was sitting on a mat at his feet, but he did not resent her presence. To him she was coolness rather than heat; a quietly burning candle rather than a consuming fire. Perhaps it was because she was so utterly different from Nefretiri that he no longer begrudged her the place she now occupied in his life. Yet in some way she seemed to fit into the pattern of his love for the young princess. She was the child they might have begotten from their wild passion, the moments of tranquillity that might have followed in the wake of satisfied desire.

She sat now very quietly, her dark slender body perfectly at ease. She was not unpredictable, like Nefretiri. He knew that she would sit like that, nearly motionless, for hours, if his mood demanded quiet. But when she did move, it would be with a calm, deliberate sureness which sprang from a deep inner consciousness of poise and rhythm. Sometimes she wore jewelry, but not today. She seemed to know

166

instinctively when ornaments, or lack of them, would suit his mood. Once, going for a walk along the riverbank in the starlight, she had bedecked herself from head to foot with shining bangles—bracelets, anklets, a dozen necklaces, a high tiara with almost as many jewels as the milky way. It was the only time he had ever known her to look like a queen, and there had been none but him to see her. Usually, as now and on their wedding night, she wore a simple tunic of white linen which left her slender brown arms and lower limbs completely free but, unlike the transparently fine, tight-fitting garment of the Egyptian woman, concealed all but the vaguest contours of her small, pointed breasts.

Queer, he reflected occasionally, that on that first night he could have thought her nothing but a child! His soldiers still thought so. He had caught their vulgar quips, seen their mocking, slanting glances as they had swaggered through the Nubian villages in the wake of a buxom female. But they had not felt the tremulous urgency of her lips nor lain by her side...

"I just did a strange thing," he said abruptly.

"Yes," she replied. "I know. I was watching from the tent. Why did you do it?"

"I—don't know. I didn't stop to think, I guess. I just saw him lying there on the ground the way—the way—"

"Yes?" Her voice encouraged without insisting.

Until he told her the story of the young Shasu whom he had tried to set free he had not realized how close the memory lay to the threshold of his mind. When he had finished, the palms of his hands were as wet with sweat as on the morning when he had seen the limp body hanging beneath the circling black shadows.

"I understand," said Tharbis gently. "And when you saw the slave being beaten today it brought it all back. You had to do what you did, to make up for what you failed to do long ago. Now perhaps you will be free!"

He looked at her wonderingly. Where had she got her uncanny gift for understanding? From the moody, tempestuous Nubian queen who had been her mother? From the clever Sinuhe, who, Moses suspected, had in a careless moment sired her? Or from her own quiet contemplation of the savage but strangely harmonious landscape of her childhood?

"They are calling me a fool," said Moses. "Before nightfall every soldier in camp will be laughing behind my back."

"Suppose they are," replied Tharbis evenly. "Did you listen to their scoffing when you marched across the desert? If you wished—" Beneath the smoothness of her voice there was that sudden note of reckless wildness, like the distant sound of the cataracts. "If you wished, you could free every prisoner in camp."

Because of that note Moses held his head high when he left the tent for his evening round of the encampment. If there was whispering among the men, it subsided at sight of his determined features.

Tutu, waiting in a convenient shadow, ready with stern syllables of reproof, drew back. Moses' mood of rebellion obviously persisted. A pity, too. His first really unpredictable action since leaving Thebes. But a servant of Amon could not afford to be even slightly unpredictable. A man who asked questions was bad enough, but one who went about freeing slaves—However, the river also veered off into surprising detours after it seemed well settled in its channel. By the whiskers of Bast, he had actually come to like the fellow! After all, the sun had been terribly hot.

"The orders of the general have been carried out," reported Ahmose respectfully after one glance at his face. "The slave was taken to the edge of camp and given a good parting—" About to say "kick," he hastily changed his mind. "A good parting supply of drink and victuals. Let's just hope," he added with more boldness, "the other slaves don't get any ideas. They outnumber us ten to one."

"I'm going to inspect them now," replied Moses briefly.

It amused him to feel Ahmose's wary glance following him as he turned toward the prisoners' pens. He was conscious of other eyes straining curiously after him through the dusk. Fools! Did they think he was going to repeat his performance? They did not know why he had done it, and if they had, they would not have understood like Tharbis. How right she had been! It was himself he had set free, not a slave for whose black hide he cared no more than for one of those eternally wheeling vultures!

Where was the miserable creature now, he wondered. He hoped the soldiers had given him plenty of food and water. But why should he care? What difference did it make to him whether the boy ever reached home or not? It was for his own sake that he had set him free, so that he would never again have to remember...

The stench of the prisoners came to his nostrils. He could hear the shifting of their chains, the constant movement of their bodies. It was the same stench, the same restlessness that had assailed his senses that other night long ago in the desert encampment. The years between might not have been. No, not quite the same. For these were his own prisoners. Except for him they would be back in their mud huts, tilling their thin little strips of green, bending their backs to the creaking shaduf. Well—they had been slaves before, hadn't they? At least in the pharaoh's service they would get enough to eat, even if the rations were often belated. A hungry slave was little good at dragging a thousand-ton monolith. No difference? Scarcely any at all. He laughed aloud, mirthlessly. Merely the difference between a bird chained to a golden post and one winging its way up and up, its white wings glinting in the sunlight!

If you wished, you could free every prisoner in camp.

The voice of Tharbis was again in his ears. Why not? He had but to say the word, and the black tide would go pouring up the riverbank. His campaign would become a farce, and he would be the laughingstock of Thebes.

"Well—suppose you are," Tharbis would say quietly.

What was the matter with him? Why was he different from other men? Their flesh did not sweat, he was sure, at sight of a straining body dragging stones for Amon's temple. They felt no chafing of their own wrists when they heard the grinding of another's chains. Even the gods did not care how one man treated another—certainly not how an Egyptian treated a Nubian. Then why should he?

If you wished—

With a sudden relief he remembered why he had gone to Nubia. The prisoners were to purchase security for Amon-nebet.

If he did not take them back with him, he would betray his trust. He had no choice. Hastily he withdrew to a spot where the stench of the pens no longer reached him.

"See that the guard is doubled," he told Ahmose curtly. "And warn the sentries to keep a sharp lookout. We must not have any more escapes."

5

On the same day, almost in the same hour, two processions flowed through Thebes. One was a funeral cortege: the other, the triumphant parade of a military victor.

The seventy days of mourning had passed. Even as Isis and Anubis had prepared Osiris for his burial, so now this new Osiris had been accorded the elaborate rites of the embalmers: emptied of its viscera, lined with resins and perfumes, soaked for long weeks in brine, stuffed and padded and swathed in yards upon yards of linen bandages interspersed with amulets and magic writings, painted with white stucco, inserted in a nest of fine-wrought wooden coffins, each carved in its own human shape. Covered with flowers, surrounded by wailing females, their breasts bared to the blazing sun, it floated down the river on its gorgeous bark, a cloud of incense mounting upward with the women's lamentations.

"An incense offering to thee," chanted the funerary priest in a shrill monotone. "O Harmachis Khepri, who art in the bark of Nun, the father of the gods, in that Neshmet bark which conducts thither the god and Isis and Nephthys, and this Horus, the son of Osiris."

"Steer to the west," cried another shrill voice to the helmsman, "to the land of the justified. In peace, in peace to the west, thou praised one, come in peace!"

Up the long desert road from the river wound the long procession, following the bark of the sacred dead drawn on a great sledge by oxen; through a narrow cleft in the rocks into a barren valley where the only living creatures were the wheeling vultures; down into the cool darkness through a maze of corridors and galleries and antechambers, the light of their flaring torches revealing painted scenes of sheer perfection—the journey of the soul through its twelve hours of night, its trial, judgment, and final vindication; down—down—

What more could they do for the sacred dead? They had poured out water before him and opened his mouth with magic rites. They had laid him in a sarcophagus of alabaster, carved like a gem. They had surrounded him with thousands of little images of wood and bronze and ivory, counterparts of the slaves who would serve him in that dread land beyond the western desert. They had taken out his sinful heart and put in its place a stone scarab which could not rise up and speak against him in the judgment.

The procession was over. Back to Thebes flowed the mourning multitude, to discover to their satisfaction that another had begun. Their wails changing to shouts of acclaim, they streamed to the gate of the city, hastily gathering fresh flowers to strew in the path of the conquering hero.

Moses received their adulation with outward satisfaction but inner impatience. Just below Elephant Island he and his weary troops had put ashore at army headquarters and freshened their bedraggled appearance. They had exchanged their battered boats for newly polished chariots and sturdy oxcarts. A messenger had been dispatched to Seti. Moses knew the priests of Amon. They preferred the mammoth ugliness of the great hall at Karnak to the graceful delicacy of Seti's Abydos temple. For Amon-nebet's sake he had deliberately made his entrance into Thebes as impressive as possible.

But this was no organized welcome. Neither priest nor government official was in evidence. The crowds that surged about his chariot were merely the riffraff which any parade, however small, picks up in transit. What had happened? Many months had passed since his departure. Had Seti moved on to the north, having accomplished his purpose in Thebes? Had Amon-nebet been confirmed as crown prince and his marriage with Nefretiri consummated? Or had the message never been delivered?

Tortured with uncertainty but reluctant to ask questions of a gaping stranger, Moses rode beside Ahmose through the streets of Thebes. It seemed as if his chariot were being drawn, not by two sleek brown stallions, but by the long rows of black, naked bodies, chained one to the other, herded by the guards along the street ahead of them. He could almost sense within himself the heaviness of a block of limestone or a granite obelisk.

Uncertain of his reception at the royal palace, he had no place to go except to the barracks with the other soldiers. The palace he had formerly occupied was now, doubtless, the property of a new favorite. He was glad of that. The life he had lived there now seemed as remote as his childhood in the harem nursery.

It was Tutu who finally told him. Tutu, who gleaned bits of information from a crowd as easily as another might have caught its wilting flowers!

"The reception accorded the friend of the pharaoh is unfortunate but understandable," he murmured when Moses had barely alighted from his chariot. "After all, on the day of a royal funeral—"

"A funeral!" echoed Moses sharply. "Who—"

"A pity," continued the scribe with unmistakable relish, "that the seventy days of mourning must come to an end almost at the very hour when the victorious young prince was preparing to enter the city, that even while his chariots were being yoked to the horses for their last day's journey the mourning women were smearing earth on their faces and bared breasts—"

"*Who?*" repeated Moses with such explosive finality that Tutu drew back in alarm. Hastily and simply he made answer.

"The young prince, Amon-nebet."

Seti would not eat. The chief cook and baker and butler were at their wits' end to concoct some delicacy that would tempt his palate. Tender gazelle steaks, Charu figs steeped in sweet red wine, meltingly hot breads baked in the cunningest of shapes, even his favorite tiny onions fried in oil—all were sent back un-tasted. The Strong Bull sat alone in his inner chamber, permitting no member of his family or his courtiers to approach him.

Amon-nebet was dead. God though he was, there was nothing further that he, Seti, could do for his son. He had laid him in a chamber of his own unfinished tomb, surrounded him with every object he could possibly desire, made a life-sized statue in his image, and provided a full-time priest to keep food and drink before it at all times. During the seventy days there had been necessity if not incentive for living. Now there was none. He would do as Amon-nebet had done: simply refuse to face a future that demanded greater courage than he had to give.

Perhaps in his case the end would come more quickly. There would not be the long months of wasting away, with the terror in his eyes taking new and stranger shapes each day. If he sat quietly, refusing to let food pass his lips, it might come soon enough for him to overtake his son before he had completed his perilous journey across the Lily Lake. Amon-nebet had always been timid. Even with his ka to help him, would he be able to cajole and bluff the stern old ferryman, Face Behind, into rowing him across? Together, surely they could reach the other shore and brave its monsters. Together they would be admitted through the door of the sky by the gatekeeper of Osiris. Together the blessed Horus would lead them...

"If the Strong Bull will bend his golden horns and look upon his miserable servant, Prince Moses waits upon him."

Moses. The name had been on the lips of his son during those long weeks when most of his babblings had been unintelligible. If Moses had been here, perhaps Amon-nebet would not have died. But for some reason Moses had been sent away. Far away. Seti frowned, trying for the first time in many days to concentrate. To Nubia. To quell a revolt in that far country known as Kush. And he had succeeded. He had married a Nubian queen, and was returning with much gold and many prisoners. For Amon-nebet.

"Send him in," ordered Seti abruptly.

Moses looked down at the motionless figure and felt a swift upsurging of affection and pity. The customary phrases of homage died on his lips. He laid his hand on the thin shoulder.

"I loved him too," he said simply.

"Yes," replied Seti. He knew now that Moses had not been responsible for the unfortunate episode in the temple. If he had needed further proof, he would have found it now in the reflection of his own naked grief on the face looking down into his. "I was wrong," he continued, rousing himself with an effort to speak. "It was Ramses who made me believe you had done it, fooling me into believing he was concerned for his brother. When was Ramses ever concerned for anyone but himself?"

"It does not matter," said Moses.

"No. Nothing matters."

They talked of Amon-nebet, each deriving a peculiar solace from mingling his grief with the other's. The coldness which had enveloped Seti began to melt, giving way to an agony even more intense.

"He called for you." In the grieved father's voice there was bitter accusation of self. "Over and over he spoke your name. He said you were his strength and courage. If you had been here, you might have saved him. But where were you? In Nubia, where I sent you after gold and slaves. Gold and slaves!" he repeated, his voice rising in a shrill crescendo. "To satisfy the priests of Amon. While my son lay dying!"

"Hush!" said Moses gently. "The Son of Heaven must not reproach himself."

But Seti would not be silenced. The waters of his emotions had been too long frozen. "It was they who killed my son, the priests of Amon. They feared him because he looked like the only man who ever managed to curb their power, the only man living for centuries who has not feared them. No—" a gleam appeared in the slanting, almond-shaped eyes— "not the only one."

The realization came to him with a suddenness which again struck his spare, erect body into rigidity. He also was not afraid of the priests of Amon. Not any longer. It was for the sake of his son that he had feared. And now his son was dead. Bitter irony! The death of his son had set him free—now that he had no desire for freedom. He had nothing to keep him from living life to the full—now that he had nothing for which to live. Nothing? When that vast hierarchy which had brought about his son's death was locked in a deadly grapple for power with his own office of pharaoh? When from Thebes into all of Egypt its greedy tentacles were reaching out—

"Amon-nebet was right," he murmured, half to himself. "You are strong, and you have courage. With you to help me, Moses, we can get that northern city built. We can make Per-Ramses, not Thebes, the center of the empire. And slowly, drop by drop, we might bleed the gluttonous body of the priests of Amon. You and I together."

Deliberately Seti reached toward the silver tray resting close to his elbow, selected from it a tender onion fried in oil, and placed it in his mouth.

PART V

1

With a suddenly awakened purpose in living Seti plunged into action which would hasten the execution of his plans. The seat of government, he proclaimed, would be moved immediately to the north: first to Memphis, later, when his new city was completed, to Per-Ramses. Egypt was a world empire now, and Thebes was no longer her center.

Moses, the strong right arm in the fulfillment of his scheme, was publicly restored to favor. He was again given "the gold," that highest of all tributes, and the title of *"very* nearest friend" was conferred upon him. The palace of Amenhotep was closed. The warning rumbles of Amon, who feared lest his son might wander too far from the protection of his benevolent ram's horns, fell on deaf ears. Even the god's obdurate refusal to render approval by weighing heavily on the shoulders of his priests failed to deter Seti from his purpose. He would consult the Apis bull in Memphis, he told Amenemhat imperturbably. And, bundling his royal family into the *Star of the Two Lands*, he sailed down the river toward the City of the White Wall.

The Apis, as Seti had expected, was heartily in accord with his enterprise. Emerging through the bronze doors of his palatial stable, with his small eyes glaring viciously at his adoring worshipers and the white crescent-shaped spot which was the mark of his divinity quivering on his black flank, the sacred bovine made straight for the little door marked "Yes," in his haste almost dragging the two priests who bore the ends of his long solid-gold chain.

Sending Moses to the Delta to hasten the completion of his new city, Seti established his family in the palace at Memphis. He would have breathed a sigh of relief except for one circumstance. Tuya was in Memphis. He would have to listen again to her nagging pleas to make her son Ramses his successor to the throne. And Seti was not ready to make that promise. Not yet.

Beket was gloatingly happy. Not only was she back again in her mistress' favorite apartment, but she had another child to mother. On leaving for the Delta, Moses had entrusted his new wife, Tharbis, to his foster mother's nurse.

"Please be—kind to her," he had asked Sitra hesitantly, not quite knowing how to phrase his concern. "She—may be a queen, but she's also—well, a child. And it's not easy to be in a strange land."

Beket, who had no awe of queens, received Tharbis with open arms, lavishing upon her all the affection she had once bestowed on her mistress' foster son. She combed and pomaded and waxed the long black hair until it was as shining as polished ebony, then arranged it in endless combinations of plaits, curls, and waterfalls. She rubbed countless lotions into the soft, dusky skin and experimented with perfumes for hours on end in order to find exactly the right combination to suit the child's elusive and slightly savage beauty.

"Don't waste too much energy on her," Sitra advised dryly. "You'll have none to spare when Moses gets him a real wife—though I can hardly imagine the Princess Nefretiri's permitting a slave to tell her what foods to eat and what perfumes to use."

Beket's eyes gleamed. "He isn't married to the Princess Nefretiri yet," she replied stubbornly, "and he is married to my lady Tharbis."

Sitra looked annoyed. "But of course it was only a marriage of convenience, which means almost nothing at all. The girl is more concubine than wife."

At the first opportunity Beket procured a magic potion compounded of the milk of a lying-in woman, the urine of a pregnant cat, and other efficacious elements, which she rubbed, surreptitiously but thoroughly, into the unsuspecting Tharbis' scalp. So she wasn't a real wife, poor little mite! Maybe they'd sing a different tune when she bore Prince Moses a lusty son and heir!

Sitra was triumphant. So certain was she now of the outcome of her scheme that she could not resist flaunting her satisfaction in her rival's face. Not that she intended to disclose the details of her plan. No, she would merely sit and listen and pretend she was sharing Tuya's triumph. Her own would be all the sweeter because it was enjoyed in secret. Smiling, she entered the queen's apartment.

But when she saw Tuya lying on the massive couch, she felt no triumph. The waxen face, the pinched nostrils and bloodless lips, as brightly painted as a statue's, might already have felt the touch of the embalmer. Only the dark eyes blazing in their deep sockets were thoroughly alive.

"Don't!" said Tuya sharply before Sitra had time to open her lips. "Don't say it. I don't want to be pitied."

"I didn't come to pity you," replied Sitra gently. "Why should I? He who accomplishes what he most desires is not to be pitied."

"And you think I have accomplished what I most desire?"

"Why not?" Finding the unswerving gaze of the dark eyes oddly disconcerting, Sitra looked away. "Amon-nebet is no longer in the way of your ambitions."

Tuya laughed, and it was not a pleasant sound. "You really thought you were fooling me, didn't you? Making me think you were consumed with loyalty to my Ramses when it was your precious Moses in whose interest you were scheming and conniving!"

"You—you don't know what you're saying!" Sitra's warmth of pity changed to sudden startled coldness. "I—What could possibly have given you such a mad idea!"

Tuya's clawlike fingers plucked at the coverlet. "It's you who had the mad idea." Her voice was faint now, the words punctuated by little rasping breaths. "Thinking you could put—Moses on the throne. I know all your plans. You counted on Nefretiri being—in love with him. What if she—is! You yourself were—in love, but the Mitannian prince didn't become—pharaoh of Egypt. And neither will—Moses. No, not even if you could prove that he's really your son. And you can't—do that—not ever—because he isn't. And I—I know—who he—really is!"

Except for the stabbing thrusts of Tuya's labored breathing the room was absolutely quiet. Sitra's heart seemed to have stopped beating, "How—" she murmured faintly.

"How did I—find out—who he is? You thought you—were quite safe, didn't you? No one knew—where he had come from. Even the slaves—who had seen him that first day—had never seemed to connect the two—the child you brought one day to the palace as your son—and that other—" Tuya was speaking more easily now. The blazing eyes seemed to have kindled in her a fresh store of energy.

"At first you didn't try to keep his origin a secret," she continued more calmly. "When all the conflicting stories started, it merely amused you. It was only later, when you planned to make him pharaoh, that you tried to suppress the facts about his birth. You made certain that all the attendants who had been with you the day you found him were no longer in the royal household. But you forgot one. Memnet. And Memnet remembered."

Sitra found her voice. "And you believed her foolish blabbings," she injected scornfully. "Even if her story were true, whatever it was she told you, it would make no difference. Moses is the king's favorite. Seti leans on him as on a staff. He is second to no man in the kingdom." Recklessly Sitra flaunted before her rival all the little triumphs she had intended to keep secret. "Yes, and Nefretiri is in love with him, your own daughter, who is as stubborn as you in getting her own way. You can no more keep Moses from becoming pharaoh than—than—"

"Than you can hope to make him so," finished Tuya steadily. Her brief energy consumed, she slipped even deeper into the enveloping cushions. "I—I'm warning you—Ramses is going to be—king. Nothing can—stop him. If you try, you'll be—sorry. I'll make him king if—if I have to—" She stopped, gasping for breath, the soft linen cloth which she pressed to her mouth suddenly as crimson as her painted lips. Startled, Sitra summoned a slave. She knew that her interview with Tuya was ended.

She was not smiling when she left the queen's apartment.

2

It was the beginning of the season of growing. All along the river the fellahin were planting their crops. In the black, moist soil left by the receding waters they sowed the seed broadcast, then dragged branches across the muddy surface to cover it. Some scattered their seed over the mud flats even before the flood receded, rowing over the shallow waters in their rude papyrus boats, then driving cattle in to tread it down. Watching curiously from his cabin on the boat that bore him to the Delta, Moses saw one fellah wade into the water with a calf on his shoulders, the anxious mother following at his heels. Presently a whole herd was wallowing after her, their clumsy hoofs burying the precious seed in the rich silt

Like human beings, thought Moses grimly. *If one man is sure where he's going, no matter whether he's saint or demon, he'll always find plenty who are willing to follow.*

It had not been a good inundation, less than thirteen ells, and a fevered desperation pervaded the fellahin's every gesture. For a flood of only twelve ells meant hunger. In the fields untouched by the rising of the river, wooden plows were loosening the cracked earth, naked children following in their wake to break the hard, dry clods with mallets. With a fierce, dogged grimness the fellahin lowered and raised their gaunt arms in rhythm with the creaking shaduf, filling, hoisting, emptying, filling, hoisting, emptying. It was a losing battle from the start. Try as they would, they could not possibly slake the vast thirst of the soil with their little buckets of goats hide. It was hard enough in a good year to make their tiny plots yield enough grain to fill their children's stomachs and pay their taxes. Overhead the wheeling falcons mingled their harsh plaints with the wailing of the shaduf, and the hoopoes screamed their defiance. Only the fellahin were silent.

Last year, thought Moses irrelevantly, *Amon received over two hundred thousand bushels of grain on his feast days alone. And he owns five hundred and eighty-three thousand acres, tax exempt.*

As he passed On, the City of the Sun, Moses wished suddenly that Tharbis had come with him. He would like to show her the sacred stone where the phoenix, winging his way from the far-off lands of spices and perfumes, had built his funeral pyre and perished, to rise again out of its ashes. She would laugh delightedly, then suddenly sober, and that curious, questing look, like an alert animal trying to see in two directions at once, would come into her wide-set eyes.

"Where did he go from here?" she would ask with simple directness.

Well—and where had he gone? Was there more truth than myth in the old legend? Had wisdom flown from the altars of Egypt long ago, leaving but a pile of ashes? Moses did not stop at On, though he had intended to pay a visit to his teacher, Maruma. He went straight on into the Delta.

Seti's new city of Per-Ramses, named in honor of his father, was not progressing rapidly. Approaching it by water, along one of the eastern branches of the Nile, Moses felt a keen sense of disappointment. The walls were only half finished, the temple was a mere shell fronted by a majestic but still uncarved pylon, the royal palace barely begun. It would be months, perhaps years, before the city would be ready for occupation. Establishing his headquarters in the army barracks, Moses promptly dispatched several brief but cogent messages stamped with the royal seal and was rewarded by the early appearance of Baka, Seti's commissioner of building for the Delta.

"If the noble prince had but warned us," protested that official regretfully but without dismay, "we would have made suitable preparations for his coming."

"Yes," retorted Moses. "I suppose you would have finished the palace in time for me to occupy one of the royal suites. I'm warning you now. The pharaoh himself is coming. And it will take something more substantial than regrets to satisfy him."

Baka continued his glib apologies. There had been insuperable difficulties. He would tell the friend of the pharaoh the whole story. But not here. Over a goblet of Lebanon wine, perhaps, in his own miserable lodgings.

The miserable lodgings, Moses discovered, were a palatial residence, quite finished, in a choice section of the new city. In a cool, pillared dining hall, its walls decorated with bright paintings, he sat regarding his host with the utmost distaste. Just what was it he disliked most about Baka, he wondered. The sound of his harsh voice which reminded him of the creaking of a shaduf? The sharpness of his small, mahogany-colored eyes set too deeply in his fleshy face, like dried dates pressed firmly into a soft lump of dough? Or perhaps it was his lips, which never fully closed and seemed always to have been recently moistened by an exploring tongue. Or his hands...

"So it's these Hebrew squatters who are responsible for the delay," he commented tersely after the creaking had proceeded for some moments without interruption. "Why?"

Yes, it was his hands, Moses decided as the commissioner carefully picked from a tray the largest and most succulent of a mountain of sweetmeats. They were very small and soft, like the hands of a child, and the nails, which had been allowed to grow very long, were painted a dainty, shell-like pink. They seemed to make of the hardheaded, coarse-tongued official some hybrid creature, like the fabled sag or gryphon, with the head of one animal and the body of another.

Yes. With barely an interlude for the dipping of the bucket the creaking began again. It certainly was the Hebrews. And of all the ass-headed, swine-bellied sons and daughters of Set who had ever issued from the ill-smelling slime in which all foreigners were spawned, they were the worst. They thought that because they had been allowed to do as they pleased for a few generations, running their dirty sheep over the best pasture land of the Delta, they actually owned the place. If only they'd been treated like slaves from the start—

"It has been the policy of Egypt," Moses reminded the official curtly, "to permit nomads to come over the border. They've come for various reasons, some to escape famine, some to seek protection. It has been to the interest of Egypt to have them here as a buffer against invading armies from Asia."

"Harmhab didn't think so," replied Baka shrewdly. "He saw that in case of invasion these squatters might be a danger instead of a protection. A nice advance regiment of the enemy right inside our walls. Yes, and he did something about it. Remember? No, of course you don't. You were just about being born at the time. But he certainly killed off some of the rats. In fact, the general who directed the purge was a slight connection of yours." The small eyes gleamed maliciously.

At the subtle reference to Ramses, his foster mother's husband, Moses flushed self-consciously. He changed the subject abruptly. Hebrews or no Hebrews, he reminded Baka, his delay was reprehensible. Negligence in the service of the Strong Bull was a crime punishable by death.

Baka helped himself to another sweetmeat, his soft fingers fondling it in anticipation. Let the very nearest friend of the pharaoh not judge too hastily, he advised soothingly. Wait until he had seen the Hebrews. The stubborn fools would break their knees before they'd bend them. He had even tried Harmhab's favorite remedy for lawbreakers, picking out the most rebellious, cutting off their noses, and sending them to Tharu.

"With one exception," qualified the commissioner, a bright predatory gleam in his eye. "Let us say, rather, all but the most rebellious. You'll understand why when you see her."

"See whom?" asked Moses sharply.

Baka was evasive. The gleam might have been for the dripping sweetmeat which he still held caressingly and kept eyeing with anticipatory relish. If the friend of the pharaoh did not believe the Hebrews' ungodly beards sprouted from asses' heads, he continued, let him listen to this: Last month when the provisions had failed to arrive, a common occurrence in slave outfits like this, the stiff-necked sons and daughters of Set had *refused to work!* No rations, they had maintained stubbornly, no labor. He had ordered them whipped and tortured, but to what effect? They had merely stretched themselves on the ground and bared their backs to the lash. What was a man to do?

"Well—what did you do?" asked Moses curiously.

Still eyeing the sweetmeat, Baka ran his tongue over his lips. "Let them starve, of course," he retorted contemptuously. "When the bread and onions finally arrived, I put them under military guard, and that's where they are right now. I can be as stubborn as they can. I tell you it's unbelievable. Nothing like it ever happened in Egypt. Wait till you see. I'll show you the whole outfit tomorrow."

With a final caress of anticipation he popped the sweetmeat into his mouth. His jaws revolved slowly, and there was a faint crunching sound.

If he were a vulture, thought Moses, *he would not be satisfied with the flesh of his victim. He would consume it bones and all.*

He did not wait for the proposed tour of investigation. Early the next morning he ordered one of the army carriages and, with White Elephant as his sole companion, started on an inspection of his own.

The Valley of Goshen, near the northern edge of which Seti's new city was being built, was one of the most fertile spots in the Delta. Watered by a long canal stretching from the Nile almost to the Bitter Lakes which formed the eastern border of Egypt, it lay like an elongated emerald in its setting of bronze-gold desert. Here, scattered in sprawling clusters over a wide area from the banks of the canal almost to the outskirts of Per-Ramses, were the mud or reed huts of the squatters. Riding through one such settlement, Moses gazed at it curiously. At least, he thought, most of the interlopers had had enough sense to learn to build houses like their civilized neighbors' instead of clinging to their old black goatskin tents. It was the only custom of their barbaric nomad ancestors, however, which they seemed to have discarded. The hideous bright striped wools, most of them soiled and tattered, the untrimmed beards, the flocks of dirty, fat-tailed sheep grazing along the edges of the marshland, were all repugnant to his fastidious Egyptian tastes.

The earth swarmed with brown-skinned men. They peered at him from the cavernous mouths of open doorways, slipped like shadows through the tall grass beside the road, materialized suddenly so close to his horse's head that time after time the animal reared in fright. Faces, all unbelievably gaunt, bodies so thin that each separate bone was clearly outlined, moved with such steady continuity before his eyes that they seemed to merge into one identity.

Fools! he thought with mounting irritation. *What are they trying to do—starve themselves out of sheer spite so that Seti will have no man power to build his city? Why don't they kill their miserable sheep and eat them if they're too stubborn to pay the price of getting the pharaoh's bread and onions!*

Baka's taskmasters, he noticed, had not been neglecting their duty. Scarcely a brown back met his eye which did not show the deep teeth marks of the lash. Swollen limbs, lacerated hands and feet and lips bore mute evidence of other instruments of torture. Complete silence greeted his approach. Ahead he could hear normal sounds—a woman's scolding voice, the harsh gutturals of a sheep tender, the shrill wailing of children—but as soon as his horse and carriage came in sight every other sound died. A wall of grim faces reared itself about him, behind, ahead, on either side. He could hear White Elephant, squatting on the floor of the small, two-wheeled cart, clucking uneasily. But he felt no fear, only a deep sense of uneasiness and irritation.

"Lord printh keep eye on foreign demonth," warned White Elephant with sudden urgency. "Put whip to horth. Get out of here quick!"

Moses reached for his whip, but it was too late. With the swiftness of shadows, dark hands were reaching for his horse's bridle. The beast was rearing, pawing crazily at the air, tossing his splendid head until his glossy mane was as disheveled as the untrimmed beards of the creatures within whose iron grasp he was imprisoned; then, quivering, he stopped his struggling. White Elephant, chattering as excitedly as the monkey he resembled, was shoved rudely aside. Before he had time to analyze the situation, Moses was dragged from his carriage. Fingers with the sharpness of talons snatched at the gold collar about his neck and, unable to find its fastening, pulled and twisted until its blunt edges pressed painfully into his flesh. His carefully curled wig was torn from his head, his outer garment of fine linen wrested from his body. After his initial bewilderment he felt oddly detached and impersonal.

"Why not?" he asked himself. "This is the very thing I've expected to happen—in the mines and quarries, in the temple at Karnak. It's what I would do if I were in their place."

He was no longer surrounded by silence. The mumbling of some desert jargon was in his ears, its low threatening tones rising in pitch and increasing in tempo like an approaching storm. Presently he became conscious of one voice standing out above the others. It belonged, he noted, to a bronzed young squatter not much older than himself, obviously the ringleader in the present assault Moses knew suddenly that his fate was in the hands of this gaunt, sunburned Hebrew, whose long hair, surprisingly neat and well arranged, was as black and crisply curling as his own. He stared at him spellbound, marveling at the words tumbling from his lips, suddenly realizing that he was speaking in passable Egyptian.

"...know how it feels to be driven like cattle, to wallow in mud to your knees, to feel the sweat mingling with the blood from your tortured back! Day after day after day, without any hope of release, staggering up from your straw before dawn, dropping down on it at night, too tired to wash the filth from your flesh! Hating the sun, you whose fathers from the beginning of time have steeped their bodies in its life-giving rays, cursing it now as an instrument of death! You, there, with the well-fed stomach and the jewels around your neck! Did you ever plunge those soft ringed hands into the mud, move your aching

185

muscles to the tune of a whip—faster, faster, until every breath you drew was like hot sand drawn into your throat? No, but you're going to do it now!"

Strong hands seized Moses and dragged him through the settlement into its bordering marshland. He felt his feet plunging down a sharp incline, mud oozing about his ankles. His detached mood vanished. Hot resentment flooded through him. Struggling violently, he lashed out blindly at his captors.

"Ha!" The voice taunted. "So those arms aren't as puny as they look! Where did you get all that strength? Wielding the lash on the backs of your groveling captives? Good! You need strength to make bricks and build cities for the pharaoh. Show him, men! Somebody get him a basket! There, that's the way! You have to have mud to make bricks. You can't just stand in it. Put your hands down deep, scoop it up, fill your basket!"

Thrusting him forward, they plunged his arms into the black mud. Choked with rage, he seized it in great handfuls and flung it about him in all directions until his arms were again pinned tightly and he stood, trembling with anger but impotent.

"That's right, a lash! An Egyptian can't get bricks made without a whip. Braid some of those stiff reeds together—"

Sharp pain stung him between his shoulder blades, across his back, his thighs. He was thrust forcibly to his knees and his arms plunged again into the mud, this time to his elbows. He clamped his lips tightly together. Baka had been right. The ass-headed, swine-bellied fools! No torture was too inhuman for them. But he could be as stubborn as they. Let them tear his back to ribbons, they would not bend his will to theirs. They could plunge his hands into the mud, but they could not make him scoop it up. His will belonged to no living soul on earth except himself. He would not make a single brick for them—no, not if they killed him!

The pain pulsed through him in waves, threatening to submerge him into unconsciousness, but not quite succeeding. His flesh burned. They were trying other methods of torture now, no doubt the ones their foremen had used on them—thrusting sharp objects into his ears, twisting his arms and turning his fingers back at the knuckles. Sweat poured from his body, and he could see the mud at his feet turning a dark, sickish red-brown. His stomach was racked with nausea. Then, suddenly, he knew that he could stand it no longer.

"I—I'll do it—anything you say—" he mumbled.

He was stumbling up the bank with a loaded basket on his shoulders when he heard the woman's voice. Instantly the sound of it awakened a disagreeable memory. He was standing in his chariot, and a tall figure, startling in its beauty, was holding the bridles of his terrified horses, pouring forth such a stream of abusive language as had never before met his ears. Then, a moment later, blinded, stung to the quick with both anger and pain, he was wiping the mud out of his eyes. Her lips were pouring forth just such language now in some strange jargon, and he half expected to feel the stinging slap of mud against his face. It did not come.

Shaking the sweat from his eyes, he looked in the direction of the voice. She was just as he remembered her, except that her beautifully rounded body had become thin—straight, proud shoulders, features as purely chiseled as a new obelisk, black smoldering eyes, and skin as smoothly delicate as new rose petals. In spite of shrunken breasts and hollow cheeks she was still beautiful.

Like a tawny lioness, thought Moses, moved to admiration in spite of discomfort and resentment, *gaunt with hunger but still queen of the jungle.*

The swift barrage of words was addressed not to him but to his captors, and he noted that all, even the eloquent young man with the curly hair and beard, listened respectfully. Before he knew what was happening the heavy basket of mud was removed from his shoulders, and the same strong arms which had dragged him down were assisting him carefully from the mud hole. Again the woman opened her lips, this time in sharp command, and promptly, if a bit sullenly, several of the men departed to do her bidding. Dazed with pain and weariness, Moses dropped to the ground.

When he again became fully conscious, he was lying where he had fallen, but his body felt soothed and clean. Though his back was still sore and bruised, the pain was gone. So were his tormentors. The woman was kneeling beside him on the ground, wiping his limbs on the skirt of her dress.

"Please lie still a little longer," she said when he tried to raise himself. "I have been rubbing oil into your wounds and washing the mud from your body. I have nearly finished."

Her Egyptian was hesitant but intelligible, her voice, no longer sharpened by anger, pleasantly melodious. Seen from a closer vantage, she looked older than he had thought, his senior, perhaps, by a dozen years. The golden bloom of her skin was not that of freshly opened petals. It was the rich ripeness of full maturity.

"My brother is often hotheaded," she continued. "He is young and has many things to learn. It was he who set the other young men upon you and pulled you from your carriage. He does not yet understand that there is nothing to be gained by taking revenge on an individual. It is like striking angrily at the swelling where you have been bitten by a serpent. It does not kill the reptile nor remove his poison, and you only cause yourself more suffering in the end."

Strangely, Moses felt his resentment subsiding. He studied the woman with interest while she emptied more water from the skin and, cupping it first in her hands, capably removed the clinging mud from his feet. They were not beautiful hands. Their skin was rough and coarse, the nails broken, and no amount of water could have removed the grime embedded in their many wrinkles.

"What about refusing to make bricks because your supplies of food failed to come through in time?" asked Moses curiously. "What has it gained you except more suffering? Isn't that another instance of striking angrily at the swelling?"

"No!" Her dark eyes blazed down at him. "It's striking straight at the body of the serpent. It's the only weapon we have to fight it with— the labor of our hands. For without our labor it could not live. It's not you that we're fighting, even though you're a prince of Egypt, one of those who grows fat when the serpent is well fed. You're not the serpent, and neither are our taskmasters who wield the lash. You're just its fangs and as much its slaves as we are."

Moses stared back at her intently. The soreness of his back, the recent indignity to his person became suddenly of small importance. His mind raced to follow her. Not since his scholarly discussions with the wise Maruma had his powers of reason been so acutely challenged. Here, still eluding him but close to his grasp, were the answers to some of his most searching questions.

"You mean," he began slowly, "the serpent is—"

His own mind intercepted both question and answer. No, the serpent was not Egypt. The rich, lazy black valley bared her breasts as willingly to one suckling as to another. The tiny plots of the fellahin grew as lushly green as the vast acres of the pharaoh and the priests of Amon. The serpent was born of men. He had a human mouth and belly. And he fed on human victims. Not because he had a taste for flesh and blood. He was a kind serpent at heart. But it had taken flesh and blood to satisfy his appetite for greatness, to build his pyramids and drag his monoliths. He had not wished to make others hungry. It

188

had merely been necessary if his own belly was to be overfull. And—*he had made his gods in his own image.*

"We have to fight it in this way," said the woman earnestly. "There's nothing else we can do."

"Even if it means you'll be bitten worse?"

"Yes. Even if we all starve. Can't you see? It's not just for ourselves. We're just one link in a long chain. Someone has to suffer—sometime."

"Yes," said Moses. "I see."

And he did. With sudden startling clarity. Suppose the builders of the pyramids had refused to work unless their labors should be lightened. Suppose they had been willing to submit themselves to brutal beatings, to die, in order that a thousand years later their comrades would not be shoveling mangled flesh and bones into a mortar tray at Karnak. But they had not refused, any more than did the stooped, straining figures laboring today in the quarries and mines and tombs and temples; any more than he himself, not an hour ago...

"What makes you Hebrews different from the other slaves?" he demanded of the woman suddenly.

The black eyes flashed. "We are not slaves," she replied with dignity. "We never have been and we never shall be. You cannot make a man a slave by forcing him to make bricks, or by beating him. Only if he himself chooses."

As she continued to wash and dry his feet, Moses stared at her with an ever-deepening astonishment. He had borne a secret resentment against her for years, had exchanged words with her for fewer moments than he could count on his fingers. He was a prince of a master race, and she, in spite of her denial, was a slave. Yet there flowed between them a deep current of understanding.

Suddenly he laughed aloud. "You said your brother was hotheaded." He could not resist the sly gibe. "How about yourself? Is it only after cool reflection that you stop spirited horses, deliver a bitter tirade, and fling handfuls of mud in a passing prince's face?"

Her hands dropped his feet as if they had been leprous. She stared at him, horrified, the blood draining from her face. "You—it was *you*—"

"Yes." He returned her gaze steadily, amused at her reaction to his words. He had expected her to be apologetic, perhaps distressed, but hardly as distraught as this. He hastened to reassure her. "I'll admit I've hated you for it all these years. I've even thought of hunting you down and having you properly punished. But now—"

He stopped suddenly, startled by the look on her face. "And I— I've been letting my hands touch your body!" She sprang to her feet. "You—you'd better go now. At once. This minute. Before I— Your slave will help you to your carriage."

White Elephant was instantly at his side, supporting his bruised shoulders. Moses stood unsteadily on his feet. "But—why? I don't understand. I am the one who should be angry—"

There was suddenly no mistaking the emotion in her blazing eyes. It was neither distress nor apology, but contemptuous hatred.

"My father," she said, "was one of those—bodies you left beside the road that day. It was your chariot that killed him."

3

"The building of the city must proceed," ordered Moses with finality, "at any cost."

Yes, agreed Baka. But how? The very nearest friend of the pharaoh was most wise. What procedure did he recommend? Sending an army into Asia to secure a fresh harvest of captives? Drafting the fellahin?

Impatiently Moses walked the floor of Baka's apartment. The complacency of the man irritated him beyond words. He longed to seize one of the confections from the small hand and force it down the long throat. Yet all that the commissioner said was reasonable. Either the Hebrews must be made to work or other slaves must be secured. The fellahin had already served their term of labor during the inundation. Any other method of securing slaves involved hopeless delay. Yet the pharaoh's city must be built.

"Why not yield to the Hebrews' demand and give them their food?" he asked suddenly.

Baka looked horrified. Surely the friend of the pharaoh was jesting. Give a laboring man what he asked for! Couldn't Moses see what would happen? Tomorrow they would be sniveling and begging for something else—more authority for their Hebrew section bosses, reduced daily quotas, maybe even shorter working days!

Moses could see. "Get the section bosses of the Hebrews together," he suggested with less conviction. "Try reasoning with them."

Baka shook his head. The section bosses were all good tools of his subordinates. If he wanted to try reasoning—the commissioner's eyes narrowed craftily—why not approach the ringleader of the troublemakers?

"If you know who the leader is," said Moses curiously, "why in Amon's name haven't you disposed of him?"

"You will see," replied Baka, running his tongue over his perennially moist lips.

They followed the same route that Moses had taken on his preliminary tour of inspection, but this time a well-armed unit of the guard preceded them, and two of Baka's most rugged construction bosses followed in another chariot, their whips noticeably in evidence. Deliberately Moses kept his eyes averted from the disfigured bodies and haggard faces. He had told no one of his humiliating adventure. White Elephant had nursed him back to health in secret. He himself had invited the attack. He desired no reprisal. In fact, the woman's bitter denunciation had left him with a strange feeling of annoyance, almost of guilt, which all his reasoning powers had not been able to dissipate. It had been Ramses' fault, not his, that the horse had swerved so sharply that day. As it was, the speeding chariot had barely missed his own by a hair. If he had not pulled hard on the reins which Nefu held— There it was again, the fact which he could not escape. If he had not pulled hard on the reins, the father of that disturbing woman would still be alive. He had done it instinctively, to save himself and his chariot. He had had no thought for the men beside the road. Well— *should* he have thought of them? That was the question he was not able to answer.

"Perhaps I should tell you," said Baka when they were standing outside one of the small mud huts, "that the leader of the troublemakers of whom I spoke is—a woman. Her name is Miriam."

There was no time then to turn back. Even before his eyes became adjusted to the dimness inside and he could see the tall, arrogant body, he could feel her blazing scorn.

"Did you bring the rations?" she demanded of Baka without the slightest sign of an obeisance.

One of the two guards who had entered the hut with them thrust her roughly to her knees. "Kneel, slut, when, you speak to the commissioner," he ordered curtly. "And don't speak until you're spoken to."

The woman paid him no notice. Though she remained on her knees, there was no humility in the posture. "Did you?" she repeated.

"No," said Baka. His voice sounded almost apologetic. "I—that is, we—thought it might be advisable to discuss the matter—"

Moses looked sharply at the commissioner, and his lips curled in disgust. For Baka was looking at the kneeling figure with exactly the same anticipatory relish with which he regarded one of his toothsome confections. The broad nostrils, slightly distended, quivered like those of an animal on the scent of its prey.

The woman rose disdainfully from her knees. "If it is words you have brought," she said abruptly, "it is my brother Aaron you want, not I."

Baka watched her avidly as she crossed the room and bent over a woman who lay on a mat in the farthest corner. One glance at their faces, and the relationship between the two was obvious. Though the spare features of the elder were wasted by sickness as well as hunger, one was but the more mature counterpart of the other. There was a resemblance too between the woman on the mat and the young brother Aaron, with the black curly hair and beard, whose presence in the room had been overshadowed by that of Miriam but who now was left to face the emissaries of the pharaoh alone. He was not so scornful of imperial authority as his sister, Moses noted. He did not wait for the guards to thrust him into a kneeling posture, and his eloquent tongue remained discreetly bridled.

He is worried for fear I will tell Baka about his part in the assault, thought Moses, observing his wary glances. *He's brave enough when he has stout backs and strong arms behind him, but now—*

The other male occupant of the hut bore no resemblance to the rest of the family. Big and square and stolid, his thick brown hair and beard framing a face in which all emotions were guarded behind unsmiling lips and watchful, intelligent eyes, he might have been a sturdy reef breaking and steadying the swift, stormy currents of these other more emotional personalities. The husband of the woman called Miriam, decided Moses. And was the slender, black-eyed girl with the two tiny scarecrow faces peering out from behind her skirt Aaron's wife?

The air in the unventilated hut was so close he could hardly breathe. Acrid smoke from the sheep-dung fire smoldering in the center of the floor stung both eyes and nostrils. Whiskers of Bast! Did all these people live together in this one cramped room and its small adjoining courtyard? There was barely room to stretch enough mats for their beds on the hard earthen floor.

The discussion between Baka and Aaron was worse than ineffectual. The commissioner understood no technique except threat and bluff, and the young Hebrew was too clever to be bluffed and too stubborn to yield to bombastic threatening. What he might have done if he had been alone was unpredictable, but with his sister's towering strength just behind him, her will breathing his less ardent convictions into flame, his obstinacy increased and Moses' admiration with it.

"No, no, no! How many thousand times must we say it! We have earned our rations and we shall not make another brick until we have them. It's our right as human beings, and we'll fight for it as long as we've a drop of blood left in our bodies."

Baka's face was purple. "Rights!" he snarled. "Human beings! By Amon, next thing the asses will be calling themselves men! Curses on you for the stupid herd of swine you are!" He gestured to the two construction bosses, who had been standing just inside the door. They stepped forward with alacrity, whips uncoiled.

The young Hebrew bit his lips as the first stroke descended on his body. Moses could see a drop of blood ooze from their tight, thin line and flow slowly into his beard. But no sound issued from them. He knew he should be glad to see the youth suffer the same indignity he himself had been made to endure. But he felt no satisfaction. As blow after blow descended sweat stood on his own forehead, and the palms of his hands felt clammy to his clamped fingers. Except for the whining of the lash and its sickening thud there was no sound in the room. Even the two children, their faces pressed against their mother's thighs, made no whimper. The woman on the mat lay tense, hands clenched tightly at her sides. With every thud of the lash a quiver passed through her wasted body, but she made no sound. They were not lacking in emotion, Moses knew. The eyes of the woman Miriam, standing motionless, a disdainful smile on her lips, were even now blazing with such passion as he had never before seen. What strange capacity for endurance kept them silent?

He was filled with disgust. The sheer stupidity of Baka was unbelievable. What in Amon's name did he think he was accomplishing by pounding an able-bodied man to pulp? Proving his mastery? But it was the man's will he wanted to master, not his body. Did he think you could change a man's mind by beating him?

"Stop that!" he commanded suddenly, reaching for the lash. He turned to Baka. "Which do you want," he demanded tersely, "dead Hebrews or bricks?"

"Why—bricks," replied the foreman, mouth agape.

"All right, then. Why don't you get them?"

"That's what I'm trying—"

"No, you're not," snapped Moses. He turned to the kneeling figure, but it was to the woman that he spoke. "We need bricks," he said simply, "to build a city. You need food, the food that you have rightfully earned. You won't work until you get it. Baka refuses to give it to you until you work. All right. Bring your workmen to the brickfields tomorrow morning. Baka will bring your rations to the same place. You will receive them the minute you are ready to begin working. Is that satisfactory?"

"Yes," replied the woman instantly.

"Why—yes," agreed Baka, amazed that the matter could be arranged so simply. He rubbed his small soft hands together. "Prince Moses is most wise. A very excellent suggestion."

The sudden silence was startling. So intense was it that it could be heard as well as felt. It was the sick woman who broke it. Lifting herself with difficulty on her elbows, she stared at Moses intently.

"Prince— What did you say?" she whispered.

"He said," interposed Miriam swiftly, "that our visitor, the prince, had made a wise suggestion. Now that the matter is settled, our esteemed guests will not wish to remain longer in an atmosphere so demeaning to their sacred persons. The hut of a despised squatter is no suitable setting for a prince of Egypt."

The utter contempt with which she spoke made the words an insult rather than an expression of abasement. A hot rejoinder rose to Moses' lips. The arrogance of the woman was insufferable. What right had she to blame him for an accident that had been unavoidable? Then he lowered his gaze to the face of the woman lying on the mat, and the hot words died on his lips. Did she know that he had been responsible for the death of her husband? If not, then why should she look at him as if she were trying to absorb every detail of his features? He was sure of one thing. There was no hatred or abhorrence in her expression.

"Yes," she murmured in a voice barely audible. "Of course. I should have known."

He was still pondering her words as he rode back to Per-Ramses. What should the woman have known? That he was the sort of person who would heedlessly plow furrows through a gang of slaves? But she had not been the only one to look at him strangely. The silence, the sudden bombardment of startled, intent eyes had come directly after Baka's pronouncement of his name. Why?

"Well—what do you think of her?"

Moses looked bewildered. "Think—what—"

"Fancy finding Hathor herself in a herd of asses," mused Baka, smacking his lips with gustatory satisfaction. "And without her cow's head! This job of commissioner may have its compensations."

Moses eyed the man with disgust. "If you know what is good for you," he said curtly, "you will keep away from that woman."

Baka's eyebrows lifted. "Does that mean I have a rival?"

"Yes," said Moses, purposely misunderstanding. "The big square fellow with the brown beard. If I'm not mistaken, the woman's husband. Or," he continued pointedly, "doesn't the husband of a squatter have the prior right?"

He knew the instant he had said it that the question was ridiculous. A squatter had no rights at all.

From some repository in his garments Baka produced a sweetmeat. Holding it in his right hand and balancing himself with his left, he contemplated it pleasurably for some moments before depositing it in his mouth. His teeth closed on it with a hard, crunching sound.

"Thanks for warning me," he said blandly.

4

Tuya was dead. Up the road toward the cliffs of the western desert swung another long procession, this time turning south into the Valley of the Queens. The wailing of the women echoed and re-echoed through the barren wasteland, as familiarly attuned to its wild desolation as the howling of Anubis, the jackal. And, like the cry of its desert counterpart, it bore, mingled with its shrill lamentation, a weird note of triumph.

For not all who followed in her funerary procession grieved wholeheartedly for Tuya. The eyes of her daughter Nefretiri, following dutifully behind the swaying oxcart, were less bright with tears than with plans for a future laden with long-awaited opportunity. Sitra, gingerly applying earth to her immaculate flesh, felt a relief such as she had not experienced since her last visit to Tuya's apartment months before. The still, painted lips would never reveal her secret. Even the threat which they had once uttered seemed as powerless as the great, carved, gold-encrusted bier topped by the brooding wings of the vulture goddess Mut. *I shall get my way if I have to die and journey to the land beyond the Lily Lake.* If Sitra remembered them now, it was with only the vaguest of misgivings. Long before the re-embodied queen had found her way by the mystic charts concealed in her many swathings, Sitra's goal would have been achieved. For Nefretiri was possessed of as strong a will as Tuya's, and she had no Lily Lake to cross.

No, nor even a river to navigate. "Tonight I shall wear my mother's jewels," she told Memnet calmly. "The openwork collar of gold with the vultures and royal sphinxes, and bracelets and anklets to match. And her favorite perfume. And you are to do my hair the way she liked hers best, in two thick masses falling over the shoulders. I want you to make me look exactly like my mother."

"But—" The old nurse looked bewildered. Her slow wits, never able to keep pace with the whims of her unpredictable charge, found this new caprice even more confusing than usual.

"Is it so strange that I want to look like my mother?" demanded Nefretiri. "She was a very beautiful woman."

"Indeed she was, the poor little lotus blossom." Memnet's tears flowed afresh. "If I were sure that was the only reason you wanted to do it and that you weren't up to one of your tricks!"

The girl was more patient than usual. "What trick could I possibly be up to? After all, I'm her daughter. Why shouldn't I want to look like her?"

Satisfied but still bewildered, the old nurse fulfilled her young mistress's commands, reverently, as one performing a last service for the dead, sniffing the beloved perfumes, fondling the little jars and bottles and vials until Nefretiri was driven nearly mad with impatience.

"Memnet! You lumbering hippopotamus! Hurry, can't you? If you keep puttering much longer, it will be too late."

"Too late for what?"

"Oh—nothing important. Anyway, it's no concern of yours."

The tear-dimmed eyes blinked suspiciously. "You are up to some trick. I might have known."

Nefretiri stamped her foot. "Memnet, if you don't do what I tell you and stop mumbling—"

"If its nothing important," replied the nurse stubbornly, "then there's no hurry." Stolidly and without haste she continued to brush the

196

smooth black hair and roll it on her fingers. "At least it isn't one of those tricks you and your clever cousin Moses used to scheme together. Thank the good Hathor, he's too far away to stir up trouble now!"

"Why do you hate Moses so?" asked Nefretiri curiously. "He was never any more responsible for the tricks we used to play on you than I was. And you don't hate me, do you?"

Memnet's thin lips drew into a tight line. "Some people that were born respectable," she said grimly, "have the ill luck to turn into slaves. Others that were born on peasants' stools manage to get themselves made princes. There isn't any justice in this world."

"We were talking about Moses," retorted Nefretiri tartly. "And he wasn't born on a peasant's stool."

"Oh—wasn't he?" The small eyes gleamed. "I guess maybe I could tell you a few things about that!"

The nervously tapping foot was suddenly still. "What do you mean?" asked the girl quietly.

The nurse's lips set even more tightly. She had said more than she had intended. "Nothing," she hedged. "Nothing at all. Will the princess have her hair twisted with gold threads or strung through the gold meshed loops?"

"Neither," replied the other promptly, "at present. The hair will remain just as it is until you have told me what you know about Moses."

"But—I tell you it's nothing—!"

"I shall be the judge of that."

"But—I promised your mother the queen—"

"My mother is dead now. I am your mistress."

"I—I tell you it's nothing. It's just that—that I was there when she found him."

"Where? When who found whom?"

The quiet voice was as inexorable as Tuya's had once been. Reluctantly, remembering her promise to the dead queen, Memnet told her story. When she had finished, Nefretiri sat very straight for some moments without speaking. Finally she laughed. "Memnet, what an utterly ridiculous yarn! Nobody would believe it, of course." Sobering instantly, she fixed her eyes on the old servant's. "But you're not to repeat it to anybody, Memnet, do you hear? Never! Do you swear by the sacred scarab which will be buried between your breasts that you will never let a word of this pass your lips?"

"I didn't mean it to pass my lips today," replied the old nurse aggrievedly. "And it wouldn't have except for your nagging."

"Swear it?" demanded Nefretiri ominously.

"No. And you can't frighten me into doing it, either. But I'll say this much. I promised the queen your mother that I wouldn't tell. And I intend to keep my promise, unless—" The square features set obstinately.

"Unless what?"

But Memnet's lips were clamped as tightly as two bricks in a mortared wall.

Seti felt a deep relief. He could lean back against his cushions in the kiosk overlooking the charming little lake which Amenhotep had designed for his wife Tiy and bask in its serenity. He had been afraid that sometime out of sheer weariness, like a rock constantly eroded by a persistent waterfall, his hard core of resistance might be worn away. Now he need fear no longer, for the waterfall was still. Ramses was not yet crown prince, praise be to Amon, and he had made no promises.

Half closing his eyes, he pictured Tuya as he had first known her, when his father had been a general in the armies of Harmhab and neither of them had been possessed by an emotion more violent than their pleasant but mild fancy for each other. So vivid was the recollection that he could actually see her coming along the edge of the lake toward the kiosk, her tiny, gold-sandaled feet making a bright pattern on the red gravel path. His pulses quickened first with pleasure, then with annoyance, as he noticed the jewels which encircled her slim neck and wrists and ankles. No, she was not the Tuya who had come to him as a bride, sweet, gently stimulating, docile. The high vulture cap was on her head and on her features the look of intense, acquisitive desire which he had come to know so well. Instinctively he braced himself.

Then, as the illusion persisted, sudden realization struck him. It could not be Tuya. Tuya was dead. But it was. She was coming steadily toward him, living flesh and blood, her wasted body strangely rejuvenated, mounting the steps of the kiosk

"No, no!" he gasped. "Don't—don't come any nearer!"

"It's I, father. Your daughter, Nefretiri. What's the matter? Don't you know me?"

Nefretiri. Of course. How could he have been so stupid! She had always been the living image of her mother. Probably she had deliberately made herself like Tuya in some mistaken hope of bringing comfort. Relieved but still uneasy, he made her welcome.

"No. I can't sit down. I must talk to you, father."

The voice too was like Tuya's. Its gentle insistence raised soft barriers about him, threatening to stifle him. "Well?"

"I'm a woman now, father. It's time you were thinking about a husband for me. Most of the girls of my age in the harem were married long ago."

Seti stirred restlessly. The words were Tuya's also. A few more gently soothing sentences, and she would be mentioning Ramses.

"Since Amon-nebet's death there is only one person who is worthy by birth to be united in marriage to the heiress of the throne of Egypt. It has always been my mother's wish that you should wed me to my brother Ramses and that he should succeed you on the throne."

Something seemed to burst in Seti's aching head. "No!" he protested wildly. "I won't do it. You can't make me do it. It's your mother who told you to do this to me. Can't I even be free of her nagging now she is dead? I tell you I won't—I won't—"

"Why, father!" The voice that was so much like Tuya's was gently soothing. "I'm sorry. I didn't dream—Please! Don't distress yourself so."

Tuya would have spoken like that too, withdrawing her barbs into a sheath of soft gentleness until she was ready for a further probing.

"But you know, father, you must face the problem eventually. It is time I had a husband."

The barbs were coming again. Seti braced himself, determined this time neither to yield nor to lose his temper.

"And who is there for me to wed but Ramses? Surely my father would not wed me to someone of low birth, like—like Prince Moses!"

"Moses is not of low birth," demurred Seti. "That is, we don't know that he is. If his father was a Mitannian prince, he has more royal blood in his veins than I do."

Nefretiri drew herself up to her full height. Tuya herself could not have looked more arrogantly regal. "But—the man who weds me will be the future king of Egypt. Surely you would not choose Moses—"

"Why not?" Amazing that he had not thought of it before! It would make the solution of the whole matter so simple. And it would not be the first time that a pharaoh had been succeeded by his brother. Look at the great Thutmose! And Moses was popular. The priests of Amon would think twice before they rejected the people's favorite. It looked as if Nefretiri might make a bit of objection, but he was through being dictated to by the women of his harem.

"Leave me now," he said abruptly to his daughter. "I must think."

She went as she had come, by the red gravel path along the edge of the lake. Seti, watching her proud back, would have been both amazed and confounded if he could have seen the triumph in her eyes.

5

The Hebrews were back at work. Between the marshes and the brickfields the valley swarmed again with processions of laborers, their backs bent beneath baskets oozing thick black mud. In the fields close to Per-Ramses the kneading pits where the mud was mixed with sand and bits of straw were once more alive with churning feet, and rows of black wet oblongs stretched endlessly in all directions. Four days, and the oblongs, now firm and dry, were turned on end. Seven, and other processions of toilers were moving between brickfield and city wall, huge humps of finished bricks on their backs. The air reverberated with the shouting of foremen and the whining of lashes.

Bound ostensibly on tours of inspection as a servant of the pharaoh, Moses made frequent trips to the brickfields. Sometimes he took Tutu with him, bringing back detailed reports, but usually he went alone. Not even to himself would he have admitted the real reason for his going, that he found a peculiar fascination in the brown laborers. They repelled, yet intrigued him. He despised them for their uncouthness, their untidy beards, their ugly bodies swollen with red welts and grimed with mud and sweat. He was nauseated by their odor. Each time he paid a visit to the brickfields he vowed never to repeat it. But inevitably he returned. The Hebrews were different from any other slaves he had ever known. What made them so? He had to find out the reason.

He tried to talk with some of them, but they turned to him faces almost as blankly uniform as the oblongs that sprang from their wooden molds—with one exception. They did not bear the stamp of the reigning pharaoh. The Hebrew section bosses, chosen for their loyalty to their Egyptian masters, were more communicative. One of them, a man called Dathan, as attracted by a gold collar and signet ring as a fly by sweetmeats, took every occasion to fawn upon him.

"The friend of the pharaoh has again smiled upon us with his presence," he would accost him humbly. "If his miserable slave can render any service—"

"Tell me this, Dathan," said Moses once, abruptly. "Why aren't your fellow Hebrews as sensible as you? Think of all the trouble they caused themselves by being so stiff-necked and rebellious. If your ancestors had used your good sense when they came into the country, you might all be respectable Egyptians by now."

"That's just what I tell them," agreed the Hebrew eagerly, forgetting his studied subservience. "What's the sense of keeping to the old ways, I ask them. Just because our grandfathers wore beards and kowtowed to some old desert god that nobody even knows the name of, that's no sign we have to make fools of ourselves. Some of the squatters had the sense to get out of here long ago. They've gone up the river and settled in the cities, and they've made good too, buying and selling the goods the caravans bring in. You'd recognize their names if I should tell you. Good respectable Egyptian merchants. Not slaves like us."

"You—say you have a god and don't even know his name?" asked Moses curiously.

"Well—yes and no. He—or maybe I should say *they*—have lots of names. Some people call him the Fear of Isaac, and others, the Mighty One of Jacob. I've even heard him called the Shield of Abraham. It depends on what clan you belong to. Some think they're all the same god, and others that they're all different." The Hebrew shrugged. "As for me, I don't care one way or the other. What good does a desert god do us here in Egypt? Now those gods you worship—a man can really understand them. Take the one you call Hathor. I could worship her with a relish. But this god—or gods—of ours! He's as outdated as our beards—yes, and as our thickheaded stubbornness."

"I see you've shaved off your beard," remarked Moses thoughtfully.

He was driving through one of the settlements of mud hovels, alone except for White Elephant, when the strange impulse seized him. Handing the reins to his slave, he descended from his carriage abruptly. Though the huts were all alike, he had no difficulty in finding the one he sought. He remembered it by a strange, brownish-red marking on its gatepost, which might have been made with earth or vegetable dye or even blood. Some clan symbol, he supposed.

The sick woman was alone, as he had expected. Though in the dimness he could not see her features, he sensed that she was watching him. Confusion seized him. Now that he had yielded to the impulse, he had no reasonable explanation of why he had come.

"You—you won't remember me," he said stumblingly. "I—I was here—"

"Yes," she replied. She spoke Egyptian accurately but not fluently. "I remember. You are the young man who came with Baka, the Egyptian foreman. He called you Prince Moses."

"I—I hope you will forgive me for coming back."

"An Egyptian does not ask forgiveness of a Hebrew for entering his house." There was no bitterness, only a dry humor, in her voice. "In fact, he does not ask for anything. He takes."

"I have not come to take anything," Moses assured her hastily. "I—I just happened to be passing." He fumbled for a plausible excuse. "I—I knew your family would be gone and I—I wondered if there might be s-something I could do for you."

Once the words had passed his lips he realized how ridiculous they sounded. An Egyptian prince turning out of his way to help a sick squatter! She would suspect him of some baser motive.

"Why—yes," she said, apparently without surprise. "If you would fill this gourd from the waterskin by the door, I would be grateful."

Moses filled the gourd awkwardly, for he had performed few menial tasks in his life, and held it to the woman's lips. His eyes had become accustomed to the dimness, and he could see now that she was no more like her daughter Miriam than the White Nile far above the cataracts was like its stormy, turbulent offspring. Only the physical contours were similar. The life currents that flowed through this wasted body were as deeply serene as the other's were troubled and tumultuous. And suddenly Moses knew why he had come.

"It was my chariot," he said, "that killed Miriam's father—your husband."

"Yes," she replied. "I know. Miriam told me."

"Did she—t-tell you how—"

"The young prince in the chariot behind forced you off the road. I understand that it was an accident."

"Your d-daughter hates me." The stumbling of his voice revealed to him suddenly how deep his concern had been. "She believes it was my fault."

"The young are hasty in judgment. Miriam loved her father. I loved him too. And I do not believe it."

"But—how can I be sure?" All at once the words were tumbling from his lips. "Perhaps it *was* my fault. It was my hand that pulled on the horses' reins. I did it instinctively, without thinking. But—" he hesitated only a second, his eyes probing the woman's steady gaze, *"would I have done it if they had been Egyptians?* Can you understand what I mean? They were not men to me—those brown naked figures beside the road. I was taught to believe that only Egyptians are men."

"And now," prompted the woman softly, "you believe that Hebrews also can be men? Who taught you that, my—" her voice suddenly faltered, "my friend?"

"I—don't know," replied Moses honestly. Suddenly he was telling her, hesitatingly at first, then more freely, about certain things in his life which until this moment had seemed relatively unimportant: about the young Shasu boy and the little barber's wife, who had waited all day outside the temple gate to return his jewel; about the workman who had fallen at his feet in the temple at Karnak, and the miner who had stolen a handful of water in the desert in Nubia; about the slaves whom he himself had driven back from the land of Kush. And he saw suddenly that all these threads, secretly woven together in the fabric of his experience, had become blended into an intelligible pattern.

"I don't know why I am telling you all these things," he said finally. "What is past is past. Your husband is dead. So is the Shasu boy—and the barber's child. And the workman at Karnak. And the others might as well be. What difference does it make?"

"Whether you believe they are men or animals? It makes a great deal of difference—to me."

"Then—you don't hate me for killing your husband?"

"No. I don't hate you."

"But—there is still something I haven't told you," he continued, impelled for some reason to be brutally frank. "I wanted to save the Shasu—yes. And I think I could have killed the viceroy who chained that thirsty slave within arm's length of water. And I do believe now that Hebrews are men, not animals. But—I still despise them. I abhor their long beards, their woolen garments, their ugly sheep, everything about them which is not Egyptian. I—I suppose I even despise you a little."

He watched her face apprehensively. Why should it matter to him what this woman thought of him, whether she believed him guilty of long ago, unwittingly, committing a wrong? But it did matter. He heard her catch her breath sharply, saw the color drain from her cheeks. But her eyes did not waver.

"You are honest," she said quietly. "Did they teach you that in Egypt?"

"Then—you still don't hate me for what I did?"

"Hate you? No, I—" She began to cough, and he lifted the gourd again to her lips, raising her slight body by slipping an arm beneath her shoulders.

"My son," she said, "is strong like you. I could almost imagine—"

He lowered her head gently to the mat. "You mean the one they call Aaron?"

"Yes. Aaron."

"You have other sons?"

"One other."

"Older or younger?" He did not know why he was asking. As if it mattered to him whether this Hebrew woman had one son or twenty!

"Younger. By three years. But he has not lived with us for—for a very long time. Not since he was a baby."

"No?" murmured Moses absently. With the sudden cooling of his emotion, the impulse that had led him to the little mud hut had burned itself out.

"Shall I tell you about him?" asked the woman gently.

"Why—yes, of course. If you wish."

He hoped she would make it brief. He could see through the door that his horse, under White Elephant's inexpert handling, was becoming restless. But, once she had started her amazing story, he did not glance through the door again.

It had happened years ago in the reign of Harmhab, who had decided that the rapidly multiplying squatters in the Delta, an advance contingent of the country's potential desert enemies, constituted a threat to the public safety. The purge that followed was still spoken of in terrified whispers by the Children of Joseph. It had been directed, not at adult males, toward whose unexploited man power Egypt had already been casting covetous glances, but at children. For Harmhab had been a foresighted monarch, proposing to accomplish his end by destroying, not assets, but liabilities.

During this reign of terror the woman had borne a son, fine and healthy and possessed, unfortunately, of a lusty pair of lungs. She had hidden him as long as possible from the royal police. Then, driven to desperation, she had made a small cradle out of river rushes, lined it with bitumen to make it waterproof, and, taking her daughter Miriam and the baby, had traveled north across the Delta to the easternmost branch of the river.

"Miriam carried the basket," she said reminiscently, "and I held the baby. She wanted to change with me, but I would not. I expected it would be the last time I would ever hold him. He was a very sweet baby. I can remember just how he felt in my arms. His head was warm and heavy against my shoulder, and if I turned my cheek I could brush it against his hair. He had very soft curly hair, like—like Aaron's."

They had had to travel by night only and with great care because of the police. At the sound of each approaching footstep they had left the road and hidden. Once, lacking other shelter, they had lain in the swamp on the edge of the river, half submerged by water, while a band of soldiers, returning from Bubastis, had engaged in a drunken quarrel on the road not a stone's throw from their hiding place. Afraid the touch of water would make him cry, she had held the baby high over her head, until there had been no feeling in her arms but a throbbing pain in every other muscle of her body. But the baby had not cried. And the soldiers had passed.

"One morning," she continued with sudden brevity, "we came to the borders of an Egyptian city. We put the baby in the cradle and laid it on the river among the rushes. As I had expected, the Egyptian women came there to bathe. One of them saw the basket and, like any woman, was curious. She had her servants bring it to her. When she saw the baby, she wanted him, of course. No woman could have helped it. Miriam, who was watching, was very clever. She went and asked the woman if she would like a Hebrew nurse for the child. Then Miriam came and found me. I remained with him until he was two years old. Then I left him. That is all I know. You, who are an Egyptian, know the rest of his story better than I."

"And—you never saw him again?" asked Moses, intrigued.

But the woman had turned her face to the wall and did not answer. She was still living in the past, he supposed, journeying through the darkness, perhaps, with the baby in her arms, feeling his hard little head against her shoulder, pressing her cheek against his curly hair. Quietly he left the hut.

He thought fleetingly of the woman's story as he drove back to Per-Ramses. An astonishing tale, certainly, if true. More likely the figment of a fevered imagination. Perhaps the woman had had a son once and he had died or been actually liquidated in Harmhab's purge. Unable to reconcile herself to her loss, she had reared this fantasy about his memory. But it had sounded convincing. After all, it could be. There were plenty of Asiatics masquerading as good Egyptians, some of them Hebrews, as that caviling section boss Dathan had testified. Was the little foundling still alive, he wondered. Had he by any chance brushed shoulders with him? A pity that he would never know.

6

With mingled emotions, Moses complied with Seti's summons to join the royal family at the palace in Bubastis. He was reluctant to leave Per-Ramses just now and was not yet ready to make his report to the pharaoh. He did not trust Baka, yet he could lay his finger on no specific grievance. Was the commissioner a tool of the priests of Amon? Was he using his position of authority as a comfortable sinecure where he might loll in luxury and feed his sensual appetites? Moses did not know. And unless he stayed, he could not soon find out.

But as he journeyed up the arm of the river in the vessel which Seti had dispatched for him, his mood changed to one of anticipation. The most riotous holiday in the Egyptian calendar was close at hand, the Feast of Bast. The stream was swarming with boats of all kinds and their decks crowded with people. At every tiny settlement hallos were shouted, cymbals merrily rattled, and the inhabitants summoned by coarse gibes and mocking jests to come out and dance on the banks. As the pylons and pennanted staves of Bubastis flashed flamboyant greeting, the mood of gaiety accelerated its tempo to mirthful frenzy.

Moses went straight to the palace. He knew it well, for it had been the residence headquarters of his foster father Ramses when the latter had been stationed at Tharu. His infancy had been spent here and a part of his childhood, for Sitra, even after becoming queen, had preferred it to the palace at Memphis. The vestibule was just as he remembered it, even to the nodding porter sitting with his back propped against the second of the four wooden pillars. The uraeuses twined around those pillars in the days of his childhood were still there but they had shrunk to puny rings no bigger through than a man's finger and hardly longer than his arm. Once they had been giant coils of bronze, wrist-thick and longer than the soldiers' spears whose tips had glittered high above his head. Anhu the porter had lifted him on his stooped, narrow shoulders so he could touch the red jewels that formed their gleaming eyes. He was surprised to find them now below the level of his gaze.

"May the precious Bast scratch out the eyes of this miserable ass's offspring," quavered a familiar voice, "if it is not the jewel of my bosom, Prince Moses!"

"Anhu! Is it really you? I—I can't believe—"

"That the old bones could hang together this long?" The old man chuckled as he tottered to his feet. "Well, I'd hardly attempt to straddle those princely legs across these shoulders. But I did it once. Remember?"

Moses did remember. He looked down at the wizened figure with the half-pitying, half-nostalgic sentiment of a man for his lost childhood. But the doors of the palace beckoned.

"Is—is all the royal family here?" he asked with unintentional eagerness.

"Yes. She's here." Anhu's treble rose in a sly cackle. "And I'll wager she's waiting for you too. Been out here ten times today if she has once, peeking through the lattice to see if you were coming."

Moses flushed. Was his love for Nefretiri a bawdy toy, to be bandied from hand to hand in the servants' quarters? Then he flushed again, more deeply, as he realized that it was not of Nefretiri that Anhu was speaking.

"No wonder the brother of the Strong Bull pulls at his halter in haste to be gone. It was past time they gave you a wife. And she's not a bad-looking wench, if a man prefers to pluck his lotus blooms half blown. And the darker the skin the softer, I've heard tell."

Shaken, Moses turned abruptly toward the entrance between the gold-twined pillars. Strangely, the possibility of Tharbis' having accompanied the royal family to Bubastis had not occurred to him. What emotion now did the knowledge of her presence arouse in him? He was not sure. He tried to picture in his mind the contours of her slim, smooth body, the shape of her dusky features, but he saw only softly rounded golden flesh, warm lips gently parted and curving like the rim of a wine goblet, eyes in which sunlight swam and bits of emerald glimmered. Tharbis was neither a body nor a face. She was a mood, an essence. The sudden thought of her was like a fresh wind brushing his cheek, a faint sound in his ears like the distant roaring of the cataracts.

"Shall I summon a slave to conduct the brother of the Strong Bull to his chosen destination?" quavered the old voice with a hint of mischief. "Or is the prince in too great haste?"

"It's quite unnecessary," Moses threw back swiftly. "I know my way about the palace."

He passed through the spacious dining hall, where preparations for a great feast were in progress. Aproned slaves were darting about, sprinkling and sweeping the tiled floor, twining ribbons about the pillars, filling the wine jars and wreathing them with flowers, loading the long sideboards with heaped trays of fresh fruits, breads, cakes, sweetmeats. He had sat many times at these tables as a child.

A vivid memory flashed through his mind. He was sitting beside a large man who wore a big red and white cap on his head. There were many good things in front of him to eat, and beneath him a high pile of cushions, so that his eyes came just above the level of the table. But he did not want to eat. All he wanted was to look at the queer-shaped cap, which was white inside and red outside and had a high curved handle like that of a long saucepan. When the big man took it off and put it beside him on the table, he reached out his hands and pulled it toward him, lifted it, and put it on his head. It was heavy, and it came down over his face and smelled very badly. When he could not get it off again, he began to cry.

Remembering, he smiled now, grimly. No wonder he had found himself the center of sudden confusion. For the big man had been the pharaoh, and the red and white cap had been the crown of Egypt. He could still feel the stifling darkness of that enveloping tent closing in upon him, could still smell its stale, acrid scent.

Reaching the pillared fountain hall beyond the dining room, he turned instinctively toward the women's quarters, then hesitated. Whom should he visit first? Sitra? Tharbis? Hardly Nefretiri. While he was trying to make up his mind a short, stout man came toward him, corkscrew curls bobbing about his round face, a ridiculous little fan clutched in his pudgy hand. Rahotep was well named the "king's mouth." His full lips, the upper slightly shorter than the lower, were the dominant feature in an otherwise undistinguished face. They began mouthing syllables long before any sound issued from them.

"How the brightness of Amon-Re shines on the very nearest friend of the pharaoh! The eyes of this miserable mouthpiece are dazzled by the glory they now behold. Let the lord prince but stand thus shedding his light, and there is no need of the sun! All else is as black night in his presence."

Moses looked about, seeking the source of such effulgence, but he and Rahotep were alone in the court. Bowing at regular intervals, the short, stout figure came toward him.

"The Strong Bull has been waiting many hours for the coming of his very nearest friend. His golden hoofs have become weary with his impatient pacing and his celestial eyes dim with much watching. Now that the brightness of the morning has come, he will leap up again and lift his gold horns in triumph. The Strong Bull bids his very nearest friend to come to him at once in his audience chamber and to accept this trifling token."

Moses stared at the glittering object which Rahotep held toward him. He recognized it instantly. It was a pectoral which Seti himself had often worn on state occasions, a cumbrous ornament of openwork gold plate, elaborately engraved on one side and inlaid with precious stones on the other. Emeralds, rubies, sapphires formed intricate designs of sphinx heads about the magnificent outspread wings of a flying vulture. Two enormous garnets were its eyes, and its beak a shining sliver of jet. In and out through the whole pattern twined the regal coils of a uraeus, sparkling with emerald chips. It was a jewel such as only kings were permitted to wear.

"B-but—" stammered Moses, "there's some mistake. This is not for me."

"The very nearest friend of the pharaoh is most wise," murmured Rahotep, "and this miserable mouthpiece would not dream of contradicting the golden words that flow from his lips. Nevertheless, when the Strong Bull bellows, what is the unweaned calf that he should bleat in protest? If the Golden Horus bade his miserable mouthpiece to lift the crown from his sacred head and plant it on the head of an ass, Rahotep would obey."

Rising on tiptoe, the "royal mouth" fastened the glittering pectoral about the neck of Moses.

Seti looked down the long banquet table. In spite of the cumbersome crown his head felt curiously light and clear. His limbs moved freely beneath the folds of his gold-encrusted regal robes, and the cushioned chair molded itself comfortably to his spare body. He had donned full royal dress deliberately, even to the ridiculous little pointed beard and moth-eaten lion's tail, in order that he might endow this casual feast with an atmosphere of official significance.

He had succeeded. Currents of tension flowed up and down the long table more freely than the wines which poured ceaselessly into the thin bronze drinking cups. Delicate bits of broiled gazelle meat and tender beef were neglected for more highly spiced morsels of whispered conjecture. So aware were his senses that the interplay of whispered words was almost as distinguishable as the delicate morsels of food passed by solicitous hands from one lip to another.

"I tell you, it's more than a feast doing honor to Bast! Does the Strong Bull wear his robes of state when he attends a mere banquet?"

"Notice how he has put his nearest friend, Prince Moses, on his right hand and his son, Prince Ramses, on his left? Is it one of them, do you think, that he intends to favor?"

"See the new chain that Ramses wears about his neck. It is circled in sphinxes and its great pendant is a vulture's head. A sign of kingship, or may Eset consume my dead body!"

"But the one Prince Moses wears is equally magnificent!"

"The royal scribe sits on the rug in the shadow of the Strong Bull. By the mewings of Bast, I'd like to know what he's writing!"

"We shall know before the feast is over. And meanwhile, we're not the only ones in ignorance. Look around you. See their faces."

Yes, reflected Seti with peculiar satisfaction, see their faces. It was pleasant to keep them all in suspense for this brief interval. Lifting his wine cup, he sipped sparingly, letting his glance wander over the rows of faces, plucking one here and there, casually, as one wandering through a garden plucks a flower, appraising its petals briefly, then tossing it away.

Nefretiri's. Proud, as finely chiseled as the inscription on a scarab. She had dressed to look like Tuya again tonight, plaits of hair drawn forward over each shoulder. Did she still think that by such means she could bend him to Tuya's will? Before the feast was over she would know his answer. So it was a husband she wanted, was it? Well, she would have one.

Sitra's. Flushed too deeply with rouge and wine and excitement. Tonight her gaiety was overdone. Did she think the bleary-eyed general beside her was another Mitannian prince to be captivated? At least he had found out the facts of that episode. Before making his decision, it had been necessary to know if the blood of royalty actually flowed in Moses' veins. He had asked her point-blank, and she had confessed that it was true. "Not that I have any way of proving it!"

The gold and silver platters were emptied of pistachio nuts, dates, figs, pomegranates, grapes, melons, raisins. Soft-footed slaves in tiny starched aprons slipped silently among the guests, like priests performing rites at tie altars of deity. The dancers discarded both their languor and their concealing ribbons. The music rose to new crescendos. In the center of the table appeared a huge bronze bowl filled with red wine and crowned with wreaths. Into the dining hall trooped a bevy of slaves, holding aloft a tiny mummy upon a miniature bier. Around and around the room it passed, to the rhythm of dirges and slow-marching feet.

"Drink!" wailed the flutes and harps and guitars.

"Drink!" echoed the sistrums and castanets.

"Drink!" mourned the somber beat of kettledrums.

"Drink!" cried the slaves with their ghoulish burden. "Drink and be merry, for soon you will come to this!"

The guests needed no second invitation, but Seti himself partook sparingly. The moment of climax was now fast approaching. Turning slightly, he glanced briefly at the profile on his left. Ramses'. Handsome, superbly arrogant, as usual, lips slightly curved in a secret smile, eyes narrowed in faint disdain. By the horns of Amon, did he have no anxiety concerning what was about to happen! Noticing that the proud lips were moving, Seti leaned toward his son.

"What's that you're muttering to yourself?" he asked sharply.

The arrogant head bowed slightly. "If my father, the Strong Bull, Lord of the Two Lands, the Golden One of Horus, pleases," drawled Ramses softly, "it is a poem that I conceived in one of those barren hours when the sun of the pharaoh's presence failed to shine upon me. A hymn of praise to my father, of course. Shall I repeat it to him?"

"Please do," urged Seti.

Ramses' lips seemed scarcely to move. "From the time that I was in the egg," they intoned in a voice that grew more and more resonant and penetrating—

> "From the time that I was in the egg
> The great ones sniffed the earth before me.
> When I attained the rank of eldest son and heir,
> I dealt with affairs.
> My father having appeared before the people said to me:
> I shall have him crowned king that I may see him in his splendor,
> While I am still upon this earth."

Half the table was listening before he had finished. The banqueters had been waiting long for an expected climax. Wreaths of wilting flowers were torn from perfumed heads and flung toward the drawling voice. Goblets were held crazily aloft, drunken lips unloosed.

"Hail, Ramses!"

"So it's you who are the favored one!"

"From the time that he was in the egg the great ones sniffed the earth before him!"

Smiling regretfully, the young prince rose to his feet and signaled for silence. But the shouting only grew louder.

"Hear, hear!"

"Tell us how the great ones sniffed!"

"Give us a speech, Ramses!"

Still smiling, the young prince waved deprecating fingers at them. A most regrettable mistake. Surely his friends would not think him guilty of composing such a eulogy of himself! The poem was of course a tribute to the Strong Bull, Lord of the Two Lands, the Golden Horus.

Futile rage coursed through Seti. Vaguely he realized that his moment of triumph had been stolen. But he would not have it so. By all the gods of Egypt and every other land, he would show this insufferable braggart who was master!

"Silence!" he shouted in a voice which, disappointingly, resembled neither the roar of the lion whose appendage he wore nor the bellow of the Strong Bull whose human counterpart he claimed to be. But finally it penetrated the confusion. Goblets paused in their perilous passage from table to lips, golden limbs froze into lewd tableaux, guitars quivered discordantly into silence. The Good God had spoken. Seti gestured to his scribe. The moment had come.

The scribe's voice too was disappointing. The guests listened respectfully but a bit dazedly while it pipingly informed them that in the thirteenth year of His Majesty Horus, the Strong Bull, beloved by the goddess of truth, Lord of the Diadem of the Vulture and of the Snake, full of years, great in victories, King of Upper Egypt and King of Lower Egypt, strong in truth, Chosen of Re, Son of Re, Lord of the Temple, shining daily among men as his father Re, His Sacred Majesty Seti—that in this glorious epoch of time the royal Princess Nefretiri, daughter of Seti and Tuya, became betrothed to Prince Moses, son of the Princess Sitra and...

The piping voice was drowned in the babel of excited comment.

Moses! Had their ears heard aright?

Whiskers of Bast, so it was Moses, after all, and not Ramses! Well—what difference? They could drink to one, couldn't they, as well as to the other?

How would the princess like that, to be mated to a bastard?

Hist! Who said that? Remember the prince of the Mitanni!

Moses—Ramses—Ramses—Moses. The scribe's voice had been a piping reed. Had anybody heard what he really said?

Who cared? They could drink, couldn't they, to the princess and her bridegroom?

Drink—drink—to the princess!

Drink...

212

The confused babbling in his ears, Seti looked again at his son, and Ramses returned the look, handsome, arrogant features unmoved. You see? mocked the bold eyes, Tuya's eyes. Your little scheme fell flat, didn't it? And so I win, after all. I shall always win.

Seti felt a sudden panic. He turned toward Moses for assurance and saw, not triumph, but dazed bewilderment. Ramses was right. His climax not only had fallen flat; it had not even been understood. But it was not too late. He was the Strong Bull, the Good God, the Mighty Horus. He could still make them understand.

"Silence!" he shouted again, and this time his voice left nothing to be desired. It roared like a lion. It bellowed like Apis himself, pawing the ground before the gaping multitude. And the room was silent.

Seti rose to his feet. He reached up and took the red and white crown from his brow and placed it on the head of Moses.

7

Inside the palace the climax of abandoned merriment had long been reached and passed. The huge bowl had been emptied and refilled many times. The wine stains on the white cloth had darkened to the color of dried blood. Flies swarmed like miniature vultures about abandoned rinds and cores. What few guests remained no longer graced the cushioned chairs. Their bared shoulders and delicately shod feet protruded from beneath the table or from sheltering bowers of flowers where they had withdrawn to share the recurring languor of the golden-fleshed dancers. The air was heavy with the sickish smell of decaying foods and wilting flowers.

But in the streets of the town where Moses walked alone excitement was still rising. Torches flared in the night breeze and men and women and children snake danced crazily through the streets, entwining in their coils all stragglers who got in their way. Inside small magic bubbles of light, jugglers tossed golden balls and fragile vases and glittering knives; mummers with grotesque animal heads mouthed silly lines; Negro acrobats performed amazing and terrifying feats. Bast, queen of the festival, was no longer a ribald, roguish feline, delighting in rattle and coquettish catcalls. Under the surface of the night she was beginning to prowl and snarl and show her claws. Frolicking became strife; coquetry, brute passion; and worship, frenzy. Devotees beat themselves with thorny clubs. Knives flashed. Blood flowed as freely as wine, and cries of ecstasy and pain were indistinguishable.

Moses was conscious only of noise, color, confusion, both within and without. The whirling figures, bawling voices, and magic bubbles were but physical counterparts of the emotional upheaval within himself. Even the grimmer shapes lurking in the shadows seemed but projections of his own uncertain, jeering incredulity.

Occasionally he fingered the neckpiece still hanging on his breast. This much was true then. He had been met that afternoon by the king's mouthpiece, presented with this amazing gift, and conducted to Seti's apartment, where even more amazing words...

"It is the will of Seti, the Strong Bull, the Golden Horus, that Moses, son of his mother Sitra, his nearest friend and blood brother..."

Again and again he set his feet on the ladder of unreality. The words that Seti had spoken were the rungs on which he must climb to reach the dazzling pinnacle. But had Seti really spoken them? Ah, the neckpiece again! Painfully he retraced his steps: the fumbling at his breast, the groping in his mind to find the rungs of the ladder, the setting of his feet upon them one by one.

"It is the will of Seti..."

No use. The rungs possessed no more substance than the flames of Bast's streaming torches. The interview with Seti and the words the pharaoh had spoken were as elusive as a dream.

The banquet too—had that been a dream? Painfully he tried to re-create the sights and sounds of those hours in the dining hall and to endow them with reality: the red-gold sheen of lamplight on the great bronze wine bowl; a silvery peal of Nefretiri's laughter; the savor of a delicate morsel of venison; the piquant aroma of the night-blooming white lotus; the penetrating murmur of a soft, drawling voice:

"From the time that I was in the egg the great ones sniffed the earth before me."

The moment of climax swung into reality. He was sitting on the right hand of Seti. The fingers of his right hand were closed upon the thin stem of a lotus blossom, moving slowly up and down, like the monotonous voice of the scribe reading from a new papyrus which as he unrolled it crackled with a faint sound of rustling leaves. The words too were like leaves, golden leaves, dropping one by one into the pool of his consciousness, where lying lightly on the surface they formed a wonderful, amazing pattern.

"In the thirteenth year of His Majesty Horus..."

Clear as a jewel with many facets, the supreme moment became re-created. In a luminous void before his eyes hung the features of Ramses, mocking, insolent, and, for the first time in his memory, a little frightened. The echo of the voice of Seti, louder and more authoritative than he had ever heard it, was ringing in his ears. The pharaoh was rising to his feet; he was lifting his hands to his head. And with the long holding of an indrawn breath the moment was here. Upon the brow of Moses there was a heaviness, a hardness, like the shifting of an old and very heavy burden; in his nostrils a familiar, long-remembered scent, a little stale and acrid, like unwashed garments that have remained long in a closed chest.

And suddenly the rungs of reality were beneath his feet. He was mounting them steadily, his feet sure, toward the lofty pinnacle which was the throne of Egypt.

When Moses returned to the palace, it was but a few hours to dawn. A feverish torpor hung over the streets. The city lay littered and soiled, like the deserted banquet table, while overhead the bronze bowl of the moon, now nearly emptied of its magic, held the crimson dregs of the mad night.

The last of the guests, even the most drunken, would have departed. The outer gate of bronze and cedar would be shut. He would go around to the back of the wall and let himself in by a garden gate. In fact, for the little that remained of the night he could sleep in the garden, in the kiosk overgrown with rose vines. He rather fancied the tumult among the servants in the morning: the future pharaoh of Egypt sleeping on the earth floor of a kiosk!

But there was tumult already among the servants. The cedar gate was flung wide. Torches flamed in the darkness, revealing terrified faces. There was an excited but muted clamor of voices. In the farthest corner of the outer courtyard, close to one of the round high towers, a knot of people was gathered. On the outer edge of it stood Anhu.

"What is it?" demanded Moses, touching the stooped shoulder. "What has happened?"

"Hush!" The old man put his finger to his lips. "You'll waken the pharaoh." Then aghast recognition smote his features. "Bast scratch my eyes out!" he muttered. "That I should tell the Good God's chosen one to hush!"

"What has happened?" repeated Moses.

"Let not the lord prince, the brother of Horus, concern himself. It is nothing that should disturb his rest. Some thoughtless servant fell from the top of the high tower. Let the friend of the pharaoh return to his bed before the sight offends his eyes."

Moses pushed his way through the knot of people to the blurred shape on the stone floor. Reaching over, he turned it slightly so that the face lay within the pool of torchlight. Memnet! Even in death the lips curled in contempt, and the bright eyes stared at him with their habitual disapproval. There was nothing he could do for her except to close her eyes. Servants were already standing by with reed mats and sheets and pitchers of water. Even while he stood watching they bundled the sorry remains into an enveloping swath of linen, lifted them on the mat, and bore them away; all very swiftly and quietly, for they were the same soft-footed slaves who, earlier in the night, had performed endless rites at the altars of deity. Muted of voice they made of this grim labor another priestly rite. But they would find it more difficult to wash the dark stains from the stone floor. For the rock was porous, and it had drunk deeply of the blood of the strange sacrifice. Even though they used all the water in their pitchers and scrubbed until the light of their torches was no longer needed, the eyes of the Good God, accustomed to unblemished pavements, might still be offended when he came forth to walk again among men.

Sometime, thought Moses with startled clarity, *I shall be the Good God sleeping in that dark inner room. These same priests will be protecting my eyes from ugliness, my feet from pollution, my body from all shameful contacts with common men.*

He passed through the vestibule and dining hall and on into the fountain court, where only yesterday the king's mouthpiece had hung the symbol of royalty about his neck. Again he reached through the folds of his cloak to touch its blunt edges, this time not to assure himself of its reality but to reinvoke the mood of exaltation which the incident in the courtyard had shattered. But the disdainful lips and scornful eyes of Memnet persisted in intruding between his vision and the shining pinnacle.

"Son of the Princess Sitra?" they had mocked him boldly. "Offspring of a Mitannian prince? Maybe you look like that to some people, but to me you're nothing but a bastard!"

Well—she would taunt him no more. Soon, after the brief journey to Thebes when his status would be legally proclaimed in the presence of the priesthood, no one in all Egypt would be able to taunt him. He would be the crown prince of the Two Lands, Beloved Son of Amon-Re, begotten in the womb of the divine consort Mut by the life-giving ray of the god himself.

216

There was no need now of prying the secret of his birth from a reluctant Sitra. Seti had done it for him. He was a prince. An Egyptian. A *man*. He could not help hoping that the skeptical Memnet had been listening last night behind some ribboned column when the royal scribe had inton*ed the liberating words.*

"It is the will of Seti, the Strong Bull, the Golden Horus, that Moses, son of his mother Sitra, his nearest friend and blood brother..."

It was nearly dawn when he finally went to his apartment. He noticed with annoyance that the silk curtains of the balcony beyond his bedroom were undrawn, the lamp on the alabaster stand had nearly flickered out, and White Elephant was nowhere to be seen. A pretty state of affairs if the newly appointed crown prince of the Two Lands had to turn back his own coverlet, wash his own flesh, with his own hands remove his soiled clothes and don his linen shift! White Elephant had had too much of coddling. This time he must be punished.

Moses reached for the wooden mallet which lay beside the brazen gong. It snapped back with the quick movement of his wrist, then hung poised as a faint flutter like the wing of a bird caught his eye. He became conscious then of the slight figure standing on the balcony. Except for the movement of the hand which had attracted his attention, it might have been part of the curtain's loosely hanging folds. But now he could see it clearly—silhouetted against the pale sky.

"Tharbis!" called Moses gently.

He was surprised at the surge of pleasure that swept through him. He had wanted someone to share these first high moments of his triumph, someone who possessed a child's capacity for deep wonder and enjoyment. He could have taken her with him tonight through the streets of Bubastis, and she would have endowed the somber journey with adventure. She would have been delighted with the antics of jugglers and acrobats and mummers. She would have put a grinning mask on his head, seized his hand, and drawn him into the whirling, merry coils of dancers. Her wide, marveling eyes would have supplied all the answers to his uncertainties. As she had shared with him that moment of magic when they had climbed the towers of Saba and heard blended together the music of the stars and the cataracts, so she could have climbed with him tonight up the golden rungs, shared with him the breathless vision of the shining pinnacle—could still share it!

"Tharbis!" he repeated eagerly. "Were you there in the banquet hall? Were you listening when the king's scribe read the royal edict?

Come here, child, and let me see your face. Come and tell me how it feels to be wife of the next pharaoh of Egypt!"

Again there was that faint flutter. The figure on the balcony moved out of the shadow of the curtain and came slowly toward him. Even before she was near enough so he could see her features plainly, he knew by the wild beating at his temples that it was not Tharbis.

"So," said Nefretiri evenly, "I come to you on the night of our betrothal that we may rejoice together. And when you finally return in the grayness of the dawn, the name of another woman is on your lips."

"But I—I thought you were Tharbis—"

"So it appears. And you wish to know how it feels to be the wife of the next pharaoh of Egypt. Don't you realize, my dear Moses, that it is Nefretiri who should be asked that question, not Tharbis?" Her voice, like her eyes, was soft and dark as the cape she wore. "Or perhaps it is *you* who were not listening when the king's scribe read the royal edict."

She was right. He knew that he had not been truly listening. The reality of one shining pinnacle had been too much for his unbelieving eyes. He had not even attempted to focus them upon another. Now the words rushed against his consciousness. *The royal Princess Nefretiri, daughter of Seti and Tuya, became betrothed to Prince Moses...* The lamp flared in a last effort to translate this vision also into reality. In one devouring glance, he drank of her loveliness—the sparkling, green-flecked eyes, the imperious curves of cheek and lips and throat; the smooth blackness of hair; and, where the folds of the cape fell open at the breast, a glow of golden flesh. As the light sputtered and went out, he started blindly toward her.

"Nefretiri—my own—my beloved—"

In the darkness she slipped out of his reach. "I waited a long time." Her voice sounded cool and remote, and he could not tell from what part of the room it came. "I supposed, of course, you would come to me after the banquet.

"I—I didn't believe it could be t-true." The explanation sounded lame. "It—it seemed like a dream. C-can't you understand?"

"Of course I understand." He could see a blur of movement now, feel her cool gaze upon him. "You were so busy trying to picture yourself as pharaoh of Egypt that you had no time to consider the prospect of becoming husband to Nefretiri."

"Beloved—forgive me!" Again he groped to find her, and again she eluded him. "I—I don't know what I was thinking of."

"Of Tharbis, perhaps."

"No. Believe me, she did not enter my mind until I came into this room and saw you standing there." He could see her more plainly now. She was leaning against the carved bed, fingers curved against the two massive lions' heads which formed its pattern, slim body arched slightly backward upon her braced hands, and he was certain that she invited as well as taunted him. Emotion possessed him, so intense that he could scarcely breath. He knew that in every fiber of his body he was a helpless slave of this woman. But he did not care. All that mattered was to penetrate the barrier she was raising between them, to feel her in his arms again, soft and yielding. "I—I don't know what possessed me. I should have come to you, of course. Instead, I—I went out and walked alone in the streets."

"Yes. I know. I saw you go. I was watching from the tower."

"The tower!" he repeated sharply. "You were in the tower tonight? Which one? How long were you there?"

"The—the south one." There was but the briefest hesitation in her reply. "And only for a few moments. Why—why do you ask?"

"It's fortunate you were not in the north one," returned Moses. "You might have seen a painful tragedy—or have prevented it." Briefly he told her about Memnet.

"Then—then she is really dead?"

"Yes." Though he was halfway across the room he could feel the sudden relaxation of tension in her body and reproached himself for his thoughtlessness. He should not have broken the news with such cruel abruptness. Memnet had been her nurse since childhood. Regardless of her lack of affection for the dour servant, the knowledge of her violent death would naturally arouse a deep sense of shock. "But it was over very quickly," he assured her hastily, "so let it not be a cause of too much grieving."

Again he started toward her, not with the urgency of passion, but in tenderness, to comfort her as one would comfort a child, but she whirled away from him. "Grieving!" Her voice floated back, full of scorn, from the direction of the balcony. "You don't think I'd grieve over Memnet! She was wicked, she was always telling tales that were untrue, and she deserved to die. She even told tales about you. It was a good thing if someone killed her."

"But no one killed her," explained Moses patiently. "Didn't you understand? It was an accident. She must have fallen. Perhaps she was unwell and went out for a breath of fresh air and became dizzy."

"Yes," said Nefretiri quietly, "Yes, that was it. Of course. She often complained of dizziness. And—and she walked in her sleep."

Moses followed her to the balcony. "Nefretiri!" The warmth of urgency flowed through his lips now as well as his veins. "Beloved, what are we doing? Why are we talking of people and things that do not matter!" She could not escape him here. The railing of the tiny balcony, its dainty painted columns, the dusky, yellowing light, caught her, delivering her into his eager, insistent embrace. Thirstily his lips sought the rims of the long-untasted goblet, its sweet wine entering into his body and coursing through his veins like flame. And finally he could feel her yielding, her soft contours shaping themselves subtly to his flesh, her lips becoming responsive beneath his own. But it was not as it had been among the flower beds in the garden of Mut or in his chamber the night before he had left for Kush. There was hardness beneath her softness, a stubborn core which tainted the ripe fruit of her yielding and made her kisses faintly bitter beneath his lips. Finally the hardness became resistance. She lifted her hands and pushed them against his breast.

"I suppose you have held Tharbis like that," she said coldly, "murmured those same soft words into her ears, pressed your lips so against her dark ugly flesh."

He felt exultant relief mingled with amusement. He had not supposed it possible that Nefretiri, the proudest and most beautiful woman in all Egypt, could stoop to the pettiness of jealousy. The knowledge moved him to peculiar tenderness. "No," he said gently, "you know that isn't so. I married Tharbis in order to fulfill the mission which your father entrusted to me. She is gentle and sweet and friendly, but compared with the daughter of Seti she means nothing to me."

"Then," she said calmly, "you will not mind putting her away."

"Putting her—" Moses looked bewildered. "You mean—"

"That if she means nothing to you, you will be ready and willing to give her a writing of divorcement," continued the calm voice reasonably. "Surely Prince Moses has no thought of demanding that the heiress of the throne of Egypt share her future queenship with a dark-skinned heathen."

The hands at his breast were no longer resistant. If there was any hardness now within the supple figure, it was in the green flecks which seemed to have absorbed all the soft blackness of her eyes. Moses returned her gaze steadily.

"Tharbis is my wife," he said quietly. "I took her as the price of an agreement."

"An agreement which can be easily broken," she returned with persuasive gentleness. "Surely Moses knows that there is no agreement, no law on earth, which is binding on the son of Amon-Re."

"Moses is not yet the son of Amon-Re," he parried.

"But he will be. In a few more days we shall be starting for Thebes. You will enter the great hall at Karnak—"

Deliberately Moses removed the clinging hands and turned away. And Nefretiri realized her mistake. She should not have reminded him of the unfortunate episode accompanying the last confirmation in the temple at Karnak. "You will not be doing Tharbis an injury," she hastened to assure him. "Naturally she will still live with the royal family in the palace and be well cared for. And if you wish her as a concubine—"

He turned then and faced her. She had not seen him angry since their childhood days in the nursery, and the coldness in his eyes was frightening. "Concubine!" he echoed hoarsely. "You actually think I'm the sort of man—"

The words choked in his throat. He turned on his heel and re-entered the chamber, stumbling over a low stool fashioned in the shape of a couchant lion. Pain darted upward through his shins. In the dim light he could see the bronze jaws of the overturned beast grinning up at him. The bedstead too was made in the form of lions. When he sat down on its edge, he could feel the curving smoothness of a long, sinewy back pressing into his thighs. But he was almost unaware of bodily sensation. Words dropped slowly into his consciousness with the dull resonance of stones falling into a deep well.

"I have abandoned you as wife, I am removed from you, I have no claim on earth upon you, I have said unto you, 'Make for yourself a husband in any place to which you shall go.'"

They were the words which Nefretiri demanded that he speak to Tharbis. She was not content to become his wife. She must be his only wife. She was insisting that he should break his vows made to Sinuhe by the light of his desert fire in the shadow of the walls of Saba. It was right, she said, that he should break his vows. For he was to be pharaoh of Egypt. And the pharaoh was god himself. He was bound by no vows, no laws. He was under no responsibility to any man.

God himself...under no responsibility to any man...

Soft fingers pulled the hands from his face. "I'm sorry, beloved," she whispered. "I shouldn't have mentioned it now. Later will be time enough. You are right. Why do we talk of people and things that do not matter when you and I are here at last—together!"

His lips uttered a faint, harsh sound before he swept her again into his arms. She was completely yielded to him now, her cheek warm against his, the soft-petaled goblet pressed brimming and sweet to his lips. It was within himself that there remained that stubborn core which flavored their kisses with the faintest taint of bitterness.

8

Before leaving for Thebes to celebrate the wedding of Nefretiri and Moses and to complete the ceremonies of the latter's confirmation as crown prince, Seti must visit his new city, Per-Ramses. In vain Moses tried to dissuade him. The city was not ready, he demurred. The palace was still a mere shell. It could not possibly accommodate the royal party. The temple to the god Sutekh was barely begun. It would be much better for the Strong Bull to wait until the splendors of obelisks and pylons could delight his eyes with at least a promise of future magnificence. But the Strong Bull did not care to wait. He would exult not in what was, but in what was yet to be. And if Moses wished to prepare the city for his coming, he could go ahead and do so. Let him send word after a week—a month—or whenever he was ready. But let it be soon. The Strong Bull was impatient.

Moses took Sinuhe back with him to Per-Ramses. He took him for three reasons. First, he desired his company. The leathery face, the graceful hands and gently modulated voice never intruded themselves into moments of desired solitude, but at the first summons to a shading of adventure they were always ready. On the deck of the luxurious vessel which bore them to Per-Ramses they talked together of many things: of crops and cranes and the comparative flavors of domestic and imported wines; of the strange smoking mountains in the country of the Blue Nile; of the wisdom of Ptahhotep and the laws of Hammurabi; of Ipuwer and Neferrohu, the prophets, and their dreams of an ideal king.

"'The people of his time shall rejoice,'" quoted the gently modulated voice with the vigor of a fresh wind blowing dust from an old papyrus. "'The son of man shall make his name forever and ever. Righteousness shall return to its place; unrighteousness shall be cast out.'"

Moses felt a strange leaping in his veins. *He* was to be king in Egypt. Was it possible that *he* might be the long-desired son of man promised by the ancient sage? Would *he* make his name forever and ever? But—what was righteousness?

"'He brings cooling to the flame,'" the voice continued. "'It is said he is the shepherd of all men. There is no evil in his heart. When his herds are few, he passes the day to gather them together, their hearts being fevered.'"

Moses flushed and averted his face, hoping that Sinuhe had not caught the flare of speculation in his eyes. No evil in his heart indeed! When with every oar's length of motion his tongue was endeavoring to shape the words which were the second reason for his bringing Sinuhe with him on this journey?

It was clear to him now that to mount higher toward the shining pinnacle he must put Tharbis away. Nefretiri had been adamant. She must be his first wife, for the time being his only wife, or she would be no wife at all. Remembering his own bitterness at the prospect of yielding his place as lover to Amon-nebet, he could not blame her. And he had come at last to a tolerance, if not full acceptance, of her viewpoint. He was sometime to be pharaoh of Egypt. The very words which he spoke would be divinely uttered. His body would be sacred. He could do no wrong. A pretty irony indeed if he could not take or leave any woman of his choosing! They were the arguments of Nefretiri, and he had found it both useless and unpleasant to protest against them. Confusing, also. Life became much simpler, he had discovered, if one accepted it as it came and did not ask questions.

But Sinuhe, he feared, had arrived at no such conclusions. He had acquired many unconventional ideas in his long wanderings. He might even pose some of those disagreeable questions which Moses himself had asked in those first days, before he had accustomed himself to his impending divinity: What of the agreement they had made together in the tent below the cataract? He proposed to repudiate the wife he had taken. Did he propose to repudiate also the victory of which she had been the price? Restore the city of Saba to independence? Return to the hills of Kush the gold which lay inch deep on Seti's temple columns? Send back the slaves...?

Tharbis herself had asked no questions. He had seen her but once, briefly, during his visit in Bubastis. On the morning after the banquet, Beket, his old nurse, had come to his apartment with one of his favorite raisin cakes, cooked with her own hand, and a message that he was to go directly to the lotus pool in the garden. He had tried to question her, but her masklike face had been completely unrevealing. She had looked at him with a mild clairvoyance which in earlier years had indicated a suspicion of extreme naughtiness.

"A raisin cake may not mean much to you now," she had said simply. "The taste of honey is too strong in your mouth. But someday maybe you'll be glad to have it—if you re not so big a fool you go and throw it away."

Bewildered, he had asked, "Why should I throw away a raisin cake, especially when you made it just for me?"

The wise old eyes had admonished him through the mask. "A little raisin cake is a tender thing. Just be careful of it. That's all I'm saying."

He had found Tharbis kneeling by the pool and feeding the pet geese with little balls of paste, and looking very much like a child. He had knelt beside her and they had fed the birds together, laughing at the visible progress of the round lumps down the long curving necks. It had seemed so natural being there with her that he had forgotten to be constrained because of his recent conversation with Nefretiri. When Tharbis had finished feeding the birds, she had jumped to her feet, wiped her fingers on her tunic, and raised her wide-set, alert eyes to his.

"I wanted you to know," she had said without embarrassment; "that I am glad about you and the Princess Nefretiri. I've always known that it was she you were in love with. She doesn't like me, so I know you won't be seeing me much more. Whatever you decide to do about me, I shall understand."

"I—" He stared at her miserably. "I d-don't know what to say—"

"There's nothing to say. That which was mine will be mine still. You can take nothing away that really belongs to me. The hour we spent on the tower at Saba looking at the stars, the day you gave me my first glimpse of the pyramids, the nights we lay side by side, even a few moments when we fed some birds in a garden and laughed together—they are all mine. And neither Moses my husband nor Moses the king of Egypt can take them away from me."

She had lifted herself suddenly on tiptoe, brushed her cool lips against his, and run like a child along the red gravel path toward the palace, leaving him staring after her, a sense of loss within him, as if the laughter had gone out of the morning.

The hours passed leisurely under the blue and crimson awnings of the palatial vessel, and still the carefully framed words, followed by their glib explanations, had not been uttered. "I shall wait until the slaves come to clear away the empty trays and bring the wine vessels," he would tell himself vaguely. Or: "In the hour of twilight before the lamps are lighted there will be a brief interval when we cannot see each other's faces clearly. In the darkness I shall find it easier—" Then, as the lush green swamp grass and feathered tops of papyrus gave place to the stark black deserts of the brickfields: "I shall wait until we have reached our lodgings in the city when some more opportune moment shall present itself."

Their first glimpse of Per-Ramses was even more discouraging than he had anticipated. Its walls were still ragged. The huge obelisk that had been floated down the river from Assuan was still being dragged inch by painful inch on its wooden sled up the great sloping mountain of dirt and timber and brushwood piled in front of the pylon, a vast army of antlike workers still dumping infinitesimal buckets of sand into the mammoth pit which would receive it. No temple towers or palace staves and parapets rose in glittering splendor against the burning metallic blue of the sky. Seen in the glare of noonday, its stark outlines black with sweating laborers, the city looked less like an embryo than a carrion festering in the hot sun and swarming with flies.

But the boy poet Pentaur, whom Seti had sent ahead to compose a eulogy in honor of his impending visit, plucked bravely at his lute and, with the optimism of the true artist, managed to evoke glory whence no glory existed.

"His majesty has built for himself a fortress," he quavered hopefully,

> "Great in Victory is her name.
> She lies between Palestine and Egypt,
> And is full of nourishment.
> Her appearance is as On of the South,
> And she shall endure like Memphis.
> The sun rises in her horizon
> And sets within her boundaries.
> All men forsake their towns
> And settle in her western territory.
> Amon dwells in the southern part, in the temple of Sutekh,
> But Astarte dwells toward the setting of the sun..."

Moses was not so reluctant to disclose to Sinuhe the third reason why he had brought the old adventurer to Per-Ramses.

"I want you to observe this commissioner Baka," he told him soon after their arrival. "There is something about him—I'm not sure what—which makes me distrust him. He reminds me of a snake hiding under a lotus blossom."

"And the question is," responded the other astutely, "why is he there? In other words, does he wish to devour the blossom or is he merely basking lazily in its shade? I would be inclined to say the latter. Any man who has good Charu wine to spare for his visitors dines on meat more substantial than lotus blossoms."

The news of Moses' amazing good fortune had preceded him. He was conducted to a new apartment, sumptuously furnished, adjoining Baka's own establishment. Soft carpets of Syrian weave adorned its floors. The four wine jars in the outer vestibule were, as Sinuhe promptly discovered, filled to the brim. Dark, unsmiling sons of Joseph, the marks of their service in the brickfields still raw on their brown backs, bore dainty trays with the same aloof dignity with which they had shouldered staggering burdens of dried bricks. And in their wake appeared Baka, hastily bedecked with all the jewels he possessed, ready with glib phrases of welcome. The brother of the Strong Bull must look with tolerance on his wretched servant. If only Baka had been forewarned that the chosen one of the Good God himself was to bless Per-Ramses so soon with his presence...

I came too soon, thought Moses, listening to the interminable droning which was like the creaking of a shaduf. *My coming interrupted his plans.*

"How is the building progressing?" he demanded curtly.

Baka reached for a sweetmeat. "Not badly, not badly," he assured Moses cheerfully. "The chosen one of Horus would be glad to know that the labor problem was slowly being solved. The spirit of those ass-headed, swine-bellied sons and daughters of Set seemed at last to be breaking. Oh, he had had a few minor difficulties; had been forced to shut a couple of the stiff-necked sons of iniquity in the dungeon under the new palace. Perhaps the very nearest and dearest friend and brother of the pharaoh would remember them: the two filthy-maned creatures whose presence had defiled the air in that stinking hut which they had visited."

Moses did remember. And the woman who had also been in the hut, he questioned casually, the one with the blazing eyes of Bast and the body of Hathor—presumably Baka had shut her up likewise?

The commissioner carefully extended a pink tongue and licked the melting honey from his sweetmeat. His small, mahogany-colored eyes melted also in anticipation. No, he had not laid hands upon the fiery-eyed, spitting she-cat—that is, not yet. He would postpone that pleasurable exercise of authority until—well, until the mood of the hour seemed to demand it.

"The pharaoh is coming to inspect the city," announced Moses abruptly.

The commissioner's mouth sagged. "When?"

"Within a month, certainly. Possibly within a week."

"B-but he can't! It—it's not ready!"

"Of course it's not ready!" Moses whipped him a glance full of scorn. "The walls of the palace are scarcely higher than a man's shins. The room where the king expects to sleep is as unroofed as a vulture's nest."

The flesh in which the small eyes were embedded turned the color of unbaked dough. "There—there hasn't been time—"

"There's been time enough to make your own house a fit habitation for a prince," retorted Moses.

"He may not understand that it's not my fault." The throaty creaking descended to a mere whimper. "That it's those ass-headed, swine-bellied sons and daughters—"

"No," interposed Moses evenly. "Not knowing those ass-headed, swine-bellied offspring as you and I do, he won't understand. He may even jump to the conclusion that you're not anxious to see his city in the north completed, that you find it more profitable to serve other masters than Seti."

It was a chance thrust, but it struck sparks. "B-but it's not true," protested Baka wildly. "I have worn myself to the bone in the service of the Strong Bull. Behold this wretched body. It has no other master than the pharaoh."

Moses beheld. "It has no other master," he replied contemptuously, "than its own whims and appetites. And, speaking of appetites, you'd better eat that sweetmeat."

Baka thrust the remains of the dripping morsel between his gaping lips. There was a brief pause and a sound of crunching.

"What shall I do?" he inquired more cheerfully, casting a tentative eye toward the platter.

"Nothing," replied Moses. "Just what you have been doing. Leave the city to me. I'll make it ready for the pharaoh."

From that moment Moses did not rest. He was obsessed by but one desire: to have the obelisk in place and bright pennants flying from the palace when Seti visited his new city. The royal dwelling, of course, could not be made ready for use. An embryo does not clothe itself with flesh and blood in the space of one moon. But the bones could be assembled. The pyloned gateway could attain at least the outlines of future grandeur. The walls could be reared to the height of a man's shoulder. The tall cedars which had been brought down from Lebanon and left blistering in the sun could be placed triumphantly on their feet and adorned with proud banners.

He became a stern and indefatigable taskmaster. The Egyptian construction bosses, who had enjoyed much of Baka's leisurely freedom by turning over their responsibility to Hebrew underlings, learned to dread and resent his coming. He set them impossible goals and insisted on their achieving them. Behind his back they grumbled heatedly. They might have been underlings themselves for all the respect he accorded their position. Expecting them to descend into the burning pits where the sons of Joseph were burrowing! Demanding an accurate accounting of every brick made, hauled, and laid; every shovelful of dirt extracted from the mountains on which the obelisk hung suspended; every fraction of an inch which the palace walls grew in stature!

But the walls of the palace grew, brick by sunburned brick, from the height of a man's knees to a level with his groins. The cedars of Lebanon reared themselves again proudly, one by one. The sand grew deeper in the yawning pit which was to receive the obelisk. And, with the terrifying patience of eroding winds and waters, shovelful after groaning shovelful, the sweating workers burrowed into the pile of earth beneath the recumbent giant, slowly and imperceptibly shifting the slant of its mammoth bulk, even as through long centuries of labor their brothers the elements had changed the course of rivers and shifted the contours of mountains. But here there must be no centuries. It must be done in weeks—hours—minutes—with only the whirring of lashes for the shaping winds and the dripping of sweat for the eroding waters.

Deliberately Moses kept his face averted from the toiling figures. When his glance fell upon them briefly, he saw them en masse, not as individuals; a dragging chain rather than as separate links. He saw vaguely that it was as Baka had said. The spirit of the sons of Joseph seemed to be broken. There was little now to distinguish them from those other slaves whom he had inspected in mine and quarry and temple. Their backs bent themselves to their loads of bricks not as bows which would spring back into straightness the moment the burden was removed, but as the gnarled trunks of desert acacias hunched beneath generations of winds and sandstorms. Their features were blank, unhostile, empty of rebellion. They reminded him vaguely of something, he could not recall what...until one day he saw one of the naked bodies chained to a post on the edge of the brickfields. Then he remembered. The bird had been white, not brown, and its chain had been shining gold. But, finding its cage opened, it had crawled under a pile of refuse in the back of a tent, having lost all desire to fly.

No problem was too small to command his attention. He rose before dawn, traveled ceaselessly from palace to city gate, from city gate to brickfield, keeping a stern eye on each successive step of the operations. He checked brick tallies by actual count, tested the consistency of mortar, made innumerable calculations and a thorough survey of the embryo city to its remotest cranny. It was at the end of this inspection that he paid a visit to the palace dungeon.

The guard on duty recognized him and was properly obsequious. He would be glad to accompany the friend of the pharaoh into the bowels of the earth, but he was expecting to be relieved shortly, and it was necessary for him to be at the door to render an account to his successor. If the noble prince would care to wait...

"I'll go in alone," said Moses. "That is, unless there's danger of losing my way."

There was no danger, the guard assured him. There was only one path, downward, and one room at the end of it. Taking one of the lamps from its niche in the stone wall, Moses closed the heavy stone door behind him and began the descent.

How like Baka, he thought, noting the smooth, tight walls on either side, *to make his dungeon complete before he started on his palace!*

The passage was narrow, and it descended at an abrupt angle, like the inclined shaft of a tomb. He looked along its walls, half expecting to see pictures in the dimness, setting forth the voyages of the soul through its twelve hours of night. But there were no pictures. And in the dark cavity at the bottom of the final flight of steps there were no heaped masses of treasure, no hundreds of little models and images to labor for the incarcerated bodies in the hereafter. He thought at first there was nothing at all. Then, as he stepped tentatively forward, he sensed rather than saw the two shapes lying on the floor. Moving toward them, he held his torch high. At first glance he thought Baka must have made a mistake. These were not the two men whom he had seen in the room of the small hut. The blinking eyes, the matted hair, the smooth, unnaturally pallid cheeks belonged to strangers. Then recognition flared in the faces staring up into his. A harsh laugh burst from the pale lips.

"Well! Prince Moses himself! The pharaoh's pet in the flesh! Can his princely stomach really stand the stench of the dungeon?"

Moses' hand gripped hard on the handle of the torch. It took all his self-restraint to keep him from flinging it in the mocking face. He knew now why he had not recognized the man Aaron and his companion. Baka had punished them with the supreme indignity. He had shaved off their beards! Disgusted, Moses turned to leave the dungeon. To his mortification he had difficulty in locating the narrow door where he had entered and finally had to grope his way by feeling along the wall with his hands. It was cold as a snake's belly and damp to the touch.

When finally he reached the outer door at the end of the long upward passage, he was actually running. Hastily, without replacing the torch in its niche, he pushed it open. Hot sunlit air burst against his face, and he stood for a moment drawing deep breaths of it into his nostrils. The new guard, lounging against the skeleton wall of the palace, looked up at him, stared, lifted his fingers to his lips and emitted a shrill whistle. Moses was completely unprepared for his swift assault. Dazed, he felt himself flung hard against the closed door, the torch thrown from his hands, and his arms pinned securely at his sides. Instinctively he began to struggle. Lifting his right knee, he pushed it with all his might into the man's chest. In response to the whistle two other guards came running.

"Hold him!" gasped the first, his breath almost knocked out of him by the force of the knee thrust. "He's a—vicious brute. One of those accursed Hebrew prisoners—thought he could—get away."

Now that he knew the reason for the unexpected assault, Moses ceased resisting. Amusement almost triumphed over resentment. It would be worth the indignity to see their faces when they discovered his identity. But when he announced that he was Prince Moses, brother of the pharaoh, the guard laughed and spat squarely in his face. Prince Moses, was he? Why didn't he tell an even better one and claim to be the Good God himself? By the udders of Hathor, he guessed he knew the two asses' heads that had been rotting in the dungeon for the last moon! He'd fed them often enough. And he'd swear by any god anybody wanted to name that this was one of them. Fine dress or no fine dress, this was one of the heathen carcasses that belonged in the dungeon, and if it wasn't back there before a man could count the hairs of Bast's whiskers...

Moses felt no more amusement. Enraged, he struggled against his captors, but, strong though he was, it was three against one. Seizing the other torch from its niche, they bore him, still struggling, down the steep passageway. Entering the single chamber of the dungeon, the guard held his torch high. It gave a sudden lurch, and almost fell.

"Sweet Hathor bless my soul! He—he's still there on the floor! May Amon help us!"

"You'll need his help," said Moses grimly, "and sweet Hathor's too. When the pharaoh hears that you've brought dishonor—"

He stopped, realizing that the guards were staring at him, lifting and lowering the torch so that it shone, first on his face, then on that of the man lying on the floor.

"By Amon, they *are* alike!"

"I swear they could have budded from the same womb and suckled at the same breasts!"

"Mother Isis help us. It's a man's ka we're seeing!"

Laughter burst from the man on the floor. He raised himself to his elbows, and his dark eyes, catching the reflection of the torch, blazed like those of an animal.

"So he looks like me, does he? The mighty Prince Moses sees his own image in the face of a despised son of Joseph! Well, why shouldn't he? Is it so strange for a man to look like his brother?"

The three guards were inarticulate with terror. Out in the sunlight again they groveled in the earth before the very nearest friend of the pharaoh. They called upon all the gods to smite them blind and cut out their tongues as punishment for their stupidity. They implored the chosen one of the Good God to spare the lives of his miserable slaves.

Moses neither saw nor heard them. Though the noon sun was hot upon him, he felt no heat. His body was still cold with the dampness of the dungeon.

9

He was not the blood brother of the pharaoh. He was not an Egyptian. He was not even a *man*. He was one of the despised sons of Joseph.

Sitra had lied to Seti. He was not her son. Neither the blood of the royal Mitanni nor the blood of the pharaohs flowed in his veins. He was a foundling whom she had discovered by chance and in a moment of womanly weakness befriended. He was the outcast child of an outcast people.

Strange how all the scattered pieces suddenly fitted together, like broken bits of pottery with parts of a picture painted on them! The sojourn of Sitra in Bubastis not too many miles from the Valley of Goshen; the purge of Harmhab; the long, deep silence; the startled cry of a sick woman when Prince Moses' name had been mentioned; the strange story that had poured from her lips; the face-to-face encounter in the dungeon. The pieces had leaped together without warning, leaving no jagged edges to mar the stark outlines of the picture. For hours now he had been staring at it. Not hours. Days. Years. An eon. An eternity.

It had been high noon when he had gone into the dungeon. Looking up now at the sky, he was bewildered to note that the sun was still only halfway between the horizon and the zenith. It was the hour when he should be rising from his midday rest, calling for a skin of wine cooled in a well of deep water. Today, obviously, he had had no midday rest, no cooling goblet. No matter. Neither had the Children of Joseph. No; say rather the other Children of Joseph.

He was surprised to find himself in the act of making his usual tours of inspection, taking tallies, issuing sharp commands. It would be another month at least before he could summon Seti; two before they could make the trip to Thebes. Even so they would be in the southern capital in ample time for the Feast of Opet, when Seti planned his confirmation.

What's that he was saying? Confirmation? The bit of shard on which he was scribbling thrust its sharp edges into his palm. A Hebrew confirmed as crown prince of Egypt! Well—why not? There had been shepherd kings on the throne of the Two Lands before. For a hundred years at least they had reigned. Perhaps they had been ancestors of these same Children of Joseph.

A beardless, submissive, slightly crafty face came within his range of vision. Moses remembered it vaguely. It belonged to a Hebrew section boss named Dathan.

"If the nearest friend and brother of the pharaoh would be so kind as to remember a little conversation he deigned to have with his servant some time ago—"

"Yes," replied Moses curtly. "I remember it. I asked you why more of your stubborn kin didn't follow your wise example in conforming to the ways of their adopted country. But you didn't give me a good answer."

"Because there is none," responded Dathan promptly. "Stupidity is not explainable. But—it may very well be dangerous."

"What do you mean?" demanded Moses, wondering what the subservient creature would do if he were to announce suddenly: "You think you're talking to a prince of Egypt, don't you? Well, you're not. I'm blood of your own miserable blood, do you hear? I'm a Hebrew!"

"I mean that it would be well for that mighty one who shall sit on the throne of the Two Lands to have both eyes and ears among the Children of Joseph."

"I see," said Moses. "And you would like to be those eyes and ears. At a price, of course. I—will remember."

His blood was burning and his fists were clenched when he turned and walked away. Belong to that despicable brood of asses and cravens? Heaven forbid! Indeed, heaven had forbidden. Had it not taken him out of the swamp where he had been spawned and made him in everything but birth Egyptian? Why then should he be so concerned? His position was secure. In the eyes of all Egypt he was the son of Sitra, the brother of Seti, the betrothed of the daughter of the pharaoh. Who could or would prove it otherwise? Not Sitra, certainly. She had already perjured herself to make his name honorable. Beket? Hardly, though she undoubtedly knew the truth. *Memnet! Memnet had known!* Her small eyes and thin, curling lips had told him so over and over again. But Memnet was dead. She had fallen from a balcony on the very night that his position had become assured. Her lips had been closed.

He stopped suddenly in his tracks, knowing that Memnet had been deliberately silenced. How? And by whom? Had someone been standing behind her on the balcony—someone who *knew*—and who knew that Memnet knew? Sitra would have known. And Beket. Nefretiri had been on the balcony that night. She had hesitated when he had asked her which one. But Nefretiri did not know. Or—did she?

"Is—is she really dead?... She was wicked, she was always telling tales that were untrue. She deserved to die. She even told tales about you."

Moses' brain whirled. Sitra—Beket—Nefretiri. No matter. It was done. His secret was safe. Someone had cared enough about him to kill in order to preserve it. Swiftly his fears veered to those others whose knowledge might endanger his position. The guards who had seen the likeness? Their blunder had stricken them dumb with terror. Aaron, Miriam, his—the woman lying on the pallet? No, they would not tell his secret. And if they did, who would believe them? He was safe. He was still Prince Moses, the chosen one of Seti, the future pharaoh of Egypt. He could go back to his apartment and sip cool wine and chat pleasantly with Sinuhe and forget that this day had ever been.

He did go back finally but not until after the brickfields had been deserted, their rows upon rows of flat black oblongs stretching like a death city of mastabas in the waning moonlight. The virgin obelisk hung on its mountain like the suspended arm of a balance, set to weigh the heart of a giant in the last judgment, the shadow of an immense brooding Thoth in the background. On the broad marsh below the walls of the new city sprawled the makeshift encampment of the laborers, their tiny scattered fires glowing like stars in a world turned suddenly upside down. Since it was impossible for most of them to return to their huts in the Valley of Goshen between the coming of starlight and dawn, they cooked their meager rations over a small blaze of dried grass or dung, rolled themselves in dirty sheepskins, and slept on the ground wherever they chanced to fall.

To his chagrin he had to pass through one of these impromptu encampments in order to reach the city gate. The odor of sweat and cooked onions and oily sheepskins was heavy on the air. He had to step carefully to keep from stumbling over the sprawled bodies. But his presence was not conspicuous. Egyptian underlings were everywhere in evidence, shouting orders, bawling names from roll calls, punctuating curt questions with the familiar whine of whips.

Merciful Amon! thought Moses. *Can't we even eat our bread in peace or lie down on the bare ground at night without—*

He stopped aghast. A coldness deeper than that of the dungeon crept slowly up through his body. Amon help him, all the gods of Egypt deliver him, what had he said!

We...

Sinuhe, as usual, was sipping wine. "You're late," he remarked cheerfully before looking at Moses' face. "White Elephant has already served me an excellent supper. I'll have him—Ah!"

"I have to go away," said Moses, "on a rather long journey. Don't ask me why. I—I'm not quite sure yet myself."

"You look as if you'd just come from a long journey," observed Sinuhe quietly. "Where are you going?"

"To—toward Tharu."

"It's a long way to Tharu."

"I know. I may not go all the way—tonight."

"Some confidential business, I suppose, for the pharaoh." The curious eyes, intent on the ravaged face, supposed no such thing. "Are you sure it won't wait till morning?"

"Very sure."

"You're taking White Elephant, I presume?" The question in the softly modulated voice denied the presumption.

"No. It's—very confidential business. And—Sinuhe?"

"Yes, my son?"

Moses' eyes flashed their gratitude. The old man had never called him that before. "If—if I shouldn't get back by the time the obelisk is in place, send word to Seti that the city is ready. I shall be back before long, of course, but—just in case—"

"I understand. Just in case. But—listen, my son!"

"Yes?" Moses waited, his body a still, empty question mark.

The old man laughed and shrugged. "No—don't listen. A fine one Sinuhe would be to keep a man from going on a journey when his heart bids him go!"

He was not surprised to find the door of the hut open and a dim light burning inside. Nothing surprised him any more. His eyes went straight to those of the woman lying on the mat.

"Why didn't you tell me?" he said.

He moved toward her, but before he had taken more than a few steps the woman called Miriam was in front of him, her blazing eyes two sharp dagger points halting his progress.

"*You!*" she whipped out at him scornfully. "What are you doing here? Wasn't it enough for you to—kill him?"

He stared back at her. The words too had become daggers, their significance striking deep into the most sensitive fibers of his being. Not until this moment had he realized the implication of his relationship to this household. *The man he had killed had been his own father.* No wonder this woman despised him. Suddenly he felt like laughing, but the sound that escaped his lips was not laughter. In all his long hours of mental wrestling this was one eventuality that he had not considered. What a crowning master stroke of this day's genius for bitter ironies; that he should be despised and cast out by his own despised and outcast people!

"Come here," said the sick woman quietly.

The blazing dagger points shifted slowly, reluctantly; were replaced by two steadily glowing lamps. He found himself moving toward them, standing beside the mat, dropping suddenly to his knees beside it. The woman reached out her hand and pushed back a strand of curling hair from his damp forehead.

"You're tired," she said gently, "and hungry. There's a little wooden stool almost at your feet. Miriam, bring some bread and a cup of fresh goat's milk. Your brother has come home."

10

The judgment scales were tipping. As the lashings were removed from the huge wooden sled on which the mammoth monolith had been dragged up its improvised mountain, there was a harsh creaking and splintering of wood, a fierce grinding as of stone being crushed to powder, and the heart of the giant weighed steadily downward into the waiting pit of sand. But there was no Thoth, god of justice, brooding in the background. The sky was unmarred by shadow. Except in the small chamber beneath the mountain where through a tiny opening into the pit the shovels of the workmen nibbled feverishly at the yawning maw of sand, these was no spot of shade beneath the vast blazing canopy. And here the heat was that of a baking kiln. Men labored until they fell and were dragged out, fainting and exhausted. Slowly, imperceptibly, hour after hour, day after day, sand drained from the huge pit like tiny grains sifting through an hourglass, and the inclined shaft settled deeper and deeper, until it rested finally on the huge concrete base that had been prepared for it.

Moses straightened his shoulders and wiped the sweat out of his eyes. He was still weak and trembling, his heart pounding like hammer thrusts in his chest. For he was one of those who had remained in the furnace until the last grains of sand had filtered through the tiny opening. There was little feeling in his arms, and he stared at them fixedly for a moment to assure himself that they were still whole and in place. The right hand and arm of the laborer beside him had been caught by the settling shaft and crushed flat to the elbow. The man's streaming had resounded through the small chamber until one of his comrades, using the blunt edge of his shovel, had mercifully ended his misery.

Seeing his own whole right arm and hand, Moses was seized by an overpowering nausea, and for a few moments he was violently sick. Spent and weak, he stood dazed, trying to adjust himself to his surroundings, and his eyes encountered the smooth, upright shaft of granite. Up and up they traveled until they reached the dazzling gold tip, almost as bright in its reflected glory as the sun itself. Pain throbbed behind his eyeballs, but he did not turn aside his gaze. From the blazing focus light burst forth in all directions, splintering into a thousand darting spear thrusts of radiance, each one ending in a tiny outstretched hand.

"Aton!" he murmured. Half-remembered phrases rose to his lips.

> "Thy dawning is beautiful in the horizon of heaven,
>   O living Aton, Beginning of life..."

It was here again, the moment of near perception which he had experienced in the temple at Akhetaton, which he had striven over and over again to recapture: the intense burning radiance, the flooding sense of warmth within and without, the awareness that was almost comprehension. Surely now again he was on the verge of discovery. He would know if the benign presence that had warmed the spirit of the gentle Ikhnaton was the answer to his questions.

"Aton!" he repeated. "O living Aton, Beginning —"

The throbbing pain pounded like mallets against his temples. The golden rays with their little outstretched hands became thousands of tiny flails beating mercilessly upon his flesh. The burning focus descended from its lofty height; entered into his body, became a devouring fire licking at the sources of life itself. His eyes half blinded with pain, he stared until the blazing core of radiance was finally washed away with healing tears. Then he threw back his head and laughed aloud. Benign presence? Beneficent heat which enfolded all mankind in its embrace? To the gentle Ikhnaton, perhaps, sitting in the cool kiosks of his garden. Not to his laboring fellah or the slave toiling in his brickfield! They would sing a different hymn!

> "Thy dawning is grievous in the horizon of heaven,
>   O cruel Aton, Devourer of life..."

"Listen here, you swine's offal! What do you think you're here for, to lean on your shovel and gape at the sunshine? Get your eyes on the ground where they belong! By Amon, if you can't fill the cart with dirt, you'll do it with your rotting carcass!"

Instinctively he braced himself to the fierce rhythm of the lash. The familiar stinging pain was between his shoulder blades, in the sensitive curve of his back, in his shins. As always when the lash descended, anger tensed his muscles. His fists clenched until his nails

237

bit into his palms. It took all his self-restraint to keep him from turning on his assailant, seizing the coil from his hands, and twisting it tightly about the stocky throat. In fact he would not need the lash. Just his bare hands...Instead he picked up his shovel and thrust it deep into the mountain of earth and brushwood, emptied it into the waiting cart to which two of the Children of Joseph were harnessed; filled it and emptied it; filled...emptied... Until, like the widening ripples succeeding the fall of a stone into water, the pain became less and less concentered, and finally subsided.

Again the half-naked shapes were on either side of him, the sound of their labored breathing in his ears, the smell of their sweat in his nostrils. Even after these long weeks of toiling among them, they were still merely brown, naked shapes, possessing no individuality. He despised them no less than when he had walked among them as a prince of Egypt, careful not to soil his white garments by contact with them. In fact, a little more, if anything. Seeing a space somewhat apart from the others, he moved toward it, turning his back on them to shut out sight as well as sound and smell. But he could still hear the hoarse breathing, smell the acrid, sickening odor. When he realized that the sound emanated from his own lips, the foulness from his own flesh, he laughed again. He took a morbid pleasure in lifting his hand to his chin and feeling the blackened stubble. Another few weeks, and there would be nothing to distinguish him from the others. The dirt would have ground itself deeper into his pores, the raw flesh on his back hardened into a network of red-brown ridges. Even his beard would have grown to a respectable length. He wondered if it would be black and curling, like his brother Aaron's.

When he had taken his place among them on that first day, many of the Children of Joseph had believed that he was Aaron, paled and weakened from his sojourn in the dungeon. Their curiosity had been short-lived. Today they accepted his presence with the same stolidity as tomorrow they would accept the absence of that other whose right hand and arm lay flattened beneath the obelisk. That he chose each night to take the long trek back to his hut in Goshen rather than to wrap himself in a sheepskin and lie beside their dung embers occasioned only the briefest wonder and speculation. For it took energy both to wonder and to speculate, and they had none to spare.

Once in the beginning when his unaccustomed muscles had been sorely tortured by the day's labor, Moses had laid himself down among them. But he had not slept. The closeness of the sprawling bodies had been stifling. His unwashed flesh had itched and crawled unbearably, and the stench of the oily sheepskin had nauseated him. Fortunately the hut of Aaron and Hur was near the northern border of Goshen and within walking distance of Per-Ramses, so after that he had traveled the long, stumbling journey at night through the dark, that he might steal down to the edge of the marshes and find a shallow pool to wash himself, then enjoy a few hours sleep on his pallet.

Each night as he reported to Dathan, his section boss, for his daily ration of bread and onions, he held his head down, letting a thick mass of hair fall across his forehead Dathan's eyes wore cold and penetrating. More than once he had seen them rest upon him with a puzzled speculation that was almost recognition.

"Mosheh ben Amram?"

"The servant of Amon," mumbled Moses in reply, holding out his hand for the meager packet. He was glad the conversation must be held in Egyptian, for he could say but a few stumbling words in Hebrew. He tried to make his accent halting, as if he were speaking in a strange tongue.

Tonight Dathan did not give him his packet at once. "I have been making inquiries," he said. "There are those of the Children of Joseph who remember that Amram had another son than Aaron. But he died in infancy, in the great purge."

"I did not die," replied Moses, lowering his head still further.

"So it appears. But—I don't understand where you could have been all this time. You—your face looks familiar."

"Like my brother Aaron's," said Moses.

"Get along there, swine's snout. Take your victuals and get moving!"

Grateful for the interruption, even though it included a smart kick from the Egyptian overseer, Moses seized his packet and hastened away. He was conscious of Dathan's eyes, still puzzled, following him.

The obelisk was in place. Even though it still remained for the two mountains to be eaten away by the vast army of burrowing ants, the visit of Seti could be postponed no longer. The walls of the palace were shoulder-high. Bright banners of crimson and blue and purple streamed from the tips of the proud cedars of Lebanon. In another day Sinuhe's couriers would be on their way to Bubastis. Before another seven days Seti would come to inspect his new city. With him he would bring his daughter Nefretiri, who would soon take as her bridegroom the man who, unless he chose otherwise, would become the next pharaoh of Egypt.

As Moses traveled through the gathering darkness one thought beat persistently against his consciousness. *It was still not too late.* He could wash the grime from his body, put on his white linen garments, and take his place again among the sons of Amon. Mosheh ben Amram could disappear as completely as had Moses, prince of Egypt. It could be as if these weeks of degradation and torture had never been.

Suppose the Children of Joseph were his people. Was he making them any less poor by assuming their poverty, any more clean by aping their uncleanness? Now that he knew them better, he despised them more rather than less. The fact that he shared their uncouthness made it not less but more repulsive. It merely caused him to despise himself. Why had he yielded to the strange compulsion, obeyed the voice that had said with unmistakable clearness: *"Go down, Moses! These are your people. Share their burdens!"* Had he lightened their labors one whit by sharing them? Indeed, had he really wanted to serve them, could he not have done it far better as the crown prince of Egypt? With the king's seal he could have freed Aaron and Hur from their dungeon, increased the meager rations of bread and onions, reduced the quota of bricks demanded of each section boss—*could still do all these things!* He need merely return once more to the hut, take his white garments from the chest where they had been stored, and announce his decision. Only the woman lying on the mat would regret his going. The eyes of the dark young girl called Elisheba would light eagerly because it would promise release for her husband Aaron. Miriam would regard him with a cold scorn that would strip his motives of every trace of selflessness.

"Go, by all means!" she would spit out at him disdainfully. "But don't pretend it's for the sake of your Hebrew brothers you are going! You've done better than I thought you would. I'd have wagered when you came that you wouldn't last a moon. It will be something to smile over when you're lying in your soft bed with your princess wife and growing fat on fine foods that once for a full moon you lay on a straw pallet and ate barley bread and onions!"

But tonight Miriam was not in the hut when he entered it. Elisheba had obviously returned from the brickfields alone. She was kneeling beside the smoking fire in the center of the earthen floor stirring something that smelled like a soup of lentils. With her grimy face and untidy hair she was not a pretty picture, but Moses regarded her gratefully. Her eyes did not blaze at him scornfully through the film of smoke, nor would her words be weighted with barbs of bitterness. Tonight there would be peace in the small hut.

Now that he encountered no obstacle to his immediate departure, Moses became suddenly loath to leave. After all, there was no need for great haste in making his decision. Another night, another day...After going down to the river to bathe he would sit cross-legged before the mat of woven reeds on which the frugal supper would be laid and dip his morsels of bread into the bowl of steaming lentils.

It would taste good tonight, for he was hungry. Perhaps there would be a bit of laughter, and Aaron's children would climb on his knees. Then he would sit on the low stool beside Jochebed, his mother, and they would talk together. Perhaps she would tell him more about the strange god her ancestors had worshiped, the being whose abode they had left far behind them in the desert, whose voice was the voice of wind and storm and thunder, and whose temple was a fire-rimmed mountaintop.

"Miriam is going to see Aaron and Hur," announced Elisheba excitedly. "A message came to her while we were working in the brickfields, from the building commissioner himself."

Abruptly the room swung into sharp focus. As if the film of smoke had been blown away, Moses saw the round contours of the clay cooking pot, the bold lines of the chest of acacia wood, the eager features profiled against the glow of the fire. And he knew that for a long time, unconsciously, he had been waiting for this moment.

"Who did you say sent the message to Miriam?" he asked sharply.

"The building commissioner, Baka," replied Elisheba. In her excitement she broke into swift Hebrew. "Surely that means that he is planning to release them soon, or he wouldn't have bothered to send her a personal message. At least she's going to see them—"

"Tell me exactly what the message said," interrupted Moses sternly. "In Egyptian, not Hebrew."

"It—it said that if she wanted to see her husband and brother," repeated the girl carefully, "she was to come to the hut of Dathan on the edge of the brickfields. Tonight, after all the workers had left. If she valued their lives, she must bring no one with her. She must come alone and wait."

Moses turned toward the door. "I'll be back," he said shortly. Then he turned to the woman lying on the mat. "She may not be able to find her way home easily in the dark." He tried to make his voice sound casual. He knew that the words were no better than no explanation at all. Miriam knew her way far better than he did. "Besides, I—I want to hear about Aaron and Hur. I'll go to the edge of the brickfields and meet her."

"But—your supper." Elisheba looked distressed.

"No matter," said Jochebed quietly. "Moses is right. Don't try to stop him, Elisheba. He knows what he is doing."

Moses stumbled through the darkness without thought of the rough ground over which he traveled. Hatred for Baka and contempt of his own stupidity filled him to the exclusion of all other emotions. One by one the pieces of the ugly pattern fell neatly into place: the calculating cupidity in the commissioner's eyes, the sumptuous new apartment adjoining Baka's house, the arrest of Aaron and Hur, his own intuition that he and Sinuhe had arrived, from Baka's point of view, just a little too soon. Knowing what he did, he should have warned Miriam; no doubt would have, if her attitude of scornful indifference had not precluded all friendly intercourse between them. Probably she would not thank him now for his interference. She might even prefer the indignity of becoming Baka's mistress to that of accepting assistance from his hands. Why then should he concern himself over the fact that an Egyptian official was availing himself of a privilege which every custom and law of the land accorded him? In fact, Baka was exhibiting an extreme delicacy in the matter. If the king's building commissioner desired to take a mistress from among the daughters of Joseph, he had only to send a couple of guards and have her brought summarily to his lodgings. But it was no gentlemanly delicacy that had inspired Baka to resort to trickery. It was fear. He was almost as afraid of Miriam as he was desirous to possess her.

Moses was breathing hard when he reached the edge of the brickfields. The rows of tiny mastabas stretched endlessly in all directions. He soon found himself stumbling among them, hopelessly lost. The huts of the Hebrew section bosses were ranged along the outer edges of the fields, long distances apart, and even by daylight there would have been nothing to distinguish Dathan's hut from a dozen others. The fields were quite deserted. There was no light except from the faint glow of the rising moon, against which the obelisk, flanked by its two ragged mountains, formed a clear silhouette. Its pointing finger was Moses' only guide. He knew that Dathan's hut was somewhere to the right of the road leading up to Per-Ramses from Goshen, but each square dark shape looked like every other. He had almost decided to retrace his steps and continue on to Baka's house in the city when he heard the startled neighing of a horse. Creeping toward it cautiously, he berated himself again for his stupidity. Of course Baka would not have ventured into the brickfields alone or on foot. Had he started searching for a horse and carriage in the first place, he would have saved himself much unnecessary delay.

He circled the dark shapes warily, approaching only close enough to assure himself that it was Baka's outfit. The commissioner's inordinate vanity included his horse and carriage, and the proudly reared head silhouetted against the sky was topped by a tuft of plumes almost as intricately cheerful as that of the pharaoh's own steeds. The driver was lolling sleepily against the carriage rail.

The hut was not far away. Moses placed his hands against the mud wall and groped his way to the corner. The adjacent wall also had no opening. Carefully he moved along it, keeping his hands in constant contact with its rough surface. The single opening was in the wall beyond. He could see faint light streaming from it. Cautiously he made his way toward it.

Then, as a familiar sound came to his ears, he forgot caution and sprang toward the doorway. Dim though it was, the light of the small oil lamp blinded him and he stood blinking on the threshold. But the sound, dull and rhythmical and faintly hollow, continued in his ears. Slowly the interior of the hut swung into perspective. He was aware of one lucid moment when every object in the room was sharply chiseled on his consciousness; the lamp flaring in its niche; the network of cracks on the three black mud walls; the outlines of a wooden spade standing in a corner; the naked woman stretched on the mat; the slow arc of the man's arm as he drew it back before each rhythmic motion; the sinuous line of the lash outlined again and again on raw flesh.

Only for that moment did he see clearly. Then all the objects swam in a red haze before his eyes. The cracked surfaces surrounding him were the suddenly straitened and compressed boundaries of his own emotions. The radiance from the clay lamp was the sudden flaring of a long-smoldering impulse of hatred. The naked figure was not Miriam, his sister. It was a boy hanging from a crude gallows on the edge of the desert...a woman kneeling outside a gate with a strange mark on her forehead...a shapeless mass shoveled into a mortar tray...black swollen lips panting to the rhythm of dripping water...a white bird dragging a gold chain beneath a pile of rubbish. And the man whose hand formed a pink-tipped arc each time it wielded the lash was not Baka...

The mud walls seemed all at once to expand, the pale flare to burst into ruddy flame. Moses moved forward. Seizing the soft shoulders in a viselike grip, he swung them about. The small, mahogany-colored eyes sank deeper into the doughy flesh. The lips opened and closed, but at first no sound came.

"You—" they managed at last to gasp with that harsh throatiness which was like the creaking of a shaduf. "Who—let you—out—dungeon—"

Moses laughed. So the coward thought he was Aaron, come to take vengeance for the rape of his sister! The red haze began to throb before his eyes, flowed into a single focus that moved to a slow rhythm, like the beating of a drum. No, not like a drum. Like the steady pulsing of the shaduf. His fingers closed about it, and he felt its rhythm coursing through his own body. His grip tightened. The balls of his thumbs and fingers pressed deeper into the soft flesh, found the source of its steady, relentless beating. It slipped from beneath his grasp, but he found it again, held to it stubbornly until he had somehow stilled its rhythm. Aaron? He laughed again. No, by Amon and all the gods who had ever lived, he was not Aaron! Nor was he Moses, who had been born a slave and who had dreamed of sitting on the throne of Egypt. He was a man's crushed bones and sinews awakening into vigor and prying stones apart. He was a flattened arm and hand swelling suddenly into strength to uproot a mighty monolith. He was the fellah rising at last out of his infinite patience to still the creaking of the shaduf.

Then the mist cleared, and he saw with horror that it was Baka's throat to which his fingers clung, Baka's body which hung with limp heaviness from his grasp. With sudden revulsion he cast it violently from him. It struck the mud wall with a thud and a faint snapping sound, and it remained motionless where it fell, limbs grotesquely doubled, head hanging from its body at a sickening angle.

"You have killed him," said Miriam without emotion.

"Yes," said Moses. He stood staring at the still shape, powerless to move. It was Miriam now who assumed authority. Rising from the mat, she hastily donned the single garment which had been torn from her body during the struggle with Baka.

"Quick!" she ordered. "We have no time to waste. Dathan will have finished the errand Baka sent him on and will be returning. Here! Take this. It's a spade I found in the corner. Don't stand there staring. Take it in your hands and hold it. Put his cloak around him, and drag him over here to the door while I put out the light. What's the matter with you! You've just killed a man—an Egyptian! Hurry and do as I tell you!"

Mechanically Moses obeyed her. He wound the cloak about the still figure. He placed his hands beneath its armpits, and, with the room plunged into darkness, dragged it across the floor. But it was Miriam who led the way to the sandy ground on the edge of the brickfield, who bore more than her share of the heavy burden which they carried between them, who indicated where the hole was to be dug, who smoothed the earth over the shallow grave and packed it down with her bare feet, who went back into the hut and replaced the wooden spade in the corner, who pressed his arm in warning when they turned the corner of the building and came face to face with Dathan.

"Ah! Mosheh the son of Amram! An industrious workman indeed! I have been standing here watching him at his labors. The light of the moon is very bright."

"So bright that Dathan doubtless saw the Egyptian Baka returning to his house in the city," retorted Miriam in swift Hebrew.

"So soon?" drawled the section boss insolently. "And without his horse and carriage? The company of the lady Miriam must have been even more intoxicating than he anticipated. It is dangerous for a man to be so forgetful."

"Yes," replied Moses calmly. "Very dangerous. Let Dathan be wise and follow his example. Let him not be forgetful of the fact that he also is one of the sons of Joseph."

As soon as they were out of sight and hearing she turned to Moses. "You must go back to the city at once. Dathan knows. You won't be safe for a moment until you have become once again a prince of Egypt. Just let me tell you this before you go." Her words poured forth with a hot vibrancy. "Until tonight I hated you. I wished you had drowned the day I watched over you so carefully. But now you have made yourself one of us. With the blood of Baka our god has been pleased to wash from your hands the blood of our father Amram. Now go! And the god of the Hebrews, the Shield of Abraham, the Fear of Isaac, and the Mighty One of Jacob, will go with you."

The full moon, red as a great drop of blood, hung impaled on the tip of the obelisk. As he stumbled toward the gate of the city, Moses kept his eyes upon it. He was going, as Miriam had commanded him. But he was going alone. The god of the Hebrews, who took pleasure in washing away the stain of one man's blood with the blood of another, did not go with him. He had no desire for his presence.

The red disk swung clear of the impaling shaft, and, like a ship casting off all moorings, moved into the waiting void. Lifting his eyes, Moses found it strangely akin to his own mood. For he also moved through the darkness in a loneliness so profound that even the stars fled before it.

11

Again Moses was a prince of Egypt. His face had been shaved smooth. The red ridges on his back, tenderly rubbed with oil and bandaged by White Elephant's skillful hands, were covered by the folds of his clean linen garments. Sinuhe greeted him at breakfast with the welcome of a friend for a recently returned traveler. Had he had a pleasant trip, and had his business been completed satisfactorily? He was looking a trifle thin, Sinuhe observed, and had obviously experienced a bad sunburn. But he had returned just in time. Perhaps he had noticed that the obelisk was at last in place. Sinuhe had as yet sent no message to Seti. If Moses had not returned, he would have done so today. But there was really no hurry. Let Moses cease to walk about so restlessly. The obelisk would still be there a hundred, perhaps a thousand, years from now. Not so with this delicious Charu wine. Let Moses sit down and drink a goblet with his dear friend and brother Sinuhe.

It was as easy as that Mosheh ben Amram was gone as completely as if he had been buried in the sand on the edge of a brickfield. And Moses, the very nearest friend of the pharaoh, soon to be crown prince of Egypt, had returned. He sat down on the comfortable couch beside Sinuhe and found that the soft cushions eliminated the painful soreness in his back. He let the warmth of the wine unloose the chilled fountains within his veins and the curved rim of the lotus-shaped goblet stir his pulses with anticipation of a softer, sweeter goblet soon to be pressed against his lips. By the time the morning meal was completed the strange month just passed had become a disagreeable memory. By the time he had enjoyed another cup of wine and a leisurely conversation with Sinuhe, it was but an unpleasant dream. And when he finally entered into his usual routine of interviews and inspection, it was almost as if it had never been.

Almost—but not quite.

"Send Baka to me," he ordered the young scribe who was droning out an inaccurate report of the building operations that had been completed in his absence. "I'd like to check—" He stopped abruptly, his tongue paralyzed by a sudden coldness. "N-no," he managed to stammer when the scribe arose to do his bidding. "I—I'll see the commissioner l-later. G-go on with your report."

The voice of the scribe droned on, and the coldness in Moses' body slowly subsided. By the time the report was finished it had quite disappeared.

He plunged into the day's activities with a feverish haste and enthusiasm which left him no time to think. He dispatched a courier to Seti in Bubastis. He signed an order for the release of the two prisoners in the dungeon and sealed it with the king's seal. He made careful tours of inspection.

Only when he walked among Dathan's gang did he display the slightest reluctance. He cast but the briefest of glances at the toiling human ants burrowing in the ragged mountain. And he noted with relief that his former section boss was at the moment too busy to make his usual obsequious recognition of the friend of the pharaoh's presence.

When Dathan wielded the lash he made a thorough job of it. He was wielding it now, his victim an emaciated youth who had made the mistake of falling a third time in one morning from exhaustion. Even at a distance Moses recognized him. They had worked side by side only the previous day. He knew that the youth did not fall because he was lazy. Only yesterday he had propped the inert body against a pile of earth, covered it with his own greater height and breadth until the moments of unconsciousness had passed and the boy could again lift his shovel. *Yesterday...* But this was today. And today there had been no one to shield him.

Moses descended from his carriage. Before Dathan was aware of his presence, he was standing beside him, grasping his shoulder firmly, seizing the lash from his uplifted hand.

"Fool!" he exclaimed contemptuously. "Do you think you can put life into a sick dog by beating him to death? Have you snake's blood in your veins that you have no more loyalty to your brothers, the sons of Joseph?"

Dathan turned toward him, his face livid with fear. "May the very nearest and dearest friend of the pharaoh look kindly on his miserable servant," he whimpered. "If the noble Prince Moses will believe me, it was only for the sake of the Good God, the Son of Horus, the Strong—"

The words faded suddenly into silence. The crafty lips curled into a slow smile, "Who made you a prince and a judge over us?" demanded the Hebrew insolently. "Are you thinking of killing me also, as you did the Egyptian?"

Moses turned abruptly and went back to his carriage. He gave a curt command to his driver. Gradually, as they returned to the city, the cold panic within him melted into urgency, crystallized into a keen blade of decision. He knew that he had no time to lose.

Sinuhe had been explicit in his directions. Moses had found the place without difficulty, even in the dark. He had not supposed that there was such a spot out here in the wildness of the eastern desert, that the waters of the Great Gulf, extending upward through the long chain of the Bitter Lakes to Tharu, the fortified gateway of Egypt, became shallow enough at any point for a man to cross through them safely. But in the broad path of moonlight stretching from his feet to the opposite shore he could see thin blades of rushes pricking through the shimmering sheet of silver.

"Wait until the tide has reached its lowest ebb," the old adventurer had warned him. "And don't attempt to cross in the path of the rising moon, even though you are sure no man has followed you. Remember what Sinuhe says and wait."

Moses remembered. Impatiently he curbed his impulse to set foot at once in the shallow waters. He was sure he was safe. Hours of soundless desert stretched behind him. For miles, before dark had fallen, he had seen no signs of life except the wheeling vultures. But the tide had not yet reached its lowest ebb. The shimmering waters still lay in the path of the newly risen moon. He sat down on the bank and waited.

Thoughtfully he reviewed the preparations for his journey. Had he fastened all the loose threads in the abruptly severed pattern of a lifetime? It was not the things he was taking with him that mattered. They were already knotted in the bundle at his feet: a change of clothing like the coarse tunic he was wearing; an extra pair of sandals; a square of white cloth to protect his head from the desert sun; a full waterskin; enough food for a few days' journey. No, what mattered was the things he was leaving behind him. And not the things. The people. One by one he considered them briefly, then, like a man carefully storing his possessions in a chest, laid them away in the recesses of his mind.

Tharbis. Sinuhe. White Elephant. Sitra. Seti. His mother Jochebed. Nefretiri. Strange that in so many years a man's life should have interwoven itself with so few threads and that all could be severed so easily! Tharbis he had given into Sinuhe's care, where she had always been. A few glibly spoken words and the imprint of his seal on a bit of clay had insured her freedom.

"I have abandoned you as wife, I am removed from you, I have no claim on earth upon you, I have said unto you, 'Make for yourself a husband in any place to which you shall go.'"

To Sinuhe also he had entrusted the faithful White Elephant. "Let him think I am going on another short journey, and after I am gone, give him his freedom. And another name. Call him Phinehas, why don't you—the Nubian!"

Seti... Sitra... They would be glad enough to forget him once Dathan had told his ugly story, Nefretiri. He could do nothing but cut the threads cleanly. Not the threads. The veins through which his very lifeblood had flowed.

He was glad he had seen Jochebed once more, had knelt beside her pallet and felt her cooling hand on his forehead. She had told him where to go to find the people from whose black tents her ancestors had wandered, where he must turn his eyes to seek the strange god they had worshiped, the being whose voice was the voice of wind and storm and thunder, and whose temple was a fire-rimmed mountaintop.

With finality Moses severed the last thread. The tide had reached its lowest ebb. The moon had broken its moorings and cast itself high into the lonely, waiting void. The time had come. He picked up the bundle at his feet and stepped down into the shallow waters.

PART VI

1

After the bleached poverty of the wilderness the sight of her was like a lush oasis. He stood in the shelter of a clump of thorny acacias and watched her coming toward him up the pathless wadi, her limbs moving with the effortless grace of a young leopard. It was this free poetry of motion which had first drawn his eyes to her that day over ten years before when he had found her watering her father's flocks beside the well. She had lowered the wooden bucket from her shoulder, stooped to fill it, and emptied it into the long stone trough, all without the slightest hint of awkwardness or wasted motion. He had barely noticed the other six maidens in whose midst she had moved.

Then, as now, she had worn her long hair uncovered and bound only with a fillet of goat's hair. Among the six discreet headcloths of her soberer sisters it had glistened with tawny lights, as sleek as the coat of the leopard whose lithe grace she shared. It had been even more concealing than a headcloth, falling in rippling cascades each time she bent her head, hiding not only the lines of her features but the richly curving contours of shoulders and arms and breasts. He had waited for what had seemed an interminable interval for the first glimpse of her face.

He waited now, but with reluctance rather than anticipation. Though he still found pleasure in the sight of the tall, exquisitely flowing figure, he had long since ceased to hope that its promise would find fulfillment in her features. Nevertheless, as she came nearer, her small sandaled feet moving from rock to rock with the unerring swiftness of soft paws, his pulses quickened involuntarily, and something of the excitement of those first expectant moments filled him. She was as much a part of the strange harmony of the wilderness as its crumbling rocks and blazing sunsets and vast silences. It was inconceivable that in spirit also she should not partake of its freedom.

"Zipporah!" he called.

She paused, with the suddenly arrested motion of a wild animal quivering to a familiar sound or scent, changed her direction, and came toward the cluster of acacias. He could distinguish small details more clearly now: the rise and fall of her breasts beneath the cheery stripes of her tunic, the bright pattern of her girdle, the flexing of the muscles of her forearm as she grasped a stunted bush and pulled herself to a higher level But still be could not see her face.

"I'm coming," she called up to him. "Reach down your hands, Moses, and pull me up! You're not so prickly as these thorn bushes."

Was it his imagination, or did her voice sound less nervously high-pitched than usual? He had been away from the encampment for a long period, weeks this time rather than days. Was it impossible that the free, simple life, the wide horizons which had worked such a miracle within himself, should have changed her also?

Eagerly he reached down his hands and met the touch of warm flesh. Not until he had lifted her to a level with his shoulders and she had tossed back her hair did he gain a clear view of her features. His eagerness slowly receded. They were just as they had always been: dark, restive eyes slanted slightly at the corners, full, somewhat pouting lips, high-boned cheeks flaming with restless color. Her spirit abounded with energy as did her body, but it did not belong with the wide spaces of the wilderness. It was an energy born of rebellion, not of harmony. Moses took her in his arms and kissed her, as a man should do when he greets his wife and the mother of his children after a long absence, but not with the eagerness of youth pressing its lips to a sweet goblet.

Still holding his hands, Zipporah looked at them and frowned. "They were strong enough when you came," she said petulantly, "or you could not have driven away the rival herdsmen who were trying to take our oasis from us. But at least they felt like hands. Now they're more like the hide of a goat, and I believe they could break an iron bar in two."

"Yes," said Moses with satisfaction. "They are the hands of a shepherd. They have to be tough and strong. If I told you some of the things they have done since I saw you last—"

"You're different in other ways too," interrupted the woman. Withdrawing herself to arms length, she regarded him through narrowed lids, her restless glance flicking each detail with the haphazard energy of a child toying with a flail: his eyes, sharpened to eagle brightness but withdrawn for protection beneath increasingly lowering and prominent brows; lips whose straight firmness had become accentuated within the frame of a thick, curling black beard; skin once smooth and golden, now toughened and burned almost to the texture of leather. Or, rather, I should say you're the same now as all the other shepherds. When I saw you that first day by the well, I believed that here at last was the prince from a far country of whom I had dreamed, come to take me away from this wilderness to a city where women live in houses and have slaves to wait on them, and where the men do not grow skins as rough and black as the ugly goat hides of which they make their tents."

Suddenly the petulance left her voice. Dropping down on the ground and leaning against the trunk of one of the thorny acacias, she stretched her slender body with pantherlike grace and smiled up at him invitingly. "Let's not go down to the encampment just yet. Stay here and—and talk to me."

Moses stood looking down at her. Much as he loved it, the wilderness had been a stark, unlovely companion. The excitement he had felt at the first sight of her coming toward him up the wadi entered into him again, filling him with a longing for human fellowship which was closely akin to desire. After all, she had left the encampment amid all the excitement of the approaching spring festival and come a long way to meet him. Was it possible that he had misjudged her motives, that this time she had sought him only for himself? Perhaps if he held her in his arms now it might be as it was in the first days and nights of their marriage, when she had still seen in him the dream prince from a far country. If he closed his eyes, he might even believe that in spirit as well as in body both he and she and the vast, harmonious freedom of the wilderness were one. He sank down beside her on the stony ground.

"What—what shall we talk about?" he asked hoarsely.

She turned swiftly toward him, so that one of the sun-dappled wings of hair fell over his cheek and became threaded with his beard. "Our kinsmen have come from Ezion-geber," she said eagerly. "They sat about my father's fire last night and talked until the moon had sunk into the tops of the palm trees. And this time they brought their women with them from their houses in the city. We sat in the tent with them, and they showed us all their fine clothes and jewels and told us about the marvelous houses they dwell in at Ezion-geber. Walls of real stone instead of goat's hair, and floors covered with fine rugs such as the merchants bring down from Syria. And in the evening they sit on the tops of their houses under tents made of bright cloth and taste wonderful foreign foods from dishes wrought in strange shapes and adorned with gold and silver."

Moses pushed aside the wing of hair and rose abruptly to his feet. "Come," he said, "the sun is getting low. Let us go down to the encampment."

She pulled insistently at the sleeve of his striped cloak. "Not all the children of the Kenites are shepherds," she continued urgently. "In

Ezion-geber there are Kenites who are merchants and smiths and artisans. And—and one of the men who sat last night by the fire is very rich and powerful indeed. He is the employer of many men who bring him much wealth from the copper mines. His name is Eldad. I spoke with his wife in the tents. She—she told me that he has need of men to help him run his mines and manage his slaves. He would pay high wages for a strong man who has traveled far, especially one who has held positions of authority in such a great land as Egypt!"

"Come!" said Moses harshly. Without looking back to see that she was following, he plunged down the withered flank of the wadi, slipped on a bit of loose shale, and painfully twisted his ankle. At the sound of his sharp exclamation she was instantly beside him, prodding at the tender flesh with gentle, skillful fingers, competently folding her girdle into a bandage and binding it firmly about the injured member. Except for one shrewd and slightly mocking glance, she might have been any dutiful wife of the desert.

"You see?" her eyes taunted him with brief triumph. "You don't really belong in the wilderness. You can't walk over a slope of loose shale without slipping. Even after ten years among us you still have not learned our ways. You should have slaves to wait on you and live safely within the walls of a city, like Ezion-geber."

Aloud she said, "May Yahweh keep your feet from stumbling and protect you from all your enemies!"

Involuntarily Moses looked above the gray wall of stone forming the farther side of the wadi to the distant horizon where The Mountain reared itself, proud, aloof, mysterious, its lofty brows hidden beneath an enveloping hood of white mist. Here Yahweh, the god of his Kenite ancestors, had his abode. *His* god, for he had joined himself forever to the tribe of Jethro, his father-in-law, and made it his own. He had opened his wrists and mingled his blood with that of his wife's people, making them his brothers. The black sprawling tents which folded their dark wings and took flight from one oasis nest to another were his tents. The flocks of sheep and goats which were the common wealth and succor of the tribe were his responsibility to shepherd in return for the wealth and succor which he shared. The god whose favor they strove constantly to purchase and whose jealousy they endeavored eternally to pacify was his god.

Life had become astonishingly simple. There was no longer necessity for asking questions. The god who dwelt on the crest of The Mountain, who by day hid his face within a hood of cloud and by night wrapped himself in garments edged with fire, was quite sufficient for the needs of a humble shepherd. The frugal table which he spread on the bare floor of the wilderness was adequate to nourish but not lavish enough to engender false security or idleness. His brimming oases were all the more precious because one's lips grew parched and the tongues of the flocks were often fanned by the hot, panting breath of anticipation.

"Yahweh," they called him, this god who lived on a smoking mountaintop, whom all the wandering clans up and down tile barren region, from the hot furnace of the Arabah eastward and southward through the desolate wadies and high plateaus bordering the Great Gulf, feared and strove by ceaseless rites and formulas of magic to propitiate. Yahweh—*the one who causes to fall, the Destroyer!*

But to the shepherd who had learned his ways and was willing to abide by them, Moses had discovered through long, patient years of trial and error, Yahweh was no destroyer. Only during his early months of ignorance and ineptitude had the wilderness seemed the creation and expression of a hostile being. Then more than once, having lost his way, he had wandered for days without finding an oasis, his lips swollen with thirst, his flocks falling beside the path with blackened tongues and dragging bellies, all because he had not known how to sound for a porous rock with his staff and with a few vigorous strokes pry loose the outer scales of limestone, letting the long-hoarded treasure of pure water seep through the filtering inner layers. Faint with hunger, he had lain beneath a desert tamarisk and watched the rising sun melt the precious little globules that had exuded from the thorns and fallen on the ground among the twigs and leaves, not knowing that if he had gathered them in his goatskin pouch they would not only have assuaged his hunger but tasted pleasantly sweet, like honey, beneath his tongue. It was the flocks of that shepherd whose eye was ever alert to danger, whose hand was swift and skillful with the sling, which Yahweh protected from their enemies.

"But I haven't told you the most exciting news of all," said Zipporah eagerly, her firm young shoulder supporting his arm as they moved down the wadi. "My father has business that must be done at Ezion-geber, and I have persuaded him to let you do it for him. You are to return with the caravan of Eldad after the festival, and I am going with you. Then you can see for yourself how much better life would be as a manager of Eldad's copper mines than as a poor shepherd."

Moses felt suddenly imprisoned. He dropped the supporting arm, then winced as his weight fell on the injured ankle. "But—the sheep…" he protested with a desperation approaching panic. "I couldn't leave—"

"You've left them now, haven't you?" countered the woman smoothly.

"Yes, but only for the festival. You know the shepherds take turns watching the flocks each spring at the time of the Feast of Pesach. We find a good grazing valley where they can easily be handled in large numbers and where the danger from intruders is slight—"

"And where they can be herded together for a moon or two," finished Zipporah, "as easily as for a week. That too is all arranged. Or," her glance mocked him, "do you think you're such a skillful shepherd that you cannot trust to others the dropping and tending of your spring lambs?"

Moses flushed. He wished that it had not been his turn to attend the Feast of Pesach, that he could have remained with the other shepherds in the Valley of the Lion's Skull, where the problems a man had to face could be solved by keenness of eye and swiftness of hand. Helplessly he waited for the shoulder to be placed once more beneath his arm.

He was entering again into the world of men, and life had ceased suddenly to be simple. The friendly tents mushrooming the green surface of the valley below were symbols not of freedom but of bondage. Even the mist-wrapped Mountain brooding on the far horizon looked faintly sinister, as if the mysterious being whom it shrouded, the benign patron spirit of the wilderness, had turned into a capricious daemon who must be cajoled.

Once in his own tent, however, Moses' sense of insecurity gave place to an increasing fullness of well-being. Here also, life was safe and orderly and simple. He did not dwell in a palace, while others of his Kenite brothers were crowded into huts. The tent of Jethro himself, acknowledged by all to be chief of the tribe, differed only in size from that of his humblest clansman, and that only because it must be large enough to shelter a multitude of strangers. One did not say of the land: "This is mine. You must not pitch your tent upon it!" nor of the water that flowed into the long stone troughs at the center of the oasis: "It belongs to the Strong Bull, the Good God. If you draw from it, you must pay so many measures of barley for a tax." For both water and land belonged to Yahweh, and hence to all his people in common. When later he should eat the sacrificial meal outside the door of his tent, he would not be partaking of tender roast gazelle meat while another ate fish and a loaf of barley. Neither would his stomach be filled while another's remained empty.

Moses' two small sons, Gershom and Eliezer, were so excited over his home-coming that even the preparations for the festival outside possessed no allure. They followed him about the tent like two miniature shadows, quarreling with each other over who should bring his clean clothes from the chest, who should pour the water for his bath, and especially, who should tell him the latest news and ask him the most questions. Gershom, a sturdy lad of six with his father's dark curls and his mother's swift tongue and restive eyes, won the verbal round of the contest but was content to yield the victories involving labor to his four-year-old brother, slow of tongue like his father but stubborn as Zipporah in attaining his desires. The clean coat arrived at its destination somewhat the worse for the imprints of small soiled feet, and the wooden ewer slopped water all the way from the bulky goatskin leaning against the front tent poles to the rear corner of the sleeping quarters where Moses hastily performed his toilet.

"Will my father wear his girdle with the red and black stripes or his new embroidered one made of many colors?" inquired Gershom helpfully, magnanimously leaving to Eliezer the task of procuring the desired article, while his own tongue flowed nimbly on. Had his father left his grandfather's sheep with the other shepherds in the Valley of the Lion's Skull, and why did they call it the Valley of the Lion's Skull, anyway? Was it because there was a rock there that looked like the head of a lion, and if it was, would his father take him there sometime and show him? And how many lambs had dropped so far from his father's ewes? More than six, he hoped, which was what Jabal said had dropped from his father's. He would like to get the best of Jabal just for once. And had his father noticed how tall his older son had grown in his absence? Another notch would have to be made on the tent post, at least a finger's width higher than the other. And...and...and...

Moses listened with delight to his son's chatter. *Why did I name him Gershom?* he wondered to himself. *Neither one of us is "a stranger here." Both he and I belong in these black tents where no man calls another his lord and every man's son has an equal opportunity with every other's. I was wiser when I named Eliezer, for truly the god of my people has been my helper.*

He poured the fresh spring water over his arms and chest and back, careful to catch every drop in the wooden trough beneath his feet. It had been hard for him to learn to be frugal with water, harder even than to accustom himself to the feeling of rough woolen cloth against his flesh and of abundant hair on cheeks and chin and upper lip. The latter still gave him a faint sensation of uncleanness. The other shepherds would have hooted riotously if they could have seen him surreptitiously returning to some meager pool after they were fast asleep, to run driblets of water through his long hair and beard and then comb them with his fingers until they were as soft and silky and (he hoped) free from vermin as the fine white garments he had once worn.

His Egyptian passion for cleanliness was, it seemed, the one quality that separated him from full union with his Kenite brothers, and so completely had he discarded all allegiance to his former life that sometimes he almost despised himself for it. What was physical cleanness beside a peace of mind which enabled a man to wrap himself in his cloak at night and gaze serenely up at the stars before falling into an untroubled sleep? He knew now that in Egypt he had not had such peace of mind since the day he had seen the body of a young Shasu slave hanging between the burning blue of the sky and the hot gold of the desert.

"What are those marks on my father's back?" asked Gershom curiously. "They look like the queer ridges the wind makes in the sand. And what makes them white and not brown like the rest of his body?"

"Marks," echoed the small Eliezer, who had found it necessary to reduce speech to a minimum in order to forestall interruption. He lifted an experimental finger and traced the wavering livid grooves. "Not like sand. Snakes. Funny, crawling snakes."

"Keep your hands off!" The words burst from Moses' lips, and, lifting his hand with a sudden motion, he gave the boy's cheek a resounding slap. Instantly he was ashamed and contrite. "I'm sorry," he apologized quickly. "I didn't mean to strike you, son. I—I don't know why I did it. I—"

"I know why!" flashed Zipporah, appearing suddenly from the women's side of the tent. "For the same reason you're content to stay in this barren wilderness when you might be one of the richest and most important people in Ezion-geber. Because you're a coward. You ran away from something in Egypt, and you don't even dare to look back. You don't dare to look ahead, either. I thought when you drove away the shepherds at the well that you were different from all these spineless wretches who think the words that drip from my father's mouth are the wisdom of Yahweh himself. And instead you're worse than any of them. Go out and take a look at Eldad, why don't you, and see a man who really is a man!"

Moses heard scarcely a word of the bitter invective. His eyes were fixed with horrified intensity on the small figure whimpering into his mother's tunic. Until this moment it had been ten years since he had lost control of his emotions. He stared now at his son as once he had stared at the body of a man lying on the floor of a hut, its limbs doubled grotesquely and its head hanging at a sickening angle. His horror changed to a consuming fear. Had he really attained freedom from the past?

His hands felt nerveless as they smoothed the new embroidered girdle across his knee, creased it carefully so that its two folded edges formed, a pocket at the top, and fastened it about the waist of his striped woolen coat. He wished desperately that he were back in the Valley of the Lion's Skull, where the problems that a man must face concerned the ways of sheep and goats, not those of human beings.

2

There were evil spirits lurking to bring harm to man in the light of every full moon. But at the full moon nearest the spring equinox, when the hours of the day and the hours of the night were one, eternal vigilance must be employed against the powers of darkness. Yahweh the destroyer must be lured from his holy mountaintop and strengthened by the taste of flesh and the savor of blood to protect his people from their enemies. Yahweh the creator, opener, and replenisher of the womb, must be persuaded to visit his flocks with divine favor. Yahweh the patron deity of the Kenites must enter again, through the eating of the sacrificial sacred meal, into a holy state of oneness with his people.

As he joined with his fellow tribesmen in making ready for the solemn festival, Moses found his sense of well-being slowly returning. There was nothing here to remind him of Egypt. The eyes of the desert worshiper were blinded by no glittering splendor. To the wandering shepherd, constantly forced to seek shelter for his "blessed ones" from the sun's hot glare, night, not day, was the vessel of divine beneficence. The wild falcon floating on the purple dusk was only a falcon, not the imprisoned spirit of an avenging Horus. Here animals, and only animals, wore the heads of sheep and goats and jackals. And even the sprawling tents and kindled fires, the sole outward evidence of man's presence, were as ephemeral as the night's purple shadows.

Moses went with the other sons and sons-in-law of Jethro to draw about the outer edges of the encampment the magic circle which through the long night of danger was to keep evil spirits in abeyance. Hobab, his favorite among the sheik's sons, a youth of about fifteen years, moved soundlessly behind him.

"Is the husband of my most beautiful but most restless sister already performing the sacred dance of Pesach?" he inquired softly.

Moses started. The precautions against the unseen enemies lurking in the darkness had set his nerves on edge. "What—" he gasped.

"Have no fear," continued the youth with uncanny astuteness, his white teeth flashing in the dusk. "It's no evil spirit creeping up behind you, only I, Hobab. I merely asked my brother, why the limp?"

"I turned my ankle," replied Moses briefly, the impatience in his voice directed not at the youth but at himself. For he knew, and Hobab knew, that no true son of the desert would be careless enough to turn his ankle, nor would he permit himself to become startled.

"Too bad," countered the other easily, slipping his firm young shoulder beneath Moses' arm. "Though I'd wager my share of the roast lamb you did it on purpose. You don't like to dance any better than I."

Moses laughed, a free spontaneous sound which fell like a bright pebble into the solemn pool of silence. Jethro, a short, spare shadow at the head of the procession, halted and turned, but he uttered no word of reproof. Moses curbed his impulse. He was reminded of another time when his laughter had fallen into a solemn silence.

"Hist!" warned Hobab in a barely audible whisper. "If it had been any but the husband of my most beautiful and most restless sister, the eyes of my father would have glowed as red as the fires in which Yahweh wraps his head at night. We mustn't let them know we think it's silly to go skulking like this through the dark, drawing lines on the ground to keep out evil spirits."

Moses gazed at the youth's face in astonishment. He was always discovering the unexpected in Hobab, but of all the amazing boyish confidences he had shared, this was the most startling. "You mean— you think it is useless to try to keep out the evil spirits?" he asked slowly.

"I mean I don't believe there are any evil spirits," came back the prompt whisper. "And neither do you."

Before Moses had begun to comprehend the significance of his words, Hobab had changed the subject. "I've been on a long journey since I saw you last," he whispered excitedly, his dark, slightly slanting eyes gleaming almost as brightly as his white teeth. He was as beautiful in body as his sister Zipporah and as restless. But it was not the restlessness of discontent. He was as much a part of this stark country as the fiery sunsets, or the white-winged vultures wheeling above the shaggy oases. Although Hobab was not a shepherd, his lean brown body and adventurous spirit were in perfect harmony with the wilderness. Like all the sons of Jethro, he had chosen to become a worker of metals rather than a keeper of flocks and with his brothers traveled from one desert encampment to another among the various tribes of the Midianites, plying his trade.

"Where?" asked Moses reluctantly, his mind still unable to cope with the amazing words but loath to relinquish the attempt.

"In the desert country far beyond Ezion-geber. If I were a sheik like my father, I'd leave this region where the pastures are so poor and the flocks have to be moved so constantly. There are wadies there on the edge of the desert where whole tribes could camp for years within only a few hours travel of each other. You should have seen one spring we found at a place called Kadesh! It flows from the rock in three streams, each one the thickness of a man's arm. I think I'll try to persuade my father to move his tents there."

"No!" exclaimed Moses sharply.

The youth's eyes, bright with the glint of campfires studding the darkness, probed his curiously. "Why not?"

"Because—" Moses' voice stumbled, "this is where we belong. There is peace here—and security. I wish I need never leave this wilderness again."

"Yet you are going to Ezion-geber," returned Hobab quietly.

"Who told you?" There was sudden panic in Moses' intense whisper.

He could feel the youth beside him smiling into the darkness. "Who do you think? Ah—you've guessed it! My most beautiful and most restless sister."

"I don't believe there are any evil spirits. And neither do you."
As Moses, in company with the head of every other family in the encampment, stood before his tent and slew the first-born lamb of his flock, the astounding words echoed and re-echoed through his mind. Were they true? Had the youth with the sure feet and canny eyes

apprehended some momentous change within him of which he himself was as yet but dimly conscious? No, Yahweh forbid! He was through asking questions about gods and men. Questioning brought nothing but trouble. Until ten years ago he had questioned all his life, and where had it led him? To a moment of bitter climax in a stifling room, where he had gazed in horror at a twisted shape of his own making, a supreme and awful question mark.

The bleating of the dying lambs sounded a terrified din in his ears, a wild medley of separate voices. Of course there were evil spirits. They lurked in the rock crevices where you led your flocks, and crept into your tent after darkness had fallen, and passed over your prostrate figure in whirling, blinding columns of sand. They lingered about the bodies of your dead tribesmen so that in the presence of death you must be ever watchful, removing your sandals and donning sackcloth that your clothes might not be polluted; covering your mouth that your spirit might not be drawn out by their spirits; strewing ashes over your head that you might make yourself unrecognizable to the dead. Certainly he believed in evil spirits. He *must* believe in them—or relinquish his blessed sense of quietude. If he asked questions about them, he must ask them also about Yahweh.

Hastily and in sudden panic he plunged his bronze knife into the warm, limp body, drained the blood of the newly slain lamb into a wooden ewer, and flung it on the center tent post. His fingers trembled so that most of it spilled on the ground.

"Be careful," cautioned Zipporah sharply, drawing her gaily colored coat closer to her limbs. "You almost spattered my new holiday dress. And, look, you did get stains all over the rug! Must you be clumsy with your hands too, as well as your feet?"

Moses scarcely heard her. Again and again he dashed the bright rich tongues of crimson against the upright center post, against the two other posts flanking the entrance on either side. They ran down in rivulets, sank into the dry, seamed surface of thorny acacia so thoroughly that only a few driblets trickled down into the thirsty sand. Zipporah stared at him with a mounting wonder not unmingled with dismay.

"What—what in heaven's name has happened to you!" she demanded in a low voice, glancing warily toward neighboring tents to assure herself that they were not attracting undue attention. "You're supposed to smear blood on your tent posts, not drown them in it! Don't forget there are important visitors in the camp tonight. Do you want them thinking the evil spirits are within the sacred circle instead of without?"

Moses splashed the last few drops from the ewer. "One cannot be too careful," he muttered. "The evil ones—"

But the sharp, taunting voice had steadied his senses. He laid aside the ewer, wiped the bronze blade of his knife on a bit of goatskin, and replaced it in the leather sheath hanging from his girdle. Then he looked at his wife. Never had she seemed more beautiful. Even on the day when he had first seen her at the well, all the poetry of this free wilderness in which he had found release seemed to take substance within the lovely contours of her body.

Unlike most of the daughters of the desert, she had not grown thick and heavy with the bearing of children. The woolen tunic which she had woven with her own hands, its customary stripes of brown and black and ocher interspersed with bold bars of scarlet, seemed more revealing than a close-fitting tunic of transparent linen. High color flamed in her cheeks. The dancing firelight was in her slanting eyes and full red lips, which, bereft of their customary pout, were slightly parted and gently curving.

Looking at her, Moses felt the unmistakable stirring of anticipation and desire. The night of the festival was here. The full moon hung, red as blood, above the black tent tops. Already the drums were sounding the weird, halting rhythm of the limping dance which accompanied the Feast of Pesach. Fool, to worry over the existence of evil spirits when here within the compass of a woman's seductiveness lay the answer to all a man's questions!

"Zipporah!" he called, but her eyes were roaming eagerly about the encampment, and apparently she did not hear him.

His fingers ached suddenly to stroke her hair, to discover if it was as soft to the touch as he remembered it, and he moved toward her around the circle of firelight. Then, as his figure passed between her and the light, the rays of the newly risen moon fell full upon her hair, splintering it into glinting facets of copper and jade and ebony, like the dappled skin of a snake's back, and he retreated slowly, his fingers falling nervelessly at his sides.

"Hurry!" commanded Zipporah sharply, stamping her small foot on the ground. "They're starting the dance. Get the lamb ready to roast so I can put it on the spits above the fire. I've bribed my sister Tamah's oldest girl to tend it. Look, Moses! See that big, thickset man standing in the door of my father's tent? That's Eldad, the man I was telling you about. Hurry, can't you? How can I win for you a fine rich future in Ezion-geber if you're not even willing to help?"

Watching her later as she swung into the irregular rhythm of the dance, Moses again chided himself for having been a fool. It was easy to follow her progress in the maze of whirling figures, even after the drums had quickened their halting tempo and the first somber, limping motions of the dancers increased in excitement and momentum until they finally approached a leaping frenzy. In the shadowy coiling human chain she was like one of the scarlet stripes in her own garment, a vivid dash of color in a pattern of neutral shades. She managed to make even the halting limp a thing of grace and beauty. It was easy to follow her progress also for another reason: the presence of the awkward, thickset shadow moving always as close to her as the intricate steps of the dance would permit.

Our noble kinsman Eldad, thought Moses grimly. Then, his lips twisting with sudden humor: *I'll wager he's panting like a sheep dog that has been chasing a frisky jackal through a waterless wadi!*

The new coat, the heightened color and smiling lips had all been for Eldad, of course. The irony of it was that it was not Eldad she wanted. It was a position for him, Moses, helping to run Eldad's copper mines in Ezion-geber!

But he would not go. No one could make him, not even Jethro. Jethro would understand. The sheik was his friend. Throughout the past ten years they had been closer to each other than father and son. Tomorrow Moses would go to him when he sat before his tent to render judgment for the people of his tribe. Then he would return to his flocks in the Valley of the Lion's Skull. The wilderness was where he belonged. For no reason and no person on earth would he relinquish his precious heritage of freedom.

The dance grew even wilder. Faster and faster whirled the shadowy figures. The familiar night odors of the desert encampment—sharp, acrid smells of drying leather and unwashed sheepskins and animal-scented human flesh, mingled with the moist sweet tangs of wet sand and spring crocuses and flowering date palms—were all absorbed in the penetrating savor of burning fat and roasting flesh. Overhead the moon, paler now and somewhat shrunken, lay motionless and empty on its tablecloth of violet damask, waiting to receive the sacrificial meal which men and their god would sit down and eat together.

Moses felt a small, sticky hand tuck itself into his and looked down into the curious eyes of his son Gershom.

"Why does my father stand by himself while my mother does the dance of Pesach?"

"My ankle is hurt," Moses reminded him briefly.

"Jabal says we have to eat all the little lamb," continued the child eagerly. "He says there mustn't be anything left of it, not even a little scrap. But I didn't believe him. I don't believe anything unless my father tells me it is true."

Moses stifled a sudden chuckle. "This time Jabal is right," he told his son gravely, "however much it may pain us to admit it. The little lamb must be consumed entirely before the setting of the moon— flesh, bones, skin, and entrails. Not even the tiniest piece must remain."

"Why not?"

"Because—" Moses' voice was edged with faint annoyance, "because it is Yahweh's wish that we should do so."

"And is Yahweh coming to eat it with us?" Suddenly the eager questions poured from the childish lips. "Will he get here soon? How shall we know when he is here? Will he bring the fire with him from The Mountain? Will we see him with our own eyes? Can we hear him talk? And why does Yahweh say we must get rid of the little lamb, bones and all? Why—"

"Be quiet!" commanded Moses with such sharpness that the flow of words froze into startled silence. "Don't ask questions, do you hear? It will bring you nothing but trouble and misfortune, and you'll never find the answers."

The boy dropped his hand and slipped away in the darkness. *Now,* thought Moses bitterly, *I have frightened away both my sons. And why? Only because I desire to live at peace and let others do likewise.*

Deliberately he turned his back on the dancers caught in the imprisoning meshes of moonlight. Questions. Could a man find no release? Blindly he started to walk toward a group of his fellow tribesmen seated about a fire, not knowing that he was heading for a plunge into that very past which he was trying to escape.

The men around the fire were members of that wandering company of metalworkers with whom the boy Hobab traveled. Two of them were blood sons of Jethro. Their bodies were weary with much journeying and hungry for the taste of flesh, for they had not tasted meat since the last festival six moons before. Later, after the sacrificial meal had been totally consumed, they would join with their kinsmen in the rhythms of Pesach and dance fast and furiously until the moon sank into the pale vestibules of dawn. But now their muscular bodies were surfeited with motion. Even their tongues begrudged the effort of conversation. Yet occasionally one of them spoke. And the words that fell from his lips, though sparing in number, were as audible as dry seeds shaken in an empty gourd.

"...a good spring, the shepherds say..."

"...lambs dropping already like the sweet bubbles of the tamarisk..."

"Who said the rumbling of Yahweh boded misfortune?"

"Better look in the other direction for the rumblings of misfortune!"

"Yea, Egypt!"

"...what good a hundred more lambs if we have to feed them into the pharaoh's fat belly?"

"...demanding more copper from Ezion-geber..."

"...prices go any higher, we'll be driven out of business..."

"...evil day for the sons of the desert when Seti died and this Ramses became pharaoh..."

They were startled out of their comfortable torpor by the sight of the tall figure thrusting itself into their midst, its intent features thrown into bold relief by the light of the fire.

"Did you say Seti is dead?"

There was a brief silence, broken by Lahad, the oldest son of Jethro. "So," he remarked leisurely, pulling himself into an upright position, "the husband of our favored sister Zipporah has deigned to walk among us. Moses—" his thick lips curled about the word, "the Egyptian!"

"Is it true?" demanded Moses.

Lahad's eyes narrowed mockingly. "Impossible that the favorite of our father Jethro has been kept in ignorance of a matter which so closely concerns his somewhat—er—doubtful past!"

"I've been with the sheep in the hills," explained Moses curtly.

"Ah, then that explains it." There was a faint hissing sound as Lahad spat into the fire. "Perhaps now that Seti is dead there is no longer need for the husband of our sister to deprive the fair black country of his presence? Perhaps the new king Ramses is awaiting him this moment with outstretched arms! A pity indeed if he should feel called upon to leave us!"

As Moses left the group, he scarcely noticed their disagreeable laughter. The sons of Jethro had always been jealous of the favor accorded him by their father and of his popularity among the other tribesmen. He was conscious only of the startling piece of news, and even upon that he could not at the moment concentrate. For that he needed a place of solitude.

Figures were silhouetted against the entrance of his own tent, his two small sons and the young granddaughter of Jethro tending the roasting lamb above the fire. He moved on through the widening circles of tents, into the outer darkness where lay the imaginary line across which no evil spirit (please Yahweh!) could pass. Through his stout sandals he felt the soft grass of the oasis change slowly to dry sand and hard stubble. Here at last was the solitude he sought.

Seti was dead. Suddenly the ten years of silence, the long miles of intervening desert, were as nothing. Step by step he followed the nest of coffins up the long western road into the Valley of the Kings' Tomb, through the wide lofty door, down the rock-hewn steps that led to the first inclined corridor. Strange he could even remember the number of them from his tours of inspection! Twenty-seven. Down into the great hall and vaulted chamber with their manifold formulas and pictures of the journey of the soul... Down... Down... Dampness beneath his feet, the coolness of smooth rock beneath his hands...into the deep silent chamber with its polished sarcophagus of alabaster.

Seti was dead. And Ramses was sitting on his throne. So the arrogant young prince had got his way after all. *"From the time that I was in the egg the great ones sniffed..."* No doubt he had also taken Nefretiri as his bride. Deliberately Moses took the thought from his mind and examined it, but he felt neither ecstasy nor pain. In fact, he felt nothing at all.

Seti was dead. And suddenly Moses' solitude was broken, peopled with a dozen familiar shapes from the past. Miriam, Aaron, his mother Jochebed...The four walls of the small hut pressed close about him. What would the passing of one pharaoh and the coming of another mean to them? Would their life be made harder or easier—if, indeed, they still possessed life! Ten years was a long time in a country where human flesh was cheaper than mortar. Sitra, Amon-nebet, Sinuhe, Tharbis...

For the first time in years his young Kushite wife stood living and breathing by his side, dusky face with its alert eyes and small pert nose upturned to his in eager questioning. He was startled by the reality of her presence and by the sudden tumult which it aroused within himself. He could even hear her voice, low and warm and filled with faint musical cadences.

PART VI

"I like your wilderness, Moses. It's wide, so you can stretch out your arms and not feel as if you're touching the ends of the earth the way you do in Egypt. If I lived here long enough, I believe I could learn to fly. And listen, Moses! If you listen very hard, you can hear—"

Moses listened, and it seemed that there did come to his ears a faint rushing sound, like the distant music of the cataracts. He reached out his hand to grasp hers, as he had done that night long ago on the turret above Saba, but his groping fingers felt no touch of responsive flesh. She was gone. The warm spring night seemed suddenly to have grown cold about him.

Seti was dead. Ramses, his son, sat on the throne of the Two Lands. And how did this concern him, Moses? He must face it at last. If he wished, he could go back now without danger to his own country. The killing of Baka would have been long since forgotten. Ramses, serene in his impregnable security as the Strong Bull, Lord of the Two Lands, the Golden Horus, and the Good God himself, would no longer find in him a cause for jealousy. It was, in fact, conceivable that in his sublime egotism he might welcome the presence of a rival prince who had once aspired to his own state of lofty eminence and lost. If he wished, Moses could return to his own country either as a Hebrew or as an Egyptian. As a Hebrew—Yahweh forbid! The very thought caused the scars on his back to throb with pain as if they had been inflicted only yesterday. But as an Egyptian...

It would be pleasant to shave off his unruly beard and feel again the cleanness of linen garments, to sit on a high deck beneath bright awnings and watch the green shore drift past with its tombs and its palaces, its naked brown bodies bent to the ceaselessly creaking shaduf. No, no! Yahweh again forbid! He could hear the sound of it now, beating in his ears, throbbing against his temples. *Who...what... why...who...what...* No, not the shaduf! Never again the shaduf or the bent brown bodies or the sound of stone grinding against stone! Never again, please Yahweh, the eternal questioning!

His own country? This was his country. Suddenly he stretched his arms wide, exulting in the knowledge of the vastness of space embracing his body from every side. He dug the toe of his sandal into the sandy ground, taking keen pleasure in the feeling of rough earth and stubble against his flesh. He lifted his face and let the coolness of the dark envelop his being again in the floodwaters of peace and security.

Seti was dead. And Ramses his son sat on the throne of Egypt. What did it mean? Nothing, except a faint stirring of regret, like the

270

fluttering of a breeze through the dried leaves of a dead tamarisk. Nothing, thank Yahweh, at all!

Ten years ago he would not have noticed the dark shape crouched in the shadows behind the outer circle of tents. But now his eyes were those of a shepherd, trained to probe the darkness for even slighter movements than the rolling of a pebble or the flicker of a snake's uncoiling body. Approaching it as quickly as his lame ankle would permit, he found the crouching form to be a man, huddled deep in his enveloping cloak, his features a shapeless blur in the moonlight.

"Who are you?" demanded Moses sharply. "What are you doing here?"

A pair of terrified eyes detached themselves from the blur. "Don't tell him I'm here! Don't—for Yahweh's sake!—don't let him know—"

"Don't let who know?" asked Moses more gently.

"Eldad. He saw me last night when we brought the first-born lambs to Jethro to receive Yahweh's approval. He pretended not to recognize me, but he did. I could see it in his eyes and the way his lips turned up at one corner. He knows, I tell you! He—"

"Hush!" warned Moses. "If you don't want people to know you're here, you won't help the situation by shouting." He turned the blurred features so that the moonlight fell full upon them and leaned closer. "Why—you're Jared!" he exclaimed. "Remember me—Moses, the son-in-law of Jethro? We pitched our tents side by side at the last festival of shearing."

"Yes, I know." The man spoke more calmly now. "I knew when you spoke. I remembered your voice."

"And why are you afraid of Eldad?" inquired Moses.

"Because he wants to take me back to the copper mines. He claims I still owe him labor for his feeding and sheltering me after I slipped in the mines and broke my leg."

"And do you?"

"No, no, it's impossible. I labored for him two full years after that, and he gave me only enough food to keep barely alive. He would have made a slave of me, holding always over my head the debt he claimed I owed him. I ran away and sought shelter with the tribe of Jethro, not knowing that it was Eldad's tribe."

"Are you a Midianite by birth?"

"Yes. But I did not dare to return to my own tribe. I thought Eldad would be certain to find me. Yahweh help me—"

"Yahweh will help you," Moses assured him earnestly. "If you are a Midianite either by birth or by the blood rite, Yahweh is your god. And Jethro is his priest, who makes known the will of the god for his people and determines the obligations of one man toward another. Tomorrow Jethro sits in judgment before his tent. You must come there with Eldad."

"No!" The terrified eyes again detached themselves. "As soon as the moon is set and it is safe to cross the line into the abode of the evil ones who dwell in darkness, I shall run away. He shall not find me!"

"No, for you must find him," said Moses. "If your cause is just, you have nothing to fear. Have you never heard Jethro render the judgments of Yahweh?"

"Yes, but Eldad is rich and powerful. He always gets his way."

"Not with Yahweh," replied Moses sternly. "There are no rich and poor among the people of the wilderness. Have you not heard Jethro say that in the sight of the god all men are alike?"

They returned to the encampment together, the arm of Moses placed comfortingly about the shoulders of the man called Jared.

3

The Feast of Pesach was ended. With the coming of dawn the firstlings of the flocks set apart for the worship of the god had been utterly consumed, even to the smallest bone and tiniest fragment of skin clinging to the tender roasted flesh. That which first opened the womb had been given to the god, whose it rightfully was by the custom and creed of long centuries, and Yahweh had graciously come from his holy Mountain and partaken of the meal of fellowship with his people.

Nor did he depart again at once from their midst but lingered benignly among them, causing his presence to be sensed even more potently than usual in the Tent of Meeting where he was accustomed to hold intercourse with his worshipers through their priest Jethro. Pitched in the exact center of the encampment, close to no other abode except that of the sheik-priest himself, the sacred tent of tryst was on this day after the great feast the center of all eyes, the embodiment of all fears and aspirations.

For Yahweh was actually *within* the Tent of Meeting. Could they not see the evidences of his presence with their own eyes? Had not the hood of flame on the holy Mountain fled into dimness beneath the light of the full moon? Had not the halo of cloud about its lofty brow seemed to disintegrate at the coming of the sun as if the god who wore it were for the moment absent from his throne? And did not the pillar of incense smoke rising from Jethro's early-morning offering climb at first straight into the air, then bend and coil itself about the sacred Tent of Meeting?

Yes, Yahweh had graciously chosen to remain with his people and commune with Jethro in the rendering of judgments. The roof of crimson-dyed sheep's skins, the lengths of goat's-hair fabric draped about the four sides and turned back in front to reveal the sacred entrance curtain, were all that hid the divine being from their mortal eyes. Feet which but a few hours previously had yielded themselves in wild abandon to the savage syncopation of the drums now stepped warily, careful to keep well outside the limits of the circle drawn about the holy place. Voices that had shouted bold cheers and uttered loud incantations were muted to tones of excited but hushed apprehension.

"Will Jethro go in unto him, do you think? Or will he simply judge by repeating the *toroth*, as usual?"

"No, no, son, not so close! If you so much as set one foot across that line, something terrible will happen! Do you want the god to smite you dead?"

"Have you seen the new curtain that hangs over the entrance? A gift, they say, from Eldad, our rich kinsman from Ezion-geber."

"Eldad? I used to know him when he was nothing but a shepherd like the rest of us, and a poor one at that. Why should he be so blessed of Yahweh?"

"See? It has threads of real gold woven into strange patterns on a background of blue and crimson and purple, of the stuffs the merchants out of Egypt and Damascus spread from their packs. Will Yahweh like it, think you, to have his tent decked with finery like those of heathen gods?"

"He's staying here with us! Isn't that proof enough he likes it?"

"According to Eldad, we're fools to stay here tending sheep when we might be making ourselves rich like..."

Moses took no part in their murmurings. He barely glanced at the new curtain, its bright fabrics contrasting strangely with the rough black goat's-hair flaps turned back above it. His eyes were fixed on the dark triangular opening through which at any moment Jethro would issue.

He remembered the first time he had looked upon the tent of Jethro. It had been his first experience with desert hospitality. Jethro himself had come running to meet him, apologizing extravagantly because the young Egyptian who had protected his daughters from the bullying of some rival tribesmen and drawn water for their flocks had not been summoned at once to break bread in his tent.

"Thanks be to Yahweh our God, who has blessed us with the sunlight of your presence! Enter into my tent; it is yours. My sons and daughters are yours. I shall gladly sacrifice them if it will give you pleasure. Abide with me, I pray you, for all eternity."

As it happened, Moses had accepted this invitation with more literal significance than had been intended. He had dwelt in the tent of Jethro, if not for all eternity, at least until Zipporah, with the help of her sisters and the other women of the sheik's household, had woven the long tight strips of goat's hair which were to form the roof of their own tent, sewed them into a broad waterproof textile, stretched it upon its nine sturdy poles of acacia wood, and driven home the tent pins. Night after night he had lain on his coarse straw mat wrapped in his great woolen coat and talked with Jethro until near the coming of the dawn. Never had he felt such kinship with any living person, not with Maruma nor with Amon-nebet, nor with Sinuhe; no, not even in those brief illuminating hours when he had locked spirits with the aged priest, Merire. They had talked of the ways of a man with his god and of the ways of men with men and of the ways of a shepherd with his sheep. And it was as if the two paths by which they had journeyed, the one graven deep with the footprints of kings and the other sculptured from the desert's solitude, had had for their common goal the converging with each other.

"Look!" the man called Jared clutched his arm nervously. "There he comes! Yahweh have mercy on me and defend me from my enemies!"

"He will," returned Moses confidently.

Even after ten years he felt again the excitement which had first filled him at sight of the slight figure now emerging from the tent. Jethro did not hold his position of sheik over a lusty desert tribe by reason of superior size or strength. In height he came barely to Moses' shoulder, and his spare body seemed lost in the voluminous folds of his woolen cloak. But it was not the slightness of frailty. His frugality of bone and flesh was that of the wilderness itself, its rocky substructure pared by the disciplining elements almost to its very marrow, its thin soil whipped and toughened until the sparse, tenacious life it brought forth seemed to possess the very substance of eternity.

In fact, to Moses, Jethro *was* the wilderness, as, by some strange alchemy of the unconscious, Baka, the man whom he had killed, had become Egypt. After the fat, lazy somnolence of the sun drunken valley, the spare, disciplined body of the priest of Yahweh had seemed from the first moment of their meeting not only the symbol but the very actuality of the new freedom he had sought and found.

"He's going to the Tent of Meeting," observed Jared worriedly. "Is it not his custom to sit before his own tent to judge the people?"

Moses glanced down curiously at the figure by his side. Jared was not a small man, though shorter than himself. His shoulders were broad, and a tight knot of muscles bulged beneath the bare skin of his forearm. But he was quivering like a reed in the wind. It was not like the sons of the Kenites to show fear or uncertainty. Something had happened to this man in the copper mines of Ezion-geber. Suddenly Moses felt an almost uncontrollable desire to strip aside the coat, to satisfy himself that the brown flesh beneath was unmarked by whitened furrows and ridges. But he said only: "It is Yahweh who renders judgment. Jethro must first commune with him in order that he may be sure he speaks the will of the god."

"How will he find out what is the will of Yahweh?" questioned Jared fearfully. "By throwing the sacred stones which say yea and nay?"

"Perhaps," replied Moses. "But Jethro has been a priest so long and knows the will of Yahweh so well that he usually judges from his own wisdom and knowledge of the *toroth*, the laws which through long usage and repetition have been handed down from priest to priest through many generations."

Jared's foot traced a nervous pattern in the sand. "I had rather he judged my case by his own wisdom," he said worriedly. "Yahweh may remember that Eldad has just given him a new curtain for his tent. I know Jethro, that his head cannot be turned by crimson cloth and fine embroideries, but I'm not so sure of how Yahweh will feel about it."

The impulse to reprimand the man for his irreverence died on Moses' lips. Who was he to berate another human being because he dared to question!

"Wait and see," he said simply.

As the morning passed and Jethro sat on the hard earth before his tent judging the members of his tribe, Moses forgot Jared. Fascinated as always by any form of legal procedure, he listened to the details of one small dispute after another, marveling at the wisdom and simplicity with which this sheik of the desert dispensed justice to his people. In Egypt they would have thought him a strange sort of judge. He sat in no hall of columns or "excellent gateway," wore no image of Maat, the goddess of truth, about his neck. There were no scribes, no written statements by plaintiff and defendant. But the words he spoke were final, and there was pith as well as reason in his sane and often caustic judgments. The losing party in a dispute might leave the scene looking sheepish or shamed or even penitent, but seldom angry or disgruntled.

"So Jonadab accuses Maacah of stealing his new girdle which his wife made him for the festival. Very well. Let Maacah remove the disputed article... Ah! A nice piece of weaving. I don't wonder that you both desire it. Now, while I hold it here behind me, let both Jonadab and Maacah describe its pattern, both the color of the warp threads and that of the woof... Ha! I thought so. No man is a fit judge of his own clothes. Let the wives of Jonadab and Maacah be brought, and to her who can best describe the pattern her hands fashioned let the girdle be given. And next time be sure you know your own property before you accuse others of theft!"

"Certainly, Nadab, my son, you are entitled to a tooth from the mouth of Joab, who knocked out one of yours accidentally with a stone from his sling. But be sure that you likewise use a stone, and may Yahweh make your aim sure! For if you take two instead of one, the battle will be on again, and you will both soon be wishing you could chew good hard bread again!"

"If the wife of Hosah the son of Adab bears him no fruit from her womb, surely he shall be given another wife in due time. But let it first be ascertained that it is truly his spirit that faints within him for sons and not his body that yearns after the flesh of a certain maiden. Come to me again, Hosah, after another twelve-month."

"Eldad, son of our kinsman Eliezer, now resident in Ezion-geber, complains that our fellow tribesman Jared unlawfully deserted his post of labor while still in debt to his employer and demands return of said Jared..."

Moses stiffened. His eyes converged on the two men who now stood before Jethro for judgment, to all appearance the embodiment of innocence and guilt: the one smiling and confident, pleading his case with glib assurance, the other trembling and hesitant, the very earnestness of his defense an apparent acceptance of defeat.

But Jethro will not be fooled, Moses told himself with grim satisfaction. *He knows an honest man when he sees one.*

In spite of his confidence, his interest was intense. It was he who had persuaded Jared to go with him last night to Eldad's tent, demanding that the priest be permitted to render judgment on their disagreement. Eldad had frowned, shrugged his shoulders, then smilingly agreed. The smile had been for Moses, not for Jared. He knew his rights in the matter, but if it would please the husband of the most beautiful daughter of Jethro, he would be glad to go to a little extra trouble to obtain them. Yes, he would even permit the troublesome Jared to spend the night in freedom, if Moses would be his surety.

The man's arrogant self-confidence infuriated Moses. He longed for the inevitable moment when the decision of Jethro would wipe the fatuous smile from the round face. But Jethro seemed in no hurry. He sat stroking his short stubby gray beard, his eyes narrowed to fine slits. Fuming with impatience, Moses moved closer and stood behind Jared.

"I must go to consult Yahweh," announced the priest finally, rising from his mat. "The case is not clear."

"Not clear!" blurted Moses. "Did not the priest, my father, hear this man's testimony, how he broke his leg in the service of Eldad and then labored for him two full years to pay for the miserable food and shelter he had received while he could not work? And then to say it's not a clear c-case—!"

His voice choked in his throat, and he fell silent, aghast at his own audacity. The curious onlookers that were gathered about the tent of Jethro gasped. Never before in the tribe's memory had anyone dared publicly to question the sheik's authority in judgment. Only Jethro looked undisturbed.

"My son is well instructed in the laws of peoples who live by far more complicated codes than the Kenites," he observed mildly. "I must inquire if he recalls any code which gives a judge the right to render his decision on the sole testimony of one man, without witnesses?"

"B-but—" Moses felt the blood rushing to his face. Words choked in his throat. He knew that he had not only committed an unpardonable offense but also made a fool of himself—and before Eldad! Only Jethro's kindly, desert-bred courtesy had saved him from the rebuke which was deserved. "I—I b-beg the sheik's pardon," he managed finally to stammer.

Without reply the priest turned and, moving with an innate dignity, traversed the sacred space about the Tent of Meeting, lifted the new embroidered curtain, and passed inside.

Jared flung himself at Moses' feet, his nervousness reduced to terrified incoherence. "You said—no need to fear—no doubt of what the priest would say—Yahweh always just—better if I had run away—curses on the day I met you—better if I had died—Yahweh have mercy and deliver—" His voice rose suddenly to a shrill cry. "Hear me, Yahweh! Listen to me just this once instead of him, even if he did buy you the new curtain! Believe me, Yahweh, I'd have bought you one if I could! I'll do anything you say, only don't send me back—"

"Hush! Quiet yourself, Jared! Do you think you'll help your cause by shouting?" Stern words finally curbed the shrill outburst into unintelligible whimpers. Moses forcibly loosened the fingers from their viselike grip on his garments and held them firmly in his own. "Listen to me! I told you Jethro would judge your case justly, and he will. Didn't you hear him say he was going to consult Yahweh? Is the god less likely to render a wise decision than his priest? Here! Sit down on the ground and control yourself."

Lifting his eyes, he met Eldad's amused gaze. "The husband of the most beautiful daughter of Jethro is a most—shall we say—interesting person? I begin to anticipate the hours that we shall spend together. They give promise at least of variety."

"The hours we—" Moses stared back at him, bewildered.

"Or should I have said days? Or even, perhaps, weeks? The son-in-law of the wise Jethro is returning with me, I understand, to Ezion-geber and is to remain there for some time as my guest, his most beautiful wife accompanying him."

Moses made no reply. At the moment the trip to Ezion-geber was far in the future, and the present was all that mattered. His gaze fixed itself on the embroidered curtain with a concentration so intense that it seemed it must penetrate the mystery behind it. What was happening in the Tent of Meeting? Did Jethro know himself to be in the actual presence of Yahweh? And how was he going about it to discover the divine will? Was he taking from the folds of his breast the small flat stones that were white on one side and black on the other? Was he holding them in his hands and shaking them gently, his lips moving in a prayer of supplication that the god might answer yea or nay according as his wisdom chose? Was he casting them upon the small altar of stone...?

Suddenly the rich embroidered curtain changed before his eyes. Its network of gold threads, catching the blaze of the morning sun, broke into a hundred dazzling foci and almost as many shapes: crescents and winged disks and lions and bulls and grinning sphinxes, falcons with spreading pinions and pointed, glittering obelisks. He was back in the temple court at On, watching the shining bark of Re being borne aloft on the shoulders of his white-robed priests, a wagon piled high with gifts moving slowly in its wake. A sea of excited faces was swimming before his eyes, only one of them, that of the donor of the gifts, indifferent. Slowly the bark was moving forward, approaching the magic spot where the obelisk cast its shadow, and he felt suspense rising within him like physical pain. It pounded within his chest, laid tight fingers on his throat. *Would the god make himself heavy...?*

"I have communed with Yahweh, and he has made known to me his will in this matter."

Moses plunged abruptly into the present, amazed to discover that Jethro had returned and was sitting again before his tent. The crowd of curious onlookers had grown. He found himself surrounded by a sea of tense, excited faces, only one of them, that of Eldad, amusedly indifferent.

"It is the will of Yahweh," continued the priest confidently, "that Jared return to Ezion-geber with his employer Eldad, to labor again in the copper mines until such time as he shall have discharged his debt."

The remainder of the day seemed interminable. Moses found both human society and solitude equally unbearable. One purpose possessed him. He repeated it over and over to himself, sometimes aloud, sometimes with a mere silent movement of his lips: *I must see Jethro alone. I must talk with him. I must ask him...* But here he always finished, retreating in panic like a horse driven again and again to the leaping point of an obstacle which every instinct warns him not to pass. For beyond this point lay questioning. It was inevitable. He could not escape it. Nor could he escape the compulsion that lashed him again to the starting point, set his feet doggedly in the same narrow path of decision: *I must see Jethro—I must talk—*

But as the day passed it became increasingly clear that he could not see his father-in-law alone. At noon the priest was still judging among his people. Then came the hours of rest, when the tent of the hospitable sheik was as filled with guests as a quiver with arrows. After the midday rest there might be a further rendering of judgments until sundown; then the evening meal and more festivities.

Constant physical motion became a necessity. If he remained quiet for a moment, his mind inevitably began to function, and he did not want to think. Time enough for that later when he had had his talk with Jethro and ascertained for a certainty...He walked endlessly about the encampment, exchanging perfunctory greetings and uttering pleasant holiday inanities, all with his lips and forgotten the moment they were spoken.

"Peace to you, Jabal... Aye, the lambs are dropping well. Never has Yahweh blessed the wombs of his ewes with such fullness... I hear you have a new son, Jonadab. May Yahweh make the fruit of your loins as the sands of the desert!... Yea, the sons of Amalek are more hungry for plunder than usual this year. May Yahweh defend us from those who would lay waste our tents and despoil our flocks!"

Yahweh—Yahweh—Yahweh! Could he not even pass the time of day with a fellow tribesman without whipping into flame the tumult in his mind? Yesterday the word had been as a soothing balm on his lips. Now it stung like a draught of bitter, brackish waters.

"What in Yahweh's name has entered into you!" complained Zipporah, the bright satisfaction in her eyes not for Moses but for the new girdle she was hastily weaving. "You'd better go in and rest with the children. You'll get that ankle so sore it won't heal before our trip to Ezion-geber."

At another time Moses would have wondered where she had secured the filaments of gold that she wove into the crimson threads of her girdle, but not today. Conscious suddenly of his throbbing ankle, he entered the tent, where the two boys, as wide awake as hungry falcons and as restless, were impatiently awaiting the end of their enforced rest. Gershom's eyes widened with predatory eagerness, while questions sprang from his lips like the bubbling of a fountain.

"Will my father lie down on the mat beside us? Will he tell us now why Yahweh wishes us to get rid of all the little lamb, even to the tiniest bone? Jabal says—"

Hastily Moses withdrew from the tent and in spite of his aching ankle walked swiftly to the outermost edge of the encampment, where there were no faces to remind him of Jared's, desperate and accusing, no voices to which he must reply, nothing to interrupt his constant pacing. It was here, much later, that one of the small grandsons of Jethro found him.

"Oh, here you are, Uncle Moses! I've looked everywhere. My grandfather sends word that he would see you alone, right now, in his tent."

Jethro looked up as the tall figure entered. Though the dim space was lighted solely by the glowing fire outside, his keen gaze noted the labored breathing, the tense lips, the bloodshot eyes.

"My son—"

"There's something I must ask you," blurted Moses without the customary greeting. "I've been waiting all day. I have to know. Tell me—"

Jethro raised a deprecating hand. "Certainly. The beloved husband of my daughter shall ask me anything he chooses. But not until the guest whom I have bidden to my tent is seated and given to eat and drink and has exchanged with me the blessings of Yahweh."

Moses flushed as the gentle but pertinent rebuke hit its mark. "I—I b-beg the sheik's pardon," he stammered for the second time that day. "I—don't know what possessed me. I—guess I've driven myself half crazy with uncertainty."

"And with pain too, if I'm not mistaken. Here, sit down on the mat beside me and let me see that ankle."

"It's nothing—"

"Let me be the judge of that."

As Jethro proceeded to wash the swollen member, dress it with a cooling poultice of herbs, and bind it with a strip of wool torn from his own headcloth, Moses felt the tumult within him diminish. The touch of the soothing, competent fingers, the familiar shapes and sounds and smells of the sheltered spot where he had first found peace and security—all helped to release the pressure on his taut nerves. He yielded himself gratefully to the pungent, shadowy warmth, the fellowship that was like the converging of two oddly variant paths, one with the other.

"Now," said Jethro, when they had shared a meal of bread and goat's milk, "I am ready. The matter for which I summoned you can wait. Ask me what you will, my son."

Suddenly Moses realized the enormity of the question he had determined to ask the priest of Yahweh. "I—it was nothing," he stammered.

"Nothing?" Jethro's eyes were quizzical. "You call it nothing which burns a man's eyelids red and consumes his breath and causes him to tread on hot coals of pain? Come now, my son, I insist that you tell me."

"It—it was the case of Jared," confessed Moses reluctantly. "I—I merely wondered if—if you were really sure your judgment was the will of Yahweh. I—had to know."

There! It was out. He had had the audacity to question the honor of the priest. Jethro would refuse to answer him, of course, would fling him out of the tent as he deserved, punish him publicly before the whole encampment. But it was not fear of punishment that caused him to await the priest's reply with a tenseness that was close to panic. It was the apprehension that as a result of Jethro's anger *he would never know the answer.*

But Jethro was not angry. "Is it not always the duty of the priest to determine for a surety the will of his god?" he responded gently.

"Then you mean you—you actually threw the—the sacred stones?" Moses knew that his audacity was almost as great as if he had attempted to penetrate the holy place beneath the crimson leather covering. Surely now Jethro would flame with righteous anger and banish the blasphemer from his tent, perhaps from the encampment.

"Certainly," replied the priest quietly. "In what other manner would one discover the will of Yahweh?" Leaning forward, he placed his hand on Moses' knee in a gesture that combined both firmness and affection. "Listen, my son. The time has come when I must speak frankly to you, even as a father. It is not by accident that Yahweh hides his face from the sight of man within a deep hood of mist and fire. There are mysteries of a god's being which even his priest cannot penetrate. The ways of the gods are not like the ways of men. The wise man attempts neither to climb upward through the mists nor to walk boldly into the holy dimness of the Tent of Meeting. Do you understand, my son?"

"Yes," said Moses. His lips twisted ironically. If Jethro only knew how well he understood! (*"Don't ask questions, my son. It does not bring happiness. I know... When Re has spoken, is it for Maruma to inquire?... And if Amon chooses to make one man rich and another hungry, who are we to question... The will of the Good God pharaoh, is it not the law?"*)

"Yes," he repeated. "I understand."

"It is the tribe that is important in the sight of Yahweh," continued Jethro earnestly. "When the tribe prospers, then its members are blessed. The part is of value only as it contributes to the well-being of the whole. Remember that, my son, when you are a priest and sheik among the sons of Yahweh."

"When I am—*what!*"

The words sprang unbidden to Moses' lips, like a muscle's startled reflex. "Surely you must know," went on the voice imperturbably, "that there is that within you which can make you a leader of men. I saw it the moment you entered my tent. A voice spoke in my ears, 'This is he who should sometime be sheik and priest over my people in your place.' Call it the voice of Yahweh or not, as you may choose. It spoke to me then, and it still speaks."

"B-but—it's impossible!" At a great distance Moses heard something that sounded like his own voice blurting protest. There was no will behind the words. It was as if his body, unaware of the mortal confusion which it harbored, were continuing in some strange way to function without his spirit. "I—I don't want to be a leader of men. I want to be just what I am—a shepherd. And—and even if I did, they wouldn't want me. This isn't Egypt, remember. In the desert a man becomes sheik only because of his qualities of leadership and by common consent."

"Exactly," replied Jethro calmly. "And does the green shoot in whose fibers flows the quickening sap of the date palm turn itself at will into a stunted thorny acacia?"

The smoke from the evening offering of incense rose straight up into the clear coppery dusk. To the worshipers gathered outside the sacred circle, their faces devoutly lifted toward The Mountain, it seemed that its wraithlike substance met and mingled and became one with that far-off, mysterious hood of cloud and fire.

"Yahweh has left his tent," they said to each other in whispers. "He has risen again into the air and returned to his sacred Mountain."

And afterward, as they walked about the circle to go back to their tents, their steps were a little less wary, their laughter a little louder and more carefree. For although there had been comfort in the knowledge that the god was close at hand when there were evil spirits in the offing, it was undeniable that his presence had placed upon them a certain strain, not unconnected, perhaps, with the fact that the prescribed space about the holy imminence might be violated only under pain of death. Surely a wayward foot was less easily detected from a distant mountaintop!

Moses sat very still in the entrance of his tent, the necessity for motion quite gone from his body. Strangely enough he found a certain relief in the knowledge that he need resist no longer. His mind felt suddenly fresh and clean. Zipporah, watching him out of the corners of her slanting eyes, frowned slightly and nervously fingered the bright golden threads of her new girdle. Even after the drums had begun to beat their slow, insistent invitation, she seemed in no hurry to leave. For the first time since Moses' return she was uncertain of the success of her plan.

"I—I heard Eldad say today that—that his caravan is leaving on the third day at dawn," she broached hesitantly.

"Yes," said Moses. "I know."

"My father said that—that he was going to speak to you."

"He has already done so."

"And—and you—"

"Don't worry. I have told Jethro that I will perform his errand."

Strange how unimportant it had suddenly become to him that he was to go to Ezion-geber! The new pharaoh, Jethro had explained worriedly, was demanding submission and heavy tribute from all the desert tribes. If they hoped to obtain leniency, messengers must be sent to the city at once to meet his envoys. Moses was the man to go. He knew the language of Egypt and the ways of diplomacy. Moses had agreed, almost without emotion. The trip to Ezion-geber could no longer rob him of a peace of mind which he no longer possessed!

After Zipporah had gone to join the dancers, as swift and eager in her relief as a playful young leopard, Gershom came and sat down beside him.

"Would my father tell me now why it is that Yahweh says we must get rid of all the little lamb, even the teeniest little bone?"

Moses put his arm about the small bony shoulders. "Your father would tell you if he could," he said honestly. "But the fact is, son, he doesn't know himself."

The round eyes were unbelieving. "You mean there are things my—my father doesn't know?"

"Many things," replied Moses gravely. "You see, I'm really just like you, son—always asking questions. And, like you, I mean to find the answers."

He sat and watched the moon rise like a bubble blown from the parched purple lips of the wilderness. In its flooding radiance The Mountain fled suddenly into even deeper mystery, as if drawing its flame-edged hood closer about its face. Moses stared at it grimly. There was no use deceiving himself. If Jethro was right, then Yahweh was just like all the other gods he had worshiped, then questioned, then despised; making themselves heavy with approval for those who brought them gifts; caring much for the way men treated them but not one whit for the way men treated each other. Yahweh had his incense, his sacred circle, his new curtain. What did it matter to him that a man called Jared was cowering in the dark, his hands chained to a tent post, cursing the poor trusting fool who had promised him justice?

If Jethro was right.

4

When he caught his first glimpse of Prince Nehsi, the man who had been dispatched into Asia as Ramses' envoy, Moses was scarcely able to stifle the exclamation that rose to his lips. One concern instantly possessed him. He must not be recognized. When his turn finally came to approach the seat of council in the city gate where the noble servant of the pharaoh had established his headquarters, he lowered his face so that his headcloth fell well over his forehead and kept his eyes modestly downcast, as befitted a humble son of the desert in the presence of the great ones of earth; hence his failure to notice the features of the scribe sitting on a well-padded segment of the stone platform not far from the envoy's feet.

"To the servant of Ramses, Son of Amon, pharaoh of Egypt and lord of all the lands of the east and west unto the ends of the deserts, from his humble and dutiful servant Jethro, son of Yahweh, sheik of the tribe of the Kenites of the land and peoples of Midian..."

Moses uttered an audible gasp, which he had difficulty in changing discreetly into a cough. He stole a sidelong glance at the squatting figure to make sure that his ears had not deceived him. No, there was no mistaking that familiar figure, even with ten more years of meticulous grooming and excellent nourishment added to its plump contours.

"Tutu!" his lips mouthed the exclamation soundlessly.

As the well-remembered voice proceeded with its customary smoothness to the end of Jethro's message, Moses hastily revised his plans. First, he must not bargain for a lower tribute as he had intended. And, secondly, he must not speak a word of Egyptian. Just why it had suddenly become so important that he escape detection he could not have told.

"Name of sheik's official messenger?" demanded the scribe abruptly.

"Mo—" The first syllable was well out of his mouth before Moses stopped aghast, ending it in an explosive choking sound. It was going to be more difficult than he had thought.

"Mosheh ben Amram," he muttered hastily.

Alarmed by the silence that followed his half-coherent announcement, Moses shot a glance at the figure seated on the stone platform, but there was nothing in the envoy's demeanor to suggest suspicion. At the moment his eyes were lowered in perusal of Jethro's message, which Moses himself had inscribed on a fine piece of leather in hieratic script, and there was ample opportunity to appraise the familiar features. Strange how little difference the ten years had made! One could imagine it was only yesterday—

"The sheik Jethro seems remarkably well instructed in the language and etiquette of Egyptian letters," observed the servant of the pharaoh, returning the small leather roll to Tutu's bands. "I would swear this was written by a true son of Amon with the education of a scribe."

Moses wet his lips. But his panic was short-lived, for the interpreter shrugged and said in Egyptian: "There are a half dozen good scribes in Ezion-geber. Any one of them would inscribe a letter for a few handfuls of dates. And for a bag of this sheik's wool they would copy the whole Book itself."

The envoy nodded. "It is unimportant. I spoke only from idle curiosity. Let the scribe read the list of items which this Jethro is sending by his messengers as a small sample of the tribute the lordly Son of Re may expect from this dutiful and obviously wealthy son of— what's the name of that queer god from whom he claims to have derived existence? Oh, yes—Yahweh. Never heard of him."

"An obscure desert deity," comforted the interpreter slightingly.

Tutu hastened to comply with the envoy's request, his unctuous voice obligingly anointing each separate item before submitting it for his chief's approval. "Twelve score of the tribe's finest rams, all yearlings, and ten score ewes, two hundred milch goats, one hundred bags of wool..."

Moses listened with mounting apprehension. The gifts already on their way from the encampment were not intended as a "sample." They represented a far greater tribute than the tribe could well afford. It was on his own recommendation that Jethro had multiplied his donation at least threefold.

"If we take too little," he had told the sheik shrewdly, "they will double or treble their demands upon us. But if our offer is generous, though less than they would have demanded, they will be content. Having much, why should they waste good soldiers to obtain little— especially if there is one to plead for us who speaks their language?"

But now he could not speak their language. Indeed, he scarcely dared speak at all for fear these two who had known him so well might remember the sound of his voice. Perhaps if he disguised it—

"P-please make the noble envoy to understand," he begged the interpreter, "that the tribe of Jethro is neither great nor rich. We are the dutiful servants of the great Ramses, but unless he leaves us flocks by which to live, how shall we serve him properly?"

The interpreter shrugged again. "The envoy knows his business," he replied indifferently.

Sweat trickled from beneath Moses' headband and lodged in beads on his heavy brows. He knew that he was failing Jethro. But he could not bring himself to speak the few words that would reopen the long-closed doorway. Perhaps, had Tutu not been there—

"The sheik Jethro seems to be a dutiful and honest subject," said the servant of the pharaoh with impersonal finality. "Since he is the only desert chieftain who has anticipated the full demands of his lord for tribute, his loyalty shall be rewarded as an example to other sheiks who are not only less co-operative but less foresighted. Let the scribe make record that only half of the offerings of Jethro, son of Yahweh, sheik of the Kenites of the land and peoples of Midian, are to be accepted. The other half will be returned to said Jethro in such manner as shall be directed by his official messenger—let's see, what was his name? Ah, yes, Mosheh. How stupid of me to have forgotten! Mosheh ben Amram,"

Moses' relief was so great that to conceal it he bowed himself to the ground even more hastily and thoroughly than the watchful guards, jealous of the honor of the absent pharaoh, would have considered necessary, thus missing completely the slow, appreciative smile on the envoy's leathery face and the amusement in his eyes.

But his relief was short-lived.

"I am giving a small feast," announced Eldad that same day as they lounged on the housetop during the afternoon rest, "for Prince Nehsi."

"Prince—" Moses looked bewildered.

"The envoy of the pharaoh, the nobleman who gave you audience this morning. Don't tell me you didn't even learn his name!"

For a few moments Moses made no response. The feeling of bewilderment persisted. His senses lulled into a golden torpor by the tropical ocean of sunlight engulfing their vine-covered shelter, he had sunk into a state of semiconsciousness in which reality was strangely intermingled with memory and fancy. The leafy arbor might well have been the green fragile roof of a dainty kiosk. All the sensuous comfort of Egypt was about and beneath his languorous body. Color swam and blazed and burst into a thousand kaleidoscopic variants between the half-closed lids of his eyes. Above his head a sky of shimmering turquoise was thrust through and through by the bright sharp jade of palm blades. About and below, the mud and stone cubes which were the dwellings of Ezion-geber descended like steps of old, yellowed ivory to the blazing sapphire pavement of the gulf waters. And on the tumbling rocky cliffs of the far and near horizons pale golds and plums and violets ran the full gamut of color to burnt orange and crimson; the rose pinks of granite merged into the deep blood reds of porphyry; while on the withered, bony flanks of the Giant's Spine, from which the city derived its name, pinks and blood reds and flaming golds were blindingly crisscrossed with bold black bars of basalt.

Moses struggled suddenly out of his torpor. "You say the Egyptian is coming—*here?*"

"Yes. I am giving a small feast in honor of our noble guest. Someone should show him that Ezion-geber is a potential center of the empire's culture, not an outpost, and I know of no other citizen who could create that desirable impression." Eldad thrust a handful of raisins between his thick lips. "Only a small company, the elders of the city, a few of the prince's more respectable attendants, such as the fat scribe and the captain of his regiment, and of course—yourself."

"Oh, no!" objected Moses in sudden panic. "You don't want me. As you say, it should be a gathering of the city's dignitaries. It should include no humble shepherds."

"Ah, but the son-in-law of Jethro is not merely a humble shepherd." The sweetness in Eldad's voice was not wholly derived from raisins. "Any man who can persuade a prince of the pharaoh to lower the tribute of his tribe by half—"

"B-but I had nothing to do with the envoy's decision," explained Moses hastily. "I said scarcely a word and not one of them in Egyptian."

"All the more remarkable," agreed the honeyed voice. "If your mere presence exerts such an effect upon Egyptian princes—"

"But I assure you my presence had nothing to do with it." In his earnestness Moses rose to his feet. "Neither the envoy nor his scribe recognized me."

"Ah, then you *did* know them!" The small black eyes which bore an odd resemblance to the disappearing raisins gleamed triumphantly. "I am certain now I want you at my banquet. The tribute on the copper mines has not yet been levied."

"But I tell you the—the prince, as you call him, does not know me."

"Besides," continued Eldad, "I need your help in planning the feast. I want it to be Egyptian in every detail. And we have no time to lose. It will be held tomorrow."

"B-but—it was tomorrow that we were to go into the Arabah to inspect the copper mines."

"So it was." Eldad paused for an instant as the sound of women's voices drifted up from the open courtyard below, that of Zipporah, excited and penetrating, rising insistently above the others. Then his lips began to revolve with fresh vigor, as if in prospect they were munching a substance even sweeter than raisins. "I am delighted that you show such enthusiasm for your new occupation," he said, smiling.

"B-but—you mistook my meaning! I—I haven't said—"

"The trip to the Arabah can be postponed another day," continued Eldad imperturbably.

Moses was silent. Eldad reminded him of some place, some circumstance, some person, perhaps a combination of all three, but he could not think what it was. He knew only that it was vaguely associated with darkness, with four walls pressing suffocatingly about him, with a confusing awakening of emotions of which not the least was fear.

The feast was by no means the ordeal he had anticipated, in spite of the fact—or, possibly, because of it—that as a model of Egyptian decorum it was a ridiculous failure. He took a morbid pleasure in the knowledge that in the eyes of the prince and his party Eldad was making himself absurd. The flowers were coarse, rank, tropical blooms as far removed from the delicate lotus in scent and texture as were the lumbering servants from the soft-footed, crisp-aproned slaves of the Egyptian dining hall. Instead of seeping gently down to lend aroma to the guests' garlanded brows, the perfumed unguents, too liberally applied, became odorous cascades blinding the vision, tickling the nostrils, and coursing between bosoms and shoulder blades in thin, itching rivulets. The women, accustomed to eating in their own quarters after the men had been served, were either gauche and tongue-tied or, like Zipporah, pitiful in their attempts at volubility. Even the dignified city elders gazed stupidly at their bronze knives and, used to dipping their sops of bread into one common bowl and wiping their fingers on their beards, looked helplessly askance at the platters of food and dainty silver finger bowls proffered awkwardly by the servants.

He wanted it Egyptian, thought Moses, watching the perspiring Eldad struggle with a scrawny, lopsided wreath which threatened to shut out his vision. *I hope he's satisfied.*

His own position was as inconspicuous as he could have desired, at the foot of the long table, with all the elders in careful order of precedence above him. As he had requested, he had been presented to guests obscurely as Ben Amram and been accorded less than perfunctory interest. His eyes studiously avoided the familiar face beside Eldad's. He did not trust the possible disclosures of even the briefest interchange of glances. They had shared too many things in common.

But whatever the feast's deficiencies, the wine was excellent. Moses knew without glancing at the guest of honor that the thin lips were caressing each other with gustatory enjoyment, the bright slanting eyes agleam with satisfaction. As the meal progressed, it became increasingly unimportant whether the thin sweet streams from the vineyards of Lebanon issued from goatskin bags or golden jugs twined with wreaths of lotus. Presently the elders of Ezion-geber were locked in fond embrace with their dear brothers, the Egyptian guardsmen, and, whatever their natal customs, dipping into a common bowl. As the conversation became less and less intelligible, the services of the interpreter became more and more unnecessary. The women ceased to be gauche and tongue-tied and became as adept at advertising their natural charms as the most brazen of the pharaoh's dancers, and the feast gave every indication of degenerating into a finale that was typically Egyptian in form, length, and content.

Noting that Zipporah had left her place for one close to the admiring Eldad, Moses rose suddenly to his feet. The room, already hot, now seemed stifling. He slipped out of the room into the inner court and on through the vestibule into the outer court beyond. He was halfway up the stairs leading to the housetop before the compulsion for flight had yielded to an even more constraining impulse of relief. Continuing upward more leisurely, he drew deep breaths of the night air. The pounding urgency at his temples subsided, but so slowly that he failed to hear the soft footsteps of the figure that followed him up the stairs.

"So you really thought I didn't know you, Mosheh ben Amram?"

Moses wheeled. "Sinuhe!" he exclaimed automatically.

"No, not Sinuhe. Nehsi." There was a note of ruefulness in the gently modulated voice. "All good things have to die, including the

290

spirit of adventure. It's a mark of old age to attempt to recapture the most loathsome sensations of one's youth. I never told you, did I, that I was a younger brother of Harmhab? He made a prince of me, much to my disgust. I stood it as long as possible, then ran away—as you did."

"But not for the same reason, I hope," returned Moses, feeling suddenly as if a fresh draught of blood, warm and vigorous, had been poured into his veins.

"Yes," replied the Egyptian calmly, "for exactly the same reason. Oh, don't misunderstand me. I didn't kill a man. You think that's why you ran away, don't you? No, it was only the immediate occasion of the act. If you hadn't been forced to go then, you would have gone sooner or later. There was something in you, as in me, which made it inevitable. We are made of the same stuff, you and I."

"With one difference," said Moses. "We both ran away, yes. But I shall not return."

Prince Nehsi's eyes, almost as bright as the stars that clustered above the housetop, glimmered briefly.

"We shall see," he said with enigmatic brevity. He drew Moses toward a stone bench close to the parapet. "Come, my son. In spite of the preoccupation of our friends—and otherwise—below, we have no time to lose. Ten years is a long distance for even my nimble tongue to traverse, and yours was never noted for its agility. Begin at the beginning and tell me all that has happened."

Time had never been of consequence in the presence of Nehsi, and now for Moses, the sense of space vanished also. They were back again in the open court of the palace at Saba...pacing the deck of a river boat in the sultry dark...lying beside spray-drenched embers and shouting to each other above the roar of the cataracts. It was easy to talk to Nehsi. Words sprang eagerly and fluently from his lips, became clusters of tents moving like black brooding wings across the face of the wilderness, became narrow rocky paths and steep, rain-swept wadies marking the shepherd's ceaseless but rewarding struggle to find provender for his flocks and peace for his own spirit in a country of intense meagerness and solitude. He told all that had happened to him in the past ten years, failing, however, to mention the two personalities that, with the exception of Jethro, had been most important in the shaping of his new life since he had left Egypt: Yahweh and Zipporah.

"You have a very beautiful wife," commented Nehsi quietly.

"Then you—" Moses felt the hot color staining his cheeks. "How—"

"I asked the interpreter during the feast, and he in turn put the question to our amiable host."

"She wants me to stay here in Ezion-geber and become manager of Eldad's copper mines," blurted Moses, relieved to share at least a part of his burden of confusion.

"Yes. I could see that she wanted something of the sort. She is to be pitied, like all women who have the misfortune to love men like you and me. They are like the tumbling streams which try ever to blend themselves with the Blue Nile, the father of waters. In spite of their tempestuous currents and mighty origins, some of them mightier than his, they can never shape his course. They are either lost, absorbed completely, or compelled by their obduracy to turn back into themselves and seek new channels. Only one, the White Nile, has ever truly merged her being with his, lost nothing, retained nothing. And she is as strong in her serenity as he in his brutal singleness of purpose. Only for a little space does she seem to be lost, submerged. Then the quiet, relentless courage which conquered a thousand miles of choking sands begins again to assert itself. And they become one, neither complete without the other, both stronger than the sum of each. Even the blueness and the whiteness mingle, and, behold, the fruitfulness which they create together is Egypt."

Moses' lips became suddenly dry. "Tharbis!" they shaped soundlessly. "Tell me about Tharbis!" But the words did not come.

"I see you have also a mountain of fire," said Nehsi, changing the subject abruptly, "And I suppose the god who dwells at its pinnacle is the one your people worship."

"Why—yes." Moses was startled out of his tortured constraint. "But how—"

"Every mountain of fire has its god," continued the old adventurer imperturbably. "There are many of them in the country where the father of waters has his birth."

"But Yahweh is different!" protested Moses earnestly, his gaze turning to the glowing, fire-rimmed core from which all the night's star-drenched radiance seemed to spring. "He's not like any other god. He—"

"How?" demanded Nehsi, as Moses' voice faltered into silence. "How is he different?" Receiving no reply, he continued a little wearily, it seemed. "All gods are different—and all the same. Some get their way by one means, some another. But all are exacting and capricious masters. And all have their price. Even the Strong Bull, the Golden Horus, the Good God himself. Especially the Good God himself."

They talked then of Egypt and of Ramses, the new pharaoh, who had determined (for a very large price indeed) to extend his protective godhood over as many as possible of earth's benighted peoples.

"The capital is definitely to be moved to the Delta," said Nehsi, "as soon as the new city Per-Ramses is finally completed. Another store city closer to the canal is also under construction. Where Seti required ten bricks of his builders, Ramses, as you may have guessed, requires twenty."

Moses was filled with a sudden coldness. The moment he had been dreading, the moment for the avoidance of which, he knew now, he had striven to escape detection, had come. He wet his dry lips. "And—my people, the Hebrews?"

Nehsi was silent for a long time. When he finally spoke, his voice was harsh. "Don't ask," he advised with brutal brevity. Then after a pause, more gently: "Just thank your god, who is so different from all others, that you are no longer one of them. And if it is any comfort to you, your brother Aaron still lives. I saw that he was released, as you directed. And I am almost sure I saw him less than a moon ago, when I rode through the brickfields."

They fell again into silence. Moses became conscious of movement, of the relentless passing of time, as if the stars were treading past, in swift-marching tempo, above their heads. Suppose someone came; suppose Nehsi, thinking their conversation finished, were to rise from the bench and leave him there, the question still unspoken.

"And—Tharbis?"

He could not believe that he had actually uttered the words until Nehsi said quietly: "Tharbis is well. When you left she was a child. Now she is a woman."

"Then—then she is—still—"

"Still in the royal palace? Yes. The unpleasant scandal which resulted after your killing of the Egyptian did her no actual injury. Sitra's slave, Beket, kept her under cover for a while. When I regained my princely title, I acknowledged her as my daughter. It was at about the same time, also, that an official of noble birth requested her hand in marriage."

The stars ceased their martial treading, and Moses' pounding pulses diminished so suddenly in tempo that he was conscious of no motion within him. The housetop, the gold-studded darkness, even the familiar figure beside him, seemed hung in a cold, luminous void. He shivered.

"Shall we go down?" he asked abruptly. "Eldad will never forgive me for keeping you here so long. Unless I persuade you to reduce the tribute on his copper mines," he added with sudden bitterness.

Heat hovered over the raw gash of the Arabah like a palpable substance, winding itself in ever-tightening coils about one's forehead and neck and chest, beating tiny flails against the drums of one's temples with every jolting step.

"I admit it's not a pleasant trip," remarked Eldad cheerfully as they remounted their asses after the midday rest on the second day. "But don't worry. I shall expect you to make only occasional tours of inspection. Most of your duties will be connected with the refinery at Ezion-geber. And even they will not be too confining."

Moses glanced curiously at the stocky figure astride the plodding ass. *They should change places,* he told himself grimly. And indeed Eldad looked quite capable of hoisting the tired beast to his shoulders. His vigor had apparently risen in direct ratio with the temperature. It was easy to see why he had left his original occupation as a shepherd. He looked uncomfortable but not unhappy. The sweat pouring from his thickset body seemed to drain it, not of vigor, but of lethargy. As he rode, a stream of raisins, like bits of charcoal fed into a smelter, flowed constantly into his mouth from an apparently inexhaustible store in the folds of his girdle. Watching him, Moses was again reminded of something, he could not tell what; but his curved fingers suddenly dug so deeply into his ass's bridle rein that the beast swerved sharply to one side.

"As I told you, a house will be provided for you close to my own in the city. Not stone, like mine, to be sure, but you'll find it comfortable. Your attractive wife seems to think it will suit your needs very nicely."

Why was Eldad so anxious to secure his services, Moses wondered, that he should hold before him, a complete stranger, such alluring prospects. Surely not because of his acquaintance with the Egyptian envoy, because until two days ago Eldad had possessed no knowledge of such a connection. Why, then? Grimly Moses faced the alternative. Zipporah, of course. He was surprised to discover that the fact aroused within him almost no emotion whatever, except, possibly, pity. For the man who looked upon Zipporah with desire was doomed to share only her own restive frustration. She was the receiver, never the giver. In return for his fine mud house, Eldad would receive only light words and smiling blandishments. It would be almost worth staying in Ezion-geber to watch his smug self-sufficiency change slowly to discomfiture.

Well—why not? Moses was beginning to feel drained of resistance. Peace and freedom were no longer to be found in the wilderness. The long hours when he would have nothing to do but watch his sheep and torment his mind with questions had suddenly become intolerable. At least here The Mountain with its eternal question mark would be removed from his vision!

By midafternoon they were passing great heaps of slag piled on the floor of the wadi, and soon clusters of miners' huts came into view. Their shapeless mud walls seamed and blistered by the sun and half buried beneath a litter of shingle and human refuse, they looked like the foul excretions of a flock of giant birds. The open-faced mine, honeycombed into the terraced cliff above, was aswarm with dark, naked figures.

Moses felt a sudden nauseating faintness. As they passed the maw of a huge smelter into which raw ores were being fed for their first roasting, a blast of hot air assailed them. He was filled with an intense relief when Eldad, leaving behind that part of the caravan which was loaded with provisions for the miners, rode straight on through the crowded settlement. They camped that night beside a gushing spring a few miles up the wadi, where the air was indescribably sweet with the odor of moist green grass and acacia leaves.

"Those miners must be fools," he murmured as he wrapped himself in his enveloping cloak and lay down beside Eldad, "to build their ugly huts down there in all that filth and heat when there's a cool spot like this within walking distance of their day's work!" Receiving no reply, he sank into a pleasant drowsiness, a dazzle of starlight pricking through his half-closed lids and the music of running water in his ears.

Riding to inspect the mines the next morning, he counseled himself not to permit a recurrence of those distasteful emotions which so often in years past had presaged his most unpleasant hours of questioning. This was neither the quarries of Egypt nor the gold mines of Nubia. The toilers burrowing into this glowing crescent of rock were not slaves. They were free men, working at an occupation of their own choice and paid both in rations and wages for their labor. Moses had seen with his own eyes the loading of the pack asses at Ezion-geber. Not food rations alone had gone into those bulging panniers, but woolen yarns, coats and cloaks, sandals of good quality and workmanship, pottery, copper cooking pots, and even a few trinkets and Egyptian scarabs! Poorly paid laborers could not possibly purchase such articles. If free men chose to burrow like ants into a mountain and bury themselves in filth and ugliness, why should he waste his sympathy upon them?

Eldad went straight to the commissary's hut, where they found the young subordinate who had been in charge of the provisions and merchandise lolling, foolishly drunk, in the midst of his empty panniers. He grinned stupidly up at his employer. "Good bishness," he greeted thickly. "Good newsh for mosht eshellent shon Yahweh— All shold out—"

"Where are the records?" demanded Eldad sharply, his face turning a fiery, threatening red. "If you've let somebody get away with them—"

"Here!" Hastily the young man produced from beneath his cloak a bulging goatskin. "All right here! Don't get exshited!"

Eldad seized the sack, untied its neck, and drew out a few fragments of broken pottery. The fire in his face subsided. "All right. But next time save your celebration until these are safe in my hands. There are a hundred men who would think nothing of killing to get their dirty claws on these."

"Very good. Nexsht time remember. But shon Yahweh should have come earlier. Misht exshitement. Another runaway."

The fires leaped again in Eldad's cheeks. "Another one!" Seizing Moses' arm, he pulled him in the direction of a second hut, larger than the others and slightly removed from the prevailing filth. "Those foremen of mine, lazy swine! As drunk as the commissary, I'll wager! Now they've let another of the sly devils get away!"

"But—hasn't a man the right to go if he chooses? I don't see—"

Eldad shot Moses a shrewd glance. "You will soon enough, since you're going to be my manager. How do you think these dirty rats pay for the stuff that filled those panniers? With copper rings and ingots? Don't be a fool, my friend. Most of them owe me so many hours of labor they'll rot of old age before they settle their accounts."

In spite of the intense heat Moses felt a sudden coldness. Crossing the encampment behind Eldad, he stumbled on a pile of loose shingle and turned his weakened ankle. The swift surge of pain, mingled with the enveloping stench, made him violently sick. His body feeling wracked and weightless, he finally followed Eldad into the chief foreman's tent.

The runaway had been caught and brought back to the encampment. He was lying flat on the dirt floor, a thick gag in his mouth, arms and legs bound tightly with withes, and Eldad was looking down at him. The chief foreman was making voluble apologies.

"...the first one that's slipped by us in a moon, and you must admit the boys got him quickly..."

"All right, all right." Eldad gestured impatiently. "He's back, and you know what to do with him. Let's have action, not words."

Moses looked at the trussed figure. He was relieved, for some reason, to see that it was not Jared. The two guards who had captured the runaway unwound the withes, removed the gag, and swung him roughly to his feet. Instantly he turned on Eldad. The guards swiftly pinned his flailing arms, but they could not immediately silence his swollen tongue.

"You dirty swine! Someday one of us is going to kill you! Sending your honey-tongued slaves through all our tribes, whispering fine promises in our ears of how free we'd be if we came and worked in your mines, how we wouldn't have to share everything we owned with the rest of the tribe! Why didn't you tell us you'd never let us get out of debt to you once we got started? You call this freedom! What do you suppose we care how much we can call our own if we have to pay for it the rest of our lives! I tell you—"

The shrill protest ended in a gurgle. Eldad shrugged. "Take him away. You know what to do with him."

"In Egypt," said Moses suddenly, "the sons of Amon flog their runaway slaves."

"The sons of Yahweh are kinder," replied Eldad. "If you're curious, go along and see what we do with them. You'll need to know soon enough. Then come back here to me."

Moses followed the chief foreman and his guards across the encampment toward the squat mud building which housed the smelting furnace. He had gone but half the distance before the heat became almost unbearable. A line of naked figures was transporting buckets of charcoal from a huge pile on the edge of the encampment, dumping them within a few feet of the building, then withdrawing as quickly as possible. Unbelievably, other naked figures emerged from the low entrance, their bodies silhouetted against the red glow inside, snatched up the buckets, and disappeared, one after the other, through the opening. One of them, Moses saw, was Jared. The waves of heat seemed suddenly redolent with the smell of burning flesh.

When he returned to the chief foreman's hut, Eldad was sitting alone on a mat inside, his profile to the entrance. His hand made frequent trips from his girdle to his mouth, and his jaws were slowly revolving. It was not memory but a sudden blinding surge of emotion which told Moses of whom the thickset man reminded him. The four walls of a hut were pressing close about him. Red mist swam before his eyes. The strength of white-hot metal was coursing through his arms, his wrists, his finger tips. He moved silently forward.

Then suddenly the mist cleared. He dropped his clenched hands. It was not Baka sitting on the mat. Baka was dead. Someone had killed him long ago. Someone with the mind of a child. Someone who had believed that by killing a man one could kill the evil which he had designed and accomplished.

"I have come back," said Moses quietly.

5

Zipporah first stormed, then sulked on the way from Ezion-geber back home to Jethro's encampment.

"There was no need of your returning with the caravan! There were plenty of tribesmen to take care of the flocks and bags of wool when my father *sent* them to the city. Why should you consider yourself so indispensable now that there are only half as many?"

"News travels fast among the desert tribes," replied Moses. "There isn't a band of marauders within sight of The Mountain that doesn't know our offered tribute was reduced by half. You think they won't be on the watch for our return?"

"And I suppose you think you could rout them all single-handed!"

"No. But I think I could help my fellow tribesmen rout them." Briefly Moses reached under his girdle and fingered the short bronze dagger which he had purchased at the foundry in Ezion-geber. "It wouldn't be the first time I'd been called upon to lead a company of soldiers. Though I'll admit I'm better with a lance than a short-sword."

Zipporah regarded him with that momentary respect which a reminder of his Egyptian heritage always had power to elicit. However, her former grievance soon asserted itself. "At least you might have left me in Ezion-geber to get our new house settled! We'll be returning so soon it seems foolish for both of us to make the journey. And you could have packed our few possessions and managed the children quite as well without me."

Moses fixed his attention on the spiral of smoke rising from the brazier of burning coals hoisted on a long pole and borne aloft by the leader of the caravan. Like the harassed herdsmen, he also felt the need of some lodestar to hold him to the course he had chosen.

"We are not returning to Ezion-geber," he replied quietly.

While the storm of her fury beat against him, he remained still, like a rock unmoved by the tempestuous waters of the cataracts. So detached was he that he scarcely noticed when the waves subsided into silent but angry little currents of animosity. Since the day he had let his clenched hands fall at his sides in the small hut far up the valley of the Arabah, he had felt curiously alone. He knew that he was not like other men. Indeed, he was a stranger even to himself. His questioning had brought him finally into a state of complete loneliness. The lusty herdsmen in his caravan seemed no longer his fellow tribesmen. Had they looked once into his tormented mind, seen the questions that lay strewn there, they would have shied away as instinctively as a mother ewe from a nest of serpents. Why could he not find sufficiency in the things that satisfied them: water, a bowl of curds, nights full of hot, reckless satiety, a god who liked the smell of a roasting lamb but was coolly indifferent! Deliberately Moses kept his eyes averted from the mist-wreathed Mountain. For even Yahweh was a stranger. Especially Yahweh.

At sunset on the second day they drove their flocks into a secluded wadi the protection of whose narrow entrance and sheer high walls compensated for its sparseness of vegetation. The herdsmen, wearied with constant watching, abandoned themselves to joyful relaxation. A small shift would be quite sufficient to guard the entrance, from which a clear view was to be had of the surrounding country. In the lea of one of the stone flanges sheltering the opening a fire could be safely kindled from the brazier's glowing coals and burned without attracting undue attention. "Take care," Moses warned Jonadab, the chief herdsman. "The sons of Amalek are crafty, remember. Just because we need fewer guards is no sign those few should relax their vigilance."

Jonadab shrugged. Throughout the journey he had found Moses' assumption of responsibility a cause for secret resentment. He had managed very well with twice as many head on the first trip and with no advice, either, from the sheik's precious little diplomat. "We know what we're about," he replied curtly. "If you don't like the way we act, go make yourself a nice soft bed and lie in it. But I'll wager a full wineskin you don't get that skittish little ewe of yours to share it!"

Moses chose to ignore the insult, deciding also not to attempt its disproof. After the evening meal he made a bed of twigs and dried grass for Zipporah on a broad ledge well removed from the merrymakers about the fire and, wrapping himself in his cloak, lay down on the same ledge some distance away. The sulky silence turned into a fretful murmur.

"You might at least have told me before we left Ezion-geber! Then I needn't have—"

Deliberately Moses closed his ears. Lying close to the edge of the rocky shelf, he was able to command a clear view of the wadi, or as much of the wadi as the leaping flames illumined. The gray-yellow-white strata of the sheer rock walls formed natural reflectors, and the fire was blazing high. Reckless in the knowledge that by tomorrow night they would be at the encampment, the herdsmen were piling on all the fuel left in the panniers. In spite of the sheltering flanges, Moses thought uneasily, it would be visible at quite a distance. And the full wineskins purchased in the city market were becoming equally depleted. But why worry? There were sentries constantly on watch. And the wadi formed an apparently impregnable shelter. He wished fleetingly that he had followed it to its farther end to make sure that the shadowy rock wall was actually the dead end it appeared. But it was only a passing thought. The troubled murmur of Zipporah mingled with the too penetrating voices of the revelers and the rat-tat of tiny pounding hoofs, like rain on a sheet of metal. And Moses slept.

He came suddenly awake, instantly conscious that all was not well. The fire had died to embers, but the moon had risen, and the wadi was faintly illumined from one end to the other. It must have been an unnatural stirring among the flocks which had awakened him. He lay still and watchful, trying to recapture the sounds. Then they came again, from far up at the other end of the wadi, the troubled bleating of a ewe, the nervously accelerated drumming of hard, small feet. Then he saw a dark shape moving furtively as a shadow along the outer edge of the flocks...another...and another.

His shrill warning cry rent the silence like a sharp dagger thrust. "Ai-yah! Ai-ya-ah! Ai-ya-a-ah!"

In the red glow of the embers below, the recumbent figures stirred, but slowly, for they were drunk both with wine and heavy sleep.

"The sons of Amalek!" cried Moses, already scrambling down from the ledge. "They're driving out the flocks—other end of wadi! Up! After them in Yahweh's name!"

Once aroused, they were only a few seconds behind him. The walls seized their hoarse cries and re-echoed them as from a sounding board, magnifying the mere score to a hundred voices. "After them!" "Ai-yah!" "Thought they could trick us, the bloody swine!" "Ai-yah! Ai-ya-ah!" "Yahweh sharpen our knives and put blood upon them!"

As Moses slipped along the edge of the wadi between the rock wall and the heaving sea of bodies, one of the dark shadows loomed in front of him. Grimly he quickened his steps, reached forward with a swift thrust of his dagger. The blade sank into sickening softness. There was a harsh sound, ending abruptly, and a writhing, then sudden stillness at his feet. On his swift journey up the wadi he encountered another fleeing shadow...and still another. And each time his steps were fleet and the thrust of his dagger sure.

The sons of Amalek had intended to surprise the sons of Yahweh and had themselves been surprised. The narrow cleft in the sheer wall through which they had planned to drive the flocks in small installments during the night became for themselves a death trap. Caught in a swirling flood of terrified sheep which knew and obeyed their own shepherds' voices, the marauders were at the mercy of their pursuers, stimulated to a savage brutality by the memory of many more successful maraudings. The coats of the milling sheep were stained red with their blood. The few of them who escaped slaughter in the narrow cleft were pursued into the next wadi and, if not slain, given a chase they would not soon forget.

Weary, bloody, triumphant, the sons of Yahweh returned to the dying embers of their fire. There would be no more sleep that night. The wine of victory was a more heady intoxicant than any they had been able to obtain in Ezion-geber. Someone found the half-rotten stump of an old acacia, and after some coaxing the fire again blazed high. While they dressed and bandaged their wounds and cleaned their daggers, they reviewed the details of the night's adventure, polishing them with an eye for future recitation. If any remembered that it was Moses who had sounded the alarm, they neglected to mention it. According to each man's testimony just two personalities had been responsible for the victory: himself and Yahweh.

"...killed five men, I tell you. I swear I counted them!"

"When I lost my knife in the struggle, I just seized my shepherd's stick..."

"Thanks be to Yahweh, who delivers us from our enemies!"

"...said to myself when we lay down, we were in for trouble. That's why I was ready..."

"Come, let's shout again! Lift up your voices to Yahweh, who has delivered us!... Louder!"

"Praises to Yahweh, who has saved his blessed ones!"

Their shouts came to Moses' ears as he walked up and down outside the wadi's narrow entrance. They had forgotten that a sentry was still needed, and he was glad, for it gave him an excuse to be alone. He also had a knife to clean and his own wounds to bind. But he wanted no exultant eyes to watch him do it. It was his victory. He had sounded the alarm, led the attack, probably killed more than any of his comrades. But he did not feel triumphant.

So Yahweh had saved his "blessed ones." But what of his human flocks, those with whose lives he had made himself one? What, for example, of Jared? Even the poorest of human shepherds would risk his life not for his flock alone but for its weakest member. Was Yahweh a better shepherd of sheep than of men?

Deliberately Moses lifted his eyes toward the distant Mountain and looked at it long and steadily. To his intent gaze it seemed suddenly to blaze with renewed vigor, as if fuel were being fed thick and fast into its burning core, the benign radiance of its fire-rimmed hood flaring into a hot, ugly crimson, like the red glow from the bowels of a smelting furnace.

Zipporah was gone. Even when he was but half awake, before Gershom came to arouse him, Moses sensed the change within the tent. The feeling of restlessness had gone from it.

"If my father would but open his eyes, I have many things to tell him."

"What things?" murmured Moses.

"The caravan is gone. The place where their asses were tethered is empty. They must have gone very early, because Eliezer and I were up with the first teeniest ray of sunlight, and they were gone before that. And my mother isn't here, either. We've looked everywhere for her, all over the camp. And Aunt Milcah says we are to eat our morning curds and dates at her tent. Will my father tell me where my mother has gone and why we are to eat our curds at Aunt Milcah's?"

Moses rose from his mat. Deliberately he adjusted his coat and rebound his girdle, poured a little water from the goatskin into the ewer and washed his face and hands. It was like her, he thought, to leave the goatskin full of cool, fresh water, even though it had meant a long walk to the spring by a dark and possibly dangerous path. It was like her also to have made her own woman's half of the tent as spotlessly neat for her departure as for the coming of a visiting sheik. Zipporah had always prided herself on being the perfect housewife.

Moses lifted the cover of the chest automatically, knowing exactly what he would find: his own and his children's change of garments carefully cleaned and folded, a bare rectangle of yellow acacia wood where hers had been. He was closing it when a shadow darkened the entrance of the tent.

"I—suppose you're wondering where she's gone."

It was Milcah, the oldest of Jethro's seven daughters. "The most dependable," people said of her as they said of Zipporah. "The most beautiful," but in that tone of voice reserved for a dull-gray sky rather than a glowing sunset. Standing in the entrance of the tent, silhouetted against the morning brightness, she looked as devoid of color as a stretch of wind-blown desert. But Moses noticed suddenly, gratefully, that her eyes were the same clear liquid brown as Jethro's.

"I know," he replied. "She has gone with the caravan of wool merchants which is journeying to Petra by way of Ezion-geber."

"Then you—you knew all the time."

"No." He spoke slowly, carefully—had he known? "Not until Gershom came this morning and told me she had gone."

"I tried to stop her; please believe me I did." The brown eyes pleaded with him earnestly. "When I threatened to tell you or father, she told me that if I did, she would—would kill herself. She—she said she would rather be dead than stay here any longer in this wilderness when—when there was a man like Eldad who—who wanted—"

"Don't reproach yourself," interposed Moses, realizing that the disclosure was causing Milcah more pain than himself. "You could not have prevented her going. And I should have known. She had already decided to return before we left Ezion-geber. The caravan passing through merely gave her an earlier opportunity than she expected."

Yes, he should have known. *You might at least have told me before we left Ezion-geber! Then I needn't have...*" Deliberately he had closed both his eyes and his ears. Why? And suddenly he knew why; knew by the complete absence of emotion within him.

"She—she asked me to take care of the children." Milcah's voice was barely audible. "I—I could take them to my husband's tent, or—or, if you wished, I—my husband and I—we could—come to yours—"

"Yes, why don't you?" responded Moses gratefully. "You must be crowded living with all the other sons and daughters of Bildad in that one small tent. That is," he regarded her plain, flushed features anxiously, "if you're sure we wouldn't be too much of a burden."

She watched him cross the encampment toward Jethro's tent, her small pointed face breaking into a smile which made it almost beautiful. A burden? The children of Moses? To a childless woman who had loved him since she and her six sisters had first seen him, weary and begrimed, beside a well and he had drawn water for their flocks?

"No," said Jethro slowly, "I suppose you are right. We cannot go after her. All we can do is wait."

"For what?" inquired Moses coldly. "Until Eldad either tires of her charms or discovers that promises are of little value without fulfillment?"

Jethro looked suddenly old. "She was not the one I would have picked out for you," he said gently. "But, remember, she was the one you would have. She is your wife."

"Not any longer," replied Moses. Words fell glibly from his lips as if he had repeated them only yesterday. "I have abandoned you as wife, I am removed from you, I have no claim on earth upon you, I have said unto you, 'Make for yourself a husband in any place to which you shall go.'" And by the look on Jethro's face he knew that he had said them in the language of the Kenites, not in that of Egypt.

Jethro bowed his head. "As you will. Yahweh will cast no blame upon you. How could you do otherwise? She is no longer your wife." The brown eyes kindled. "But she is still my daughter. And you are still my son."

Moses would have returned at once to his flocks in the wilderness had not the band of wandering musicians and storytellers arrived just when they did, pitching their ragged tents outside the rim of the encampment, like beggars before a city gate. Not that they were treated like beggars! At the first news of their arrival, festive garments were again dragged from chests, for once more there would be dancing at night around the fires. Women kneaded their bread and hoed their tiny plots of barley to the tune of plaintive pipes and lyres. Children gathered about the makeshift shelters, staring at the gaily dressed singers and dancers, begging the old man with the silvery voice and the long white beard for "just one more story."

"There's a queer man or maybe an animal in their tents," Gershom reported after one of these expeditions. "He's so thin we all call him 'Bones.' And he just sits on the ground without saying anything. And..." here the boy watched his father warily— "and he has funny marks on his back, like those on the back of my father, only red instead of—"

So swiftly did Moses put aside the goatskin pouch he was packing for his journey that Gershom took to his heels in alarm and so had difficulty in overtaking his father before the latter reached the musicians' tents.

"Where did you find him?" demanded Moses abruptly.

The musician looked up from his task of stringing a small wooden lyre with sheep's gut, and shrugged. "Him? He just came wandering into our camp one day from over there," he gestured vaguely toward the west, "and we fed him. Can't talk, just sits like that. The little ones call him 'Bones.' Good name for him."

Moses looked down at the apparition, noting every unwholesome detail: vacant eyes, clawlike hands, dry brown skin sagging from one bone to another like a tent hung loosely on its poles. Deliberately he reached over and lifted the ragged folds of cloth covering the shoulders. His muscles tightened. Slowly he repeated a few words in Shasu, watching the vacant eyes narrowly for some flicker of response, but there was none. He tried Egyptian, Canaanite, even a few syllables resembling those he had heard from Kheta lips, but each time he was rewarded with only an empty stare. Then, at last, he leaned very close to the emaciated face.

"Peace to you, son of Joseph," he said softly in Hebrew.

There was a flicker of motion in the vacant pits, so slight as to be barely perceptible, then emptiness again.

"I'm taking him to my tent," said Moses to the musician. "I'll take good care of him. You needn't worry."

"Worry! About him?" The shrugging shoulders expressed both relief and incredulity, "Sure. Take him and good riddance, and Yahweh be praised who made you such a fool!"

With Milcah's help Moses ministered to the painfully emaciated body and still more painfully bewildered spirit. He coaxed gourd after gourd of rich goat's milk between the reluctant lips and sat for hours patiently rubbing oil into the lacerated back. The stranger was younger than he had thought at first, his hollow cheeks only faintly brushed with golden down. The slowly rounding limbs assumed surprisingly youthful contours.

He must have come straight across the desert as I did, thought Moses. *Only he had not the good fortune to encounter as many friendly tribes along the way. These are not old wounds. Less than a month ago he was with my own people in Egypt.*

To Milcah he said: "A few days more of your good food and care, and he will be ready to go with me into the wilderness. It is where he needs to go to find peace. I know."

And finally the day came when he said, "We shall go tomorrow."

The stranger was still pitifully thin, but in his eyes vagueness had given place to awareness. He seemed to listen intelligently when Moses spoke to him in his limited Hebrew, and occasionally he would nod or shake his head. But he spoke no words in return.

"Go out," Milcah urged Moses with an anxious glance at his own drawn features, "and listen to the music and the storytelling. Surely I can be trusted to tend him for an hour."

Moses went reluctantly. He was in no mood for festivity. All over the encampment tents were emptying. Men, women, and children in holiday dress were hurrying toward the open space where a great fire was lighted. Moses moved among them as a stranger. For years he had believed them to be his people, their god to be his god, but he had been mistaken. What had he in common with the people of Yahweh? Had their firm flesh ever known the stroke of a lash? Had their wrists ever been bound, their feet chained together, their shoulders bent like a straining bow fitted with leaden arrows?

In the center of a firelit space a minstrel's voice was raised in the ancient lament of some long-forgotten sheik who in a moment of bloodthirsty exuberance had managed to make himself immortal.

> "Adah and Zillah, hear my saying,
>   Wives of Lamech, listen my speaking,
>   For a man have I slain for my wounding,
>   And a youth for my striking.
>   If sevenfold Cain shall be avenged,
>   Then Lamech seventy and seven."

The women swayed and beat their breasts as had the wives of Lamech long before them, voicing the savage refrain in a chorus as shrill and harsh as the cry of the white-winged scavenger and as old as the desert law of blood revenge.

> "If sevenfold Cain shall be avenged,
>   Then Lamech seventy and seven."

Moses moved on to the smaller groups gathered about lesser fires, where the bards and storytellers repeated old folk tales of the race,

306

which had been handed down from lip to lip through uncounted generations. One group listened, enthralled, to a long prose narrative about a man called Noah, who in a time of flood had once built a huge boat to save both animals and men from destruction; another, to a fanciful, highly captivating tale of how evil had first come into the world of men through the machinations of a wily but suspiciously human-acting serpent.

How like man, thought Moses with indulgent irony, *to find some way of shifting his responsibility!*

He wandered on to the largest of all the groups, gathered about a man so old that his flesh and bones seemed transparent in the glow of the fire. Here absolute stillness prevailed, for it was necessary almost to hold one's breath in order to hear the low words issuing from the bloodless lips. It was fitting that the tales he told should stretch their roots into the beginnings of all things. His very brow seemed damp with the mists of some primeval chaos, his own elusive breath the essence of the eternal mystery.

"In the beginning, when Yahweh began to create the earth and the heaven," murmured the voice which was like a gentle wind riffling the palm leaves, "the world was a desolate waste of darkness and wind and water..."

Memory stirred within Moses. He was back in the harem nursery in the palace at Memphis, sitting in a circle of children, lips parted, eyes wide in suspense, while another storyteller, almost as old as this one, sang of another god and in another language.

> "The Master of Everything saith after his forming:
> I am he who was formed as Khepri...
> The heaven had not been formed,
> The earth had not been formed,
> The ground had not been created
> For the reptiles in that place.
> I raised myself among them in the abyss, out of its inertness..."

Moses dropped to his knees, shifting his weight slowly backward upon his feet and ankles, joining the silent group. How stupid he had been to think that these were not his people! He was one with them as he had been one with those others sitting with their small legs crossed on that circle of soft, embroidered cushions; as he had been one with his blood brothers, the Children of Joseph, squatting in a hot, smoky hut and listening to glowing legends of the Shield of Abraham, the

Fear of Isaac, or the Mighty One of Jacob. He was one with them all—
Hebrews, Egyptians, Kenites, and who could tell how many others!—
all who had ever asked the questions, Wherefore? Whence? and
Whither? and sat like children, lips parted, eyes wide and tense, waiting
breathless to know the answers.

Then suddenly it came; not, as he had sometimes dreamed of its
coming, with a blaze of light or a crashing of drums and cymbals, but
quietly, almost in a whisper, like the dropping of a leaf or a soft footfall
that might easily have passed unnoticed.

"Then said Yahweh, I shall make man in my own likeness, to be
master over the wild beasts and the tame beasts and the reptiles which I
have made. And Yahweh made man in his own likeness; in the likeness
of Yahweh he made him, both male and female he made them. In the
likeness of Yahweh he made them both."

Moses looked about him at the rapt faces in the circle of firelight,
but there was nothing in any one of them to indicate that the most
momentous words of all time had just been uttered. They were just as
they had been before the words were spoken, children waiting eagerly
to hear the end of an unfinished story.

Rising, he moved away noiselessly, kept moving until he felt the
roughness of sand and wild broom beneath his feet, the freshness of
the desert night against his cheeks. Even then he did not stop, only
slackened his pace. Not until he had reached a spot where even the
faintest echo of the wailing voices no longer reached his ears and the
last glow of the fire had vanished, did he cease all motion. Then at last,
in a stillness so profound that even time seemed to be caught and held
in its waiting void, he lifted his face toward The Mountain.

"Yahweh," voiced his spirit soundlessly.

He knew that it did not matter by what name he called it, this
truth which he had just discovered. He could have apprehended it as
well in Egypt and called it Re or Aton. Or in Syria, and named it El.
But he had not found it in Egypt or in Syria. Indeed, in spite of all his
seeking, he had not found it at all. It had come to him out of the wide
spaces of the wilderness. And its name was Yahweh.

Strange that all the truth one had spent a lifetime in seeking
should be compassed in such simple words! *And Yahweh made man in his
own likeness.* It was like gazing for long torturing hours at a distorted
image through a glass and then beholding it suddenly in perfect focus.
For if God the Creator had made man in his own likeness, then every
man was as important in his sight as every other. None had the right to
place a burden on another's shoulders or to lay a lash across his back.

Or to kill. Or to steal. Or to seek mastery by any means over either his body or his spirit.

"*It is the tribe that is important in the sight of Yahweh,*" Jethro the priest had said. "*When the tribe prospers, then its members are blessed. The part is of value only as it contributes to the well-being of the whole.*"

But Jethro was wrong. It was the human being that was of supreme importance. Only in as much as its weakest member prospered could the whole be blessed. The tribe—or family, or clan, or nation—was of value only as it contributed to the well-being of *all* its members.

And the little black and white stones were wrong. For they had made the strong master of the weak. Even though they had been cast in the name of Yahweh and by the hand of his priest, they had been wrong. They would have been wrong *even if they had been cast by the hand of Yahweh himself!*

The wilderness had ceased to be a silent, solitary place. Like a man awakening from a long sleep, Moses felt a sudden quickening rebirth in all his senses. The stars sang in his ears. He stretched his arms wide. Beneath his steady gaze The Mountain became a close, warm, living entity. Its fire-rimmed crest was no longer a concealing hood nor the ugly red flare from the bowels of a smelting furnace. It was a glowing, radiant pillar like that which rose at night from the brazier of living coals borne aloft by the leader of a caravan, to guide the way across a pathless desert.

6

After he returned to his flocks in the wilderness, Moses was possessed by but a single purpose. Once he had achieved it, he was certain he would find the serenity which had always been his goal. Surprisingly, it had not come with his illuminating experience that night outside the encampment. Following the first pure ecstasy of discovery there had been awakened within him a strange unrest. It was as if he had drunk deeply of refreshing water and still not found his thirst quite quenched; or climbed to the top of a high mountain only to discover that his eyes were so blinded with dust that he could not see the view.

He told no one of the thing he intended to do. The other herdsmen would be horrified. It was conceivable that they might forcibly prevent him from fulfilling his purpose. They would be afraid not merely for his own safety but for themselves, for the thing he intended to do might well bring the vengeance of the god upon them all. So he planned with the utmost caution, his every word and action contributing to the slow shaping of circumstances by which he would finally attain his objective.

"When we break camp this time, why not go south instead of north?"

"No doubt we'll find greener wadies farther on. If we stay here, the sheep will grow lichens instead of wool!"

"Surely the nearer we approach to The Mountain, the greater the favor Yahweh will bestow upon us!"

"It is the sons of Amalek who should be fearful of this region, not the sons of Yahweh. Let us not cower because of the god's nearness but rather rejoice in his protection!"

But though his eyes were ever focused on the slowly approaching goal, he possessed another interest almost equally consuming. For he must bring peace to the man called "Bones" as well as to himself. By now the name was less applicable. The generous feedings of goat's milk had brought not only roundness but vigor to the young Hebrew. As a herdsman he had been an apt and willing pupil. The acquired skills of long generations of nomad shepherds were in his blood. He was soon as clever with the sling as any of the grandsons of Jethro and as swift to detect the flicking of a serpent's head within the grass. But still he refused to speak, and the look of tortured memory in his eyes was worse than the vagueness it had replaced.

"You are safe now," Moses said to him over and over in Hebrew while they were walking beside the flocks or lying side by side wrapped in their cloaks at night. "It's all over. You need never go back. Let it pass from your mind and be as if it had never been. You are safe now."

He knew that the youth understood what he said, at first by the desperation in his eyes, later by the unintelligible sounds that issued from his lips. Then finally, when they were camped one night within only a few days' journey of The Mountain, the sounds suddenly became words.

"*Safe*—" It burst from his lips with a harshness like the tearing of cloth.

"Yes," repeated Moses eagerly. "Safe. It's all over, I tell you. I know, because I also escaped. You'll find peace here, as I did. Just try to forget."

310

"No! Not—forget—" The words seemed wrenched from the still far too slender body. "Not—safety—"

"I know how you feel," said Moses calmly, not yet daring to call attention to the miracle of speech. "I felt that way too when I first came to the wilderness. I would waken at night hearing the sound of the foremen's voices, feeling the strokes of the lash. It was months before I could sleep through a whole night without coming wide awake, over and over, my whole body trembling and wet with sweat. But it will pass. The wilderness is a wise and patient physician. You will forget, as I did."

"But I don't—want to forget. I don't want—safety!"

"Hush!" Moses spoke soothingly, "Don't think about it now. Just lie still, here in the cool quietness of the night. We'll talk about it again in the morning."

But the floodgates had been unloosed. The accumulated burdens of unspoken fears and torments came pouring forth, at first jerkily, then with a tumultuous abandon. "How can I—lie here—safe—when they're—down there—being lashed and driven—treated like cattle instead of men—no, not like cattle, they think cattle are sacred—I could at least have stayed with them, taken my share of the lashes, not run away and left my brothers—yes, my brothers, I tell you, two of them, one older and one younger than I am, and I ran away and left them, God of Abraham forgive me—left them to take my share of the beatings while I'm lying here safe, you tell me to forget—"

Helplessly Moses lay still and listened, the flood submerging him, until finally the tempestuous flow abated. Even then, when from sheer weariness the youth fell into a troubled sleep, words still trickled from his lips.

"Safe—when they're—down there—God of Abraham—forgive—"

Moses did not sleep. He turned and twisted on the hard ground, unable to find a position where some small stone or hummock of rough grass did not bruise his flesh. For the first time in years there was a faint throbbing of pain in his back. He longed for morning so that he could put into operation fresh plans for the fulfillment of his purpose. He was very close now to attaining it. But the shepherds were beginning to grumble. The nearer they came to The Mountain, they complained, the sparser grew the vegetation. A pretty good sign that Yahweh didn't want them to come any closer!

Finally, resigned to restlessness, he lay on his back and looked steadily at the looming pyramid with its strangely glowing core. It too seemed possessed of disquiet. Faint but unmistakable sounds issued from its mysterious recesses, sighings and groanings as of a spirit in torment. Moses stared, eyes wide with a fierce intensity, his own restlessness seeming to merge itself into some vaster, more profound disquiet. Was there no peace even in the heart of Yahweh himself!

When he finally slept, it was only to dream that he was lying on the edge of a burning pit, from which dark naked figures were attempting to climb by digging their fingers and toes into the rocky sides. Occasionally one would almost reach the top, and he would stretch down to grasp its hands, only to see it plunge back into the glowing depths. Always it had a face, and he could see its features clearly: Aaron's, Miriam's, Jared's, that of the young Shasu boy outlined against the glaring sun. He kept hearing muttered words, not knowing that they came from his own lips.

"How can I lie here—safe—when they're down there—lashed and driven—not like cattle—cattle are sacred—ran away and left my brothers—ran away, I tell you—ran away—"

"No!" The head herdsman was obdurate. "Not a step nearer. We've gone too far already. I don't know what ever made us come in this direction. You can see the god is angry with us. If you listen hard, you can even hear his voice protesting. And the feed is growing scarcer with every hour's travel."

The decisive moment had come. "I once heard it said," proffered Moses with a calmness that betrayed nothing of his inward tumult, "that to the west of The Mountain the hills level into a sort of plain, where a flock might find excellent pasturage. It looks reasonable, don't you think, for the slope on that side is much gentler."

"Well—yes, perhaps—but—"

"Then let me take part of the flocks," continued Moses hastily, "and travel in that direction. Even if the vegetation is as scarce there as here, we shall at least be utilizing all the country affords. And it will leave so much more here for the rest of the flocks."

The herdsman considered. "But—I had planned to start back at once. I tell you I don't like being so close. It makes a man feel uncomfortable."

"There's even less vegetation behind us," Moses reminded him. "And the winter rains are still a long way off. Shouldn't we make the most of this country while we're here?"

He had his way. Taking part of the flocks and a few herdsmen more daring than the others, Moses traveled in a long swinging circle toward The Mountain, keeping always in a southwesterly direction.

Vegetation continued to be sparse, but the flocks were accustomed to scarcity. When he had finally located a fairly green valley near an adequate spring, he called his undershepherd aside and said casually: "I'd like to do a little prospecting over to the west of The Mountain. I might be gone several days. I have a feeling there may be better pastures there than here, but I want to make sure before we take the flocks."

The undershepherd looked frightened. "You're leaving us alone?"

"Only for a little while." Now that his goal was so near, Moses had difficulty in keeping the agitation from his voice. "And you have enough herdsmen to give the sheep full protection. At least you don't need to fear attack from marauders. Even the sons of Amalek would hardly dare approach so near the dwelling place of the Destroyer."

It was the wrong thing to say. The undershepherd's fright changed swiftly to panic. "B-but—then we oughtn't to be here ourselves! I knew we shouldn't have come so far! Let's go back—"

"The good shepherd of Yahweh is safer here than anywhere else in the wilderness," explained Moses patiently. "Think you that in the very shadow of his presence the god would let harm come to his blessed ones?"

It took an hour of earnest argument to change the panic into a grudging confidence. "But—" the word prefaced a last weak protest— "surely you're taking someone with you—at least the queer one you call 'Bones'?"

"No. I am going alone."

Now that the final obstacle had been removed Moses felt a curious calm. Rising before dawn, he was on his way long before the encampment was astir, taking with him only the barest necessities: shepherd's staff and sling, a small skin of goat's milk, another of water, and a few dates and raisins. He moved with a sense of having infinite time at his disposal. For it was the end of a journey that he was undertaking, not the beginning. All his life he had been traveling this same lonely path leading through a wilderness toward some ultimate reality in which his questioning spirit could at last find peace.

When night came, he was so close to The Mountain that a stone from his sling could easily have bounded from one of its lower rocky ledges. It had been a longer and more difficult journey than he had expected, but he had finally emerged, just at sunset, into the broad plain which he had expected to find at the west of The Mountain, treeless and sparsely sown with vegetation, but a veritable paradise after the wasteland through which he had journeyed.

He was so weary that he lay down to rest without stopping to eat or to make a fire. In fact, he felt little need for either one. His body was fed and warmed by a consuming purpose, and for the moment he had no fear. The possibility of prowling animals was as remote from his mind as that of the sun's failure to rise.

Though he found it impossible to sleep, his eyes followed without impatience the slow swinging of the stars toward the far horizon. High above his head the fire-edged pillar glowed in a still, shining vapor, more mysterious in its nearness than when seen from a distance. Aloof and disembodied, the solid earth beneath it dissolved into darkness; it too seemed to lie motionless in a void, spirit without body, existence without reason or purpose.

Moses was glad for the hours of solitude. When a man was about to enter into the presence of a god, he had need to prepare himself. What would happen, he wondered, curious rather than fearful, when he set foot on the holy Mountain? Would Yahweh really smite him dead as every desert dweller firmly believed? If so, it was the last time he would lie wrapped in his cloak on the ground, looking at the stars. If Yahweh was that kind of god, he hoped it would be the last time.

There was another reason also why he was glad he could not sleep. For if he slept he might dream again that he was lying on the edge of the burning pit. Each time the dream became more intricate in detail and the figures climbing toward him revealed more and more familiar faces. But after tonight there would be no such unquiet dreams. In the presence of the ultimate truth he would surely find serenity.

He watched the pale dawn reach into the black void. The Mountain again took form. Silhouetted against the yellowing sky, it seemed austere, forbidding. Moses' heart sank. Why should the god have chosen such a terrifying place for his habitation? A fitting home, perhaps, for one who called himself the Destroyer but not for the Creator of all things who had made man in his own likeness! One by one the lesser surrounding peaks reared their heads proudly and donned bright turbans of sunlight. But The Mountain remained towering and aloof, untouched by any radiance save that which emanated from its own mysterious crest.

Moses rose from the ground, removed his clothes, and, using all the remaining water in his small goatskin, bathed himself from head to foot before reclothing himself in his soiled garments. Then, as outwardly calm as if he had been going to release the flocks from their night's shelter, but inwardly quivering with excitement, he moved steadily across the plain. No one knew better than he the enormity of the act he contemplated. He was about to enter into the most holy place of the temple where the image of Re was hidden; to lift the curtain of Amon's sacred bark; to tear aside with rude fingers the mummy wrappings of Osiris. Only for an instant, when the rough prong of rock was less than a hand's breadth from his grasp, did he hesitate.

"Smite me, Yahweh, if you must," he cried soundlessly. "But not yet—not until I've climbed The Mountain!"

Laying his hand firmly on the rock, and finding a crevice for his foot, he swung himself clear of the ground and slowly, one cautious step at a time, worked his way up over the first sheer ledge.

Hours later he cried out again, this time audibly: "Smite me now, Yahweh. Don't torment me any longer. If this is your face that I am seeing, then blind my eyes that I may not look more closely! If this is your voice, stop my ears that I may become deaf! Only let me find peace—"

The jagged walls of the ravine up which he crawled tossed the burning rays of the sun back and forth like jugglers toying with gleaming rapiers. Heat hovered over its narrow, ovenlike depression in throbbing waves. The winds that had risen at noon and blown incessantly across the open wastes up which he had traveled, clutching at his garments, whipping sand and dust into his eyes, were here also, their scorched breath filling the deep crevice like air drawn into an open flue.

He did not know how long he had been climbing. He supposed it was afternoon of the same day, but he could not be sure. There had been periods of intense blackness which might have been either nights or moments. He was vaguely aware of thirst and of other bodily discomforts—blistered feet and hands, knees lacerated from crawling over slippery rocks, the scratching of rough garments clinging to his soaked skin. But they were not important. His search was all that mattered, his search after peace which was leading him into greater agony of spirit than he had ever known.

"Smite me, Yahweh!" he cried again. "Blind me that I may not see—"

But Yahweh did not smite him. And in spite of the blinding dust and barbs of sunlight his vision remained clear and penetrating. He saw every unlovely detail with merciless clarity; the jagged rocks contorted into grotesque shapes, their black surfaces slashed by occasional bare strata of limestone; the twisted limbs of a thorny acacia; the shadow of a vulture's outspread wings. Groanings and mutterings as of a soul in mortal torment filled his ears, whether his own or another's he could not tell. He was no longer a separate entity but a part of some vast activity whose nature he could not even comprehend.

He had long ago lost all sense of direction. He could see neither the plain from which he had come nor the top of The Mountain for which he was bound. His one purpose, to keep traveling upward, became an obsession. He chose the steepest approach to each new eminence, refused to side pass even the most formidable barrier at a cost of retracing his steps. Sometimes in an upright position, sometimes on hands and knees or with his body stretched full length on the ground, he made his way through the furnacelike grooves, over the strange transfixed stream beds which were as smooth as glass and as black as ebony, up the sheer sides of cliffs with only a few jutting prongs of rock for a foothold, up...always up...Until finally his feet could discover no more sloping surfaces to climb, his hands no more jagged edges of rock, no more twisted branches of thorny acacia to which they might cling.

If he had found restlessness below, here he encountered turmoil. Winds swept against him with a violence that drove him to his knees. Light flashed before his eyes like blazing scimitars. Heat laid steaming compresses on his throbbing temples, fell like a moist but unsatisfying rain on his parched lips. The earth stirred beneath his body. He realized vaguely that it was sunset and that his whole world, complete but indescribably small, was spread before his eyes. Midian was a cluster of toy rock piles, Ezion-geber a fleck of dust on the tip of a blue blade. The desert of his journeying as a fugitive lay like a small outspread palm, skin-flaked and leprose. And Egypt... Egypt was the invisible black earth on which the blazing sunset fires were kindled far beyond the horizon.

Night fell swiftly, plunging the mountaintop into a weird half-light which changed its turmoil into chaos. In spite of his exhaustion Moses made his way forward, moving now on hands and knees so that he might not stumble into one of the many crevices. He was very near the goal now. Only a little farther and he would look on the mystery that lay hidden within the glowing pillar. He would look upon it, and that would be the end, for he was sure now that no human being could enter into a knowledge of its reality and live.

"Smite me, Yahweh!" he cried again. "I know now that you must. But not yet. Please—not until I've discovered a little more of truth!"

Hot mists swam before his eyes and entered his nostrils, making it difficult to breathe. Winds lashed him mercilessly. The earth reeled unsteadily. Was it, perhaps, the primeval chaos of which the old minstrel had sung? *"In the beginning, when Yahweh began to create the earth and the heaven, the world was a desolate waste of darkness and wind and water..."*

He must have slept finally, for he dreamed again that he was lying on the edge of the burning pit. At first there were no dark naked figures, only the undulating mass of molten fire, brighter and more terrifying than he had ever yet conceived it. Then suddenly they were there, climbing toward him out of the abyss, clinging to its black smooth sides, and he was reaching down his hands, struggling, agonizing, to reach them. This time there were more than Aaron and Miriam and Jared and the young Shasu boy. They came in unending swarms through the burning waters, out of the reddened mists— prisoners of war, their bodies lashed together, gold miners of Nubia, slaves from the temple at Karnak, fellahin bent like taut bows to the shaduf, Hebrews with burdens of bricks on their backs.

"Come down, Moses!" they called up to him. *"Come down and help us!"*

No, *no!* So sharply did his whole being recoil from the thought that he awakened from his dream, if dream it was. But he still lay staring into a glowing pit, its depths troubled by such profound disquiet that it might have contained all the naked bodies absorbed into one.

And Moses knew suddenly that his search was over. He had entered the holy place, lifted the sacred curtain, torn aside the divine wrappings. And he recoiled in horror from the truth he had discovered. For there was not only restlessness in the heart of God the Creator, There was an agony so intense that it constantly consumed his very being!

Yahweh did not smite him. He had reserved for this supreme audacity an even more effective punishment: to let him live.

When morning came Moses started to make his way down The Mountain. Descent was surprisingly easy. Viewed from above, the deeply gashed grooves became paths rather than obstructions. Late in the afternoon, he had reached the edge of the bleak windblown waste about halfway down The Mountain where he slaked his thirst and filled his waterskin at a small spring. A few stunted acacias nearby gave a meager shelter from the sun. Wearily he sank down beneath one of them, and, since it was already near sunset, decided that it was as good a place as any to spend the night. There was little purpose now in any of his motions. Probably there never would be again. He would go back to his flocks, he supposed, and for the endless years that might remain to him perform the routine duties of a shepherd. Perhaps if he always kept in the wilderness, he would finally forget the toiling figures, and if he refused to look at The Mountain, he might even cease in time to remember its disturbing secret. He would become hard and bitterly resistant, like the stunted acacia that stood alone on the bleak waste some distance from his shelter, its gaunt arms twisted by the winds, its meager leaves darting sharp, defiant thrusts at the enemies assaulting it on every hand.

Even as he watched he saw one such enemy approaching. Emerging from the hot sucking funnels of the precipitous ravines, the winds flung themselves together with a violent impact, locked in furious combat, then, unexpectedly joining forces, went hurtling away, a huge twisting spiral of sand and dust. Seizing the lonely acacia in its turbulent embrace, it clung to the bare, gaunt arms in mad swirling frenzy. At the same instant the setting sun thrust its bright slanting sword into the battle. There was a moment's bitter conflict, then sun and earth and wind flung themselves together in one swift ecstasy of union. The spikes of the thorn tree leaped into flame. The swift-whirling spiral of dust and sand became a pillar of golden smoke, shot through with fire. While Moses gazed spellbound, the tree burned before his eyes, yet it was not consumed. Then, as abruptly as it had come into being, the brief ecstasy of union passed. The fury of the winds subsided. The sun's rays paled. The tree was again a lonely acacia, gaunt and ugly in the midst of a desolate waste.

Moses rose from the ground. He slipped off his sandals.

"Yahweh," he whispered.

He lifted his face to the driving wind, opened his eyes wide toward the sunset's blazing core, and felt the whirling dust which was his own tortured spirit kindle into burning awareness. Blind fool that he had been! Yahweh on a mountaintop imprisoned in a glowing pit? When he, Moses, had just beheld divinity created out of dust, unspeakable beauty born out of agonizing conflict? Understanding swept through him like a flame. Yahweh had not finished his work of creation. He was still trying, patiently and in desperate agony of spirit, to create man in his own likeness. He would never cease trying until he had fulfilled his purpose, *even though his own being became consumed in the attempt!*

Night came, and Moses slept. And as he slept he dreamed that he lay again on the edge of the burning pit and that a voice which he had never heard was crying in his ears:

"Come down, Moses!"

"Who—who are you?" he stammered, knowing very well the answer.

"Yahweh, the Eternal!"

He trembled, "B-but—I can't see you! There is n-nothing, no one in the p-pit. Wh-where are you?"

"Down in Egypt with your brothers." The voice was so faint he could scarcely hear it. *"In the copper mines of the Arabah. With my sons in the temple at Karnak. Come down to us, Moses!"*

"No, no! Not that!" In his sleep he tossed and twisted on the hard ground. "You c-couldn't ask me— Why, I—I just couldn't do it!... No! No, I tell you! Who am I to do this thing? I—I can't even speak well... Besides, I'm a free man, made in your own likeness. Would you have me become a slave again?... What's that? You mean that a man truly made in your likeness must share your agony and help create...Yes! Yes, I see!... Have mercy on me, for I understand. At last I understand!..."

"Come down Moses!"

PART VII

1

"The Children of Joseph are an abomination of filth," complained the foreman, lending emphasis to his statement by a sharp thrust of his lash. "They are the miserable offspring of a swine that has lain down with an ass. They are the sputum which Ptah cast from his mouth in a moment of sickness. They—"

"Agreed," returned the commissioner of buildings for the new store city of Per-Atum. "But why this sudden—"

"And the gang of workmen under the section boss Dathan," continued the foreman with another savage bite at the dust, "are the worst of all."

The commissioner, who had once been only a foreman himself, looked surprised. "But surely you must be mistaken. Dathan's gang used to be the least troublesome of any in this outfit."

"Not any more."

"What's the matter? Don't they turn out their quota of bricks?"

"Oh—yes. Dathan sees to that. He's more loyal to the interests of the pharaoh than the Grand Viziers themselves."

"You mean to the interests of Dathan," commented the commissioner, his lips curling. "What's all the trouble about, then, if they're turning out bricks?"

"Let the commissioner see for himself," replied the foreman, his limp lash seeming to spring into sudden resilience, like a snake sensing its approaching prey. "We are about to inspect the gang of Dathan now. You'll see what I mean."

The commissioner saw. "What's got into them?" he inquired curtly after a few moments of silent appraisal.

"Let the wise official inform his humble foreman," was the sarcastic rejoinder.

"They look and act," said the commissioner slowly, "as if—as if they thought they were Egyptians. And not fellahin, either. I thought we'd got that idea out of them ten years ago."

"You see?" The foreman was triumphant. "There is something different about them. Remember the trouble we had with them when you and I were first sent up here to superintend the gangs? Remember all the demands they made? They acted just like this, as if they owned the earth."

"I remember." The eyes of the commissioner narrowed reflectively. "And if I'm not mistaken, there was a woman——"

"By Amon, you're right, there was! But that was over ten years ago. You can't tell me even Hathor herself could work in the brickfields that long and have life enough left to do any trouble-making! She was probably dead long ago."

"You think so? Look there."

The foreman looked, then gaped, "Breasts and thighs of Hathor! Did I say dead?"

"Call Dathan," the commissioner ordered.

"But you're not——" Meeting the cool eyes of his superior, the foreman continued lamely and with increased respect. "Surely the wise official has no wish to start trouble such as we had ten years ago with these sons of iniquity! And, after all, we don't know that it is the woman——"

"I said, call Dathan"

The obsequious manner of the section boss was tinctured with a slight uneasiness. "The Children of Joseph are indeed blessed," he murmured affably, bending himself to the ground, "in the presence of the servants of the pharaoh. We rejoice in making ourselves as the mean clay beneath the feet of our noble lords, even as the——"

"You don't act it," interrupted the commissioner sourly.

Dathan paled. "The—the servant of the pharaoh jests?"

"You'll soon find I'm not jesting! Don't you teach your workmen to bow when they pass an Egyptian official?"

"B-by all the gods, I swear I do!" Dathan was visibly sweating.

"Apparently you need a little help. Call back that young swine who just walked past us with the load of bricks"

The young Hebrew was hastily recalled. He stood before the two Egyptians, naked except for a rag of loincloth, as straight as a spear and as unbending.

"Tell him to prostrate himself," ordered the commissioner tersely.

Dathan gave a sharp command in Hebrew, and the young workman replied but made no motion to comply with the order.

"What does he say?" demanded the commissioner.

The sweat ran down Dathan's face and dripped from his beardless chin. "He—he says that—that no man made in the likeness of a god should—should prostrate himself before another man——"

"He—*what!*" The commissioner stared, nonplused. "Say that again." Then slowly his eyes narrowed. "Find out who told him that," he ordered finally.

There was a further interchange of Hebrew. "A man called Mosheh ben Amram," reported Dathan, a sudden gleam of satisfaction in his eyes.

"You know him?"

"He's a laborer in my gang."

The commissioner turned to the foreman abruptly. "Teach this offal from a swine's belly to pay proper respect to a real man when he sees one," he ordered curtly, then turned to Dathan. "And you bring me this Mosheh—what do you call him? I want to take a look at him."

After watching with satisfaction while the offending Hebrew was forcibly prostrated and flogged, the commissioner turned his attention to the waiting figure. Startled, he noted every detail of the lean, powerful limbs, the slim waist and broad shoulders, the curling black beard. Being a short man, he was obliged to raise his eyes considerably to complete his inspection. What he saw startled him still further. So darkly sunburned was the flesh within the frame of hair and beard that they appeared almost to form one continuous pattern. The eyes too were black and deeply recessed beneath overhanging brows. It gave one the uncomfortable sensation of standing in sunlight and being watched by some invisible creature deep within a cave.

Always slightly disconcerted in the presence of superior physical height, the commissioner was so taken aback by the new-comer's appearance that he barely noticed that he received only the courtesy due one Egyptian from another of equal rank, not the deep servile bow of the slave to his superior.

"Wh-what became of Dathan?" he stuttered almost in panic. "How does he think I'm going to talk to this heathen swine without an interpreter?"

"The commissioner desired the presence of Mosheh ben Amram?" inquired the tall Hebrew in perfect Egyptian.

The official hastily assembled the fragments of his composure. He fixed his eyes severely on the eagle-bright cavities. "Yes. I most certainly do. I—I understand that you've been filling the heads of these miserable sons of Joseph with foolish notions about some heathen god."

"Each people has its own peculiar deity," returned the Hebrew courteously. "Surely the sons of the great Amon-Re would not consider the god of the Children of Joseph worthy of their attention."

325

"B-but—I understand you're feeding them some crazy notion that—that they're made in this god's likeness, or some such foolishness!"

The Hebrew bowed. "And if the worshipers of Sobk the crocodile or of Buto the serpent desire to conceive themselves as being created in the image of their gods, do the magnanimous sons of Amon deny them that privilege?"

The commissioner flushed. While on the surface there was nothing offensive in the Hebrew's grave, courteous rejoinders, the Egyptian nourished an uncomfortable suspicion that if he could only see deeply enough he would find laughter in the eagle-bright pits. Suddenly he remembered with relief an oversight which a few moments earlier had seemed unimportant.

"Give him a good lashing," he ordered the foreman abruptly, "one that he won't forget in a hurry. Perhaps if he learns to make proper obeisance to his superiors, he'll be more careful what sort of advice he gives his equals. And if the back of the miserable god whose image he bears smarts also, so much the better!"

He was still flushed, partly with discomfiture, partly with satisfaction, when he left Dathan's section to continue his inspections.

"A less clever man," he told the foreman, almost adding "like yourself," "would have clapped that insolent upstart into a dungeon. I'll wager two copper rings that's what you expected me to do."

"Oh, no, certainly not!" protested the foreman, who had expected that very thing.

"In a dungeon," exulted the commissioner, "he would be a hero in the eyes of his fellow workmen. Now he's a fool."

"I—don't exactly see—"

"Of course you don't. That's why—" He almost finished— "why you're a foreman and not a commissioner." "That's why you'd lose your wager. What do you suppose those miserable Hebrews back there think now of the man who told them they're made like a god? 'A fine god,' they'll say, 'to be like! Does he let the gods of Egypt cut his back to ribbons?'" The commissioner laughed triumphantly. "If he were in a dungeon, they couldn't witness his humiliation."

The foreman laughed too but less loudly. "Then you think this Hebrew is harmless?"

The commissioner sobered. "Hardly. Any fool who goes around saying that a common laborer is made in the likeness of a god is dangerous. How long will the palanquin continue to ride steady if the

326

slaves who bear it on their shoulders get the idea they're as good as the man inside!"

"But surely you need not go tonight," protested Miriam, vigorously rubbing sheep's grease into the ugly red welts. "An hour more or less among the people will make very little difference."

"Or a year," threw in Aaron bitterly, looking with morose fascination at the flaming ribbons of bruised flesh. "It's nearly a twelvemonth since we started our midnight expeditions. And what do we get for it! Sneers—laughter—mudslinging! Sometimes I think the Egyptians are right when they call the sons of Joseph swine. They'd rather wallow in the mud than try to crawl out on good solid ground. How in Yahweh's name can you do anything to save a man from oppression if he doesn't even want to be saved!"

Moses winced. Miriam was not a gentle person. Her every motion, even the application of a soothing lotion, was vigorous, and it felt as if she were rubbing salt instead of balm into his bruised flesh. The hot little room swam about his aching head. The flogging that afternoon was one of the worst he had ever received. But it was the sullen glances of his fellow workmen which had caused him the most pain, just as now it was the bitter words of Aaron rather than his throbbing back that brought intense nausea to the pit of his stomach. He had heard some of their gibes, sensed others that had not been intended for his ears.

"Must be a powerful god, this Yahweh he's always prating about! Couldn't even save him from a flogging!"

"Made in the likeness of a god, are we? Maybe so, but what god? I've heard of some that had asses' heads."

"Who is this Mosheh, anyway? How do we know he's really Aaron's brother? Maybe he isn't a Hebrew at all. He talks like a foreigner."

"We've swallowed all his fine words, and what has it got us? More floggings than any other section in the outfit!"

"I say we've listened to him long enough. Who does he think he is, anyway, coming in here and telling us we don't even know the name of the god we've been worshiping or what he's like! What do you say we tell him a few things—or maybe show him..."

"There!" said Miriam, giving a final twist to the bandage. "You should feel better in the morning."

"If he lasts that long," interposed Aaron's younger son Abihu, who always managed somehow to inject a merry note into the household. "I've had one of those healing poultices, and I'm not sure I wouldn't prefer the flogging. What do you make them of—thistles?"

No one laughed, though there was a flicker of sympathy in Elisheba's dark eyes. Nadab, Aaron's oldest son, and Hur, Miriam's husband, seldom exhibited emotion of any kind. Soberly now they continued to eat their frugal meal of bread and onions and goat's milk, too weary to expend more than the minimum of energy required to lift the food to their lips. Not so with Miriam. After the long hours in the brickfields, she was as tireless as the strips of elephant hide which had plied their exhaustless energy on the backs of the Children of Joseph. With one continuous motion she wiped the grease from her hands, spread a reed mat in the corner of the room, and filled an empty gourd with goat's milk.

"Drink that," she directed Moses briskly. "Then you're going to lie down and try to sleep. As Aaron says, one night more or less will make very little difference."

Obediently Moses lifted the gourd and drank sparingly. His eyes traveled gratefully toward the unfolded mat, though even after a year's time he could not see a mat lying in that particular corner without feeling a vague sense of loss at the absence of Jochebed. Not that he wished her alive again, Yahweh forbid! Wincing with pain, he sat down on its edge, the room still reeling about his head. The figures of the four men squatted around the kettle of food lurched about him in the yellow blur of lamplight, then slowly steadied: his brother Aaron, lean and hunched and nervous, long thin fingers constantly in motion in spite of his fatigue; Hur, stolid and silent, his thick brown hair and beard framing his square face like a lion's ruff; Nadab and Abihu, Aaron's sons, the one gravely somber, the other irrepressibly fun-loving, but both gaunt and stooped like old men and as beardless as their two small brothers sleeping on their mat in the corner. It was the sight of them which finally banished his sense of confusion. He rose again unsteadily to his feet

"What am I thinking of, sitting here like this! The night is half gone. Come, Aaron. If we wait longer, they'll all be asleep."

"Better asleep than slinging mud and stones," observed Aaron cryptically. Nevertheless, he rose promptly, wiping his mouth on the back of his hand. Turning a deaf ear to Miriam's protests, Moses donned his woolen coat, grimacing with pain as he bound it with his girdle, slipped his feet into his sandals, and moved unsteadily toward the door.

"You've forgotten your staff," Abihu reminded him gently.

Miriam made an exclamation of impatience. "Suppose he has! Why on earth he thinks he needs a shepherd's staff to talk to a few men outside their huts—! What does he think the Children of Joseph are? A flock of sheep?" However, she took the staff from the corner where it stood, and placed it in her brother's hand. "There, I hope now you're satisfied."

Moses' fingers closed about it firmly. As he walked through the darkness beside Aaron, it steadied not only his steps but the tortured confusion of his mind. The hard, smooth acacia wood beneath his fingers was the one tangible link between him and the wilderness. He had carried it with him on his lonely journey up The Mountain. It had become the symbol of his purpose in living. *What does he think the Children of Joseph are? A flock of sheep?*

"Where shall we go tonight?" asked Aaron without enthusiasm.

"Anywhere," replied Moses. "It doesn't matter."

"You're right, it doesn't matter," threw back his brother bitterly. "We've gone without our sleep every night for a twelvemonth so we could tell people who don't want to be told that there's a god who would like to help save them, when you can see for yourself they don't want to be saved!"

"They are too wretched to know what they want," replied Moses. "They are like sheep that have fed on thorns so long they can't stomach good grass when you try to feed it to them."

"Then why try?" demanded Aaron.

Moses did not reply. They moved along cautiously in the darkness, past clusters of mud huts which, in the days when the squatters were independent shepherds, had been neat and thrifty but which now swelled the black surface of the valley like a festering rash. The few sheep and goats that had survived the years of neglect shared the same crowded shelters as their human comrades and contributed to the same filth. Few of the huts were blessed with the discipline of an indomitable Miriam. In many of them fires or lamps were never kindled. Returning at night from the brickfields of the new city of Per-Atum, which was close at hand, in such utter weariness that they had no taste for food or fellowship, they wolfed their few scraps of bread, onions, and goat's milk (if they were fortunate enough to have it), &ellipsis; ground and fell asleep. Occasionally a few, more ambitious than the rest, would light a fire of dried dung, and a group would sprawl around it.

"There," said Moses, spying one such firefly among the anthills of huts. They moved toward it, watching it grow into a pale-yellow circle surrounded by shadows.

One of the reclining figures glanced up and saw them. "Look! Here comes the god-possessed one."

Several of the group raised themselves on their elbows. A few bestirred themselves sufficiently to make brief, satirical comments.

"Still wants to save us, I suppose." "I hear he got away once and came back. I always thought he was crazy, and that proves it." "Doesn't he ever sleep, he and that brother of his? They say he wanders about every night, as long as he can find anybody to talk to." "Must we listen to him again? God of Abraham, deliver us!"

"God will deliver us," said Moses quietly. He sat down among them. "That is exactly what I have been trying to tell you all these months. The heart of Yahweh is turned toward all his people who are oppressed. When they suffer he suffers with them."

"I haven't seen him around getting his back in the way of any lashes," commented one of the sprawling figures.

"If he's so anxious to help us," mumbled another, too weary even to turn his head that his words might be intelligible, "why doesn't he— do something—"

"Can't you understand?" The words came easily to Moses' lips tonight, perhaps because the throbbing pain in his back made him less conscious of a sense of diffidence. Instead of letting Aaron speak for him, as he often did, he became the center of the group himself. Besides, Aaron was not in the mood to convince anyone of new truth tonight. He himself needed to be convinced.

"Listen to me!" said Moses earnestly. "How can Yahweh truly become our god unless we are ready and willing to become his people? Can the father become a family in himself, or can the children be bound together without the father? Unless each, both father and son, fulfills his responsibility to the other, there can be no true family. So must it be with Yahweh and his people."

"We already have a god," broke in one of the men sleepily, "and his name isn't Yahweh. It's the Shield of Abraham."

"You mean the Fear of Isaac," corrected another halfheartedly.

"Yahweh *is* the Shield of Abraham," said Moses with impassioned eagerness, "and the Fear of Isaac, and the Mighty One of Jacob."

There was a moment's pregnant silence, then a voice drawled softly, "If you're so anxious to help us, Mosheh ben Amram, why don't you go up to the palace at Per-Ramses and ask the pharaoh to set us free?"

"That is exactly what I intend to do," replied Moses quietly, "as soon as the Children of Joseph become the sons and daughters of Yahweh."

Then they reared themselves on their elbows or sat bolt upright and stared at him. For a moment something like hope almost flared in their eyes. Finally someone laughed, a raw harsh sound. 'Now we *know* the son of Amram is a fool!" hissed a voice derisively.

"You see?" said Aaron bitterly as they made their way back to the hut much later. "We can talk to them until the flesh falls from their bones, and their skeletons will still rise up to deride us. Every night it's just the same. I'll admit you managed to convince Miriam and me with mere talking after you came back, and heaven knows we've stood behind you. But can't you see it's different with us? We were born of a Kenite mother, and belief in Yahweh was nurtured in us with the milk we suckled at her breast."

"If only I could work with all the outfits!" deplored Moses, in answer more to his own bewildered questioning than to his brother's. "In the men we've lived with every day there is a difference. Even the commissioner noticed it. They—they hold their heads high again, act as if they really believed they were men made in the likeness of God."

"They won't long if all they get for it is red welts on their backs," retorted his brother, "and I won't blame them. If Yahweh is as interested in us as you say he is, why in heaven's name doesn't he do something?"

"You too?" accused Moses with sudden keen distress.

"If only he'd give us some sign!" lamented Aaron. "Something people could see with their eyes, so they would know he's more powerful than other gods!"

Moses' fingers clenched about the thin staff of acacia wood.

Bitterness welled up within him. "I suppose if I could perform some silly feat of magic like the priests of the Egyptians, I'd have them all flocking after me!" he exclaimed harshly. "If, for instance, I could—could throw this rod down on the ground and have it turn into a s-snake—" The words choked in his throat.

In the darkness he could feel Aaron's eyes turn toward him with sudden canny alertness. "If you could do that," came the soft but significant answer, "you could turn the Children of Joseph into the loyal sons and daughters of Yahweh in an hour's time."

"B-but—" Moses' senses were again whirling, threatening to plunge him into even deeper confusion than either pain or frustration had created.

"Can you?" demanded Aaron with sudden bluntness.

Dathan did not report the absence of Mosheh ben Amram to the Egyptian foreman. Instead he went to considerable pains to conceal it. He hoped that Ben Amram had repeated his performance of ten years before and run away for good. And he wanted to give him plenty of time to make his flight successful before the deadly pursuit techniques of the Egyptian military machine should be set in motion.

"He's been a thorn in my flesh ever since he returned a little over a year ago," he complained to his brother Abiram some time after Moses' disappearance. "This talk he feeds out to the men is poison to the morale. Give a workman the notion he's cut to divine specifications, and how long do you think he's going to take kindly to having a lash wound around his godlike back? If you ask me, the Egyptians have the right idea when it comes to religion. They tell their miserable fellahin that maybe they're hungry here, but in the next world they'll be living on roast gazelle meat and honey cakes. Yes, and they even make them pay for it right here and now!"

Abiram nodded, as well as he could with his neck astride the curving saddle of a wooden pillow. The two brothers were in perfect agreement. Both, by dint of much currying of favor, had worked their way into the good graces of their oppressors sufficiently to become section bosses, and both had ambitions to rise still further. They had built themselves a mud hut as close to the foremen's quarters as they had dared, shaved off their beards, donned Egyptian linens, and affected as many other customs of their superiors as possible.

"How long has Ben Amram been gone?" inquired Abiram.

"Two days," was the reply. "Long enough to get across the Bitter Lakes and well into the desert."

"And when the foreman finally discovers his absence—?" prompted the other helpfully.

Dathan's narrow face seemed to contract into even tighter outlines. "Whatever happens, it will be worth it. I shan't be surprised if the foreman is as happy to see him gone as I am."

Dathan's satisfaction lasted for seven days. On the eighth morning Mosheh ben Amram appeared at his post in the brickfields and proceeded with his labor as usual. The section boss could not punish him without admitting his own silent collusion in the offense. He could not even report the fact of the runaway's return. The only course open to him was a most humiliating and vexatious one: to act as if nothing whatever had happened.

Aaron led the way when they started out on their expedition the night after Moses' return. There was a gleam in his eyes and a squareness to his shoulders which had not been evident since the first nights of their journeyings. But he did not walk close to Moses, and he was careful to keep himself always on the lefthand side.

"You're sure?" he whispered soon after they stepped into the bright moonlight, his eyes drawn with fascination to the slender column in his brother's hand. "It—it will stay just like that except—except when—"

"Yes," replied Moses briefly.

He did not share Aaron's excitement. His steps lagged as they passed among the darkened huts. Even though he had been gone little more than a week, he found it hard to bring the present scene into the close perspective of reality. He had taken a long, deep excursion into the past. The sound of a once familiar and much-loved voice was in his ears; the glitter of an age-old and unforgettable pageantry still dazzled his eyes. He remembered few of the actual details of his journey, the obscure paths by which he had come at last to On, the devices he had employed to discover if his old teacher Maruma was still alive and then to maneuver himself into his presence. Only two memories of the trip possessed concrete reality: the words he had exchanged with the aged priest in his temple apartment, and the moments when he had stood again in the stifling cubicle before the cage of woven rushes.

"So," the familiar voice had sagely summarized, "you believe you have discovered new truth, which the people whom you wish to benefit by it will not accept. A very old and common complaint, my son. They expect you to give them some sign—as if truth itself were not enough!—something they can see and touch, or, better yet, something they would not dare to touch, like—shall we say?—a serpent crawling on the ground or a hand smitten suddenly with leprosy."

"But," Moses had interjected, all his profound disquiet suddenly breaking to the surface, "how could I? It would be denying the very truth I've discovered. The Yahweh I worship isn't that kind of god!"

"No." Manama's voice was sad and tired, and his filmed eyes, now completely blind, seemed to retreat further into their deeply curtained recesses. "And neither is the Re I worship. But there are many Res and doubtless many Yahwehs—as many as there are people who call themselves their followers. If a man covers his eyes and refuses to look at the sun, which is better? To let him walk in darkness or to give him a poor flickering torch to light his way? Come, my son. I know what you want, and I am glad to give it to you."

Even after he had followed Maruma into the stifling cubicle and his decision had been made, Moses had still been unconvinced. He was unconvinced now as he walked beside Aaron through the sultry darkness, his hand cupped about a smooth, cool resilience. His mind felt earth-bound and impassive, like the torpid air he breathed. If for but a single moment he could have stood on a high mountain with the sun in his eyes and the winds against his face...

"Here!" said Aaron suddenly. "Yahweh is indeed with us. There must be at least a score of men in the circle of that fire."

They were greeted by the usual derisive or indifferent comments. "Look! The nightwalkers again!" "The sons of the great Yahweh are abroad!" "Wake me up when he's finished his babbling!"

Aaron was more eloquent than usual. His voice drew the sordid firelight scene into its alchemy, changing the ragged garments of the night to velvet and the leaping tongues of the fire to images of molten gold. Listening to his eager words, Moses wondered uneasily if it were really Yahweh, god of the lofty Mountain, of whom he spoke, or some cloistered Amon hidden behind the tight, dusty curtains of his sacred box.

"Listen to me, sons of Joseph. Open your ears to the voice of Yahweh. I have heard the sound of your wailing from my far-off mountaintop. I have beheld your sufferings, how greatly you are oppressed. And I have sent unto you Moses my servant and Aaron his mouthpiece, that they may be lips and hands and feet for me in the task that I have sworn to perform. Listen to them, for they have come in my name to help you deliver yourselves from the hands of your oppressors."

"We're listening," commented one of the men cryptically. "What good does it do to listen? Nothing happens."

"Aye, we've been listening for a year, but we're still slaves, aren't we?"

"If this Yahweh is really the Shield of Abraham and the Fear of Isaac, let him prove it to us. Why doesn't he show us a sign?"

"Yes... Let him prove it!... Show us a sign—a sign!"

"Then open your eyes, and you shall be given a sign," proclaimed Aaron in a ringing voice, pointing dramatically to the thin black column in his brother's hand. "Know then that Yahweh, the god of your fathers, the god of Abraham and of Isaac and of Jacob has appeared to his servant Moses!"

The moment had come. Moses' fingers clung as if paralyzed to the slender object in his hand. He was unconscious of releasing their pressure, yet suddenly it was there on the ground between him and the carelessly sprawling figures, thin and black and vibrant in the red glow of the fire. There was a moment's silence like an indrawn breath, then shouts of amazement and terror as the sprawling figures struggled to their feet.

"A snake!" "God of Abraham, help us!" "Look out! It's coming toward us!" "Take it away!" "It's their Yahweh coming to take vengeance on us!" "We'll believe in your god—anything! Only take it away!"

The news spread through the darkened huts like fever through an infected body. By dawn of the next day there was scarcely one of the Children of Joseph that had not heard of the amazing things that had taken place.

"Hear what Moses the son of Amram has done!" "It's the power of a new god come among us!" "Not a new god but the god of our fathers, the Shield of Abraham, and the Fear of Isaac and the Mighty One of Jacob!"

"Moses also reached his hand into the bosom of his coat and it came out white with leprosy, then he put it back into the bosom of his coat and drew it out fresh and whole again!"

"It is the work of Yahweh our god, who has heard our cry from his far mountain and has come to help us!" "Yahweh! All praise be unto Yahweh!"

"Let the Children of Joseph shout unto Yahweh! Let us cry aloud unto him who has heard our voice and has come to deliver us from the hand of our oppressors!"

"You see?" said Aaron, smiling triumphantly. "We have accomplished in a single night what we could not have done in years, perhaps ever. Surely what we did was the will of Yahweh."

Moses made no reply. But after he had replaced the serpent in the tightly woven reed cage which he had brought from On and hidden behind the hut under a heap of marsh grass, he went down to the river and washed his hands, scrubbing his right palm with small particles of sand until the skin felt raw. And even then he wondered if it was clean enough to touch his shepherd's rod.

2

Prince Nehsi knew at last that he was growing old, for on the evening of the eventful day he found himself dreading, not welcoming, new adventure. He would have preferred to lie down quietly between fresh sheets, a fan gently agitating his few thin wisps of hair, and ponder the significance of the day's strange happenings. But instead he must permit himself to be bathed and dressed in clean garments, fussy with innumerable pleats, bury his comfortably cooling pate within a wig, and attend one of Ramses' insufferably stuffy banquets.

However, he was genuinely worried. It was not like Ramses to plan banquets on the spur of the moment. The question was, Which of the day's three unusual events had caused the pharaoh to depart from his usual customs? The message from Thebes that a hundred-foot slab of black granite for the king's new statue was on its way down the river toward Per-Ramses? The arrival of the tame lion, "Tearer-to-Pieces-of-His-Enemies," which was to accompany the pharaoh on his future military exploits? Or the visit of the two Hebrews to the palace that afternoon?

Either of the first two would in the eyes of Ramses make an admirable excuse for a banquet. Ramses despised the obvious. Therefore, Nehsi feared, it was the third event, the visit of the Hebrews, which had prompted the unexpected celebration.

He was almost sure of it when he saw the select company which Ramses had assembled about him at the banquet table. A small, carefully chosen group generally indicated a desire to perpetrate some clever scheme which often involved the humiliation of one or more of the privileged guests. Slipping into his cushioned chair, Nehsi glanced hastily about at the assembled party, and his heart sank. Was it possible that the presence of all three of the women who had figured in Moses' Egyptian career—Nefretiri, Sitra, and Tharbis—was a mere coincidence? Yet, he reassured himself, it must be. Even eyes as keen and clever as Ramses' could not have detected in the dark, heavily bearded Asiatic who had come and gone that afternoon any features remotely resembling those which had once belonged to an Egyptian prince!

"Yet yours did," memory prompted him significantly.

The feast had obviously been prepared in a hurry, for all the bizarre surprises which usually characterized the young pharaoh's social events were lacking. The bread was merely bread, baked in the most conventional of forms. The dancers were prosaic creatures who knew no other arts than rhythm and seduction. Even the gifts presented at the door were but simple jewels or scarabs, undistinguished for originality.

As usual at his informal feasts, Ramses insisted on having his small son Amon-herkhop, the first fruit of his not too prolific union with Nefretiri, sit beside him at table. The childish features, barely visible above the table top, were absurdly like his own, and he took an inordinate pleasure in making the likeness even more pronounced. A tall red and white cap resembling the royal crown adorned the small head, and a heavy gold collar exactly like that which circled his own full throat shone like a sunburst about the small neck. Amon-herkhop was a sickly child, and already, with the feast barely begun, his overburdened head swayed on its stem like a drooping flower. Nefretiri watched him constantly, her beautiful features as tense as if she were attempting to balance a heavy weight on her own head, the small green particles in her black eyes as hard as flecks of ice.

Nehsi, who in his coveted capacity of fan bearer on the king's right hand occupied a seat close to the pharaoh, watched for the climax. He had not long to wait. Scarcely had the crisply aproned slaves proffered the silver finger bowls at the end of the first course when Ramses displayed the symptoms which prefaced his inevitable monopoly of the conversation. With the sudden arching of his brows the golden cobra above his forehead seemed to rear its head. A slight quiver passed from the high cheekbones to the narrowed nostrils. The slate-colored eyes began to gleam with amusement.

Instantly the two attendants who had been watching for the signal held up their hands. The music of harps and lyres ceased as suddenly as if their strings had been cut. Dancers froze like statues, and all heads were turned with expectancy toward the proud, smiling visage—all, that is, except two. Prince Amon-herkhop had fallen asleep, and Nefretiri was staring at him, her face hard and expressionless, as if it had been carved of golden metal.

Here Ramses introduced his surprise, for when his full, curving lips parted, the usual self-lauding monologue was not forthcoming.

"Tell the guests about the outstanding event of the day, Nehsi," he drawled negligently.

Hastily the fan bearer gathered his wits together. Rising, he bowed low, first to the pharaoh, then, less abjectly, to the assembled company.

"The Good God, the Strong Bull, His Majesty the Golden Horus," he announced glibly, "refers to the message that came only this morning from Thebes. The mountains have at last stretched themselves prostrate before the lord of all the earth. The virgin stone has given herself unto the will of man, that out of her loins might spring the full-grown image of—"

"Not the granite, Nehsi," interrupted Ramses good-humoredly.

The prince hesitated only an instant. "Of course. How stupid of this blundering ass! The Lord of the Two Lands refers to the arrival of the king of beasts—"

"No, not the lion, Nehsi. You know what I mean."

The king's fan bearer feigned astonishment. "But surely the Lord of the Vulture and the Snake cannot be referring to the visit of the two miserable squatters!"

"At last," came the soft drawl. "I began to think the prince's memory was failing. Listen now, my friends, for this is one of the funniest things you ever heard."

It was even worse than Nehsi had expected. But his wrinkled features betrayed no emotion. "The Good God is remarkable in his sense of humor, as in all other divine qualities," he continued with smooth humility. "His discerning eyes behold whimsy where his miserable servants see only the drab and unimportant. Two men came to the palace today and sought audience with the king—"

"Men?" mocked Ramses.

"The Son of Re forgive me! Two creatures, shall I say? Yet not creatures, either, for the creature presupposes a creator. And not animals, for both the bird and the beast are at times the chosen vessels of the gods—"

"Here! Let me tell it!" interrupted Ramses. And Nehsi, lapsing gratefully into silence, smiled to himself. It sometimes amused him, how easy it was to mold the Good God to his will.

The slate-colored eyes swept about the politely attentive circle. "Two of these wretched squatters such as you've all seen swarming like ants in the brickfields and on construction jobs. I always wanted to get a good look at them, so when I heard this couple was outside I ordered them sent in. Hebrews, these two scarecrows called themselves. What a pair! Skins hard and tough as elephants' hides, beards like a crop of marsh grass, and I'll wager plenty of small game in them too!" His loud laughter was echoed by a series of polite titters.

"And what do you suppose the sons of pollution wanted! You'll laugh when you hear this. Time off from work so the whole filthy brood could go vacationing in the desert! Wanted to have a feast of some kind for their god. But that isn't all by any means. Wait till you hear—"

"Let me take him to his room," broke in Nefretiri suddenly.

The courtiers gasped. Impossible that even the queen could interrupt one of the divinely inspired monologues and remain extant! Ramses turned slowly toward his wife, and they measured each other silently, proud, handsome features cast in the same hard, expressionless mold.

"Can't you see you're torturing the child, keeping him here with that heavy thing on his head? He should have been in bed long ago!"

The expected bolt of lightning failed to fall. Without deigning to make reply, Ramses jolted his young son into wakefulness, then continued with his monologue. "Wait till you hear what else these asses' offspring did! Listen, Amon-herkhop! You'll enjoy this story too. To show what a powerful god they have and to frighten me, I suppose, into letting them take this vacation, one of them threw an ebony rod on the floor and made the thing turn into a snake."

For the first time there was a murmur of genuine interest among the courtiers. Ramses' eyes sparkled with the satisfaction of the natural-born showman. "What did I do, you ask? Summoned some of the priests of Buto, of course. With their rods they made the magic of this rawboned scarecrow look like child's play."

As if losing interest in the whole matter, the pharaoh slouched in his chair and reached negligently for his bowl of wine. Then suddenly he roused himself. "Oh, I almost forgot to tell you," he drawled casually. "Speaking of this rawboned scarecrow—he's not such a stranger as you think. There isn't a person here at table this evening who doesn't know him well. He used to call himself—*Prince Moses.*"

His eyes gleamed over the rim of the lifted wine bowl, observing with satisfaction each shocked, incredulous glance, each startled gesture; observing with special enjoyment the crimson tongue which darted across the tablecloth from Nefretiri's suddenly overturned goblet.

So, marveled Prince Nehsi, noting the queen's stricken face, *Ramses has been jealous of him all these years! That is the reason we are here and the reason why he let her interruption go unchallenged. He had a far more clever punishment in store.*

But it was to Tharbis, farther down the table, that his glance hastened. Good! His fears had apparently been groundless. There was nothing in her manner to indicate that she was unduly disturbed or even excited. Her piquant face was slightly lifted, and it wore that detached, listening look which he knew so well. A small, secretive smile curved her lips. Back in her beloved world of the cataracts again, thought Nehsi tenderly. Relief eased the tension of fear that had seized him at sight of the tall familiar figure entering the pharaoh's court. She had so far forgotten him that his name no longer had power to awaken painful memories. He would not be able to hurt her again.

Turning, Nehsi found the slate-colored eyes regarding him with cool amusement. "You thought I didn't recognize him," said Ramses, smiling in mocking triumph, "but you were wrong. You see—*I never forget a face.*"

The Children of Joseph did not profit by the visit of Moses and Aaron to the palace in Per-Ramses. The pharaoh saw to that. And he took pains that Prince Nehsi should be by his side when he dictated his orders to the royal scribe.

"To the commissioners of buildings for the Delta: Inasmuch as discontent and rebellion, those qualities which breed in idleness, have been observed among certain of the laborers in your jurisdiction, it is obvious that you have been too lax in your treatment and too lenient in your demands. Hereafter let—" the eyes of the pharaoh narrowed reflectively— "let these squatters not be furnished with straw for the binding and lining of their bricks. Let them be forced either to gather straw for themselves or to make bricks without it. But their quotas shall not be diminished, and their own construction bosses shall be held accountable for such quotas."

While the brush of the scribe was whispering across the papyrus, Ramses turned triumphantly to Nehsi. "Not a bad idea, what? If we keep them busy—and tired—they won't have enough energy left to remember they have a god, much less to plan trips into the desert to kowtow to him!"

Nehsi bowed. "The mind of the Golden Horus outshines the brilliance of the sun itself," he marveled glibly. "The mediocre intellect of a Nehsi would have merely added to their quotas of bricks. Only the supermind of a Strong Bull could have conceived a punishment so original as this which the son of the ram-headed one has devised."

"As for the two mud-spawned river rats who started all the trouble—" continued the supermind musingly.

"Surely," interposed his fan bearer hastily, "the Lord of the Vulture and the Snake will put them where they can devise no further mischief—say, in the deepest of dungeons—"

"Ah," murmured the pharaoh, who had been considering doing exactly that, "again it is the mediocre intellect, such as Nehsi's, which would so reason. No, I shall not put them in the deepest of dungeons. I shall leave them right where they are. Their fellow Hebrews will take care of them. When they are groveling on their hands and knees to find bits of straw, do you think they are likely to forget who put them there?"

"The wisdom of the offspring of Amon is amazing," replied Nehsi with genuine respect. For once, he feared, he had made a mistake. Moses would have been safer in a dungeon.

It was Miriam who saw them coming and overheard what they planned to do. As she knelt in the black earth on the bank of the canal waiting impatiently for the water to flow into her partly submerged goatskin, their dark figures moving along the path just above were clearly outlined in the moonlight. She crouched lower among the reeds and waited for them to pass, their bare feet scarcely less audible on the hard ground than their softly murmuring voices. But Miriam's ears were good. As soon as the dark shadows had passed, she dropped the waterskin, crept silently up the bank, and ran with the sureness and fleetness of an animal. Even though the route she followed was longer than the canal path, there was no one yet in sight when she arrived at the hut.

"Quick!" she gasped. "You, Moses and Aaron—run as fast and as far as you can! Dathan and Abiram are coming—and a crowd of men with them. I heard them talking. They're going to—stone you— Hurry! Put out the light before they see you leaving!"

Moses started up from the mat where he had wearily flung himself after his return from the brickfields. He caught a brief glimpse of Aaron's face, pale and twisted with terror, before the room was plunged in darkness. Firm fingers were closed about his arms, pulling him toward the door, pushing him out into the blur of moonlight.

"Toward the canal!" hissed Miriam. "In the place where I fill the waterskins. They'll never look there. Lie down among the reeds. I'll come when it's safe."

Moses found himself running through the darkness at Aaron's side. It was not until he saw the moonlight on the waters that he realized what he was doing. He stopped suddenly. "Wait for me down there among the reeds," he told Aaron abruptly. "I've just remembered something that I must do."

`He returned to the hut along the same circuitous path by which he had left it, approaching it from the rear. In the pale glow he could plainly see the figure bending over the pile of dried grasses where the cage of woven reeds lay hidden. He went toward it swiftly.

"No," he whispered sharply, placing firm fingers on Miriam's outstretched arm. "You're not to touch it, do you hear!"

She wheeled toward him. "You! But—What are you doing here?" she demanded in a shrill whisper. "I thought you'd gone—"

"I came back," replied Moses briefly.

"Are you mad?" Her eyes were bright dagger thrusts in the moonlight. "They're out in front of the hut now, waiting, deciding what to do. They think we're all inside, asleep. Oh, you fool! Why didn't you run while you had the chance?"

"I did run once," returned Moses steadily. "This time I'm staying."

The thatched roof threw its shadow about him as he moved around the corner of the hut. The cluster of dark figures was plainly visible. Even as he stood watching, it separated, became a loosely knit chain.

"Mosheh!" called a voice, which Moses recognized as Dathan's. "Mosheh ben Amram! We know you're in there. Will you come out to us, or shall we come in after you?"

Moses moved into the moonlit space in front of the hut, where he would be plainly visible. "Here I am," he said quietly. "What do you want?"

Having considered him trapped behind the hut's single entrance, they were somewhat taken aback by his sudden and obviously voluntary appearance. But the startled silence was only momentary.

"You!" shouted another voice boldly. "We want you and your brother Aaron."

"Why?" asked Moses, moving toward them into even brighter moonlight. Their features were still indistinguishable, and he sensed rather than saw the sudden clenching of fingers about various hard objects held in their hands.

"You know why," said Dathan. "You've stirred up trouble among us. Things were bad enough before for the Children of Joseph, but since you and your meddlesome brother went to the pharaoh they've been a thousand times worse. He's taken away the straw for us to work with yet expects us to turn out our full quota of bricks as before. And it's all your fault. Why didn't you mind your business and leave us alone?"

Deliberately Moses stared at the dark shape from which the voice issued, until the features of the round, beardless face became clearly outlined in the moonlight. "I know you, Dathan, son of Eliab," he said sternly. "It's not the plight of the Children of Joseph which has brought you here tonight. It's the fear that your own position as pet slave of the oppressors may prove to be less profitable than you had hoped. That's why you're standing here in the dark with those stones in your hands, you and your brother Abiram and the other section bosses you've brought with you."

"We're not all section bosses," threw back Dathan belligerently. "A lot of the laborers are just as tired of your meddling as we are. They've swallowed all this fine talk you've been feeding them about a god who wants every man to be free, and what has it got them? More lashings, more backbreaking hours, working all night now as well as all day! What we want to know is, where is this Yahweh who's so anxious to save us?"

The shadowy chain tightened, and Moses was conscious of a low, threatening murmur. "That's right, where is he?" called another voice defiantly, and suddenly he was being bombarded with derisive taunts and accusations,

"How about all those fine promises you made us?"

"Made in the likeness of Yahweh, are we? Is our god then a slave of other gods?"

"If he's so anxious to have us free, why doesn't he do something about it?"

"It's Mosheh who has brought all this trouble upon us, Mosheh ben Amram!"

A missile spun through the air, then another, and another. Moses felt a sharp pain in his arm, then a blow on his shoulder which sent him reeling to his knees. Crouching low, he lifted both hands to cover his face. But he knew that it was only a matter of moments. They were too far away to take accurate aim, but nothing would prevent their closing in upon him. And in the bright moonlight he was a perfect target.

While he waited for the enveloping blackness which was sure to come, his mind functioned with amazing clearness. So this was to be the end. He had dreamed of helping to save a people, and he had been unable even to save himself. He could understand all too well why they wanted to kill him. Their hands were clenched about their fragments of dried bricks as his had once clenched about the throat of Baka. He wished he had time to show them that the way they had chosen was all wrong, that they were grappling with the shadow of their problem instead of with its substance. Somehow he must teach them patience, the agonizing patience of the Being he had met face to face on the

343

mountaintop—he *must* teach them! It would take months, years, perhaps a lifetime, and he had only a moment. Suddenly compulsion seized him. He could not die. He had work to do.

Too immersed in his thoughts to notice that the raining of missiles had ceased, he struggled to his feet. "Men of Joseph—" he cried, but his voice was drowned by their excited screams.

"Look! It's the god sign!"

"It's come to take vengeance on us!"

"Yahweh save us! We didn't mean to kill him!"

"Quick! Run before it's too late! Yahweh is coming! Flee!"

They fled, still screaming. Turning, Moses saw Miriam standing in the center of the open space. To his dazed vision one of her arms looked strangely elongated. It seemed to stretch itself endlessly, writhing and twisting and coiling itself about her body. Then suddenly she cast it from her, and it slid away, its slim undulating shape patterned with scintillating inlays of bright silver.

"No!" cried Moses in consternation. "What have you done!"

He picked up one of the fragments of brick lying at his feet and hurled it with all his strength at the slithering shape. His was the aim of the shepherd, trained to pick the head unerringly from the body of a coiled snake. But he took no chances. He threw again, and again. The slim shape paused, quivered convulsively, and lay still.

"There!" exclaimed Moses hoarsely. "It's gone. It was a thing of evil. It does not belong with Yahweh. It will never lift its ungodly head again."

"It saved your life," Miriam reminded him with calm triumph. Stooping, she lifted the inert shape into her capable hands. "And it frightened them enough so they won't return again in a hurry. But just in case they do, I'd better make sure that the thing is buried properly. I'll get Hur to help me."

Moses' vision again blurred. His whole body throbbed with pain. But that night he walked to the edge of the desert above the green Valley of Goshen. He stood again, as on that eventful night in Midian, with the harshness of sand beneath his feet, the freshness of the wilderness against his face. He had been both blind and a fool. For who but a blind man would believe that to a god who demanded justice among men attainment of the goal was all that mattered? And who but a fool would expect to create truth by falsehood, justice by injustice, the salvation of life by its destruction? Even Ikhnaton, long ago, had been wiser than he, for he had brought his Aton out of the dark, redolent chambers of fear and necromancy into the bright sunlight.

"Yahweh!" spoke Moses aloud, lifting his face to the cool fresh vigor of the night. He felt as if his spirit had again been swept clean.

3

It was the season of the inundation. The tears of Isis, flowing for her beloved Osiris, had again wakened death into life. On the "Night of the Teardrop," when there came that first infinitesimal rising of the river, there rose also a vast sigh of relief, which changed swiftly to a prayer of thanksgiving, a shout of rejoicing.

"Thanks be to the Good God pharaoh," proclaimed the fellahin with an awakening of hope in their own parched and shrunken bodies, "for he has commanded the Nile to rise, and the Nile has obeyed his voice."

Even in his new palace in Per-Ramses, it seemed, far from Silsileh, where the thin, sluggish stream threatened to lose itself in the abysses of the underworld, the power of the Good God was unabated. Hapi, about to die, had listened to the voice of his lord and son, and responded. He was stirring in his sleep, stretching his shrunken corpse. Soon with all the virile power of his awakened manhood he would take bodily possession of his beloved, the black thirsty earth.

And the desires of men also began to quicken. Already the fellahin tasted in prospect the free food and drink that would be doled out to them at the time of the great flood festival, and with the slow swelling of Hapi they felt in their own tired bodies an eager stirring for similar life-giving fulfillment. In the banquet halls of the more fortunate, harps and lutes throbbed with an ever-mounting ecstasy, and the naked dancers sang seductively:

> "Hear the holy waters flowing,
> Re is come, for all to see,
> But my heart is sick with longing
> Till my brother comes to me.
> I shall see him when the waters
> Hurry through the opened ways,
> Give him wreaths for wreaths of flowers,
> Loose my hair for him to praise.
> Happier than pharaoh's daughters,
> When I lie in his embrace."

Reluctantly Ramses boarded his pleasure vessel, the *Star of the Two Lands*, and sailed up the river to Thebes, in order that his divine countenance might lend further refulgence to the procession which would greet the river-god in his hour of supreme fulfillment. Nehsi and others of his courtiers accompanied him, but the women of the harem remained in Per-Ramses. From the start the gods refused to lend their favor to the expedition. Ramses had set his heart on having Amon-herkhop ride with him in the procession, but on the very eve of their departure the boy had been stricken with a fever, and Nefretiri, who had strongly opposed the whole proceeding, had withdrawn to his bedside with an anxiety not unmixed with triumph. At Memphis the Apis bull stubbornly declined to pursue the tempting aromas which emanated from the little stall marked "Yes." The prospect of an encounter with the priests of Amon was always enough to put the pharaoh in an ill humor. These further misfortunes transformed the divine countenance into a thundercloud.

"Thirteen ells," prophesied the priests of the Nilometers, reading the year's future in the crystal of their marble wells. And Ramses frowned again. He had hoped for at least fifteen to make possible a sharp increase in taxes.

"Perhaps," remarked Tutu the scribe to his master Prince Nehsi, "it is those accursed Hebrews who are to blame for all this misfortune."

Nehsi shot him a quick, startled glance. "Where for Amon's sake did you get that idea!" he demanded. For Anion's sake! The words repeated themselves in his mind like an answer to his own question. He had always suspected the nearsighted but canny scribe of being a spy for the priests of Amon.

"Has it not occurred to the friend of the pharaoh that misfortune entered the palace with those two wretched squatters?" replied Tutu innocently. "The Strong Bull would have done well to let the filthy brood go to the desert—yes, and stay there. Good riddance, I'd say, and I know a lot of others who would agree with me."

"No doubt," returned Nehsi, his keen eyes narrowing reflectively. Of course. The priests of Amon would be delighted to get the Hebrews out of Egypt, together with all the other squatters whose labor was enabling Ramses to transfer the capital from Thebes to the Delta. He filed the item away in his mind for future reference.

Even the benign Hapi, upon whose swollen breasts the *Star of the Two Lands* was borne, did not present a pleasing aspect to the eyes of the Good God at whose command he had risen out of his long sleep. The nearer the vessel approached to Thebes the more jaundiced and unpleasant his countenance became.

"You call this water!" stormed Ramses, wrinkling his elegant features in distaste as his servant proffered him a finger bowl. "I might as well wash my hands in mud." He turned to Nehsi with the petulance of a child appealing to its nurse. "What's the matter with the stuff?"

The prince looked thoughtfully over the side of the vessel. The color and aspect of the river had been perplexing him for some time. He was familiar with the country from which the Blue Nile had sprung and accumulated its rich burden of silt and refuse, but the swirling red-brown waters contained more than ordinary deposits. Only once, long ago, had he seen anything like it. A suspicion had begun to grow in his mind, but he was not ready to impart it.

"The deposits of red marl do seem to be heavier than usual this year," he commented briefly.

At Thebes the countenance of Hapi was like that of a sick man, bloated and burning with a raging fever. Ramses took one look at the ewer filled with river water from Elephant Island in which he must symbolically wash himself in preparation for the festival and recoiled in horror.

"Blood!" he exclaimed with abhorrence. "For Amon's sake, take it away!"

The sharp outcry of the pharaoh was echoed all over Thebes, and, as the red-brown flood swept slowly downward on the bosom of Hapi, re-echoed all over Egypt.

"Blood! Great Amon help us, the water of the Nile has turned to blood!"

It was fit for neither washing nor drinking. Hastily men dug holes in the black earth above the high-water mark of the swollen river and strove to satisfy their thirst from the muddy pools that appeared at the bottom. Better to drink dirt of a familiar hue, they reasoned, than that whose origin was unknown.

Nehsi watched and waited and kept his own counsel. He was sure now that his suspicions were correct. Only once did he attempt to voice them.

"There are strange mountains in the country above the joining of the rivers," he said to Ramses. "Their heads seem to be on fire, and sometimes they open their mouths and vomit forth rocks and hot liquids and that which looks like boiling mud."

The pharaoh only glanced at him askance and remarked grimly: "Better keep away from that Charu wine, Nehsi. It's *your* head that's on fire. If you don't watch out, you'll be belching boiling mud yourself."

But there was no humor in the comment. Ramses' nerves were as raw as the backs of his balkiest slaves. He considered the polluted river a personal affront. And when presently there was added to its pollution the stench of vast quantities of dead fish whose bloated bellies tossed like tiny whitecaps on the surface of the red-brown flood, the wrath of the Good God knew no bounds. The unfortunate servants who waited on him trembled for their heads. When the day of the festival came, he refused to cross the river to the temple of Karnak, shutting himself in his apartment with numerous scribes of the toilet to administer frequent dosages of perfumes and Charu wine that the divine senses might be deadened to the pervasive odors.

So it was that he was one of the last persons in Thebes to hear the excited murmurings that were flooding the surrounding country as thoroughly as the mysteriously malignant Hapi. But when they did finally penetrate to his chambers, he fairly exploded.

"What's this I hear," he thundered to an increasingly apprehensive Nehsi, "about the Hebrews being to blame for the Nile's pollution? Of all the insane poppycock! I'll have the head of every demented upstart who's dared to even whisper such drivel!"

Nehsi bowed long and low, his wrinkled forehead seeking both delay and wisdom in the deep soft nap of the carpet.

"Then the Strong Bull must be prepared to massacre at least half the population of Thebes," he said finally.

"*What!* You mean—"

"I mean that the rumor is very widespread, to say the least."

"B-but—" For probably the first time in his life the pharaoh was at a loss for words. "It—it's impossible. The Hebrews are in the Delta, five hundred miles away. Most of these people never heard of them."

"Less than a moon ago that would have been the truth," returned Nehsi, "but not now."

"What are they saying?" demanded Ramses.

"That the god of the Hebrews has sent this evil upon us because the pharaoh did not permit his people to go into the desert to placate him with sacrifices." The slate-colored eyes shrank into thin hard slits. "Ah! I begin to see. Who in Egypt would like to see the Hebrews out of the way?"

"Who, indeed?" murmured Nehsi.

"But how," continued Ramses significantly, "would the priests of Amon know about the visit of the Hebrews to the palace unless someone told them? *Someone who was there!*"

Nehsi returned the pharaoh's suspicious gaze steadily. "I swear by Maat it was not my lord's fan bearer."

"Then who?" demanded Ramses bluntly.

But Nehsi was silent.

The henchmen of the priests of Amon were masters of the art of propaganda. In the market place, on the water front, even in the courtyards and pantries of the royal palace itself, they sowed their sly seeds of suggestion, and the terror of the people provided fertile soil. Ramses found himself besieged on every hand. He was wakened at night by a mob outside the palace gates demanding that he send word to the Delta for the Hebrews to be ejected at once from the country. Messengers with letters from his most important courtiers waited on him whenever he set foot outside his apartment. Even in the privacy of his chamber his chief anointer ventured to accost him.

"If the Strong Bull would but permit the Hebrews to depart into the desert as they request, this terrible plague—"

"No, no!" stormed Ramses. Summarily dismissing the noble dispenser of fragrant oils, he summoned Nehsi. "Close the doors," he ordered his fan bearer. "I'll go without food, I'll let my body remain unwashed, but I will not listen to any more of this nonsense. And I'll not let the Hebrews go, not if the high priest of Amon himself comes and begs me on his knees. Besides," the slate-colored eyes narrowed shrewdly, "the river is becoming daily more fresh and clean, is it not?"

"Yes," replied Nehsi briefly.

He opened his mouth again to warn the pharaoh, then reconsidered and closed it. As well, perhaps, to let Ramses himself discover that the matter was not yet ended. He had tried once to share his experience in the country of the fire mountains and had been dubbed an imbecile. Did people always have to see with their eyes and feel with their hands to accept truth as reality? And how long must a man live and how far must he travel, to learn that a polluted river was the beginning and not the end of trouble?

When presently he went into the palace garden and noticed that the face of the sun looked vague and that there were tiny black particles in the air, he almost spoke again.

When the mountains of fire belch their strange burdens into the air, it becomes sometimes so dark that a man cannot see his hand before his face. It is like

dust and ashes in one's mouth and in the pores of one's skin and in the breath that
one draws into one's body. If in the country of the father of waters there were such
a darkness and the wind should bear it northward on its breast...

But he did not say the words. For he remembered the looks of
suspicion and incredulity which he had seen always in the faces of men
when he had told them of wonders which their own eyes had not seen.
And he remembered also that the children of the land of the Blue Nile,
who had seen such wonders with their eyes, fled from them in horror,
crying; "It is the god! He is angry with us. He has sent this plague upon
us to destroy us!"

The black particles increased in number during that day and the
next and the next, until even Ramses, still remaining obstinately in his
chamber, found himself enveloped in a vague cloud. It settled in a fine
film on every smooth polished surface, mixed itself with his food so
that he could taste and crunch it between his teeth, ground into his
sensitive pores, and entered with the air he breathed into his body.

"What—!" he gasped. "By Amon and all the gods," he swore
hoarsely, "if someone doesn't clean this mess away—! Nehsi! Send
Nehsi to me!" he choked finally in a burst of panic.

"Did the Strong Bull summon his servant?"

"Nehsi! What is this—this dastardly mess? I—I can't even see
you. Let—let's get out of this prison, where we can breathe! The—the
garden—"

"The Son of Heaven could see and breathe no better were he in
the bright sunlight of his garden."

"What—what is it, Nehsi?"

"Perhaps the divine recipient of all wisdom would do better to
inquire what his people say it is."

"What— These confounded claws about my throat! I can't
breathe! What are they saying, Nehsi?"

"That it is the god of the Hebrews who has sent calamity again
upon us."

"More work of the priests of Amon, a plague smite their fat, lazy
bodies!"

"A plague seems already to have smitten them, my lord."

"They've probably made all this mess with their own magic! I'll
show them. If they think they can play tricks on the Good God—"

The Strong Bull's vehemence plunged him into a fit of coughing.
He gasped and choked and spluttered, while his fan bearer ventured an
unprecedented violation of his sanctity by pounding him on the back.
The eyes, peering through the black cloud, were for the first time in

Nehsi's memory bewildered and uncertain. "Do—do you think it's the god of the Hebrews, Nehsi?" "Surely the wisdom of the Son of Heaven is mightier than that of a humble fan bearer."

Ramses drew a long breath, which made him choke again. "All right. Let—let the fat gluttons have their way! I don't care whether it's their—magic or the trick of some strange god, if I can—can only see and breathe again. Go to the Delta, Nehsi, and tell the confounded squatters they can take their vacation in the desert. But if they know what's good for them, they'd better not go too far!"

4

"A message for Mosheh ben Amram!" announced Dathan with a respect that savored almost of humility.

At first Moses did not recognize the man who stood before him. Beyond a fleeting observation that he was unusually short, that he was faultlessly dressed in the most modish and immaculate of linens, and that the hand which gave him the message was as black as his own mud-stained ones, he gave him scant attention. His interest was entirely for the thin roll of papyrus. Breaking its seal and removing the outer covering, he unrolled the thin, tubular shape and spread it flat. The neat brush marks were unmistakably familiar. Tutu's.

"Tell the noble Prince Nehsi," said Moses, "that I will come—"

Raising his eyes, he stopped abruptly. "White Elephant!" he exclaimed in amazement.

"Not White Elephant! Phinehath! Lord printh named mitherable black man Phinehath himthelf when he gave him freedom. Lord printh go away, Phinehath been dead long, long time. Now lord printh come back, Phinehath alive again!"

Moses' eyelids stung. The devotion shining in the homely features was blinding in its intensity. Conscious suddenly of his mud-stained flesh and bedraggled breechclout, he felt himself also overwhelmed with emotion, compounded equally of tenderness and mirth. Lord prince indeed! The little Nubian was actually prostrating himself, dragging his spotless, pleated white skirts in the dirt, pawing awkwardly in the air for the fold of a garment which he might raise to his lips. Moses seized both the black hands in his own and lifted Phinehas to his feet.

"All right. Phinehas it is. But never kneel to me again, and don't call me lord prince. Who ever heard of a slave in fine linen and his master in a breechclout! We're just friends, understand?"

The black head nodded in violent acquiescence, its carefully curled wig seeming suddenly to acquire the animation of a bobbing ostrich plume. "Phinehath understand. Come to take lord printh to palathe. Thtay and wait till lord printh ready."

Moses encountered no difficulty in obtaining permission to leave. The propaganda of the priests of Amon had flowed down the river on the bosom of the unwholesome red-brown flood. It had ridden on the same northbound wind that had sown the sooty particles, though not as thickly as at Thebes, in the winding streets and marts of Memphis, the glittering courts of On, and even the splayed green richness of the Delta. It had come to the ears of the Egyptian foremen of the Children of Joseph and entered with a peculiar wariness into their eyes and with a certain delicate restraint into the fingers that curved themselves about the thin strips of elephant hide. Even the commissioners of building for the new cities of Per-Ramses and Per-Atum were a bit less rigid in their habits of inspection. For where the whims of a god were concerned, especially a strange one whose powers were as yet highly problematic, it was well to observe caution— at least, until the Good God should have given some indication of his will.

The foreman inspected the papyrus with an indifference that changed swiftly to both respect and wariness. Certainly Mosheh ben Amram could be excused from his labors in order to obey the summons of the friend of the pharaoh. Of course—here the foreman hemmed and hawed—it would be necessary for one of the guards to accompany him to Per-Ramses, not as a restrictive measure, he must understand, but merely to see that he arrived there safely. Naturally any person who was sufficiently important to receive a summons from Prince Nehsi— The Amram must understand his position—

Moses did understand perfectly. The foreman did not know whether the summons was honorary or punitive. If honorary, the guard could later be defined as an escort; if punitive, as a policeman. It was a clever decision. The foreman was not so lacking in cunning as the commissioner had thought.

"Well!" challenged Prince Nehsi, his bright eyes sparkling. "So this is the man who holds the writhing serpent of Egypt by the tail!"

Would the priests of Amon have been so ready to pit their wits against the pharaoh, he wondered, if they had first seen this son of a strange god whose cause they espoused? Even he was somewhat startled and taken aback by the man's appearance. When he had first seen him in Nubia, Moses had been like the Blue Nile in his youthful prime, storm-fed and tempestuous and full of conflicts. In Midian he had been struggling to find his way through choking sands and between sheer black rocks and over thundering cataracts. Now he was the mature river in the full sweeping tide of his splendid virility, his conflicts passed, his goal at last well defined, supreme in his mastery over men because he had made himself their slave.

Nehsi gazed for some moments in silence at the lean, deeply burned features, the lips which were like the straight line of a bird's flight across the desert, the eyes which were as clear and unagitated in their deep bony clefts as two rock-hewn mountain pools. A pity, he thought fleetingly, that the chin whose rugged squareness he well remembered must be buried beneath a beard, beautifully black and curling though it was. Hastily he reconsidered his intended approach to the subject. This was not a man to whom one gave advice or fatherly counsel. He looked again through the curtained portico to the outer entrance of his apartment, where Phinehas stood on guard. He had chosen this balcony for his interview with Moses because of its absolute privacy. This was one juicy morsel into which Tutu must not set his small white teeth.

The priests of Amon are blaming the Hebrews for these misfortunes which have lately struck the country," Nehsi said abruptly.

"Yes," replied Moses. "I know."

"Naturally they don't think the Hebrews are really to blame," continued Nehsi. "You and I both know what their purpose is, to balk Ramses' building operations in the Delta."

"Yes," returned Moses again. "I guessed that, of course."

Nehsi extended his fingers toward a wreathed jug of wine sitting on the small table beside him, then withdrew them. "Ramses sent me back from Thebes," he went on concisely, "with orders to permit the Hebrews to leave Egypt as they requested for the purpose of keeping a festival in the desert outside our borders. I came as fast as I could, but before I arrived a message reached me by fast courier. As I had expected, the pharaoh had changed his mind. He is not remaining in Thebes for the Feast of Opet. In fact, he is on his way now to Per-Ramses. Even were I to disregard the message, you could not possibly get outside the country before his arrival."

The eyes of the man facing him across the balcony were grateful but inscrutable. "And even if we could," said Moses, "we are not yet ready to go."

"I stood beside a stream in the mountains of the upper Nile," began Nehsi slowly, his gaze fixed cautiously on the other's face, "when one of the fire mountains was casting forth strange and terrible vomitings from its mouth. And the waters at my feet became thick with a boiling mud and red like blood, and I saw the white bellies of dead fish floating upon them. And later the air about me became dark with fine particles of dust and soot so that I could hardly see my hand before my face."

To his intense relief he saw the familiar kindling in the keen dark eyes. "And you believe that's what happened this time?" demanded Moses eagerly.

Nehsi relaxed, smiling, against his cushioned chair. He reached confidently for the wreathed jug, poured himself a goblet of wine, and drank long and deeply. "And I was afraid you too would call me a madman or an imbecile! I thought you might even believe this foolish babble that all these misfortunes were the work of your little desert god. But now that I know you're not a fool like the rest, I can tell you a few things which may make it possible for you to achieve your purpose, whatever it is."

"What things?" asked Moses.

Nehsi glanced again cautiously toward the watchful Phinehas, then lowered his voice. "The misfortunes are not yet over," he said significantly. "I have lived a long time, and my eyes and feet have not been idle. One truth only have I found in all my searchings, and this is it. *One thing always follows another.* Day comes after night, and not because the priests of On have prevailed upon Re to come forth out of his deep abyss. The sun rises in the far southland without their help. I believe—" Here Nehsi lowered his voice almost to a whisper, "I believe it would rise just the same if there were no priests of Re—*yes, even if there were no Re.*"

"Go on," said Moses, his eyes brightened to a glowing intensity.

"Growing follows inundation," Nehsi continued, "and harvest follows growing. But not because Osiris died and was restored to life, or because men have persuaded the gods by their own example to be fertile. And when the river becomes polluted so that the fish within it die and frogs crawl out of it to escape—"

"Yes?" prompted Moses.

"I am an old man, and I have seen it happen many times. After the frogs come swarms of flies, and after the flies come sicknesses which enter into the bodies of animals and men, sparing neither the sacred beasts in the temples nor the first-born of the nobleman in his palace, so that men say: 'Behold, such and such a god is angry. We must give him a maiden to delight him!' or, 'We must let his children go to sacrifice to him in the desert!' But they are wrong. It is not because the gods are angry."

"Why, then?" demanded Moses.

"I—I don't know that," confessed Nehsi, his voice faltering. "I never traveled quite far enough to discover. I know only that there's something—call it what you will—which makes one thing follow another, so that when night comes a man can say with confidence, 'The day will come.' It—it's in the very nature of things."

"And when one man makes a slave of another," said Moses with quiet deliberation, "as surely as night follows day, he sows the seeds of his own undoing. For there is also that in the being of things which enables a man, even though he is enslaved, to say, 'Freedom will surely come.'"

This time it was Nehsi's glance that kindled. "Go on," he demanded tersely.

Moses rose and moved slowly to the delicately wrought railing of the balcony, his tall figure as straight as one of the gaily painted wooden pillars upholding the bright-blue canopy. From where he stood he could see the resplendent skeleton of Ramses' still unfinished city, the gold tip of the obelisk which his own sweating body had helped to raise, its broad, flat base still resting on the crushed flesh and bone of a human hand. Moses turned again toward Nehsi.

"You say there is something dependable in the nature of things," he said quietly, "something that makes one thing inevitably follow another. Suppose, Nehsi, we give that something a name. *Suppose we call it—Yahweh!*"

As Moses walked along the edge of the pool in the royal garden, his heart beat fast with an excitement not aroused by his significant interview with the friend of the pharaoh.

"A certain person requests that you come to the little kiosk at the end of the garden pool," Nehsi had told him casually when their visit was ended. "I think you will find her there waiting."

As the white walls and bright red roof of the graceful building flashed their greeting through the dark foliage of the fig and pomegranate trees, his throat felt as dry as the gravel on which he walked. Her face as he remembered it, small and softly oval, eyes wide and curious, sprang toward him out of every cluster of leaves. What should he say to her after all these years? Words came beating against the portals of his lips, words that he knew now he should have spoken long ago.

My own, my beloved, you are everything that is sweet and beautiful, the warmth of the sunshine, the perfume of the lotus blossoms, the laughing music of the cataracts. I love you, I think I have always loved you, my beloved, my own...

The words froze suddenly, still unspoken, as he remembered that she was not his own. He had voiced other words, solemn, irrevocable words which had given her the right to become the wife of another. *"I have abandoned you as wife, I am removed from you, I have no claim on earth upon you."*

What could he say to her? He was still pondering when he found himself without preparation in the pillared entrance of the kiosk.

Tharbis—

But the woman sitting on the crimson cushion in the midst of the floor's blue and silver tiles, her gaze fixed intently on the child playing at her feet, was not Tharbis. Before she noticed his presence Moses had opportunity to study the chiseled lines of the profile beneath the heavy vulture headdress. They were as proud and beautiful as ever, but, though the child at her feet was laughing merrily at the toy cat he held in his hands, there was no hint of laughter in the firm line of her lips. And even before she turned he knew that the little flecks of green and gold no longer danced in the warm jet of her eyes. Instead they lay like hard bits of sand at the bottom of a cold, black pool.

"Nefretiri," he said gently.

She looked at him, unstartled but without recognition. "Nefretiri," he repeated, "don't you know me? It's I, Moses."

"Moses!" He saw eagerness flame then in her face as she rose, but it was not the eagerness of recognition. Her imperious gaze barely noted the familiar strangeness of his features but traveled instead to his empty hands. "Where is it?" she demanded abruptly.

"Where—what—" He stared back at her in bewilderment.

"The rod! The thing you perform all your magic with. Where is it, Moses?"

"Why—I—what—"

"They say you throw it on the ground and it becomes a snake. Then you pick it up and it becomes a rod again. You stretch it out over the river, and all the waters of Egypt become red like blood. You stretch it out again, and frogs come up out of the river and the marshes and fill the whole land. They say you can do anything with your rod." She was suddenly beside him, her hand on his arm, her eyes no longer hard and imperious, but naked and vulnerable. "Could—could you make my child well and strong with it, Moses?"

Suddenly he was standing in a room in the temple at On, listening to a stammering, pleading voice and watching the blood drip slowly from a wounded wrist to the soft nap of a carpet. The tense desperation in the little barber's face had been exactly the same as that which now confronted him in the features of the queen of Egypt.

"Cool Breeze," he murmured aloud.

"What—"

"The child's name," he hastened to explain.

"No. Not Cool Breeze. Amon-herkhop. Please do something, Moses. I've tried everything. He's had all the best physicians of Egypt. Always he wears an amulet about his neck and a charm hidden in his breast, but still the evil ones enter into his body. See how thin he is? And he has scarcely enough strength in his arms to lift his toys."

Moses' eyes turned toward the small figure on the tiled floor, and something twisted within him. Except for his pitiful thinness the child was just about the size of his own Eliezer. A friendly smile brightened his pinched features, and his black eyes danced with tiny particles of green and gold.

"Come down here," he ordered imperiously in a voice which sounded like piping through a thin reed. "Your hair's in the wrong place. It's on the front side of your head instead of the back. Come down here and let me fix it."

Moses stooped obediently and let the childish fingers tug at his beard. But Nefretiri was right. There was no strength in his puny arms.

"It won't come out, son," he said, laughing, but with a huskiness in his voice. "You see, it's meant to be there. That's the way men wear their hair in the country that I come from."

"Where?" demanded the son of Ramses.

"Out in the eastern desert, beyond the rising of the sun."

The green flecks sparkled. "I want to go there. Take me."

"No!" The cry burst involuntarily from Nefretiri's lips. "Don't say such things! The gods might hear."

As Moses rose, she came again to his side and seized his arm so tightly that he could feel the sharpness of her nails biting into his flesh. "Please, Moses! You—you loved me once, remember? If things had been different, he might have been your son. I—I'll do anything you say, make you rich again, if that's what you want, or—or go to Ramses and ask him for a favor for you—anything, I tell you! Only make my son well and strong with your magic rod!"

Emotion swept through Moses. He wanted suddenly to take her in his arms, not as he had done formerly, with passion, but tenderly, holding her close within strong arms as he might have held Gershom or Eliezer, shielding her from the words his own lips were about to utter.

"I'm sorry, Nefretiri," he said gently. "I'd give him some of my own strength if I could. But there's nothing I can do. There is no magic rod."

After he had told her, she did not storm and stamp her small sandaled foot as she would have done once. She sat very quietly on the long divan of ebony and ivory, slowly tracing with her fingers the outlines of the vacantly staring sphinx's head on its gracefully carved arm.

She'll still be there, thought Moses, his pitying eyes resting on her for a long moment before he turned to leave the kiosk, *when her attendants come with their fans and little trays and that bright envy in their eyes which even the comfortable and well-fed invariably accord those whom they deem more fortunate than themselves. She'll remain there without moving*, like—memory stirred again within him—*like the mother of Cool Breeze kneeling with her face against the post outside the gate.*

He had a strange feeling that if he were to lift the heavy folds of the vulture headdress, with its protruding beak and sheltering wings, he would find the imprint of a sphinx's head on the smooth, fair flesh of her forehead.

5

The Children of Joseph were preparing for a journey. Though they went by day to the brickfields, starting long before daylight and returning long after dark, they learned to throw themselves on their mats, sleep for a few merciful hours, then rouse themselves to work feverishly at tasks strange to most of them, all evidence of which must be obliterated before the sounding, hours before dawn, of the signals for assembly.

Fingers which for years had shaped themselves to the handles of wooden mud scoops and the sharp edges of sun-dried bricks learned again or for the first time the delicate art of weaving cloth from wool and goat's hair. In the smoky dimness of the mud huts, their entrances carefully hung with skins to hide the light of the flaring lamps, long black strips of tent cloth slowly took shape and were sewed tightly together. Bundles of raw wool, sheared hastily from the backs of long-neglected sheep, were washed and carded and spun and woven into heavy durable strips and squares, later to be cut and folded and sewed into cloaks. Old leaking goatskins were patched and rubbed with grease to restore their softness, new ones made by sewing up the leg holes of dried hides. Members of each family spelled each other at the feverish activity, several working while the others slept, one always placed on guard outside the hut, another primed to extinguish the lamp at an instant's notice.

They learned to converse with each other by day in brief, sometimes wordless, code, not trusting their section bosses to keep their secrets, although some of them, including Dathan and Abiram, had indicated a sympathetic interest in the crusade for freedom.

"I dreamed the lash was on my back last night," one man would mutter to his neighbor in indication that he thought he had heard one of the foremen prowling about the huts. Or, "By nightfall the son of Amram will have his basket again full of bricks," meaning, "we shall meet for another parley in Aaron's hut tonight."

Though the propaganda of the priests of Amon continued to seep through the narrow bottleneck at On into the broad mouth of the Delta, the cautious leniency of the Egyptian foremen had given place to an even harsher surveillance. Ramses had returned from Thebes more determined than ever to complete his building projects in the north, all his faculties sharpened to an edge of ruthlessness. For a few moments in Thebes, his divine nostrils outraged by the choking black particles, he had rendered brief capitulation to the priests of Amon, but an unobstructed larynx had soon restored his obstinacy.

The unpleasant redundancy of frogs, distasteful as it had been to his sensitive perceptions, had made little impression on the hard shell of his determination. Only for the briefest of intervals, when several of the more adventurous amphibians had found their way into the cabin of the *Star of the Two Lands* and lodged between his sheets, had he swerved slightly from his purpose. A surplus of frogs, while distasteful, was a common enough pestilence in the season of inundation, and a frog was, after all, just a frog.

Even worse than the pestilence itself had been its after effects, the heaps of decaying animal matter that had offended the divine eyes and nostrils whenever the royal vessel had approached the shore. He had arrived at Per-Ramses inspired with but one purpose: to make the Hebrews suffer with every inch of their despicable bodies for the inconvenience which their god might or might not have caused him.

But when the pestilence of insects came, he almost wavered in his purpose. The frogs had confined themselves largely to the lowlands and mud huts along the river. Not so the mosquitoes that came swarming from the heaps of decaying carcasses. The palace in Per-Ramses, close to the marshes, received the full brunt of their assault. The walls of the royal apartment were generously ventilated and unscreened, and the divine skin was tender.

"If I thought the priests of Amon were right and the god of those miserable ass-headed squatters was really responsible for this business," he exploded wrathfully to Nehsi, "I'd—I'd—"

"Doubtless the Strong Bull, who can do no wrong, would deem it wise to grant their request," interposed the fan bearer quickly. "After all, as the Son of Heaven has so often observed, they are more of a liability than an asset. Occupying, as they do, the richest farming country in Egypt, yet using it only as a pasture ground for sheep—"

"By Amon, that's right!" The slate-colored eyes, already narrowed into thin slits by mosquito bites, sharpened like keen metal edges. "You have an idea there, Nehsi! I mean—I believe I have often expressed that very sentiment."

"If the Hebrews were no longer in Egypt," proceeded Nehsi swiftly, "the son of wisdom could turn Goshen into a rich farming country. He could complete the canal—"

"The son of wisdom can turn Goshen into a rich farming country," countered Ramses, "without the Hebrews' leaving Egypt. Let them move their huts out into the desert. It will serve them right, whether their god is responsible for these confounded mosquitoes or not!"

Cursing the half dozen fan wielders who were engaged in agonized battle with the swarming, predatory multitude, the Good God lifted a swollen arm to brush several buzzingly persistent blockade runners from the divine but bloated countenance. "By the heart and bowels of Ptah!" he exclaimed violently. "For every one of these accursed insects that has had the audacity to sting the Son of Heaven, the back of every miserable Hebrew in Goshen shall be stung by a lash stroke. No, not one. Twenty!"

So it was that the Children of Joseph were given scourgings such as they had not known since the days when they had been young in bondage and had refused to do the bidding of their Egyptian masters. But again, as in those earlier days, their heads were unbowed and the cries that escaped their lips sounded above their anguish a faint trumpet note of triumph.

Strangely enough, Moses felt the sufferings of his people more acutely than they themselves seemed to. Wherever he went, their tortured bodies cried out to him, accused him voicelessly in accents that penetrated to the sensitive core of his being, while his ears heard only the excited, triumphant acclamations that escaped their lips.

"Look! There he is! And his back is bleeding from the lashes, just like ours. Why does he let them smite him? Why doesn't he just take his rod and hold it over the heads of the Egyptians, even as he held it over the waters and turned them to blood?"

"What misfortune will he bring upon them next, I wonder? And why does it take him so long to save us? If Yahweh has promised to deliver us, why doesn't he do it more quickly?"

In the dimness of their huts, also, the words falling from their lips wove themselves into tales far longer and sturdier than the strips of black goat's hair that took shape beneath their hands.

"...and then Yahweh told Moses to go to the pharaoh and say: 'Let my people go and worship. If you refuse to let them go, I will plague all your country with frogs. They shall crawl into your palace, into your bedroom, into your bed, into the houses of your officers, into ovens and kneading boards, crawling all over you and your people.'"

"Then the pharaoh called Moses to him," another voice would take up the tale excitedly, "and said, 'Make your god take away the frogs and I will let your people go to sacrifice.' And Moses said, 'Tell me when you want the frogs taken away.' And the pharaoh said, 'Tomorrow.' So the frogs died out of the houses and the courtyards and the fields. They were piled up in heaps, till the whole land stank with them. But did the pharaoh let the people of Yahweh go? No! He stiffened himself like his new ninety-foot statue!"

"Then Yahweh said to Moses: 'Go to the pharaoh early in the morning and tell him this from me: "Let my people go and worship me, or I will send swarms of mosquitoes on you and your people—"'"

"Not mosquitoes. Gnats."

"What do you mean—gnats! Mosquitoes, I tell you. I ought to know. I got bitten by plenty of them working on the wall at Per-

Ramses! So Moses stretched out his rod again, and all the dust in all the land of Egypt turned into mosquitoes. And the pharaoh said..."

Moses listened in silence. At first he had tried to tell them the truth, but, like Nehsi, he had found it was no use. No one would believe him.

"What does it matter?" Aaron demanded bluntly. "Suppose it hasn't happened just the way they think it has. What's the difference? You told them Yahweh would deliver us, and he's doing it. At least, we hope he is. Don't the Egyptians themselves say it's the power of Yahweh working through your rod? Why shouldn't we believe it?"

But Moses continued to suffer torment both in mind and body, and not only for the Children of Joseph, who were being lashed and driven because of the vengeance he, Moses, was said to have administered by the power of Yahweh. He suffered with the fellahin of Egypt, who were bearing the brunt of the misfortunes. His flesh quivered and smarted at thought of the swarming pests filling the little mud huts along the riverbanks. And when later, in the season when the barley was in the ear and the flax was in flower, there came terrific thunderstorms, with showers of devastating hail...

"It is the god of the Hebrews again," proclaimed the priests of Amon, contemplating in genuine alarm a sadly depleted income from their thousands of sharecroppers. "We will have no peace until these miserable squatters are out of the country."

"Thanks be to Yahweh," exclaimed the Children of Joseph, "and to his servant Moses who makes known his power over our oppressors! Hail, Moses! Show us the rod that brought the thunder and hail over the land of Egypt. Tell us what you said to the pharaoh!"

But Moses was silent He was thinking of the fellahin tilling their tiny green plots of flax and barley, emptying and filling, emptying and filling their small leather buckets in fevered desperation, hoping against hope that a few handfuls of their flattened crops might be salvaged. His stomach twisted with actual pangs of hunger, and in his ears there was a discord like the ceaseless creaking of the shaduf.

Ramses, whose new granaries in Per-Ramses were bulging, observed this latest misfortune with amusement rather than concern. It was wheat he needed, anyway, rather than barley, for his approaching campaigns in Syria. Barley, or the lack of it, was a poor man's problem.

But when as a result of the strange sicknesses that had fallen upon many animals and human beings after the swarming of insects, the Apis bull of Memphis was stricken, the Good God grew pale with terror, and his limbs trembled. For the Apis was the divine prototype of the Strong Bull himself.

"Send for the Hebrews," he ordered Nehsi, even before issuing directions for the sacred burial. "Let the priests have their way. I can stand frogs and mosquitoes, even dust filling my eyes, but when they begin striking at our gods—!"

When Moses and Aaron stood again before him in the audience chamber of the palace at Per-Ramses, his distaste was tempered with respect. But already he was beginning to regret his hasty decision.

"Why must you go outside the borders of Egypt to sacrifice to this god of yours?" he parried. "Why can't you and these miserable squatters of yours do it right here?"

A gleam of amusement lighted the black, cavernous pools into which he gazed. "It is the custom of the peoples of the desert to sacrifice a bull or a ram to their gods," replied Moses evenly to the king's mouthpiece. "Would the Son of Amon, the ram-headed one, look upon the defilement of his sacred counterpart at the hands of despised foreigners? Or would the Strong Bull see his namesake laid upon an altar?"

Ramses paled again, the horrible suspicion having suddenly entered his mind that the god of the Hebrews, famished for his desired victim, had laid hold on the Apis in its place.

"All right, get out!" he ordered harshly. "Take your miserable brood and go and worship your god. And if you ever show your treacherous face in my presence again, I—I swear I'll have your life!"

"The Son of Amon need have no fear," responded Moses quietly. "Unless he himself desires it, he need never look on my face again."

But after the Hebrews had left the presence of the pharaoh, Nehsi sent a message to Moses: "Wait. Ramses will again change his mind. If you go now, he will overtake you before you can get out of the country."

And it was so. For as soon as the Strong Bull had arranged for the embalming and burial of the late Apis in a huge granite sarcophagus in the Serapeum at Memphis, the importance of the tragedy began to wane. Another and better Apis would soon be found, with not only a white crescent spot on his side but perhaps also a white triangle on his forehead or a flying vulture patch on his back or a black lump under his tongue. The recent incumbent, he remembered, had not been too co-operative. Perhaps Ptah himself had smitten him.

"Send a regiment after those accursed Hebrews," he ordered Nehsi petulantly, "and bring them back to their brickmaking. Tell their foremen to flog every one of them twenty strokes for every hour he was away from his job. Maybe that will cure them of wanting to go off and worship their little desert god!"

Nehsi bowed low, so low that the smile on his wrinkled brown face was completely hidden from the slate-colored eyes. "The sagacity of the Son of Amon is beyond this small minds comprehension. His commands are so wise—but also so unnecessary. Not for a single hour have the Hebrews left their labors."

6

The season of growing became the season of harvest, and the dreaded locusts swept into the long green valley from the southern deserts. Over many places in the land they settled like a thick, hovering darkness, stripping the grain from the stalk, the foliage from the trees, and leaving desolation, as always, in their wake.

They will blame us for this too, thought Moses, watching the dense black cloud sweep over his head on a sea-borne wind. *It is as Nehsi said. One thing follows another, as day follows night. Is it important when a man wakens and feels the sunlight on his face that he should know just how it comes and why he is singled out to receive its warmth and radiance? No. It is what he does with the priceless hours of the day that matters.*

From that moment he ceased his introspection and became a man of action. After his day's labor in the brickfields he moved constantly among the Children of Joseph, reorganizing their loosely knit clans, gathering the heads of families around him and training them as, when a general, he had trained his captains, appointing leaders and assigning responsibilities to each.

"Be ready," was the burden of his admonitions, "at any moment of the day or night. Remember always that you are men, made in the likeness of Yahweh. He wants us to be free. When the time comes for us to march, nothing shall stop us."

"Be ready." The words passed through the clusters of huts like fire leaping from one clump of dried marsh grass to another. The newly woven fabrics for tents and garments were rolled into bundles convenient for carrying; goatskin bags containing sufficient food for a week's journey were kept continually replenished. The few sheep and goats still extant after the long years of neglect were pastured close to the huts at all times. And at every moment of the night some member of each family kept himself constantly alert.

If Moses was the strong will and Aaron the voice which incited purpose into the Children of Joseph, Miriam was the flame which kindled that purpose into glowing ardor. She gathered groups of gaunt, weary women about her and showed them how to make crude tambourines by stretching goatskins tightly over halves of gourds. She taught them the words of old folk songs learned at her mother's knee and struck others from the tinder of her ripe imagination. Sometimes, in the dim smoky seclusion of a hut, she even persuaded the tired, mud-stained feet to move in awkward rhythm with her own triumphant, unwearied body.

It was the coming of Phinehas, formerly known as White Elephant, that brought dissension into the house of the sons of Amram. The little Nubian appeared one day at Moses' side, clean linen garments exchanged for a simple breechclout, black face ecstatically split almost from ear to ear.

"Phinehath not go back to palathe. Thtay here with lord printh. Dig in mud and make brickth. Phinehath go now where lord printh go."

Moses welcomed him gratefully. Side by side they dug mud from the marshes, staggered with their backbreaking baskets along the road to the brickfields, churned the thick black ooze in the kneading pits, stooped for endless hours filling their molds and emptying them, filling and emptying, then staggered with still heavier backbreaking loads to the walls of Ramses' new store city before returning after starlight, drunk with weariness but with a long night of activity still before them, to the hut.

From the first moment, Miriam looked on Phinehas with displeasure. "Who does he think he is, coming in here as if he had a right to all the freedom we're struggling to win! The Children of Joseph are Yahweh's people, not the Nubians. You'd think by the way he acts that he belonged here!"

"He does belong," replied Moses quietly. "From now on wherever I go, he goes too. And he doesn't need to win his freedom. He earned it long ago."

But Miriam refused to be silenced. "It's not only this Phinehas," she proceeded bluntly. "You're letting other squatters who haven't a drop of Joseph's blood in their veins be received into the clans. They say there are even some Egyptian peasants who have sneaked into the valley believing they can have a part in our deliverance. Next thing they'll be thinking they're men like us, made in the likeness of—"

She stopped suddenly, lifting her hands to her throat in an instinctive gesture of protection. For the look in his eyes was like that which she had seen in them long ago in the hut on the edge of the brickfields, only this time it was directed at her, not at Baka. After that she remained silent, and when Phinehas was about the hut rebellion no longer flared in her eyes. She kept it concealed beneath a penitent film of ashes, where it was ready at the slightest breath to burst into flame again.

As the days grew slowly longer and the time approached when the hours of daylight would equal those of darkness, Aaron was in his element. The Children of Joseph were to make a feast to Yahweh. Eagerly he inquired of Moses all the details of the Feast of Pesach, how the lambs for the sacrifice were chosen, in what manner they were killed, the exact words and gestures that accompanied the sprinkling of the blood on the tent posts.

"It is the fellowship with Yahweh which is important," Moses told him at last with some impatience, "not what kind of knife we use to kill the lamb or how many drops we sprinkle on the doorpost. In the meal that we eat together we become one as the members of the family are one. Yahweh becomes our god and we become his people."

But Aaron continued to ask questions, and the directions he issued to the head of each family were elaborate in detail. The sacrifice to be made might be either a lamb or a kid, but it must be the first-born of a flock, and it must not have a single blemish. It must be killed at a certain time, between sunset and dark on the night of the full moon nearest the spring equinox, and cooked in a certain manner, not boiled but roasted over the fire, head and legs and all. Blood must be smeared on the two doorposts of each hut and on each lintel, in order to keep out the evil spirits that might be roaming the land, and for the same reason all families must remain indoors until the setting of the moon, when the evil ones would have passed by.

Most of the Children of Joseph needed no second warning. The sicknesses that had followed in the wake of the polluted waters and swarming insects were still raging throughout Egypt, and, while they had not as yet penetrated the more secluded Valley of Goshen, a healthy state of fear prevailed. As far as it was possible they followed Aaron's complicated directions to the letter, although the neglected flocks failed to supply the requisite number of new lambs or kids without blemish. They hoped desperately that Yahweh would not notice the substitutions.

The night came. The victims had been killed, their blood sprinkled on the doorposts, and the meal partially eaten when the message arrived from the pharaoh. "I must go to the palace at once," said Moses.

Aaron hastily laid aside his generous portion of roast lamb and wiped his fingers on his coat sleeve. "And I shall go with you."

"But—the feast—" protested Moses. "It is barely begun."

"Nadab will continue in my place," Aaron assured him with decision. Having bitterly resented Moses' assumption of leadership in their previous interview with the pharaoh, he was determined not to have such a mistake repeated.

Ramses had sent a carriage and an armed guard to conduct Moses to the palace. In spite of the bright moonlight, progress was slow, and to Moses, with Aaron's excited speculations constantly in his ears, the journey seemed interminable. Whatever the reason for the summons, he would have preferred facing the pharaoh alone. He knew instinctively that it was an occasion for neither glibness nor triumph, and the voice sounding in his ears was overflowing with both.

"Will it happen tonight, do you think? Will Yahweh show his power at last over the workers of iniquity? Perhaps it is the Destroyer himself who is abroad in the darkness instead of the spirits of evil. Can't you almost feel his cold breath on your cheeks?"

Remembering the terrible heat that had seared and scorched his flesh on The Mountain, Moses smiled grimly. But he made no comment. Cold or hot, what did it matter? If a man's god was nothing but a destroyer...

Nehsi met them in the small pillared hall beyond the outer vestibule, his brown wrinkled features, as usual, uncommunicative.

"The son of Joseph is most kind," he murmured, casting a quizzical glance at Aaron. "And it was most thoughtful of his brother to accompany him that he might not be alone on his journey through the darkness." He turned to one of the servants. "See that the brother of Mosheh ben Amram is made comfortable and refreshed with wine and cakes while I conduct the guest of the pharaoh into the divine presence"

"But—" Aaron opened his mouth to protest, then after another glance at Nehsi closed it. "I'll wait here in the vestibule," he said sulkily.

As soon as they were out of sight and hearing Nehsi turned to Moses. "It's the son of Ramses," he said tersely. "The sickness came upon him three days ago."

Before they had passed through the great dining hall into the court leading to the women's quarters, they heard the sound of grieving. At first it was no more than a faint shudder, then came a murmuring and a rushing of feet, followed by the shrill wailing of women's voices.

"We are too late," remarked Nehsi briefly.

As they went on through the pillared court, figures darted swiftly past them from the women's apartments, beating their bared breasts and wailing. The room which they entered was strangely quiet after the tumult of the court. It was obviously the queen's own chamber. Except for the slight waxen form lying on the huge carved bed, it contained but two people, a man and a woman, both almost as still as the waxen figure. The woman sat motionless on a stool in exactly the same position as Moses had last seen her in the kiosk, her beautiful features frozen into contours of stone. The man stood close to the bed, his face twisted like a crumpled mask. For the first time in his life Moses felt a stirring of pity toward Ramses.

He really loved the boy, he thought, *as he's never loved a living soul except himself.*

The mask turned slowly toward him, twisted into still more unfamiliar contours, even stranger in its distortion of fear than in that of grief.

"You!" exclaimed Ramses harshly. "Why should you come here— now? Haven't you—done enough—"

"You sent for him yourself." The voice seemed to issue from the woman without any visible movement of her lips. "Don't you remember? You thought you could make him change the mind of his god before it was too late. I told you it was no use. When Moses makes up his mind, he does not change it."

"Yes," muttered the lips of the mask. "I—I did send for him."

"It was you who killed him," continued the disembodied voice without emotion. "The priests gave you plenty of warning. They told you over and over to get rid of those horrible squatters. But did you heed them? No. You sold the life of your own son for a handful of miserable slaves."

"But I—I didn't know. I—I thought—"

"You thought" said Moses with deadly quietness, "that as long as you yourself experienced no pain, the sufferings of others were unimportant. Now you know what it is to suffer. You thought you were a master, and now you find you are nothing but a slave. You thought you were the Good God himself, and now you know that you are only a man, a miserable and unhappy one."

The features of the mask twisted again violently, as if suddenly crumpled in the palm of a heavy hand. "You—what—how dare you—"

"The question is," continued Moses with inexorable calmness, "what are you going to do with this new knowledge? Blame whatever gods you will for bringing suffering upon you, for what you do with it you will have none but yourself to blame, whether it makes you the most merciful pharaoh of Egypt or the most ruthless. Are you going to use it, or let it use you?"

The crumpled mask disintegrated, revealing features set in even harder, more arrogant lines than ever before. The eyes, naked and vulnerable, were all that remained to give evidence of the torment of fear and grief still seething within. Ramses pointed a shaking finger.

"Get out!" he shouted hoarsely. "Take your little desert god and your miserable squatters and leave me in peace! And don't come back—don't ever come back, any of you! You've done nothing but torment me since the day we went into the desert to hunt for that wretched bird. Get out! Get out, I say!"

Aaron was no longer waiting. He had returned to the carriage in haste, a servant explained, and been driven away, without partaking of the wine and cakes, when the news had only begun to spread through the palace that the first-born of the pharaoh had been stricken.

Nehsi summoned another carriage for Moses, "This is the moment you've been waiting for," he said tersely in parting. "Don't ask questions. Take it. Use it. And don't thank me," he added hastily, noting the unmistakable gratitude in the eyes above the opening lips. "Thank whoever or whatever it is that makes one thing follow another."

The new day was yellowing faintly in the east when Moses rode among the huts. In his brief moments of advantage Aaron had done his work well. Fear no longer stalked the valley. Triumph had swept through, devouring it like a flame. The time for concealment and subterfuge had passed. Lamps blazing through open doorways showed dark figures hastily gathering their few possessions together. The air throbbed with the sounds of restless, scraping hoofs and running feet. As the news of Moses' arrival swept through the settlements, figures swarmed about his carriage. Voices long muted to whispers broke into bold cries of rejoicing.

"Hail, Moses, servant of Yahweh!"

"Blessed be Yahweh, who has smitten the first-born of all the Egyptians!"

"The night is past. The Destroyer has passed over us and left us unharmed, but he has brought death to all the land of Egypt."

"Instead of the first-born of our flocks he has taken for himself the first-born of the Egyptians!"

"Thanks be to Yahweh, who has slain all the first-born in Egypt from the eldest son of the pharaoh on the throne to the eldest son of the slave girl at the mill! Thanks be to Moses his servant, who has turned the wrath of Yahweh upon our oppressors!"

Moses descended from his carriage before the hut of Amram. He saw that Miriam and Aaron and all the household were waiting, packed and girded, for a journey. The moment had come.

"Don't ask questions. Take it. Use it."

He gave the command to march.

7

The Children of Joseph were encamped in the desert beyond Per-Atum beside the Sea of Reeds. It was at the same spot where Moses had sat long ago waiting for the tide to ebb and for the moon to rise.

He was waiting again now, in an agony of impatience such as he had never before known. For this time more than his own life and future was at stake. The fate of a great host hung on the frail threads of his limited wisdom and understanding. He was a shepherd with a frightened, undisciplined flock dependent on him for their very life and safety.

"Yahweh help me!" he turned his face silently toward the narrow golden path that stretched across the shimmering waters. "What have I done! In order to give them freedom, am I only leading them into greater bondage?"

Because he felt like a shepherd and needed all the inner strength he could summon, he took his rod with him as he went among the knots of figures crouched about their fires. But he soon discovered that this was a mistake. At sight of the rod their eyes gleamed with a fascination that was half eagerness and half terror.

"The rod!" they murmured, excited speculation leaping from group to group. "Moses is carrying the rod!" "What will he do with it next?" "Is he going to use it to get us across the Bitter Lakes?" "If Moses has his rod, why doesn't he save us from all danger?"

Moses moved among them, attempting to allay their fears. "The waters will go down," he told them patiently. "Presently they will become so shallow that we can easily make our way across. But we must wait until the tide is at its lowest ebb."

They did not understand him. Most of them knew little of tides and seas, and they thought it was by the magic of his rod that the waters were to become lowered. "Do it now!" they urged. "Why must we wait? If the Egyptians follow us, we shall be trapped like animals between the desert and the sea!"

In spite of their impatience and uncertainty, their mood was still one of triumph. The night of their liberation was still not far behind them. Though they longed to be across the final barrier of shimmering moonlit waters, they were not too concerned with approaching danger. If the pharaoh came, Moses would wield his rod, and Yahweh would again deliver them. By the same reasoning they were united in a joyous, flagrant disregard of their leaders' stern injunctions to observe frugality. All over the encampment, fires flared with carefree abandon. Already the small supplies of dried dung which they had brought with them were half depleted, and the meager stores of food were being dispensed lavishly as at a feast. Why not? When they were gone, Moses would be there with his rod, and the being who had killed all the first-born in Egypt for their sakes would surely not let his chosen people go cold or hungry.

In an open space among the fires a group of women were singing and dancing, one voice rising clearly above the others, one figure the whirling, glowing focus about which all the rest revolved. At sight of Moses, Miriam left the center of the group abruptly, and instantly the song became a lifeless repetition, the dance an awkward parade of wooden puppets.

"Have you seen the mob streaming after us?" she greeted him, her black eyes flashing. "Half the riffraff of Egypt must be trailing at our heels."

"I've just finished a tour of the encampment," returned Moses, "and I've seen most of the late-comers, if that's what you mean."

"Surely you're not going to let them go with us!"

"Why not?"

"Why not!" Her fingers beat an impatient tattoo on the tight skin of her tambourin. "Most of them are no more the sons of Joseph than—than—"

"Than Phinehas the Nubian?" supplied Moses quietly.

"Yes. Than Phinehas the Nubian." She flung the words back at him defiantly, emphasizing each one with a sharp drumbeat, "Bedouin, stupid Shasu from the desert, Egyptian fellahin! What have they done to deserve our freedom?"

"Toiled in the brickfields and mines and quarries," countered Moses, his voice still low and even but with a sudden warning glint in his eyes. "Bent their shoulders to the buckets of the shaduf, felt the coil of a lash on their backs. What more have we done?"

"It's different with us," replied Miriam swiftly. "We're the people of Yahweh. Didn't you yourself tell us that he had created us in his own likeness and no one had a right to enslave us?"

The glow of the surrounding fires swam before Moses' eyes, and the tumult of the encampment became like rushing winds in his ears and a groaning of the earth beneath his feet. He was crawling again to the edge of an abyss on a mountaintop, gazing into the glowing core of a more intense disquiet than he had ever yet conceived. Through the red mist he saw Miriam's face, proud and blazing and contemptuous. But the emotion that seized him was not anger. It was agony, concern, a vast, profound patience.

"I told you that Yahweh had created *man,* not the Hebrews, in his likeness."

Miriam's eyes continued to flash their contempt. "And not only Bedouin, Shasu, and Egyptians! I even saw one of the black daughters of Kush slinking about on the edge of the encampment. Surely you don't expect the Children of Joseph to mingle themselves—"

Moses turned abruptly and left her standing, the hot protests still pouring in a torrent from her lips. Without thought or direction he made his way among the little groups gathered about the fires, heedless of greetings or questions, and, seeing the look on his face, none tried to stop him. Not until he found himself alone on the bank beside the Sea of Reeds did the tumult within him subside.

The wind was rising, a brisk east wind which carried on its breath both the salt tang of the sea and the hot raw smell of the desert. It shattered the glassy surface of the water, splintering it into a million silver fragments. The tide, at last on the ebb, had barely begun to turn. The night would be spent before he could again give the command to march. And when the time did come, the utmost haste would be necessary. If the strong wind held, the waters might remain shallow a little longer, but at best the time when it would be possible to traverse the narrow lake bed on foot would be distressingly short, perhaps barely an hour. Would he have done better, he wondered, to attempt a passage of the frontier at Tharu by way of the fortified bridge? No. Certainly not. He knew the officers at Tharu. They would have required official passports from every unit in the company, including the sheep and goats. And every inch of the land frontier from the northern end of the Bitter Lakes to Tharu was equally impassable. This was the only way.

The moonlight seized each slender reed in the waters at his feet and turned it into a thrusting dagger. The splintered waves glinted in its silver radiance like knife blades sharpened to a keen cutting edge. Beyond, bold and black and as impenetrable as a hard piebald shield, loomed the grim contours of the desert. Alone, without encumbrance, he had found them difficult barriers to cross on his journey into Midian. He could still feel the sucking of the waters about his ankles, the desert's blistering heat by day and its intense coldness by night, the fear and desperation which had hounded him on his long drifting journey from one oasis, one nomad settlement, to another. If it had been difficult for one, what would it be...

Confronted suddenly with a full comprehension of the task he had undertaken, he was seized with panic and dismay. Wave after wave of terror and despair swept over him. What had he done? Of what appalling megalomania had he made himself guilty, believing that the Creator of all things had chosen him to aid in the accomplishment of his designs! Deliberately he had made himself responsible for the destiny of hundreds of human beings. And he had done it under false pretenses, though, heaven knew, not intentionally! There was scarcely a soul in the vast, unruly horde dogging his heels but believed there was magic in his rod which would satisfy all their hunger, assuage all their thirst, protect them from all their enemies, lead them straight into a land of freedom and plenty where every desire would be fulfilled.

"Yahweh help me!" he cried again soundlessly. "Show me what to do! For they think I am strong, and I'm weaker even than they are themselves. I'm only a man, and they believe that I'm a god!"

Never in his life before had he felt so acutely alone. There was not a soul in all the encampment with whom he could share the burden that pressed so heavily upon him. Aaron was concerned only with petty details. Miriam was certainly not in complete sympathy with his ultimate objective. Even the faithful Phinehas had disappeared. He had insisted, against Moses' protest, on building him a small shelter on a hillock somewhat apart from the encampment, making a rude tent of a few upright sticks and an armful of skins and laying a small fire of dried dung.

"But I shan't have time for rest. And if I should lie down for an hour, I'd just throw my coat about me."

"Lord printh come here," the little Nubian had persisted stubbornly. "Long journey ahead. Lord printh need retht. Phinehath make everything ready. Then Phinehath go."

"Go!" There had been consternation in Moses' voice. "Go where? And why?"

But Phinehas had divulged neither his purpose nor his destination. He had only slipped away quietly. And why not? Moses asked himself with a poignant sense of emptiness. Why should anyone in his right mind choose to follow a mad fool who had the presumption to believe he could become a savior of men? His brief, stormy interview with Miriam had done more than widen the gulf between them. It had reminded him that he was putting behind him forever the only human relationship which, he knew now, might have afforded him complete understanding and fulfillment.

"I even saw one of the black daughters of Kush..."

With Tharbis he could have shared the terrible uncertainly that now possessed him, and she would have understood. He would hardly have needed to put it into words. She had always understood, about the Shasu boy and the prisoners, about the restlessness of his spirit and his hunger for truth, even about his love for Nefretiri.

As long as he remained in Egypt, there was always a chance that he might see her again. Now only a few more hours, and he would be leaving Egypt forever. The tide was slowly but surely ebbing. And the wind felt cold against his body.

When finally he moved back through the encampment, the fires were burning low. The dancing and singing had ceased. Wearied by the excitement and long marching, the Children of Joseph lay huddled among their scanty possessions, the only sounds of restlessness issuing from the flocks and herds in the center of the encampment.

We must waken them soon, thought Moses. *Better, perhaps, for them to be roused by the whip and the snarl of a foreman! Yahweh forgive me if I am waking them to something worse!*

In spite of its bitter introspection, his mind was functioning with mechanical alertness, planning even the most trivial detail of the departure from Egypt. He checked again the orderly arrangement of the clans, the key position of the leader in each one, even the disposal of the few articles of baggage. For when the time came to march, all must move with the rhythmic precision of the shaduf. In spite of their heritage, they were not yet men of the desert. They slept too heavily, too carelessly, as if they were far too confident of awaking in safety. But they would learn. After a few nights in the wilderness of Shur, with the fires of hostile tribes glowing on the near horizon and the yellow eyes of jackals and hyenas glimmering in the outer darkness...

His practiced ear picked out of the confusion of animal sounds the faint bleatings of a calf and young lamb and registered them gratefully in his mind. Good! They would lead the cattle and sheep through the shallow waters instead of driving them. Even as the fellah of Egypt persuaded the cattle to trample the seed into his submerged fields by hoisting a young calf to his shoulders and permitting the mother to follow...

He moved on into the outer fringes of the encampment where were the late-comers of whom Miriam had complained. Many of them, as she had intimated, were not of the Children of Joseph. In the light of the newly kindled fires he saw the brown flat features of Shasu slaves, the stooped shoulders and stolid faces of Egyptian fellahin, the thick lips and sloping foreheads of Nubians.

"I even saw one of the black daughters of Kush..."

The sudden hammering of his pulses belied his mind's cool reasoning. Of course. In this mixed company there would be more than one black daughter of Kush. And, besides, she would look as much like an Egyptian as a Kushite. Nevertheless, he scanned each firelit face with an eagerness that approached obsession. Presently he imagined he was seeing her features everywhere, each shadow the soft duskiness of her cheek, each winking flame the brightness of her eyes. Hastily, to spare himself further torment, he moved out into the darkness beyond the encampment, but even here he was not free. It was all his senses now which deceived him, not just his eyes. She was here in her entirety, walking beside him, piquant face lifted to the wind, lips parted, pert nose sniffing the salt tang of the air. He could feel the touch of her hand, hear the sharp intake of her breath.

"Is that the sea I smell, Moses? It smells just as I imagined it would. Take me to it, Moses—quickly!"

So vivid was his consciousness of her nearness that he actually heard in his ears the sound of her voice, but he was no longer treading the rough desert ground beside the Sea of Reeds, and she was no longer by his side. He was sitting in the palace hall at Saba, waiting, listening to the clear voice of the bride—his bride—lifted to her bridegroom in the wedding song.

> "I come to you as the flower turns to the sun;
>   As the mountain stream hears from afar the song of the river
>   And hastens to merge its flow with the Father of Waters;
>   As the wild duck harks to the trumpet call of her mate
>   And mounts up to meet him on swift wings;
>   Like a bird homing to its nest, I come to you!"

Because the voice did not seem to issue from his inner consciousness, as had the other words spoken by his side, he moved blindly in the direction from which he thought it came, his feet stumbling on the hard, sandy ground, the voice, full and rich as the sound of the river in floodtime, flowing with the wind against his face.

He saw suddenly that he had come to the hillside where Phinehas had made the little shelter of animal skins and that the fire had been kindled. A woman was standing beside the fire. The words of the song were issuing from her lips. He could not see her face, but in some indefinable way he knew that her skin was soft and dusky as the night's violet shadows. She was no more the slender figure that had been walking at his side than the full-blown lotus is the tight green bud from which it issued. Yet he knew they were the same. He moved softly toward her, fearful lest, being the creation of his desire, she might vanish before she had finished her song.

> "My heart is a pathless waste, a fireless hearth,
>   The parched earth panting for the flood's embrace,
>   Until I see your face, beloved; then lo,
>   The rushing tide, the flame, the sweet oasis,
>   A garden of flowers which are yours for the plucking!
>   I come to you, my love! I come to you!"

He was so close to her now that if he had reached out his hand he could almost have touched the hard rough fabric of her coat. It was a woolen coat such as the Hebrews wore, and it was woven in alternating stripes of brown, black, and ocher. Strange that he should see her so now, when in all his former imaginings she had worn the loose garment of white linen in which he had first seen her! Strange too that this time his mind had created her body in the ripe fullness of maturity when he had never before conceived of it as anything but a child's! What of the

376

face hidden beneath the shielding folds of the headdress? Was that different too? Suddenly he had to know.

"Tharbis!" he spoke hoarsely.

She did not vanish as he had expected. Instead she turned, and the warm firelight leaped with the swiftness of his own hungry gaze to embrace her features. He saw with gratitude that they were unchanged. The soft dusky skin, the parted lips, the wide eyes searching his with an almost unbearable intensity...

"Tharbis!" he cried again in reckless risk of dispelling the vision. "Beloved—please don't go! Don't vanish again. Wait!"

She uttered a little cry and came swiftly toward him. His arms closed about her. And suddenly there was a wild rushing in his ears like the roar of the cataracts. For it was no creation of dreams that he held in his arms. Gratefully, almost with reverence, he pressed his mouth to the sweet full goblet of her lips.

"But—I still don't see—"

"My father sent you a message," said Tharbis. "Perhaps after you read it you will understand."

Moses broke the seal of the thin roll, unfolded the small strip of papyrus, and held it close to the light of the fire, his hands trembling so that he could hardly read.

"My son," the black flowing script greeted him simply. "I am sending her by a trusted friend to your tent, which, I understand, is, according to the manner of the peoples of the desert, equivalent to a marriage ceremony. But this is unimportant, for she has always been your wife. Remember what I told you that night in Ezion-geber? I said only that an official of noble birth had *requested* her hand in marriage. The request was not granted. She has always been yours from the moment she looked from the battlements of Saba and saw you. I hoped when you returned to Egypt that you would never see her again. She had already suffered enough through you. But I have changed my mind. Say, rather, *you* have changed my mind, you and your Yahweh. I know now that suffering is not an evil thing—at least when experienced willingly for the sake of another. I know, because you have showed me. If your Yahweh is like you, or, I should say, if you are like him, I believe he is a god I would be proud to follow.

"But I am not coming with you. At least, not now. I believe I can help your cause more by remaining in Egypt. Ramses has already begun to repent his decision. Believe me, I shall do everything in my power to keep him from pursuing you, but I may fail. Go now, as soon as you can, and as swiftly."

As Moses slowly rerolled the papyrus, his eyes met those of a black grinning face peering around the makeshift tent.

"Lord printh not know where Phinehath go. Phinehath meet lady Tharbith and bring here. Not good for lord printh to be alone."

The black features merged themselves again into the night shadows.

"It was all arranged long ago," explained Tharbis softly. "I saw you the day you and your brother came first to the palace. And I knew then that when the time came I was going with you—that is, if you wanted me. I couldn't be sure of that until just now, when I saw your face."

He drew her closer, pushing the folds of her headdress aside and burying his face in the clean fragrance of her hair. "Forgive me, beloved," he murmured huskily. "Forgive me for not always having wanted you."

Later, lying by his side in the shadows of the small, makeshift shelter, she lifted her face suddenly, and sniffed the air. "Is that the sea I smell, Moses? It smells just as I imagined it would, the way cataracts sound. Take me to it, Moses, quickly, and show me! But first tell me about your god—*our* god. Is it true, what my father says, that it is he who created all that exists and who makes one thing follow another? And did you climb one of the great fire mountains to look for him? And did you really find him, or are you still searching? Oh, Moses, tell me all about it quickly! There is so much I must know!"

While the Children of Joseph slept and the embers of their dying fires tossed in the wind, the man and the woman walked on the shores of the Bitter Lakes which stretched from the Great Sea almost to the gates of Tharu. And together they relived the years which one had spent in the desert and the other in the palace. And together they climbed The Mountain, mingling their spirits in a strangely liberating fellowship of earth and flame and sun and wind. And together they descended.

Sleep fled suddenly from the encampment. The news swept with fresh gusts of wind from fire to fire, clan to clan, whipping both dulled emotions and dying embers into flame. The terrified features of a sentry took shape before Moses' eyes in the wan moonlight.

"Yahweh help us, they're on our heels! They've got us cornered like rats."

"Who?" demanded Moses sharply. "What has happened?"

"The armies of the pharaoh. They've followed us. They're only a few paces away, beyond those dunes to the north. I tell you they've got us trapped!"

"Go back to your post," ordered Moses sternly, "and stay there. This is no time for panic." He turned swiftly toward the woman at his side, "So Ramses has changed his mind again, I might have known. It's still not too late. I'll send you back to Per-Ramses with Phinehas."

Her eyes met his scornfully. "You think I'm that kind of person, running away at the first sign of danger? Listen!" Lifting both hands to his shoulders, she continued earnestly: "My father knew this was likely to happen. He tried hard to prevent it. But he entrusted me with a message to give you in case it did. He said: 'Tell Moses that if the Egyptians come after him in pursuit, I shall be with them, and I shall do everything in my power to save him and his people. Everything. Tell him to go forward as quickly as possible, just as he had planned.' Does that make sense?"

"Yes," said Moses.

"What are you going to do?"

"Cross the sea into the desert," he replied briefly. "The tide is running out fast. See how the white sand shows already through the shoals? It runs in a long bar clear across these narrows to the other side. Your father told me about this place long ago. And the wind is with us. If it holds and we hurry, we can almost pass over on bare ground to the opposite shore."

He took her once more in his arms and kissed her, then turned toward the confused and frightened host. He no longer felt panic or dismay. He moved toward his task with the calm certainty of a man who has clearly visioned its goal from a high mountaintop and is ready to descend into the deepest valley to attain it

Dawn was breaking when the last of the Children of Joseph and their motley following stepped into the shallow waters of the Sea of Reeds. For two hours or more the long dark procession of men, women, and children, sheep, goats, and cattle had moved ceaselessly as the ebbing and flowing of the tide and, it had seemed to Moses' agonized vision, far more slowly. At the time of the first crossing the moon had still swung high above the ragged horizon of the western desert. Now it was but a pale, shrunken disk barely visible in the sickly grayness of a haggard twilight.

Mercifully the wind had held through the night, but now with the coming of dawn its strength was waning. As Moses stepped into the waters this last time he no longer had to brace his body against its boisterous resistance. But with the lessening of pressure from above there seemed to come an additional hostility from the waters below. He could feel them sucking at his ankles, tugging at his knees, even pulling at the garments tucked high into his girdle. This, his last crossing was going to be the hardest of all.

He could not have counted on his fingers the number of times he had already made the journey through the shallow waters to the opposite shore. First, leading the way for the timid, floundering leaders of the procession; later, bearing the tempting bait of a lamb or a kid or a newborn calf on his shoulders; again and again returning to repeat the crossing wholly or in part, guiding the faltering steps of the old, encouraging the slow, threatening the laggard, attempting to instill into the unwieldy host something of his own fevered desperation.

They had not recognized the need for haste and for quiet. In spite of his sharp orders to sheiks of clans and heads of families, after the first few timorous crossings a spirit of leisurely jubilance had prevailed, and the roisterous wind had seized and magnified their excited, exultant shouting.

"Sing praises to Yahweh who has saved us again from our enemies!"

"Moses stretched out his rod over the sea, and the waters parted! Yea, they fell away on the left hand and on the right, making the bare ground to appear!"

"Thanks be to Yahweh and to Moses, who has delivered us with his rod!"

It was not with songs and praises that they had greeted him a few hours before, Moses remembered, when he had gone among them after their rude awakening. Their shrill complaints and recriminations still rang in his ears.

"Was it because there were no graves in Egypt that you have brought us to die in the desert?"

"Where is Yahweh now, we'd like to know? If we are his people, why does he do this to us?"

"Better to be slaves to the Egyptians than to die here in the desert like rats!"

Well, he had got them safely across, all but these last stragglers, and apparently the Egyptians, encamped beyond the dunes, had not discovered their departure. Thanks to Nehsi, no doubt! The old veteran had probably convinced the captains of the pursuing army that their quarry, once discovered, was as safely within their grasp as a netful of fish and that any sounds of tumult which reached their ears were evidence of terror and not of triumph. Not that it mattered a great deal whether the pursuit came now or later! It was a short journey up the shore of the Bitter Lakes to Tharu. Unless Nehsi was able to perform some miracle of persuasion, the soldiers of the pharaoh would have tracked down the fugitives before they were a day's march out of Egypt.

Moses stumbled and almost fell. The waters tightened their cold tentacles about his knees. So weary was he that he longed to stretch himself in the cool trough of the waves and let their darkness cover him. Black arms reached out and enveloped him, but instead of dragging him down they seemed strangely to uphold his body and propel him forward.

"Lord printh help many through thea. Now lord printh need help himthelf. Lord printh lean hard on poor thlave."

"Phinehas!" exclaimed Moses gratefully. "You're always there when I need you. But remember, it's not slave. Never slave again. Just friend—and brother."

He moved forward more easily now, the strength of the tireless Nubian seeming to bring him a renewal of energy. They were halfway across when the noise of shouting rose in their ears above the swelling of the waves. Moses looked back. In the half-light of dawn the outlines of chariots, the confused movements of horses and lancers and bowmen were plainly visible. His first reaction was one of gratitude and exultation. Nehsi had managed to keep their pursuers diverted until the last stragglers had been practically assured a safe crossing. Already they were out of range of Egyptian arrows. A few more moments and the long, creeping body of fugitives would have dragged its last weary coil out of the water's clinging tentacles. Behind lay Egypt, slavery, the shadows of a night almost ended. Ahead, beyond the shallow, troubled waters, were freedom and a sky already fast yellowing with dawn.

"Forward!" he shouted, cupping his hands and trying to make his voice carry against the wind. "And faster! Pass the word along!"

They obeyed wearily, bending their backs as doggedly to the choking sands and waves as once they had curved them to the dragging weight of a hundred-ton monolith. But they found it impossible to move much faster. Obediently they repeated his admonition, "Forward! Faster!" but without enthusiasm. It took all the energy they could muster merely to lift one foot above the other.

At least they would have a few hours to prepare themselves, Moses told himself, hastily estimating the time it would take for the detachment of soldiers and chariots to retrace their steps along the Bitter Lakes to Tharu and down through the desert on the other side. But of what avail would be a few hours in preparing an unwieldy company of untrained, weaponless men, impeded by women and children, flocks and herds, to defend themselves against even a small contingent of the pharaoh's skilled and well-armed soldiers! Already he could hear the sound of their accusing voices.

"Was it because there were no graves in Egypt that you have brought us to die in the desert?"

Above the noise of the wind and waters Moses heard suddenly the wailing of the Children of Joseph. What! Were they weeping for their dead already? The wailing became lamenting. Its burden was caught up and relayed by the long line of fugitives still pressing through the shallow waters.

"They're coming! Yahweh have mercy on us!"

"They have entered after us into the sea!"

"Yahweh has deserted us! He has surrendered us to our foes!"

Again Moses looked back. It was so. The chariots of the Egyptians had entered after them into the sea. Even at this distance he could see the tossing spray about the horses' heads, hear the cracking of whips and the sharp commands of the drivers. This, then, was to be the end. There was only one chance in a hundred that the last of the laboring procession would reach the opposite shore. They would, indeed, die like rats, choosing either to be pushed off the narrow bar into the deeper waters or to be trampled under the chariots of the Egyptian host. Surely Nehsi could have spared them this final ignominy! It should not have been hard to convince the captains that pursuit by land was preferable to the discomforts of entering the cold sea on a wind-blown dawn.

"Forward!" shouted Moses again, trying to make his voice heard above the wailing. "Faster in the name of Yahweh!"

"In the name of Yahweh!" Who was he, Moses, that he should presume to speak in the name of him who had created man in his own likeness? Was he better than the Egyptians, who had treated men like animals, laying the lash to their shoulders and heavy burdens on their backs? Deliberately he had taken into his weak hands the destinies of hundreds of human beings. Would their destruction be less agonizing, would he be less responsible for it, because he had intended their salvation?

"Lord printh hurry," urged Phinehas insistently. "Hortheth come fatht. Lord printh maybe have to jump in water and thwim."

"No," said Moses. One thing, at least, to be thankful for! He would be the first to pay the penalty for his tragic blunder. Perhaps if he placed himself directly in the path of the oncoming horses and chariots, he could retard their progress for a few more moments.

Defeat seemed suddenly incredibly easy and pleasant. There would be no more complaints and bitter wranglings. His patience would no longer be tried by Aaron's pettiness. Miriam's resentment at sight of his Kushite wife would never again have to be faced. Even the prospect of separation from Tharbis brought only a vague pang of regret. Last night their spirits had been blended in a complete and perfect fulfillment. Life had already given them its best.

With sudden clarity he saw the almost insurmountable difficulties of the task he had undertaken. Fool, blind, stupid fool, to think that he could have been equal to them! Lead a ragged, half-starved rabble across a desert? Teach them to find food and drink? Turn a mob of disgruntled slaves into confident masters of their own destiny? Weld them into a united people? Imbue them somehow with that inner compulsion which he had found alone on a mountaintop? Had he not been so utterly weary, he would have laughed aloud. He, Moses, believing himself equal to such a task, guilty of such incredible presumption that he conceived himself as capable of helping Yahweh create man in his own likeness? Yahweh forbid! Indeed, Yahweh—or some other instrument of destiny—was at this moment forbidding. The dream, the purpose, the task as yet barely begun would soon be trampled beneath the hoofs of the pharaoh's horses.

In spite of its agonized effort the procession still moved at a snail's pace. Moses turned once more and looked back. He could see the plumes in the horses' manes, the thread of a whip as it coiled through the air. The shouting of the soldiers mingled in his ears with the shrill lamenting of the Children of Joseph.

"After them!"

"Run down the filthy swine!"

Moses was sure that one of the voices sounded familiar. Unbelievable that Nehsi should have turned traitor and delivered them into the power of their pursuers! Equally incredible that he could not have found some way to prevent the captains of the pharaoh's army from plunging after them into the sea! The coldness which cut through Moses was not caused by the black waters. He waited almost with eagerness for the onslaught of the plunging horses. But it did not come.

Phinehas looked behind and chuckled. "Hortheth not go fatht in thand," he observed hopefully. "Maybe wheelth get thtuck."

But suddenly there was neither time nor energy to spend on conjectures. The dazzle of the newly risen sun was in their eyes, and, with one of those swift veerings of direction which often come at dawn, the wind was at their backs instead of in their faces. The tide waters, moving with it now instead of against it, came upon them with a rush, swirling boisterously about their knees, then mounting to their waists, and it was all they could do to keep their feet. The pursuing Egyptians were forgotten. Every faculty was concentrated on the struggle for survival.

Strength surged again through Moses' body. He no longer needed the sustaining black arms. All about him there were weaker comrades who required his aid. "Help the others," he ordered Phinehas briefly. "Don't bother any longer with me."

Doggedly he plunged forward through the deepening flood, shouting commands and encouragements, setting stumbling, half-submerged figures on their feet, rescuing those who had slipped into deeper waters, prodding the stragglers with his rod, supporting the weary, as once, a shepherd in the wilderness of Midian, he had often performed the same services for the sheep of his flock. He was no longer fearful or uncertain. These, his people, his flock, were in danger, and they had need of a shepherd's skillful, tender care.

After what seemed an endless struggle, strong hands pulled him from the water and up the bank. He noticed that the sounds of wailing and lament had ceased. Shouts of exultation rang in his ears in a paean as lusty as the glare of the newly risen sun.

"Thanks be to Yahweh and to Moses his servant, who has saved us this day out of the hand of the Egyptians!"

"Pharaoh's chariots has Yahweh drowned in the Sea of Reeds!"

"Our god is a god of war, and Yahweh is his name!"

In his anxiety for the Children of Joseph, Moses had completely forgotten their pursuers. Now he turned and looked back over the Sea of Reeds, staring incredulously. The sudden veering of the wind which had rendered their own passage so hazardous had wrought havoc with the chariots of the Egyptians. Already mired in the sand and mud, those leading the pursuit had been overwhelmed by the sudden upsurging of the incoming tide. Wildly floundering horses were only embedding their burdens deeper in the agitated waters. Lancers and bowmen and charioteers were lashing about in the waves, as frenziedly helpless in their efforts to free themselves as the plunging horses. The sun's rays, leaping from crest to crest, picked up a dazzling medley of helmets, glittering lance tips, silver harness trappings, polished woods and gleaming leathers, gold-rimmed wheel disks, all tumbled together in amazing confusion. Toward the opposite shore the more fortunate equipages were frantically reeling back through the shallower waters and being dragged up the bank to safety. A cloud of golden, sun-shot dust marked the swift retreat of the remnants of the pharaoh's host across the desert.

They will not come back, thought Moses. Even Ramses himself could not make them. We are far safer than if we had met them in battle and they had suffered inglorious defeat.

He was conscious suddenly that Tharbis stood beside him, and he knew that she was as cognizant of his thoughts as if he had spoken them aloud. She smiled at him triumphantly, even while her eyes brimmed with tears.

"It was my father who drove the foremost chariot," she said simply.

"Yes," replied Moses. "I know."

The knowledge smote his whole being like a bright, hot blade. Nehsi had known what was going to happen. As familiar with the ways of the winds and tides as with the secrets of the fire mountains in the wild country beyond the cataracts, he had deliberately led the Egyptian army to its destruction. "I am not coming with you. At least, not now. I believe I can help your cause more by remaining in Egypt." He had not only helped it. He had saved it. With the price of his own life he had purchased freedom for the Children of Joseph.

"I know now that suffering is not an evil thing—at least when experienced willingly for the sake of another. I know, because you have showed me. If your Yahweh is like you—or, I should say, if you are like him, I believe I could follow him..."

"Come," said Moses. Taking her hand, he led Tharbis along the shore of the Sea of Reeds to a high headland of sand and rock jutting out into the water. Together they climbed up the rocky incline and stood side by side, the tortured confusion of the sea behind them, the new morning sun warm on their faces.

On the shore just below, Miriam had gathered about herself a great company of women of the Children of Joseph. They were beating on their crude tambourins and singing a song she had taught them. "Sing, sing to Yahweh!" they intoned, keeping step to the quickening rhythm of both instruments and voices.

> "Sing, sing to Yahweh,
> For in triumph he rose:
> Horse and chariot
> He hurled into the sea!"

Faster and faster moved the whirling figures, the drums keeping pace with their accelerating rhythm like the beat of a racing pulse. The women were joined by other women, by men and children, until all the host of the Children of Joseph seemed to be moving in mad, ecstatic harmony with the exultant paean.

"Come down to us, Moses!" someone shouted.

"Sing and dance with us!" called another.

"Sing praises with us to Yahweh, our savior, our deliverer!"

But Moses did not hear them. For he was standing again on the threshold of discovery. Here, he knew at last, was the beginning and end of all his seeking. In the courts of Re at On, in the temple at Akhetaton, even in those torturing radiant hours on The Mountain, he had glimpsed only the shadow of the divine presence. Now at last he was looking into the blinding sunlight, the very face of the Eternal. "If your Yahweh is like you—or, I should say, if you are like him..." It was so incredibly simple! For if Yahweh had created man in his likeness, then did it not follow that in man at his best one might also behold the likeness of the Eternal? In Nehsi's deliberate sacrifice of himself for the redemption of others the profound disquiet, the agony of unrest, in the heart of the universe had become articulate. Only through the Nehsis of the world, those who were willing to suffer and become consumed for the sake of their brother men, could the Eternal fully reveal himself. Only through them could he finish the long, patient, agonizing task of his creation.

Moses felt a light touch on his arm. "They are calling for you," said Tharbis gently. "They want you to go down to them. They need you."

"Yes," said Moses.

Leaving the high place, he went down to his people.

ABOUT THE AUTHOR

Dorothy Clarke Wilson (1904-2003) was an amazingly prolific American author and playwright, who published more than 25 books and over 70 plays, as well as writing numerous essays, poems, and other literary works. Dorothy was a biblical scholar and social activist specializing primarily in biographies and religious subjects with themes running to faith, altruism, and fortitude.

Her historical fiction focused on the lives of Jesus, Moses, and other biblical figures. Prince of Egypt, perhaps her best-known novel depicted the early life of Moses, was published in 1952, and won a prize for the best religious novel of the year. More than 500,000 copies were sold and it became the primary source for Cecil B. DeMille's famous 1956 film, The Ten Commandments, starring Charlton Heston and Yul Brynner.

Ms. Wilson's biographies were mostly about women who overcame the prejudices of their time to make a difference in the world. Martha Washington, Dolley Madison, and Alice and Edith Roosevelt, as well as groundbreaking doctors and reformers such as Elizabeth Blackwell, Mary Verghese, Clara Swain, and Dorothea Dix were all topics.

Other works tackled ordinary people living under extraordinary circumstances such as Hilary Pole, a British woman with a rare, degenerative disorder. She also put pen to paper about life in rural Maine. Books on India and its people included a travelogue and a novel whose subjects were missionaries and doctors treating the "untouchables."

Dorothy Wright Clarke was born in Gardiner, Maine in 1904, the daughter of a Baptist minister and his wife. She excelled throughout school, was valedictorian of her high school graduating class and began attending Bates College at seventeen. In her senior year at Bates, Dorothy won an essay contest for "Arbitration Instead of War." This experience began her lifelong interest in activism for peace and social justice.

After graduating Phi Beta Kappa in 1925, Dorothy married a college classmate, Elwin Leander Wilson, who went on to attend Princeton Theological Seminary and the School of Theology at Boston University. After Elwin completed his graduate studies, he and Dorothy returned to Westbrook, Maine where he became a minister and she began her long and distinguished literary career.

She traveled extensively (Palestine, India, Egypt, Mexico, and England) always conducting thorough research in order to capture the authenticity of her subjects and settings. Over her lifetime, Dorothy Clarke Wilson presented over one thousand illustrated lectures, and received numerous honors—including Doctor of Letters from Bates College (1948) and the University of Maine (1984). She was the recipient of the Maryann Hartman Award from the University of Maine in 1988 and the Deborah Morton Award from Westbrook College in Portland in 1989. Other honors include the New England United Methodist Award for Excellence in Social Justice Ministry (1975); the Woman of Distinction Award of Alpha Delta Kappa (1971); the Award for Distinguished Achievement from the University of Maine at Augusta (1977); and the Achievement Award from the American Association of University Women, Maine Division (1988).

Today, deserving students attending Orono High School and the University of Maine are presented with the Dorothy Clarke Wilson Peace Award. The Maine Christian Association Board named one of its buildings, The Wilson Center, honoring her support of their organization.

Dorothy Clarke Wilson's papers (including many unpublished works) can be found in the Edmund S. Muskie Archives and in the Special Collections Library at Bates College. Ms. Wilson's work has been translated into dozens of languages and condensed into guides and digests for readers worldwide. Collectively, she is the author of 213 works in 473 publications in 17 languages with 16,154 library holdings.

Elwin, her husband, died in 1992; and her only son, Harold, died in 1977. Dorothy's own death occurred in 2003 in Orono, Maine after a brief illness.